I0773342

More Than Christmas
Tabitha Strickland

FlowersandSkulls an imprint of T Strickland Author LLC

Copyright © 2025 by FlowersandSkulls an imprint of T Strickland Author LLC

ISBN: 9798218049522

All rights reserved. No part of this publication may be reproduced, stored or transmitted in any form or by any means, electronic, mechanical, photocopying, recording, scanning, or otherwise without written permission from the publisher. It is illegal to copy this book, post it to a website, or distribute it by any other means without permission.

This novel is entirely a work of fiction. The names, characters and incidents portrayed in itare the work of the author's imagination. Any resemblance to actual persons, living or dead, events or localities is entirely coincidental.

Tabitha Strickland asserts the moral right to be identified as the author of this work.

Tabitha Strickland has no responsibility for the persistence or accuracy of URLs for external or third-party Internet Websites referred to in this publication and does not guarantee that any content on such Websites is, or will remain, accurate or appropriate. Designations used by companies to distinguish their products are often claimed as trademarks.

All brand names and product names used in this book and on its cover are trade names, service marks, trademarks and registered trademarks of their respective owners. The publishers and the book are not associated with any product or vendor mentioned in this book. None of the companies referenced within the book have endorsed the book.

There was no usage of generative artificial intelligence (AI) used in the creation of this work. This includes the cover, any internal art, editing, and revision. The author expressly forbids the use of this publication in the training of artificial intelligence(AI) technologies in any manner including, but not limited to: generating text, with or without limitations; technologies capable of generating works in the same style or genre as this publication; and technologies designed to formulate references or citations for academic styled papers or essays.

The author expressly forbids the use artificial intelligence (AI) technologies to generate any fanfiction, art, videos, reviews, or social media posts regarding this work.

Second edition

Contents

Dedication

This book is dedicated to all the people on TikTok who sat in my live streams while I edited and drove myself bonkers. Thank you for the company and the encouragement.

Prologue

Ivy heaved a sigh as she froze in the doorway that separated the closet from the bedroom. She had been tying a black, satin robe over the lingerie she'd picked up that morning when her husband's cell phone rang. She knew what that ringtone meant, and her dismay was validated when she heard Aaron's voice from the other room. Her plans were canceled, but it wasn't an uncommon occurrence. Being married to a police officer in a small town meant that calls to work could happen.

"Can't someone else go in?" she asked, though she knew the answer. "You haven't had a day off all week. I miss you."

Aaron looked up from taking his uniform shirt off the hanger. Those stunning blue eyes zeroed in on her as if finally taking in her barely concealed body. She loved the way they crinkled in apology and how his prominent ears shifted when he smirked and appreciatively tilted his head.

"I'm on standby not off, love." He pulled his shirt on. Ivy let out another heavy breath and pushed away from the door frame. "It's just for a few hours, Ives. You know how it gets on Saturday nights, especially when there's a big game." He nodded to the chair that held his vest, gear belt, and hat. "Can you put my radio on there for me?" He flopped onto the bed to pull on his boots.

Ivy plucked the radio from its charger, slid it into its holder, and expertly plugged the long mic that would wrap around his back and clip on his shoulder into the port. Then she held the ensemble out to him.

"How long will you be out?" Ivy shook her hair back when he stood to take it. Then she playfully toyed with the belt of her robe before parting it enough to let him see the pink and black surprise underneath. "Because last time you didn't get back 'til three."

"Well," he growled. Those strong hands found her waist and pulled her in. She hummed when his lips pressed into her neck. "One, no later. I made the Chief promise, so don't fall asleep on me." He nipped playfully at her ear sending waves of pleasure down her spine.

"Promise?" Ivy reached up to smooth the Velcro name tag and smiled when the light reflected off of her wedding set.

Her mom had lost her mind when she found out about Aaron's age. Fiona hadn't been too keen on the idea of her only child dating someone ten years older, but Ivy hadn't cared. She'd been smitten the instant he'd walked into that department store when she was only nineteen. He'd been the first officer on the scene to respond to the burglar alarm and found her fighting off the robber with the bank bag. That was five years ago, and she'd been his wife for the last six months.

"Aaron, do you promise?" She asked again and tugged at the lapels of his shirt.

"It's the anniversary of the night we met, Ivy Moore," he said. Those deliciously warm lips met hers, and her knees went weak at the tenderness of his kiss. "Of course, I promise. When you call your mom in a bit to check on Gavin, tell him Daddy loves him."

"It'll be Ivy Somerfield, once I get the appointment to change my name," said Ivy. She sighed when he released her, even if he had been reluctant to do so. "And I'll tell him. Then, when you get home, we can maybe get started on baby number two?" The wild flash in his eyes told her that was exactly what he'd had in mind. "Be safe."

"Always am." Aaron smiled and kissed her brow. "Lock the door behind me," he reminded her, like he did every time. She watched him pocket his cell phone, strap on his belt, then feed the microphone cord up and over his shoulder to tuck the clear earbud into his ear. He was halfway out of the room when she picked up the keys to his patrol car and jingled them.

"Forgetting something, Sergeant Somerfield?" Ivy giggled, and Aaron slapped himself on the forehead before coming back for them. "I love you," she murmured, held the keys back, and tilted her chin up for another kiss. She melted every time they played this little game when he got called in.

"I love you too." Aaron eased the keys from her hand. His almost black, close-cropped hair made his eyes seem oceanic in their hue. "See you at one." The effort he exerted to pull away and leave the room astounded her.

"I'll be here!" Ivy called after him then frowned when she heard the front door close.

Just as she promised, she went downstairs, turned the deadbolt, and flipped the switch on the knob. She watched through the window as his patrol car eased out of the drive and into traffic. Then she went back to their bedroom to call her mom and tell Gavin goodnight and that Mommy and Daddy loved him.

When all that was done, Ivy shimmied out of the lingerie and carefully folded it in a chair to slip back on when Aaron called to tell her he was almost home. She snagged the shirt he had been wearing off the floor and pulled it on over a pair of pajama pants. Then she poured herself a glass of wine from the bottle he'd bought, but they hadn't opened. Finally, she went back up to their room and laid down to watch TV.

When Aaron got called in at night, Ivy would normally bring their three-year-old son into the bed to snuggle and drift off. Now she was alone for the first time in months. The house was abnormally quiet, with Gavin away for the night, and the lack of activity,—paired with the reruns on the screen—pulled Ivy towards sleep. She decided she'd just sleep until Aaron called, then be up and changed before he got home. She closed her eyes and snuggled into his pillow.

"Ivy." Aaron's voice stirred her, and she smiled at the soft sensation of his fingers on her cheek. "Ivy, I love you."

She shot up in bed as a knock echoed from downstairs. She blinked at the empty room. Hadn't Aaron just been there?

When she picked up her cellphone, it was a quarter past one. There was a text from Aaron at eleven forty-five that said he may get to leave early because there wasn't much going on.

That was it though, no calls or voicemails.

The knock came again—three firm but quiet thuds that carried up the stairs.

Ivy kicked the covers aside and rolled her eyes with a giggle. He must've let his phone die, and he probably forgot the house keys at the station. It wouldn't be the first time.

"Coming, Sweetheart!" she called, completely ignoring the sexy outfit folded nearby. Besides, seeing her in his shirt had the same effect as any overpriced lace. Ivy slid the bolt and almost turned the knob until she realized Aaron hadn't replied.

After years of living with a police officer and being lectured about opening the door at night, Ivy peered through the glass.

Her stomach hit the floor.

It wasn't Aaron on the stoop. It was his partner from before his promotion and Gavin's godfather, Alexander Jones. The department chaplain, Penny Michaels, was at his side.

"No." As fear tore into her heart, she ripped the door open. "No! No!"

"Mrs. Moore." Alex's his face grim as they pulled their hats off. "Ivy, it is with the deepest regret that I must—" his voice caught, and Ivy's heart shattered. "That I must inform you that at fifteen minutes past midnight Sergeant...Sergeant Aaron—" his voice caught again. Those normally warm and friendly hazel eyes met hers, and they brimmed with tears. She couldn't handle it. She just couldn't. Ivy threw her arms around Alex's neck and sobbed.

"Sergeant Aaron Somerfield answered the highest call any of us can receive." Penny continued where Alex faltered, but Ivy couldn't hear her. All she could do was see those bright, blue, eyes shining down at her, feel his lips on hers as he promised to come back. All she could do was cling to her husband's best friend and feel his tears soaking her neck and shoulder as he squeezed her tightly. It felt like an eternity and a blink all at once, and every fiber of her being rejected what was being said. It wasn't real. It was just a nightmare. She'd had them before.

"Tell me I'm dreaming. Please, Alex, tell me it's not real," she sobbed and pulled back, pleading with him, but she didn't wake up. She was still standing on that stoop while tears coursed down her cheeks.

"Go and change. I'll drive you down to see him." Alex wiped her tears, but Ivy didn't feel it. She couldn't feel anything but the gaping hole in her heart. "I'll put Gavin's seat in my car."

"He's at my mom's," Ivy replied numbly.

She staggered back into the house, but she didn't close the door. It had felt empty before, but at that moment it felt cavernous—as if she was lost in the dark. With a trembling hand, she picked up her phone. Her sobs were uncontrollable as she pressed the screen.

"Mommy," she whimpered and sank to the bed. Ivy stared at the photo of Aaron on her nightstand. He was sitting with a one-year-old Gavin in front of the Christmas tree. "He's gone." She wasn't sure how she got the words out, but they came in a broken whisper.

"Ivy, you don't mean. Oh, baby." Her mom's voice sounded just as broken as she spoke. "I'll bring Gavin over right away."

"Don't. I've got to go to the station. Can I—Mommy—can I?" Ivy didn't even know how to ask, but four hours later her mother met her at the door of her apartment, and they both climbed into her bed with Gavin wedged between them.

Faith is Fickle

Ivy watched Gavin stand patiently in line to see the Santa that was seated in a massive, ornamental ball at the center of the mall. She was impressed at how well the four-year-old was behaving, given the breakdown he'd had three months earlier over the letters to Santa.

First, he'd insisted she'd write one with him. Then, he had gotten upset that his writing wasn't perfect, but he had refused to let her read his letter to help him make it neater. Lastly, he'd insisted she need to look up the address to Santa on the internet.

Ivy hadn't had the heart to tell him, when he dropped them in the mailbox before she got the stamps, that his cards wouldn't get anywhere without postage. Realistically, they wouldn't go anywhere but the trash anyway. She was glad, however, that he'd begged to see Santa, even if she had to face the Christmas Eve rush at the mall.

"I hope he didn't ask for anything we didn't order," Ivy sighed to her mother who had just walked up with a cup of coffee. "I know ordering Christmas in September is getting ahead but look at these crowds. God, there's just so many people." She took a sip to steady herself.

"You haven't handled crowds well since Aaron died,. Fiona rubbed Ivy's back gently. "I thought you went to therapy for it though."

"I did." Ivy resisted the urge to sneak over and straighten Gavin's belt. He'd insisted that she let him stand in the line and pose for the photo by himself, to show Santa that he was very serious about being good. "Just, it's been a stressful week. I almost fell off the chair decorating the tree last night. Then Gavin had a meltdown because I couldn't get him high enough to put the star on."

"You should have asked Alex to help with that," her mother replied. Ivy blew out a breath and took another long drink.

Gavin was exactly two children away from Santa. She blew him a kiss, and he blew one back before holding up the number two. She smiled at her angel, stunned for what felt like the hundredth time at how much he looked like his father. His ears, eyes, chin, and hair had all come from Aaron. Everyone else said her four-year-old had Ivy's cheeks, nose, and smile, but she didn't see it.

"Ives, are you listening?" asked Fiona interrupting her musing.

"Yes, sorry, about Alex," she said, shaking her head. "Well, he's Gavin's godfather, but he's not his father. Putting the star up is one of the few things Gav remembers doing with Aaron, and I want that memory to stay. Family traditions are important."

"I know, but Gavin won't remember if Alex does it once."

Ivy gave her a look, and Fiona busied her mouth by sipping her iced coffee. Everyone who knew them knew Gavin was unusually intelligent for a four-year-old, which was understandable given his father had been highly intelligent himself.

"You know he would, and I don't want him to lose that special memory of his dad."

"I know," chuckled her mother and wrapped her in a one-armed hug. "Speaking of which, Susan just hired this cute new guy as an accountant for the salon. I think he might be Alex's type."

"Mom, the last three guys you tried to introduce him to all failed to meet expectations," snorted Ivy. She froze when she saw Gavin climb eagerly into the lap of the mall Santa. "Ope, here he goes." She passed her mom the coffee and hurried over to stand behind the photographer.

Gavin whispered something in Santa's ear, and the man's eyes went wide. He looked over at Ivy, and what could only be described as pity filled what was visible on his beard-covered face. Hopefully, her over-enthusiastic preschooler hadn't asked for something like a tank or other bizarre item. Luckily, he only seemed to have one request, and then he posed politely for the camera.

"Come here, sweet pea," she said and waved her son over. She paused to pay for the printout picture, and they made their way back over to her mother. "Did you see who was standing by Mommy?"

"Gran!" Gavin exclaimed and took off towards his grandmother.

The only thing that Ivy had ever lamented over in her marriage was that Aaron's parents had both died when he was working on his second doctorate in his mid-twenties. While their funeral was what had brought him back to Ostcrest and convinced him to leave his job as a physics professor to work in law-enforcement in their small town, his lack of siblings and parents meant Gavin only had Ivy and her mom. He didn't seem to mind, but she knew as Gavin got older that he'd wish to have more family.

She watched as they embraced and rushed to rescue her mom from Gavin's non-stop babble about his newest robot building set.

"Okay, honey, where do you want to have lunch?"

"Oh, can we get pizza? Gran and I always get pizza on mall trips." Gavin jumped in place, his blue eyes wide and bright.

"Sounds like a plan to me," she agreed, and, after fighting their way to the food court, she helped him settle at a table with a slice of cheese pizza as big as his head.

"So, what did you ask Santa for?" asked Fiona. "Your mommy said you wouldn't let her see the letters." Ivy knew it was pointless because he hadn't even broken his silence for Alex.

"I want it to be a surprise." Gavin wiped his mouth with his sleeve. Ivy hissed and passed him a napkin. He took it and wiped his chin without missing a beat. "It'll be the best Christmas ever."

"Well, maybe your mommy doesn't like surprises. It isn't a pony, is it?" Fiona continued, and Ivy was impressed at her insistence. "Just a hint, maybe, in case Mommy or Gran needs to buy supplies."

"No hints, because it's for me and Mommy," Gavin said proudly before taking a long sip of his soda. Ivy shot her mom a confused look, and her mom sent her one right back. "Besides, he doesn't need supplies. That's silly!" He laughed and picked up his pizza. "Gran, did you know I play chess now?"

"I did not," Fiona lied and turned to give Gavin her full attention

Ivy ate quietly and tried to rack her brain for what he could want that was just as much for her as it was for him. Was it a new TV, a new car, or something else impossible? She had no clue.

"Well, baby," she interrupted his explanation of the knight's movements. "What if Santa can't bring the gift you asked for?"

"He will. Santa can do anything." Gavin's tiny voice brimmed confidence. "You and Gran said that Santa's magic can do anything."

"And we did." Ivy blew out a breath. She really hoped she could think of a way to quell his disappointment if what he asked for wasn't something she had already wrapped in her mom's apartment.

She carried that worry into the night when she had to practically wrestle Gavin off the sofa and upstairs into bed. He'd tried to insist on sleeping on the couch to see Santa. However, she needed him out of the way for her mom to come to drop off the wrapped presents that were marked as from Santa and hide them under the tree.

By the time her mom was safely asleep in the attic guest room, Ivy was exhausted. So, she checked on her sleeping son one more time before she tucked herself into bed.

"Merry Christmas, Aaron," she whispered to the photo on her nightstand and kissed the rings still snug on her left hand. "Wish you were here." Then she turned off the light and snuggled into her blankets.

She was so deeply asleep that she missed the sound of the hall door opening and a blanket being dragged along the stairs. She also didn't hear her son pick up some presents.

"None from Santa yet, yay!" The tiny whisper wasn't heard by anyone, and Gavin curled up on the couch under his blanket.

***

Nobody in the house heard the dogs bark down the street, the owl hoot as a jingling noise disturbed his silent hunt, or the sound of hooves and a sleigh on the roof. Everyone was too deep into dreams of happy times and sweet moments to hear the voices on the roof or the snorting of reindeer. They most definitely didn't hear the soft rustle of air as a red-suited man appeared in their home with a red bag clutched in his hand.

The man in the red suit paused beside the glistening tree already stacked with beautiful packages beneath its boughs. He gazed over at the small head of dark hair tucked into a blanket on the sofa.

"Gavin Moore-Somerfield," he said fondly. He knew this little one very well. His belief was so pure and powerful that his letter had practically glowed when it arrived in late October. The man in the red suit heaved a sigh, and he gently placed his bag down to open it.

"Sorry, Gavin, but there are some things even I can't do," he said as he pulled the primly wrapped gift from inside and nestled it under the tree. "This is the best I could manage." His magic was powerful, but some things were beyond his capabilities.

Then he pulled out the other present, addressed to a name he hadn't made a gift for in thirteen years. The last time he'd delivered for Ivy Moore, it had been a pair of yellow roller skates.

Hers was one he hadn't been too sure about, but she had written to him, and the pain and loss on her letter were stronger than the disbelief. Their letters had come on the same day but in different envelopes. He couldn't give Gavin what he wanted, but he thought he could at least give Ivy one final gift. Her request had taken a little searching and calling in a favor from the Amores Clan, but it had been fulfilled. He placed the tiny box on top of Gavin's.

Normally, the man left immediately upon delivery, but he lingered in the darkness. He breathed in the warm love that permeated the home, even though the pain and loss were woven throughout. The strength of this tiny, fractured family made him smile as he picked up a cookie to take a bite before drinking the milk. Finally, with a press of a finger to his nose, he was back up the narrow chimney.

"Ready, Aldwin?" Santa asked his son, who was tinkering with the updated navigation system on the sleigh. "Or are you still trying to get that thing working?" With a grunt, he hauled the bag up into the storage section.

"Yup!" Aldwin beamed before he shoved his screwdriver and glasses into his pocket and hopped back on the sleigh. "It's fully functional." He tapped the screen embedded into the dash and closed out a settings window. "I programmed it to your list, checked it twice of course, and it's running the bio checks on the reindeer now. Ruby's nose was throwing off her readings, but I worked it out." Aldwin arched an eyebrow as he took up the reins. "What, no cookies? Santa didn't get cookies?"

"You've already had a hundred and six," snorted Santa as the eight hundred- and ninety-eight-year-old sighed in disappointment. "You want to end up looking like me?" He patted his belly once. "You'll get your fill when you officially take the reins." With that, he plucked the aforementioned reins from his son's grasp and gave them a gentle flick. He laughed aloud as his team surged across the roof and launched into the air.

Aldwin pressed a button on the display, and the world bent around them, leaving the night as unbothered as it had been when they landed.

It stayed that way, quiet, peaceful, and filled with mystery as the stars and moon made their ever-winding path across the sky. As the sun crowned the eastern horizon, the homes in Santa and Aldwin's wake began to stir.

***

"Gavin," called Ivy as she checked the open bedroom and tied her house robe around her. Then she headed downstairs. She heard her mother coming down from the attic suite as she went. She yawned happily when she found her son curled up on the sofa. He had most certainly not been there when he fell asleep.

"Gavin, baby, wake up," whispered Ivy and waved at her mom who passed through the living room to go start the coffee. She kissed the stirring boy on his forehead and brushed his hair back. "Gavin, Santa came." In an instant, those summer sky eyes flew open, and he shot up with a smile. She barely had time to jerk back to avoid being hit with his head. "See, presents!" She pointed at the extra gifts tucked back behind the tree that she knew he wouldn't have seen in the dim lights. The next words out of his mouth hit her like a freight train.

"Daddy!" exclaimed Gavin, and laughter filled his voice as he jumped up, looked around, and dashed into the kitchen. "Gran, have you seen Daddy? Daddy! Daddy, where are you?"

"Gavin!" Ivy croaked and staggered to her feet. He was already up the stairs, and she heard her bedroom door fly open, as he called out again for the man who was already long gone. "Gavin, what are you doing?" she called as she made it to the stairs.

The eagerness in his little face was depleted when he dragged himself to the landing above her.

"I asked Santa for a daddy.

"Oh, baby." Ivy sank to her knees to scoop him up when he descended to her. Then she kissed his dark hair gently. "Santa can't do that. He's magic, but he's not that magic." Nobody was that magic, and that fact had broken her heart for over a year.

"Santa can't bring Daddy back. I told you that." She cupped his cheeks gently and tried so hard to pour some light back into those watery eyes.

"That's why I asked him to bring me a new one." Gavin's tears spilled over onto his cheeks. "'Nd he didn't. Because he isn't' real, is he Mommy? He's fake. Just like Lindsey said. Santa is fake!"

"Oh, honey, of course, he's real." Ivy led him back to the tree. She'd had almost two years of hiding her pain in front of him, and it came easily. So, it was nothing for her to smile and pick up a gift. A tiny box on top she didn't recognize fell over. "See, to Gavin from Santa. Open it!" She eased him to the floor and picked up the tiny box. It must have gotten mixed in at her mom's while they were wrapping; except, the tag wasn't like any they used. The handwriting was also unfamiliar, but it could have been one her mom or Alex had wrapped at a station at the mall. "And Mommy's got one. See, to Ivy from Santa."

"It's a bear, a police bear." Gavin's sigh of disappointment made Ivy rip her eyes away from the box. The bear in question was in a uniform identical to the one in the photo of Aaron on the mantle, and there, to her shock, was a name tag: A. Somerfield. Gavin stared at it for a moment, and then he threw it aside. "It's stupid!" The tears began again, and before Ivy could stop him, he fled the room.

"Just great," she sighed, leaned against the sofa, and picked up the discarded bear. Her mom came into view with a cup of coffee, but Ivy waved her off. She was grateful her mother was letting her handle this mess without outside intervention, but she still needed a moment to collect herself. Tenderly, Ivy wiped the bear's fur and hugged it. Above her, her mother shrugged and shook her head.

"It isn't from me," Fiona whispered. "Take your time. I'll start breakfast." Then her mother headed back into the kitchen.

Ivy made a mental note to ask Alex if it was from him. Fighting back her tears, she picked up the tiny box addressed to her. Carefully, she undid the ribbon and lifted the lid. There, nestled in the wrapping paper, was a chain necklace with a key charm on it.

"No, impossible," she whispered. Her heart raced as she picked it up to flip it over, and she gasped when she saw the familiar inscription.

The key to my heart is your love.

A.S.

12-25-2014

It was impossible, and she knew it. Ivy had lost that necklace six months ago while at the beach in Florida. How was it in that box? Yes, when she'd caved into Gavin's demands to write a letter to Santa, the necklace is what she had asked for, but it wasn't possible. It couldn't be possible. Her mom couldn't have had it. She wasn't even with them when Ivy had lost it. Alex had been, but Alex had been back at the hotel. It couldn't be possible, unless—

Ivy glanced over at the cookies she'd left out. She had intentionally made sure Gavin knew they were oatmeal raisins, so she could have them all to herself. He hated oatmeal raisins, but one, just one, had a bite taken out of it. The necklace slid against her palm and brought her gaze back to it. There was absolutely no way anyone could have found it.

"Gavin!" Ivy called and scrambled to her feet. "Santa is real! I promise!" She fastened the chain around her neck as she raced to the stairs and ignored her mom running into the hall. She rushed up the stairs and almost tripped over the top one. She grabbed for his door, but the knob was locked. "Baby, come on. He is real." She pleaded and shook the handle. "Gavs, let Mommy in. I promise." She leaned against the door and slid down the wood to sit on the floor. Behind it, her son's sobs echoed out.

Ivy clutched the necklace against her throat and the bear to her stomach. She couldn't understand the absolute certainty coursing through her. She was twenty-five years old, and for the first time in thirteen years, she believed in Santa Claus.

The Price of Admission

"**G**ood morning, Mum." Aldwin grinned as he strode into the kitchen. His mother, Cateline Claus, stood with a mug of hot chocolate outstretched. "That for me? Thanks!" He took it eagerly, but not before he leaned down to drop a kiss on her wrinkled cheek. Like always, she smelled of cinnamon and cookies, there was also the underlying aroma of a spring morning. The thought of spring made him freeze. "Was Grandmum Gaia over for breakfast? You didn't tell me!" He leaned against the counter and did his best not to pout. "Great Grandmum hasn't been by since June! I missed her!"

"She just popped by to remind us that autumn would start soon." Cateline reached up to pat his cheek. "Like your Dah needs reminding, but grandmums are still grandmums, even if their grandsons are over a millennium old." She turned back to her food on the stove. "Where are you off to so early? Thought you'd be down in that laboratory of yours, working on one of those new creations."

"I am, but first I'm headed to California. Lewin wants to show me this new—" Aldwin paused when his mother raised an eyebrow at him over her shoulder. He had forgotten something. He knew that look in her ancient, but ageless, chestnut eyes. "What? What did I forget?" One platinum eyebrow lifted even higher. "Hang on, autumn is almost here." Cocking his head, he surrendered to the old magic and let the vibrational energies of the human realm flow through him "It's September twentieth?" He nearly dropped his cocoa in horror at his lapse.

"Only took you ages," Cateline said and stirred the apples in the pot before her. "Your Dah's in his office. I'll be down in a bit; going to run some biscuits out to the workshop as soon as these are done." The oven beside him dinged. The door opened on its own and filled the room with the unmistakable smell of sugar, chocolate, oatmeal, and banana. His mum waved a hand, and a tray floated from the oven to a cooling rack across the room. Aldwin grinned and hurried to pluck one of the monkey-shaped snacks off the tray.

"Oh, for Gaia's sake, Aldwin! You're almost nine hundred! Don't burn yourself over biscuits!" His mother exclaimed.

"Mum, your biscuits haven't ever burned me," he said and dodged her playful swat with the apron.

Then, with a quick snatch, he acquired another warm banana-flavored treat and touched his finger to his nose. In a blink, he found himself perched in the chair beside his father, and he held out the stolen biscuit.

"Morning Dah."

"Morning Aldwin," his father answered. His rich baritone was normal to him, but Aldwin knew it held a jingle of bells and the hum of a drum to mortals. Plump fingers plucked the biscuit from Aldwin's grasp, and those sparkling, ageless, but wizened eyes met his. "You missed your Grandmum at breakfast." From the corner of his beard, a tiny butterfly fluttered out, and it left a trail of golden dust before it vanished. "If you can't tell."

"Mum told me," said Aldwin. He sat his cocoa down and stared at the scroll spread out across the aged desk. "How come you aren't using that new list I made you?"

It wasn't that Aldwin didn't love that magical smell of the parchment or the hum of wondrous energy that came with touching it and watching the names sparkle and shine, but the electronic one cut the review time in half. It also automatically calculated an algorithm that determined how close a child bordered on naughty or nice.

"I did last night, but I'm ever the traditionalist," replied Santa. One of his strong, calloused, and enchanted hands clapped on Aldwin's shoulder. "When it's your turn, you can do it your way." He watched as his father waved a hand over the scroll, and it curled up to soar across the room. "Speaking of which, it's nearly your birthday."

"I know." Aldwin sighed and braced himself for the impending lecture.

"The bag still isn't producing for you," his Dah went on. "The sleigh won't fly when you try without me, and the list won't change for you." Aldwin looked away when his father's face pulled tight under the full beard. "You've inherited all the small magic, Son, but it isn't enough. To be me, to be Santa, it all has to work together."

"I know, Dah, and I'm trying. I'm really trying." Aldwin trailed his thumb along the handle of his mug as he spoke.

He had been trying hard.

He could hear the thoughts of children. He could understand and speak every language a believer spoke to him. He could talk to the reindeer, and he could make magic happen when needed. For some reason, though, the most important vestiges of his father's legacy just hadn't manifested.

"I've even been visiting the mortal realm, incognito with Lewin for decades, trying to understand what I'm missing."

"I know you have, but being Santa isn't just about understanding humanity, Aldwin," huffed Santa. His father reached over and placed a finger on his chest. "You must feel it here. You must truly believe that you can be Santa—that you can love them all—and inspire that love and faith in return." He pulled his hand back, and, to Aldwin's surprise, a box materialized in his fathers grip. "My father is the only one who has had to do this, but it's time you learn."

Santa passed him the box, and the instant it touched Aldwin's hands, he felt it. Well, he felt the absence of it. The weight was that of letters, but the contents didn't radiate with that warming glow of believers.

"This is every child since last Christmas who has lost the faith before their time," his Dah explained.

"I can feel the loss," whispered Aldwin. He carefully opened the lid and blinked down at the neatly opened envelopes. There were at least a hundred, and they all ached with the loss of innocent belief. "What do I need to do?" he asked.

For these children, he would do it. He was ready to truly begin his training. Whatever it took, whatever the cost, he would pay it.

"Pick the one that tugs at the magic, the one that feels the emptiest to you," his father said, and those crystalline eyes flicked down to the box. "If you are truly meant to be Santa, you'll find a way to restore their faith in us." Aldwin closed the box and stood. "The Autumnal Equinox begins in two days. You'll start then. You have until Christmas Eve at midnight to restore the faith of one child. You have until your-" Aldwin cut him off.

"Until my nine hundredth birthday, or I can never become Santa. I'll just be another winter sprite, like Mum and the elves," murmured Aldwin. He clutched the box tightly to his chest. "I know. I can do this."

"Your mother wasn't always a sprite, as you know." His father's words made him pause. "She was human when we met. It was her faith, her true belief in who and what I was, that allowed her to become an immortal." His beard shifted, and Aldwin knew he was smiling. After a thousand years, their love was still as strong as the day they married. "That's how powerful the belief of an adult can be. The belief of a child, however, it is unstoppable." His father shook his head and waved a hand. "Oh and see if you can get Lewin to come along with you on this. Cupids know the mortal realm better than any of the other Ageless."

"I won't let you or them down," promised Aldwin. With that, he touched his nose and flopped down on his bed. He promptly jumped up with a yelp.

"Lewin!" he exclaimed and rolled his eyes at his best friend reclining on his pillows. He was practically naked. "Put some clothes on!"

"You missed our meeting," snickered Lewin. The man grinned and snapped his fingers. A pair of jeans and a form-fitting dress shirt replaced the silk boxers he had been wearing. "They were the cutest couple, I swear." His eyes narrowed in on the box. "That for me?"

"No, I need a favor," said Aldwin, and he dropped back onto the bed to open the box and dump the contents onto his blanket. "My Dah had to invoke the faith trials." He stared down at the hundred or so envelopes "I need you to help me fit in in the mortal realm. I'm going undercover."

"The faith trials!" Lewin cried and immediately sat up his eyes wide in shock. "But only your grandfather—what the hell Aldwin? You said the magic was getting stronger!"

"It is, but not like it should," confessed Aldwin. He picked up an envelope and weighed it in his hand. "I have to choose a child and restore their faith, but how do I pick?" Slowly, he eased the letter out.

It was a simple one, a normal one even. A little girl had asked for a pony. Magical law prevented Santa from giving live animals as gifts. All gifts had to be material, or very rarely, a miracle to the family. It couldn't be any substantial miracle by a long shot, usually something to ease the family's worry. Yes, she had lost her faith, but that was on her parents.

"I dunno," grunted Lewin, and he shrugged as he pulled a letter out. "I don't exactly pick my couples. The bow and arrows just show up, and I fire." He scanned the letter. "This kid stopped believing because Santa didn't bring him a dirt bike." One touch of the letter, and Aldwin knew it wasn't the one.

Together they flitted through the envelopes, making it to thirty when Aldwin heard Lewin sniffle and heave a sigh.

"What? What is it?" he asked, stunned to find his best friend crying softly. Cupids rarely cried from sadness because they thrived on new love and hope. "Lewin."

"I marked this boy's parents," whispered Lewin, staring down at the letter in his hand. "Gavin Moore-Somerfield, he's the only son of Ivy Moore and Aaron Somerfield. It was one of my hardest pairings." Aldwin glanced down at the paper, and he was shocked to find that there were actually two pages. "I can see their fates when I mark them, you know. They were only going to have five years together before Aaron would die, but oh, those five years were going to be so magical."

"What did Gavin ask for?" asked Aldwin. He reached out for the pages, but Lewin shifted the top one to look at the second. "What? How long is his list?"

"He only asked for one thing, but his mom, Ivy, wrote too. I almost forgot." Lewin held the letter to his nose and inhaled. Another tear rolled down his cheek. Aldwin was confused. How would Lewin know someone wrote a letter to Santa? "Your Dah asked me to find their symbol of love. She lost it on a beach in Florida. She asked for it, so I found it and gave it to him to deliver." Wiping his eyes, Lewin passed him the papers.

"But an adult's letter doesn't usually reach the barrier," muttered Aldwin as took the pages. He gasped and his heart ached deep in his chest at the pain he found on the papers. One was empty, dull, and bland like unsweetened flour. The other held just a faint glimmer, the slight spark of belief in the impossible. For the first time in his almost nine hundred years, Aldwin felt the belief of an adult.

Sure enough, the neater writing asked only for the lost necklace. It was the shaky, but perfectly spelled, block writing that asked for the impossible. Little Gavin Moore-Somerfield had asked for a new Daddy. The honest yearning was still clinging to the pages, tangible, tugging at his heart like nothing he'd ever felt, and, again, for the first time in all his life, Aldwin felt the pain of the true loss of faith and hope. "Him, it's him, Gavin Moore-Somerfield. He's my task."

"That's gonna be hard," said Lewin as he met his gaze, his eyes wary. Aldwin knew though. He could feel it deep in his soul. If he could restore this now five-year-old's belief in Christmas, he could be Santa. "Let's get started then." With a snap, a laptop appeared on Lewin's lap.

"Okay, Cupid," Aldwin said and tucked the letters into his coat. "Let's do this."

***

Across the world, Ivy Moore sat patiently in the chair across from the admission dean of Crestwood Academy.

"Honestly, Ms. Moore, Gavin would make an excellent addition to Crestwood Academy," the older woman before her said. Ivy felt her face pull up in a relieved smile through her tight cheeks. She had been pacing the halls all morning, as her son was put through a series of tests. They ranged from cognitive abilities to problem-solving, to an understanding of the base curriculum. "He's only five, but he is testing out with the scores of a ten or eleven-year-old. Not to mention, the theater teacher feels he could excel there."

"Thank you, Margaret, really," Ivy gushed. She couldn't believe it. Well, she could.

Gavin was brilliant, and he was always ahead of his age intellectually. That wasn't a surprise because he got it from his dad. Aaron could have done anything, been anything. He had a near-genius IQ, but he had left teaching physics at an ivy league college to become a police officer. He said it was the only thing that had called to his heart when he came home for his parents' funeral. He wanted to help people and protect the innocent. That had won out over everything else. "When can he start?"

"Unfortunately, we don't have any open scholarship slots until next fall," explained Margaret. Her smile was sympathetic, and Ivy's heart dropped. She had been so afraid of that. "But we are accepting paying students starting the first Monday of the month." The admissions dean slid her a folder, and Ivy picked it up. "This is the cost of attendance, uniforms, textbooks, basic school supplies, and lunches." Ivy swallowed hard as she looked down at the folder. "But starting next September, Gavin would have a guaranteed scholarship, as long as he does well academically and socially." Ivy opened the folder, and she sucked in a breath at the numbers.

"Jesus," she hissed. It would take all but three thousand dollars of what she had in savings. She had been guarding the nest egg left from Aaron's life insurance with a fervor since the house was paid off with the bulk of it. It was worth it, though, to get Gavin into the school. If she was careful with her spending, didn't miss a day of work, and forwent their weekly mom and son dinners out, she could make it without living completely paycheck to paycheck or digging to deeply into Aaron's pension payments. "Do you take card, or do I need to run to the bank?"

"Just fill out the deposit slip, and we'll draw the funds out tomorrow," said Margaret. She nodded to the folder, and Ivy pulled out the sheet. She dug a pen from her purse and quickly scrawled the banking information onto it.

"This means more to me than you can imagine," whispered Ivy. She held back the tears that had begun to fill her eyes as she slid Margaret the slip.

"I understand, Ivy. Being a mom is hard and being a single mom after everything you went through is harder," the dean said and tucked the slip away. Then she stood. "We'll mail you information about uniform fittings and such immediately, so you can have him ready to start in two weeks. I look forward to seeing his smiling face in the halls."

Ivy felt the relief course through her again, stirring her into motion, and she stepped into the waiting area. Gavin was seated quietly in a chair, coloring in his sketchbook. He'd gotten his fathers brains, but he'd gotten her artistic skills. "Hey blue eyes, you ready?"

"Mommy!" Gavin exclaimed. The sketchbook was stuffed away quickly, and he jumped off the chair to hug her. "Did I do it? Do I get to go to school here now?"

"You'll start in two weeks," replied Ivy, taking his hand to lead him down the hall to the main doors. The bright sun made her squint, but soon her vision cleared to reveal a sleek black sedan with a smiling face waiting.

"Uncle Lex!" shouted Gavin. The boy broke away to race down the stairs and leap into Alex's arms. "Guess what! I get to go to school here now!"

"Of course, you do! You're the smartest kid in the world." Alex laughed as he set Gavin down. Ivy watched her boy run around to the door and climb into the back seat. "Really, though, he got the scholarship? You submitted the application on the due date!" He grinned broadly and wrapped her in a tight embrace.

Ivy hugged Alex back as she sighed. Then she slid into the car and looked back at Gavin who had pulled his headphones out and was engrossed in some game on his tablet. "The scholarship starts next September, but I paid for the rest of the school year's tuition, so he starts next month." She opened the folder to show him the amount.

"Are you nuts?" Alex hissed and looked back at Gavin before starting the car. "Ivy, that's almost all that was left."

"I know, but what else can I do? Rockwell is threatening to expel him, Alex," she said and ran a hand through her hair. "Last week, he made the entire class cry, because he told them that Santa and all the rest were fake."

Ivy had tried for months after 'The Great Christmas Meltdown,' as her mom called it, to convince Gavin that Santa was real. It hadn't worked.

"Then yesterday, he called Miss Anderson a brick-headed moron because she mispronounced a word at story circle." Alex covered a chuckle with a cough. "It's so not funny, Lex!"

"Well, he is Aaron's son. You knew he was going to be a handful when you went into labor at two am during a thunderstorm." Alex shrugged and smiled softly at her. "But Ivy, the cost of living is only going up, and, let's face it, your art classes always dwindle this time of the year. I don't want you to have to go back to retail."

"With the benefits check, Aaron's pension, and the classes, I can do it. Money's gonna be tight, but I'll manage," insisted Ivy, but she knew he was right. While the adult education center where she taught art five days a week paid well enough for most of the year, it was based on attendance. "I can put some of my paintings online too and sell them for commissions."

"What if you rent out the attic?" asked Alex. His suggestion was not what Ivy had expected.

Aaron had only just finished renovating the attic into a larger suite before he died. They had intended to give Gavin their room and turn his room into a nursery when they conceived again. Those ideas had never come to realization, and the attic bedroom was empty except for her paintings that waited to be sold or gifted away. It was only used when Alex or her mom slept over. "You could charge a quarter of what your mortgage was, plus a portion of utilities."

"Okay, now you're talking insane." Ivy snorted and crossed her arms. "I'm not letting some stranger move into my house. What if they're a pervert or something?"

"I'll check them out for you. I can run a background check and that sort of thing." Alex reached over and squeezed her hand. "I don't want to see my best friend's girl and my godson struggling is all, and God knows you'd never let me pay for anything."

"I'll think about it." Ivy sighed. She glanced back at Gavin again. Thankfully, it seemed he had been oblivious to their conversation.

Of Cupids and Contracts

"Aldwin, you're never going to believe this." Lewin's voice filled the room. Aldwin looked up from where he was serving his mum a slice of pie. Lewin appeared in the middle of the dining room, tablet in hand. The cupid wore only a teal, sequin Speedo and matching feather boa.

"Hello Lewin," said Cateline and flicked a finger. Lewin's Speedo was covered in a tasteful toga, and his boa had vanished. "What have I told you about proper dinner wear?" Aldwin didn't bother hiding his laughter.

"Sorry Mama Claus, I was at this crazy org—" Lewin began, but Aldwin arched an eyebrow in warning. The cupid cut himself off and drew a breath. "Anyways, Aldwin, you asked me to keep tabs on any possible openings near or around the Moore's while you were working on your backstory."

"I did," replied Aldwin. He sometimes wished Lewin would just get to the point, but he knew he tended to babble himself, so he reined his irritation in.

"Well, it's your lucky day," his friend said and held up the tablet as he sat down in a chair beside him. "She just posted an ad for someone to rent a room in her house." Lewin handed him the device, and Aldwin stared down at it in shock. Her name and address were as plain as day on the screen. "It's fate, right? It must be. You pick her son as your trial, and this shows up. Come on."

"Lewin's right. Can't you feel the magic pulling?" his mother asked with a soft voice, and yes, he could. It whispered to his soul and teased at his heart, and it made him shiver.

"Yes," breathed Aldwin.

Despite being an Ageless and having spent most of his nearly nine hundred years secluded away in Yule Town, he was more than adept at modern technology. It had always been important to him to keep up with human advancements. So he found it easy to carefully craft his email, use his fabricated identity, and send an inquiry about the room. He may or may not have tweaked the advertisement with magic so that after his email was sent, all inquiries but his would be returned as un-deliverable.

"Do you think she'll be hesitant to accept a man?" he asked.

"Of course, she will. She's a believer, so she'll trust you instinctively," said Santa from the hallways. His father entered the room and smiled. "You'll have to be careful though because it will be the others in their lives that may try to rouse doubt." He clapped Lewin on the shoulder as he settled into his usual chair.

"I'll be careful. I promise," said Aldwin. The tablet beeped, and he looked down. Ivy had replied. Her email explained that she would look into the information he sent and get back to him. "Guess I should go pack."

"Forget packing," laughed Lewin. His smile was dangerous, and his hand closed around Aldwin's. "I'm taking you shopping!"

"Have fun boys," was all Aldwin heard from his mum before he found himself standing in a crowded department store in New York City.

***

A few hours later, in Ostcrest, Kansas, Ivy met Alex outside of her house to collect the laptop she'd used to place the ad.

"His entire record is clean," Alex said, and Ivy pulled her thin sweater tighter as she leaned against Alex's patrol car. "Not even a parking ticket. I asked a favor from a friend in cyber forensics in Kansas City. I had him run a trace back to the IP address, and he did a pretty thorough check of the computer. There was nothing but schematics for toys, some technology, and about eight thousand e-books." Alex handed her the laptop he'd borrowed back, and he mimicked her stance. "The guy is legitimate. He used to work for a company called N.P. Enterprises, which develops toys and educational games for kids and is based in Canada and England, but now he is teaching a theoretical physics class online."

"Bit of a jump, isn't it, toy development to physics?" asked Ivy before she slid her laptop into its bag and brushed her hair back. "You really checked into him?"

Nicholas Claus was the only one who had replied to her advertisement, which was odd. Still, after sitting down with Alex and going over her budget, it was a good plan.

"It's a family-owned company, started by his grandfather Kristoff, now owned by his father Kristofer," said Alex. Then he chuckled. Ivy stared at him, unsure of the laughter. "You get it right? Kris Claus, Nick Claus, and they have a toy company." Ivy giggled and toyed with the key charm on her necklace. "Ah, there it is. You smiled! Anyways, my break's over. I'm still picking Gavin up from daycare to take him to the chess league, right?"

"Yeah." Ivy pushed away from the car for a hug. Just like his dad, five-year-old Gavin was already well on the way to becoming a chess master. "I'm gonna go tidy up the house." When she separated from Alex she smiled, trying her best to push her nerves aside. "I'll let you know if this Nicholas Claus will be staying when you drop him off." She squeezed Alex's hands gently before he started around the car. "Be safe, Lex!"

"I'll do my best," he said and blew her a kiss before ducking into the car.

Ivy didn't have much to clean. It was mostly just Gavin's toys cluttering up the living room and the remnants of his coloring and sketching on the table, but she did want her house to look nice. Nicholas was supposed to be around to see the room at one-thirty, and it was already noon. Ivy neatly piled things up, washed the few breakfast dishes she had been ignoring, and swept the floor. She was just about to dig the vacuum out when she caught sight of the small mantle above the tiny fireplace.

"I dunno, Aaron. Am I doing the right thing?" she asked and reached up to stroke the bear next to the framed picture. "Crestwood is best for Gavin, I know. It's just... is letting a stranger move in the best idea?" The frozen lips didn't move, and those oceanic eyes stared unseeing out past her. "I'm doing my best, and Alex says it will be good." She lowered her hand and fiddled with the diamond rings she still couldn't bear to take off. "I miss you so much. I tried going out last month, you know. Everyone said it would be good for me, but you left behind shoes that I don't think anyone can fill."

Squeezing her eyes shut, Ivy tried hard to remember how Aaron's hands had felt, how strong, sure, and safe they had been. The longer he was gone, the more the memories faded. Sometimes, though, when she tried really hard, she could see the empty department store. She could feel his palm against her arm, pulling her back from the robber.

"Get out of here!" Aaron had shouted, as Alex surged forward to tackle the robber. She hadn't fled. Ivy had stayed. She had watched them restrain the man and cuff him, only to be lost in those blue eyes as they looked up and filled with shock to find her still there.

Ignoring the vacuum, Ivy moved to the kitchen. There she bagged up the trash, relined the can, and then headed outside to dump it in the main can. The recycling one was knocked over, so she bent to straighten it. Then she headed back to the stoop.

From across the street, Aldwin stared out the window of Lewin's car, as the blonde woman descended the short stairs.

"That's her?" he asked. He knew she couldn't see the vehicle, since Lewin had turned it invisible. Her face wasn't visible from his angle, but he could feel that faint glimmer of belief as it radiated from her like a lone sun ray.

"Oh yeah," hummed Lewin. "Just as beautiful as I remember too. Although," he leaned forward and made an approving sound, "she's gotten a bit curvier, probably from having a kid. Man, that is a gorgeous butt—" Aldwin smacked his arm and cut him off, though the cupid wasn't wrong.

"Lewin, focus," said Aldwin. He picked up the folder with all the documents she had requested: pay stubs, references, criminal background check, and his ID. Granted, they were all fake. He tucked them into the inner pocket of his sports coat and drew a breath. "Here we go," he said and started to get out of the car. "You coming?"

"Yup, and I'll be invisible to her. If you start to mess up, watch for my cues," said Lewin as he opened his door, and Aldwin started up the empty drive.

"Excuse me, ma'am, are you Ivy Moore?" he asked. Then he yelped in shock as she spun on the top of the stoop. He saw the tumble coming before her shoe even slipped on the rain-soaked step, and he rushed forward.

Aldwin caught her in his arms. Ivy yelped, and, when she steadied herself by grabbing his sleeves, she looked up. Time froze around him.

A shock jolted through him, striking him in his back like lightning—straight through his chest, and it sent lights across his vision. His head spun. Aldwin sucked in a breath, as his vision cleared, and he found himself drowning in mirrored swirls of caramel, honey, and amber. Time restarted.

"You okay there?" He managed to ask.

"Uh, yeah," gasped Ivy. She gave a soft shudder, and Aldwin did his best to raise her up and steady her. He released her and stepped back a bit to smile at the woman. He had never seen anyone so stunning in his life. "Thank you, um—"

"Nick Claus," said Aldwin, but he still felt unsteady in his movements. Hot, yearning, cupid's magic hummed through his core.

Lewin come from behind him staring down at his hands in shock. Aldwin's heart jerked when he saw what they held—an empty bow glistening with gold and pink dust. That same dust, invisible to mortals, came out of Aldwin's mouth like vapor on a cold morning at the same time it left Ivy's.

No, it was impossible. It couldn't be possible at all. The bow dissipated, and Lewin threw his hands up. His blue eyes went wide, and his mouth opened in silent defense. Aldwin's best friend had just shot them.

"Ivy Moore," Ivy said and extended a shaky hand. Aldwin jerked his attention back to her, his throat burning. "Well, you have quick reflexes, that's for sure. Thanks, for catching me." His fingers closed around hers, and he was surprised at how pleasant they felt when he shook her hand. Her laughter was entrancing, so intoxicating, that Aldwin felt himself grin in response before he could stop.

"Any time," he replied, dreading to find the pink tinge that spread up her cheeks absolutely endearing.

Ivy was positively beautiful, inside and out, but was it really his opinion, or was it cupid magic? On second thought, he didn't really care. Ivy's hand was soft and welcoming, and it felt wonderfully perfect in his.

"I'm sorry for startling you. I know I'm a bit early."

"It's fine really," she replied. "I'm sorry. This is so weird. Have we met before? I feel like we have."

"No, I'd definitely remember meeting you," chuckled Aldwin. He was going to murder the cupid who watched the exchange with silent laughter. Focus, Aldwin needed to focus. "I just have one of those faces." He tugged at his ear, a nervous habit he'd tried to break. Tiny flutters filled his stomach as Ivy shrugged, and then she gave a shy smile that showed just a hint of her tongue between her teeth at the corner of her mouth. "May I come in?" Blimey, her hair looked so soft, and he wondered how it'd feel slipping through his fingers.

"Right, of course," whispered Ivy, and her cheeks flushed darker. "Come on in." He wondered if it was possible that her blush could grown any redder.

"I'm going to kill you," hissed Aldwin in Ageless at Lewin, because he knew Ivy wouldn't hear anything more than a low noise, as he followed her up to the door.

"I don't control it," Lewin protested, as he fell in behind him. "The bow appears. I shoot. You know that."

"Just go," snapped Aldwin. Lewin disappeared in a puff of sparkling air.

"You say something?" Ivy asked as she turned to the man behind her. She thought she heard whispering. Then again, the air was kicking on so that may have been it.

"I sneezed," explained Nick. His cheeks darkened, and Ivy found she admired the spattering of freckles just under his eyes.

God, what was her problem? What was it about this man that had her totally off her normal behavior? It was ridiculous. Why did this moment feel so familiar? Why was she tucking her hair back and shifting her feet? Was she flirting?

She was in a department store, staring up at an amused smile, and two shining oceans danced at her in wonder.

No, she was in her entryway, but even though the man before her did have an amused smile, his eyes were brown. Why then, did she feel like she'd met him before?

"Well bless you then," she said, toed off her sneakers, and indicated he should do the same. Then she looked down, and she had to laugh. "Sneakers with a sports coat?" It was, oddly, suited to him though, and Ivy wondered how she just knew and accepted that. He wore sneakers with a sports coat like Aaron wore a leather jacket with everything. "So, this is the hall. The living room is this way. Sorry, my son's toys are sorta everywhere."

Ivy gestured at the odd assortment of science kits, architect and engineering models, and a stray tablet. Then she watched Nick's focus narrow in on the small shrine above the mantel. She swallowed and knew better than to wait for the question to be asked.

"My husband, Aaron. He was killed two years ago trying to break up a fight." She shook her hair back and fiddled with the thin sweater. "I keep it up there, so Gavin doesn't forget what he looks like."

"I'm so sorry for your loss," replied Nick. The pain of Aaron's death coursed through Ivy, and she felt her heart tighten so swiftly it stole her breath. It wasn't fresh, but it wasn't totally healed either. Would it ever be healed? It wasn't fair. "I can tell you loved him very much."

"He was my soulmate, and he was the best father too," Ivy replied. She couldn't talk about it anymore. Sometimes, the pain wasn't so bad, but it seemed that it was one of rare days where it was. "Um, the kitchen's this way." She moved past him and tried to center her thoughts on her purpose. "Not much to see. A kitchen's a kitchen."

"A kitchen is never just a kitchen," chuckled Nick. The warmth in his voice eased some of the pain. She looked over at him as he examined the kitchen.

His chestnut hair shone in the soft lights, and his smile was inviting. It beckoned her to step closer when he touched the sink. What was she doing? She didn't check people out, but goodness, he was an attractive man. She mentally slapped herself, and his words interrupted her admiration of his lithe body.

"This is what keeps the house together. Some of my happiest memories growing up are of me and my parents in the kitchen, laughing and just being together," he said.

"Right." She found it a smidge bit weird that his smile had really lit up when he ran a finger along the stove. Still, it wasn't off-putting. She wouldn't mind a bit having someone else around who knew how to cook. Maybe he had a recipe to make a five-year-old eat his broccoli. "Um, this is the dining room." She led him to the room that wasn't much more than a separate nook off the kitchen, where the back hall led to the downstairs bathroom that had become Gavin's claimed bath and the stairs. "Let's go up."

Aldwin had no qualms following Ivy up the stairs. The house was comfortable, full of warmth that couldn't be felt by the skin. It hummed with love and made him smile. It was, indeed, a true home. The landing was small, revealing four doors. Three were closed, but one was opened, just barely, and he could see a desk covered in papers and what looked like an easel. One of the doors was covered in dinosaur stickers and glow-in-the-dark stars. "You're an artist?"

"Whoops," Ivy said, pulling the door closed. "Yes, um, I teach art at the adult center downtown, and I also do private lessons." He followed her point to the dinosaur and star door. "That's Gavin's room. Mine's here." She nodded her head to the closed one across from Gavin's. "Your room is this way." Aldwin didn't miss the words that had slipped out, as if her mind was already made up. "I mean if everything you brought is in order."

"It is," he said and made sure he gave her a friendly and reassuring smile like he'd rehearsed. The shy one he got in response sent his stomach in a little flip. Ivy opened the door and flicked a switch, revealing a set of wooden stairs. He followed her up, and he felt his eyebrows raise against his will as he took it in.

The attic room wasn't just a room. It was a separate suite entirely. The bed area was tucked behind a wall, but to get to it he had to pass through a section with a rather cozy-looking love seat and table. That section of wall had been converted into a floor-to-ceiling bookcase, and it was crammed with books and globes and knickknacks. A door was opened, and one look inside showed him a spacious-looking en-suite with a garden tub and separate shower. Beside it was a closed-door that probably led to a closet.

"It's perfect," he said. His gaze fell on the bed, and instinctively he touched it. He expected to feel the tingle of happiness and joy there, but it was almost blank. The bed had been in the room a while, judging by the dust she had tried to clean off, but it had never been a permanent bed. Only the feeling of guest usage tingled in it.

"Thanks, Aaron spent months on it, but we never got to move up here," Ivy informed him. He nodded and let his hand fall off the wood frame. That explained so much. "So, what d'ya think; for the price I mean?" The suite was huge. It took up the entire length of the attic. It may as well be a studio flat. Nick reached into his coat pocket and pulled out the manila envelope with all his documentation

"I think you're seriously undercharging," said Aldwin, truthfully, and he pretended he didn't see the shock on her face. He rocked on his heels as she moved to sit on the love seat and looked over his paperwork. With her distracted, he could really take her in.

Ivy was beautiful, stunning really, with her obvious salon blonde hair and chipped nail polish. The way she chewed her lip as she read was adorable, but he could see the wear on her, how her shoulders never seemed to fully relax, and how there was just a hint of dark spots under her eyes. She was happy, that was easy to tell, but that happiness couldn't disguise the weight of anxiety, loss, and exhaustion she so obviously carried. Then he realized she still wore her wedding set. What had Lewin done?

"I can also pay the first two months in advance," he said and flicked his finger to call on the magic. He felt the weight of cash in his pocket, and he pulled it out to show her.

Ivy already knew everything he had would be clean. Alex had already double and triple-checked, but she couldn't tell him that. She looked up, finding herself momentarily stunned by the soft way he was analyzing her. The last time she had seen that look directed at her, Aaron had shooed her away from Gavin's booster seat at the table and told her to go have a glass of wine and a long bath. Why did she keep comparing them? They looked nothing alike, but somehow, they were similar.

"How do you feel about banana pancakes?" she asked, and she knew she was saying yes to the man.

"I love banana pancakes!" Nick exclaimed. She jumped on her cushion at his exuberance but smiled at his eager expression. "Bananas are my favorite. I especially love them with strawberry syrup and whipped cream, mm, with a glass of-" Ivy cut him off on instinct.

"Orange juice with pulp." The words slipped out. They startled her as much as they must have him because Nick's eyes went wide. Oh God, why had she done that? She was only asking because she'd promised Gavin breakfast for dinner.

"How'd you know?" he asked, and his exuberant smile faded to one of confusion. Ivy shot to her feet. No, she wouldn't let the tears fall.

"It's how Gavin likes it," she explained. She didn't mention it was how Aaron had, too. "We're having them for dinner. If you want to join us. Not that I'm asking if you're moving in tonight. You can, but, I—" Ivy snapped her mouth shut. She hadn't felt so flustered or out of control of her mouth since her first date with Aaron. She took the proffered cash from him.

"Will there be bacon?" asked Nick, looking as confused as she felt. Thankfully, he seemed to see she needed a subject change. "I love bacon."

"Gavin hates it, but I can cook you some," said Ivy. Aaron had hated it too. Okay, so maybe she was overreacting about how her mind was comparing them. She needed to calm down. "Then I can break the news to him about you renting the room." She headed towards the door. She had to get back to her comfort zone, and it was not this room. "The lease is downstairs."

She hurried down the stairs to her room and shut the door. There she leaned against it to gather her bearings. What the hell had she gotten herself into now?

The Mission Begins

"**W**ho're you?"

The voice of a child made Aldwin look away from where he had hung his long overcoat on the back of a chair. He had received it as a gift from Betty White at one of Lewin's parties. He had donned it while 'fetching his things' and had let the slight rain dampen it so Ivy would think he had indeed been out gathering his suitcases. In reality, he'd just taken a brief hop to Japan hoping to find Lewin. When that had been fruitless, he'd stood invisible outside long enough to get wet and then summon his stuff down from home.

A dark-haired boy with the bluest eyes Aldwin had ever seen and Ivy's cheeks and lips stared up at him from in front of a man in a uniform. There he was, Gavin Lucas Moore-Somerfield. Aldwin grinned, and he dropped to one knee to be at eye level with him.

"I'm Nick Claus. You must be Gavin. I've heard a lot about you," he said and extended a hand. The young gaze narrowed analytically, and, when Gavin shook his hand, Aldwin winced internally at the absolute lack of magic in him. He was still innocent, utterly good and blameless, but there was none of the spark that allowed young humans to see or believe in the magical.

"You smell like wet pine trees," Gavin said and pulled his hand away. "Where's my Mommy?"

"I think she went upstairs to put away your laundry," replied Aldwin. He stood and offered his hand to the man that eyed him with open caution. The man took it, and Aldwin read him. He was Alex Jones, a believer until he was ten, and Gavin's godfather. "Alex, right?"

"Exactly, I'm Gavin's godfather. Nice to meet you, Nick," grunted Alex. While there was some distrust in his mind, the detective wasn't necessarily opposed to Aldwin's presence.

"Alex!" Ivy's voice preceded her into the hall. Aldwin watched as Gavin barreled towards her with a smile, and she scooped him up, bag and all. "Hey, baby. How was chess league?"

"I won both matches!" Gavin exclaimed and pressed a kiss to her cheek, but he immediately began to wiggle. "Can I watch some TV?"

"Only a bit, then you've got to do your reading," she said. Ivy kissed his hair as she put him down, and Aldwin dodged the boy when he charged toward the living room. "You staying for dinner, Alex?

"Love to, but I'm going out on a date with Mark," explained Alex with what Aldwin assumed was an apologetic smile. Ivy's expression clearly said she didn't like this Mark person. Aldwin saw them both look at him as if waiting for a reaction, but he had none. "But call me—"

"If I need anything. Always do," said Ivy.

Aldwin gathered up his knapsack and two suitcases in his hands as they bid their farewells.

"That's all you brought?" She asked, in an obvious attempt to break the silence. "For a man who was heir to a successful company and teaches advanced science, you sure don't have a lot."

"I'm really good at packing," lied Aldwin. He had only brought down clothes and books he thought he'd need immediately. He could always call home and have his Mum or Dah send something down. Ivy's incredulous expression made him grin. The moment Gavin had hugged her, that silent weight seemed to lessen, and she was a supernova of happiness and love. It was dazzling. "Give me half a tick, and I can help with dinner."

"Oh, you don't have to," protested Ivy. She found she grew a little too warm under the excitement in Nick's gaze. "I can call you down when it's ready. Go on." She turned away and tried to ignore just how the man's wide, toothy grin made her feel a bit tingly inside. She found Gavin's bag abandoned on the counter, and she opened it to pull out his daily binder. There hadn't been any phone calls that day, and that gave her hope.

September 22, 2018

Gavin refused to play with the other kids at recess. They were imagining they were hunting a dragon. When asked why he preferred to build with the blocks, he said 'Anybody who believes in magic is a moron.'

I'd like to schedule a meeting about his behavior.

K. Anderson

"Damn it." Ivy groaned. She grabbed a pen from the drawer by the stove and signed her name with a time for the appointment. It didn't matter anyway. In two weeks, Gavin would be at a different school. She did wish, however, that he would just believe. He had an imagination, but he didn't believe. It hurt her heart that he had given up on that aspect of joy that she, herself, believed was real. There was no explanation for the necklace or the bear unless it was.

"Bad news?" Nick's voice made her jump. She hadn't expected him to be down so quick, and Ivy shoved the binder away. She was about to ask where he got off asking about her son's school notes, but he cut her off. "Sorry, that was nosey of me." He shoved his hands in his pockets, rocking up on the balls of his feet, and the apologetic smile he wore made her flicker of anger dissipate. "My mum says I shouldn't stick my nose where it doesn't belong. I'm still working on that." His British accent was like a lure, but she forced herself to ignore it.

"It's fine," huffed Ivy. She moved Gavin's bag to the peg beside the living room entryway, and the sound of a bowl being put down made her turn. "What're you doing?" She arched an eyebrow as Nick plucked the bunch of bananas from their hook. "I don't need help." She hurried forward and shooed him away. Her hands brushed his sleeve, and a strange scent wafted over her.

Nick smelled like snow-covered Christmas trees, peppermint, and some sort of incense. She hadn't smelled it earlier, but then again, she had been a little dazed. It was wonderful. Wait, what? Why had she thought that? She didn't notice when men smelled wonderful.

"Nick, do you like robots?" asked Gavin. Ivy breathed in relief at the interruption. She took the bowl away and tried to grab the bananas too.

Aldwin was thankful for Gavin's interruption. He had been frozen in place by Ivy's touch and the way her eyes had gone soft despite her protests against his help. He really needed to talk to Lewin about what had happened.

"I love robots!" He called back and surrendered the bananas to Ivy, who blinked and shook her head. Aldwin knew she felt it too, the undeniable pull of attraction, and he swallowed. "I'll just go watch TV with Gavin, yeah?" He was proud of himself for not stuttering.

"Uh, yeah, that's a good idea," croaked Ivy. She definitely needed some space to breathe, and he was more than willing to give it to her.

Aldwin flopped down next to Gavin, who had the TV on, but the boy was busy with a pile of parts for a small, brightly colored robot. "Whatcha buildin'?" he asked. Gavin was intently focused on his effort to snap an arm onto the body.

"A robot, but 's hard gettin' the arm on," the boy huffed, his words abbreviated in his effort to snap the arm into place.

"May I try?" asked Aldwin. Gavin was why he was there, after all. He was supposed to help the little boy. He grinned as the parts were surrendered.

"How come you're here? Mommy never brings strangers over," said Gavin. Okay, so the boy was clever. Aldwin had gathered he was a bit smarter than most five-year-olds, but he hadn't expected him to be so blunt.

"I'm going to live upstairs for a while. That means we're gonna be friends, right?" he asked and snapped the arm into place. Then he surrendered it back to waiting hands.

"I guess," grumbled Gavin. The young boy shrugged and rifled through some legs. "I don't really have friends. I heard Mommy tell Gran it's because I'm rude to the other kids." Aldwin wasn't quite sure how to respond to the matter-of-fact tone that sounded far too mature for five. "I want to be an astronaut when I grow up. I'm gonna fly a ship to Mars."

"Oh! That's a really good plan," encouraged Aldwin. He picked out a green leg to match the green helmet of the robot. His faith may have been gone, but Gavin did have an imagination of a different sort. That gave Aldwin hope. "When I was little, I wanted to be a pirate. Being an astronaut sounds way cooler." The boy's sweet face broke into a smile. The smell of pancakes started to fill the air, joined with the aroma of bacon. "Your mum's a good cook then?"

"The best," said Gavin. He wriggled a head onto the robot, and then he flipped it over. "Better than Gran." He took on a conspiratorial look and leaned over. "Never eat my Gran's cookies. They taste like salt. You talk funny."

"I'll keep that in mind, and I talk funny because I'm not from America," explained Aldwin. He picked up another robot body and quickly assembled it. He expected the boy to push the subject of his accent, but he didn't.

"Want to play Mars explorers with me?" the boy asked.

"Heck yeah." Aldwin laughed. If he was going to complete his trials, he needed to get Gavin's trust. One thing he had learned over nine hundred years was that the quickest way to do that was through play. He had never seen a child brighten up so quickly.

Ivy couldn't hear much over the show on the TV, but when she had peeked in just before she started the bacon, Nick had been helping Gavin with his robot toys. She was glad Gavin was being polite because most adults found his personality brusque and rude. Okay, so it drained her sometimes too, but her mom had assured her that was just a natural part of parenting.

It was the sound of giggling and cushions hitting the floor that pulled her away from where she was plating the food. Gavin had donned one of his plastic space helmets and had the TV remote in hand. He was perched like a gargoyle on the arm of the sofa. Suddenly Nick emerged from behind the wall of cushions, with an alien mask on.

"No, don't shoot! We're friendly!"

"This isn't a gun," yelped Gavin and held up the TV remote. "It's a sample scanner!" She watched as her son jumped off the sofa and landed on a throw pillow. "I'm here to learn about your people." She giggled at the way Nick pretended to duck out of sight for a moment, then peered around the sofa.

"We build robots," squeaked Nick. He produced one of Gavin's robots, holding it out. He must have seen her because he lowered the robot. "And we love banana pancakes."

"Me too!" exclaimed Gavin. He turned, face breaking into a grin, and Ivy beamed at the way he almost tripped over the pillow. "Yay for Martian Banana Pancakes!" She laughed out loud at his exuberance and snagged his helmet off as he ran past.

"Sorry, he can get a little excited sometimes," explained Ivy as she tucked the helmet under her arm. Nick pulled the mask off, took the helmet from her, and made quick work of putting the cushions back on the sofa. She was highly relieved that he was smiling and not irritated.

"Oh, it's fine. He's a smart kid." He ran a hand through his hair to fix where the mask strap had messed it up. "Like crazy smart. I've never met such an articulate five-year-old."

"Yeah, he's gifted." She gestured past her and inhaled that pleasant scent as he passed by. It made her heart flutter in an almost forgotten way, but she shoved it down. "He learned how to read and write at three. Aaron taught him." She could nearly picture them curled up on the sofa with a book, their identical eyes moving while Gavin read out the shaky words. "He actually starts at Crestwood in a week." She grabbed the plates, and before she could ask, he had picked up the cups.

"They have a whole building just for science!" Gavin piped up from his seat. "And a chess group! I love chess!" He wriggled in his chair. Those bright eyes never left the plate. "Almost as much as banana pancakes."

"Me too!" crooned Nick, matching Gavin's tone and volume as he put the cup down. Ivy swallowed her protest when he settled into Aaron's old chair. She sat the plates down and took her seat. "Maybe we can play a game sometime."

There was a bit of silence, as they all ate. Ivy was glad Gavin was taking it all in stride. She had been worried he'd pitch a fit like he had when she tried to hire an in-home babysitter instead of daycare. He hadn't been too keen on her dating, either, when her mom and Alex let it slip in front of him.

Ivy had seen the slight distrust of men Gavin had developed over during the time since his fathers death, and she was pleased to see that he was relaxed around Nick. Then again, their new tenant used to work for a toy company, and he was a teacher. Obviously, he had a way to get people to listen to him and trust him. Then, Nick spoke, and Ivy almost choked on her food.

"Gavin, it's only a few months 'til Christmas. Do you know what you're going to ask Santa for?" asked Nick, and Ivy braced herself for a tantrum.

Usually, any mention of Santa was enough to start a rant and she didn't want to scare Nick away the first night he was renting. She'd already had Gavin at a therapist to see if there was an underlying issue, but Dr. Smith had insisted that he was well adjusted and had made it through the grieving process as well as a five-year-old could. She explained that due to his intelligence, he had proven to himself that logically magic didn't exist. So long as he still had an imaginative play method and didn't become physically violent about the subject, there was no worry to continue therapy for it.

"Don't be stupid. Santa's not real," scoffed Gavin between bites. Her son didn't even look up from his plate.

"Yes he is, Gavin," insisted Ivy and offered Nick an apologetic smile. "And don't call people stupid. It's not polite." If Nick was offended, he didn't look like it. In fact, his eyes held a gleam of challenge, and he smirked. God, his smirk was earth-shattering. She shoved that thought away, determined to squash the flutter of warmth that it stirred in her chest. She wasn't ready to look at men like that, and she most definitely didn't want to feel that way about a man renting the suite that had been built for her lost marriage.

"You're mum's right. Santa is very, very real," said Aldwin. He was not upset by Gavin's rebuttal. He had expected it, but, after learning more about him, he knew how to counter. The boy was a budding scientist, so he had a plan to turn his views on his head. "Why do you think he's fake?"

"Because magic is fake, duh." Gavin rolled his eyes. He finally looked up at him, his little face full of annoyance. Aldwin grinned at the defiant challenge in his expression. It was obviously an argument the boy had won many times over with adults. "If magic is fake, then Santa is too."

"Oh, well, I dunno," tsked Aldwin and smiled over at Ivy, who watched the exchange with a nervous tightness in her features. He had a suspicion that this wasn't the first time she'd witnessed an adult try to explain things to her son. "Magic is just science we haven't figured out yet." The boy's face scrunched up in thought, and Aldwin knew he had him. Ivy's wide-eyed look and gasp of breath confirmed for him he had found a new avenue that nobody breached before.

"Huh, I didn't think of that," muttered Gavin in a surprised tone. Aldwin watched Ivy suck in and hold her breath from the corner of his eye, and he gave her his most reassuring smile. It was obvious from her expression that she wondered how he'd gotten her son to listen to anything regarding Santa. "Tell me more," the boy demanded. Aldwin winked at her, before turning his attention back to Gavin. Still, he didn't miss when she reached up to touch her necklace. He wondered if it was the one from her letter.

"Well, imagine you take a cellphone back to the fifteen hundreds." Aldwin pulled his cellphone out. "Then say you took a picture with it and showed it to the person. Do you think they would know it was science or would they see it as magic?"

"Magic," said Gavin around a bite of pancake, and his blue eyes went wide. "But we know how science makes phones work. It could be proven eventually. Santa's not the same. You can't prove Santa's real."

"Who says he isn't?" asked Aldwin. He took a bite as Gavin's face scrunched up in thoughtful silence. Finally the boy spoke.

"All the books at the library on myth...myth...mythology," began Gavin, but he didn't seem perturbed by his fumble over the word. Aldwin glanced at Ivy who watched them with worried attention. "They all said he was either based on myths of Odin or a Saint Nicholas from Turkey. That's Turkey the country, not the bird."

"Okay, and who wrote those books, humans right?" asked Aldwin. Gavin nodded. "And do humans know everything?"

"No," Gavin replied. Aldwin could see him work hard to come up with a counter-argument. "But none of it makes sense. Reindeer, sleighs, living above the Arctic circle with elves. None of it is logical." The boy waved his fork, seeming rather grown and dismissive. Aldwin suppressed another chuckle.

"That's because you're looking at it as magic and not science," corrected Aldwin. He pushed his plate aside and leaned forward. "Go on, ask me about it through science."

A Story For Dinner

"**W**hat about the population of the earth?" asked Gavin, and Ivy pushed her cup away. There had been a moment of silence when her son gathered his thoughts, but he had immediately jumped into quiz Nick. Luckily, the man seemed ready to go. "He couldn't deliver to everyone."

"Why not?" asked Nick, and Ivy found she respected the way he had turned his full attention to Gavin, posing the questions like an interview and not condescension. He leaned across the table until he was eye level with the five-year-old and kept his hands open. They were similar behaviors that Aaron had always done with their son and other children, and they were techniques she recognized from Gavin's therapist and former preschool teacher.

"The earth has over six billion people on it. I read it in a book at the library," Gavin had pushed his food away and knelt on his chair. His tiny chin rested on his palm. Honestly, it was so adorable that Ivy couldn't break the conversation up. So, she pulled the plate away from him and stacked it on hers. "How could he deliver presents to every single one?" She had been awaiting that rebuttal. So far, Nick had not missed a beat.

The man formulated responses almost as if he anticipated every question Gavin came up with. Either he had had this conversation dozens of times before, or he had been waiting to have it. Either way, he was completely focused on her son, talking to him like an adult, keeping his posture open and calm instead of closed off and domineering, that she found she had no anxiety over the discussion at all. In fact, if she didn't already believe, given her own miracle, she would have been convinced just by Nick's conviction.

"Well not everybody celebrates Christmas, so that takes a lot of people out of the delivery route," explained nick. His voice remained calm and inviting, and she could easily understand how he was a professor. "Plus, Santa only delivers to children. He might sometimes deliver to adults or older kids, but only if they write to him." She thought he glanced her way at those words, but she had apparently imagined it. He was still intently focused on Gavin. "In reality, he only delivers to somewhere between half a billion or so people."

"But how does he manage that?" Gavin scrunched his nose up as if contemplating the figure. He was a sharp kid, but the magnitude was still well over his head. Honestly, Ivy didn't understand it, but that was the glory of magic. She didn't need to know it was real to believe it. "Half a billion presents wouldn't fit on a sleigh."

"Well, he uses trans-dimensional engineering." Aldwin realized he may have gone over the kid's head when Gavin balked back with a bewildered look

Ivy giggled beside him, and Aldwin looked over to see she had pulled a leg up to rest her chin on and was watching them with a broad smile. The intensity of it made him lose his thoughts for a moment. He shook himself mentally to bring himself back to the conversation.

"It's hard to explain, but his bag is like its own dimension inside. Does that make sense?"

"Yeah...sorta....no." Gavin squished his nose up, looking so much like Aaron that Ivy's heart melted. "Hang on. So, it's bigger on the inside like the TARDIS on Doctor Who?"

"Exactly," Aldwin said with a laugh. "Anything else?" He glanced over at Ivy once more and found himself temporarily mesmerized by the way she bit her lip just so while she watched them. Her eyes met his, and he could see the twinkle of the lingering cupid magic in her gaze at the exact moment his heart skipped a beat. He blinked, and the sparkle was gone.

"How does he make it to every house on his list in twenty-four hours?" Gavin leaned back. He crossed his arms with the victorious look of a chess player declaring checkmate. He knew Gavin was capable of regaining his faith, and, when he did, that look of victory would shine with magic. Still, he had to answer the child's questions, but he wasn't worried. This was his domain. This was his life. Aldwin didn't need to do anything more than explain everything he had lived

"He bends time. Well, he doesn't bend it so much as he manipulates the time streams at synchronized points to allow him to slip between the relative dimensions," said Aldwin. Then he paused as mother and son let out a simultaneous sound.

"Huh?"

"He has something on his sleigh that allows him to find the easiest points to bend time and dimensions." Perhaps he had jumped just a little too far over their heads. Okay, he'd practically launched out of their orbit. How could he explain it? "It uses energy from time and the other dimensions to poke through the veils of each realm, like a needle in the fabric. Some of the dimensions move faster than ours." He paused to mime sliding a needle through the fabric. "So when he goes into those, he can travel at regular time there but emerge seconds later in our world. Some of the realms even allow the travel between dimensions to seem faster than light."

"But a human would be crushed if they moved between dimensions or faster than light," Gavin protested. He shook his head and raised one tiny eyebrow. Ivy bit her lip and waited for Nick's rebuttal to that. She knew she shouldn't have let Gavin watch the documentary on whether intergalactic travel would be achievable in the next hundred years. She had gotten a chance to mop the floor undisturbed, so it was a win at the time.

"But you're assuming he is human," Nick said, leaned back, and he smirked that damned smirk again. It suited his sharp features so well, and Ivy felt a flash of heat fill her chest. She picked her glass up and took a drink to quell it.

"He's an alien?" Gavin asked.

"No, he's from the realm of the Ageless," countered Nick. Ivy could tell he had Gavin's attention now. She recognized all the signs that his mind was whirring behind those piercing, blue eyes, and he leaned forward. "It's another dimension you see. Thousands of years ago, the race of the Ageless was exploring their universe, and they found a rift." Nick raised his hands and pressed them together. Ivy found herself drawn into the mystical tone his voice had taken for the story. "It was only about the size of a thread, but the eldest of them all, Gaia, was curious about the rift. So, she poked and pulled until it opened." He parted his hands and created an opening. "Then she slipped through. There she found a brand-new universe. It was only a few billion years old, practically a baby. Best of all, she found this wonderful planet we're on now with an amazing race that would eventually be called humans. Then she went back, told her people, and they ventured in."

"What happened when they came to Earth?" Gavin's voice was low with rapt wonder. Ivy couldn't blame him at all.

"Well, Gaia loved it so much, that she couldn't bear to leave. Then, she took the humans, nurtured them, and gifted them with seeds and animals from her realm. They mistook her for a goddess and called her Mother Nature." Nick's expressive voice was so rich that Ivy could almost see Gaia's smile and smell fresh flowers in the air. She breathed in, pulled her foot into the chair, and rested her chin on her knee again. His story had completely sucked her in. "Many of the others joined her. There were the Season Sisters: Spring, Summer, Autumn, and Winter, and their children, known as sprites. There were the Amores, which humans later called cupids, and many other mystical beings from lore around the world."

"So where does Santa fit into this?" Ivy asked, beyond curious about the story. She'd researched many folklores about Santa over the last year, but none had covered this. She wondered if he had invented the tale on his own. He must have. Gavin's glower at her interruption made her cover her mouth with her hand and giggle.

"Well, Gaia had never really been around Winter or her children before. See, she normally prefers Summer and Spring. Then she met one of Winter's sons. Instantly, she fell in love. They had a son of their own. He had all of Gaia's wisdom, compassion, and curiosity. He loved to travel amongst the humans."Nick's voice had dropped, and it took on the tone of someone who had years of experience telling stories. It was impossible for Ivy to not lean in closer, chin on her knee, and glance at Gavin who was just as captivated as she was.

"He found this festival centered around the Winter Solstice" Aldwin continued to weave his family's history. He could retell the story without a break. His grandmum had told it to him when he was barely fifty. "The humans would gather, decorate trees around their villages or in their homes with berries, nuts, and trinkets for the animals and sprites on the longest night of the year." He wasn't sure where to look. He knew his mission was Gavin, and the boy had fallen completely silent. Yet Ivy was just as enthralled, and her amber eyes flushed heat into his veins. He had to focus on Gavin, no matter how stunningly entranced she was.

"He was so moved that the humans had wanted to make sure his cousins and the animals were fed that night, that he had to repay them. That whole year, he traveled from town to town, whispering to children about a mystical man named Kris Kringle, who was a winter sprite. If they were very good and didn't misbehave, Kris Kringle would leave them gifts on Solstice as well. That Solstice, he did just that."

"He was the first Santa?" whispered Ivy.

Aldwin turned to face her, the look of wonder in her eyes made burning his entire being in response. He knew she was feeling something too, but not as intense. Still, he had to resist the urge to reach over and brush a lock of hair from her face.

"You mean Santa isn't human. He's from another dimension?" Gavin's question nearly broke the magic, but Aldwin turned his attention back to the boy and nodded.

"Exactly, however, since that first Santa, the line has continued. From father to son to grandson." Aldwin wanted so badly to call the magic, to show Gavin the truth then and there. It would be perfect, too easy, but he wasn't allowed to intentionally reveal himself. Gavin had to find the belief through Aldwin's efforts to earn his trust and faith. "Although, I have it on very good authority that the current Santa met a human woman a little over nine hundred years ago and fell madly in love with her. She loved him too, so much so, that Gaia and Winter turned her into a winter sprite, so they'd be together forever. They have a son. His name is Aldwin, and he is training to become the next Santa."

The silence in the room seemed to spark. Ivy swore she smelled that pine scent again, but it was intermixed with fresh baked cookies and pipe tobacco. She half expected to see snow falling beyond the window, but all she saw was the clock's reflection. It was almost Gavin's bedtime.

"But how do the rein-" Gavin began, but Ivy cut him off reluctantly.

"I think we've pestered Nick long enough," she said. She stood up and offered the man an apologetic look. "Bath time sweetheart."

"But Mom!" Gavin whined, and Ivy gave him her 'now' look. She didn't miss Nick's chuckle at the exchange. Gavin pushed away from the table and skulked to the bathroom.

"Sorry he sorta bombarded you like that," apologized Ivy as she gathered the plates and headed into the kitchen to put them in the sink. "And thanks, for being so tolerant of his questions. Most adults get frustrated when he starts trying to prove them wrong."

"Oh, it's fine," Nick said. She stepped closer to the sink so he could put the cups on the side. "His imagination is just a bit different than other kids. I'm surprised you want him to believe." His voice lowered as if afraid they'd be overheard, and Ivy had to lean in a bit to hear him. "Most parents just give up when the kids figure it out, but you didn't." His rich brown eyes skirted over her face as if she were a text he was trying to decipher. She had to look away from his gaze to find her breath again. "Why is that?"

"The magic of Christmas should be enjoyed as long as possible," Ivy explained. She hoped the sadness in her voice wasn't too audible, and she shrugged. Then she turned to rake the leftover batter into the trash. "There's so much bad in the world. I want him to believe in something purely good." She slid the now-empty bowl into the sink and heaved a sigh. Finally, she turned to look at the new addition to their house. Nick was watching her with open curiosity. "He's so smart, but I don't want him growing up too fast." The man leaned down and locked his gaze with hers. Ivy didn't think she'd ever seen such a stunning brown color in her life.

"Growing up doesn't mean you have to stop believing," Nick whispered and bumped her with an elbow. It was Ivy's turn to lean in towards him to hear his words. "I'm a grown-up, and I believe in Santa Claus." The confession had their faces so close, that Ivy found she lost her breath. His voice, so warm and calm, made her head spin as his eyes flicked between hers. "How about you, Ivy Moore? Do you believe?"

"Actually," she whispered back, and her entire body felt like it was humming. "I do. I can't explain why, but I do believe he is real." She expected a rebuttal, a laugh, or even him to roll his eyes. Instead, a toothy grin lit up his face, and Nick pulled away.

"I think between the two of us, we can restore Gavin's belief too." Nick too another step back. It almost seemed like he was running away from her, which made no sense given how close he'd gotten. "I'm going to go unpack."

"'Kay." Ivy shook her head when Nick disappeared down the hall.

What was going on with her? How did he keep managing to make her feel so alive? She hadn't felt like this in years, seven and a half years to be exact. The last time she'd felt this was the night she met Aaron. Heaven help her, she was attracted to him. She sucked in a breath, looking down at her hands gripping the sink so tightly her knuckles were white. The diamonds sparkled up at her, and she let out a sigh when guilt washed through her.

"I can't be," she whispered to nobody, and she hurried upstairs to fetch Gavin's pajamas.

Aldwin closed the door behind him, pulled out his mobile, and pressed Lewin's contact. "Oi! You, get over here now," he hissed in Ageless.

"It's not my fault!" Lewin exclaimed as soon as he popped into existence, thankfully clothed. "I told you! I don't have a choice."

Aldwin rounded on him and did his best to keep in control of his voice.

"But how?! I'm Ageless, and she's mortal! This doesn't make sense." He threw his hands up and turned to his suitcases. With a snap of his right fingers, the clothes flew to the closet and drawers. "Did you even try to look into it?"

"Where do you think I've been?" Lewin asked and ran a hand through his hair. "But there are only two other Supreme Cupids besides me, and they've never done a mortal/Ageless marking." He groaned and sat on the bed. Aldwin dropped beside him. There was something in Lewin's eyes, it may have been fear or uncertainty, he wasn't sure. "Something else happened, and I don't think you're gonna like it."

"Tell me," demanded Aldwin. He needed to know. He had to know if being marked with Ivy would somehow impede his mission or if it would help. Lewin for once seemed to flounder for words.

"I couldn't see your destinies, not past them merging in love. After the love confession, it was blank." His friend sighed. The cupid shook his head and met his eyes. "It was like when I was a Base Level Cupid, and I could mark as I pleased. Those joinings may last hours or years." Aldwin had heard this all before, but he let Lewin continue. Sometimes talking through it out loud held the solution. "We can't see destinies until we are Master cupids, you know, long-term important bindings. Supremes, we only mark soulmates. Aldwin, I can only mark the most important of soulmates, and I get my magic off the love that comes from seeing their futures."

"Is it because of my magic?" asked Aldwin. He didn't know of any other Ageless who had ever been marked. Because they lived for eons, many didn't even take life partners. Granted, the Claus line always had, but his parents hadn't been marked. They hadn't needed to be. Their unity was a choice of destiny, and it hadn't needed a nudge. "Or is it because she's, oh, I don't know-" he paused and gave an exasperated sigh before he glowered at his friend. "Grieving over her dead soulmate?"

"I don't know if it's your magic, but it's not her grief," admitted Lewin, before he drew in a shaky breath. "Just, well, let her make the first move. That's all I can advise. I can't explain it, but the magic is telling me the ball is in her court." He cocked his head, and Aldwin groaned. He knew that look. "Sorry, buddy, gotta fly. I'm needed in Quebec." With a poof, Lewin was gone.

"Well, isn't this just brilliant?" Aldwin groaned.

He flopped back on the bed. He'd been in the mortal realm alone for less than twenty-four hours, and he was in way over his head.

Sparks In The Park

Like always, the months that preceded the holidays became a blur for Ivy. One minute she was knocking on Nick's door to ask him to keep it down because her son was a light sleeper, and the next Nicholas Claus had been in her house for two weeks.

He was such an odd man, but Ivy found that having him in her home wasn't as weird as she had believed it would be. His entire presence was oddly soothing with his easy smiles and constant babble. To top it all off, Gavin had taken to him like they'd been friends forever.

She had been hesitant about it at first, but Nick had yet to lose patience with her son. From silent chess games while she finally got to finish the book she'd been working on for a month, to the pair sitting cross-legged on the floor with a bowl of popcorn between them while they watched Gavin's favorite science show, Nick never grew irritated or brusque.

Sometimes, the normality of it all caught her off guard. The way he smoothed himself into their life's routine made it feel like he'd always been a part of it. He hadn't been, of course, but still, the longer Nick Claus spent with them, the more Ivy found that her attraction to him grew.

She didn't know if he felt the same because he never mentioned it. Sometimes, though, his gaze would meet hers, and he'd smile sweetly. Other times, he'd look up from his morning coffee, take in her outfit while Gavin tied his shoes, and compliment it politely, but there was never any push behind his actions.

Ivy was slightly ashamed to admit that she looked forward to him stumbling down the stairs every morning and seeing his brilliant smile in the evenings. He was always seated at the table with his sleek laptop when they got home. She hadn't told anyone yet, not her mom, not Penny, definitely not Alex, and not even a whisper to Aaron as she curled up in bed. Those two fruitless dates from July and August hadn't given her much guilt but wondering if Nick's nimble hands would feel nice laced with hers did. She knew the guilt was silly and unwarranted, but she couldn't help it.

Everyone around her had been fine with it and even encouraged her to date. They had all told her that almost three years wasn't too early to at least try. She was young, and Gavin was still at an age where bringing in a new man wouldn't be as troublesome as it would be when he approached his teen years. So, Ivy didn't understand why her feelings for Nick had her so torn up. The support boards online for widows all said it was normal though, as she scanned through them, unable to post herself.

It hit her the hardest when it first caused her a fitful night's sleep. She'd tossed and turned, mostly because she had dreamed of Nick. The dream hadn't been anything untoward. It had just been a harmless one where they had been walking through a store. Still, it had woken her up, made her roll over to the empty side of the bed, and she snuggled into Aaron's pillow. Sleep had been elusive until three in the morning.

She groaned and pulled the covers off of her head, braced herself for the ache that came with only three hours of sleep, and wiped her sticky eyes. The headache didn't come. She squinted at the alarm clock, which blatantly told her it was Sunday morning and nearly eight. She scrambled to sit up. Gavin was always up between six and six-thirty, always, without fail. He should have either crawled in her bed for some snuggles or whined and whimpered that he was hungry.

"Gavin!" She called out. Scrambling out of bed, Ivy stumbled to the door. Was he sick? She pushed open his door, but his bed was empty. "Gavin?" She yelped and rushed to the stairs. Panic filled her as she went. She was five steps down when the smell of coffee, pancakes, bacon, and french toast greeted her, accompanied by a giggle.

"She likes the powdered sugar on them," said Gavin, and the sound of his voice made her relax. "And cinnamon."

"And you're sure she likes roses?" Nick's soft question was accompanied by the sound of glass on the counter. "Because if she doesn't, I'm gonna eat your last ice cream." Ivy tiptoed down the last few stairs and held her breath as she peeked around the corner. She wasn't sure what was waiting, but the scene before her was absolutely precious.

Gavin was perched beside the sink, finishing off an oddly shaped pancake. Beside him was a wooden tray, with a cup of coffee, a plate of french toast, and a thin vase with a pink rose in it. Nick had just put up the containers of confectioners' sugar and cinnamon.

"I don't like roses," she informed the pair. Ivy quickly brushed her hair back and silently wished she had at least worn some of her nicer pajamas. "I love them."

Aldwin spun, and his face burned at Ivy's unexpected arrival.

"Oh, good morning, Ivy. Did we wake you?" He closed the cabinet and took in her bedraggled appearance. He had thought he heard her tossing and turning, maybe even crying, the night before, but he hadn't been sure. He obviously had, given the salt tracks down her cheeks and the puffy bloodshot eyes, but she still looked absolutely adorable all rumpled and mid-yawn.

"Mommy, you ruined the surprise! I was gonna bring you breakfast in bed." Gavin announced with a pout, and the giggle that came from Ivy made Aldwin's stomach do a flip. Nothing in all the realms sounded as lovely as her joy.

"I'm sorry baby," said Ivy. She wandered further into the kitchen and kissed the boy on the head. "I woke up and you weren't in your bed. I had to make sure you were okay."

"Nick made me breakfast!" Gavin exclaimed as he pointed at the tray Aldwin had been preparing. "And I helped make you french toast!"

Those slightly reddened eyes met his, and Aldwin found himself shifting uncertainly. He hoped she wouldn't be upset with him for taking on such a task without asking.

"I was coming in about six from a jog, and Gavin came into the hall saying he was hungry." She didn't seem upset or angry, but he still offered her an apologetic smile. "Thought you might like a bit of a lie-in. So, I made him pancakes."

"Dinosaur pancakes," Gavin corrected him through a full mouth.

"Right, Gavin, dinosaur pancakes," said Aldwin. Ivy's expression softened, and her shoulders relaxed. "He wanted to bring breakfast up to you." He was just glad she hadn't asked where the flower came from. He may have told Gavin he'd gotten it from the neighbor's bushes, but, in reality, he'd magicked it while the boy went to pee.

"That's so sweet, Gavin," said Ivy with a hum of affection. He watched as she kissed Gavin's dark hair again, and Aldwin beamed. He was relieved that she didn't seem opposed to the gesture. "Thank you, too, Nick," she murmured. Then, to his surprise, she reached over and squeezed his hand. It shot warmth and excitement up his arm, and it took a herculean effort not to pull her in for a hug. "Why don't I take my little surprise to the table then, yeah?"

"Am I going to Gran's today?" asked Gavin through his last mouthful of breakfast, and Ivy picked up the tray.

"Actually, Gran went to visit cousin, Paula," replied Ivy. Aldwin had yet to meet Fiona Moore, the apparent matriarch of the little family he'd snuck his way into. "So, I thought we might go to the park and then get groceries." He couldn't help but smile when Gavin's face split into a syrup-covered grin. "What'd'ya think, sticky face?" she asked before heading towards the dining room.

"Can Nick come?" Gavin slid his plate into the sink before Aldwin could stop him. He jumped down to pursue his mum. Part of Aldwin wanted to do the same, but he decided to start loading the dishwasher instead. He still listened in though.

"Baby, I'm sure Nick has other plans," Ivy answered.

He absolutely did not, and honestly, a day in the park with the people who had swiftly became his favorite humans sounded wonderful.

"Actually." Nick's slightly nervous smile peeked around the corner and took Ivy by surprise. "I'm completely free. I don't mind if you don't." She didn't, did she? Ivy watched those chocolate eyes flicker between her and Gavin, who mirrored Nick's eager expression. "Two adults might make carrying the groceries easier." He added in with a sly tone.

"You're sure, Nick?" Ivy found she did want him to come. She'd appreciate some company on the bench while Gavin played. He nodded and smiled in that alluring way that always sent pleasant shivers down her neck. "Then I guess I can't say no." Gavin gave a yelp of victory. "Honey, why don't you go wash up and brush your teeth. Mommy's gonna eat and we'll get dressed." The boy took off with a manic giggle, leaving her alone with Nick. "You know, you can tell him no sometimes. I don't want to bother you. I'm sure you've got friends—"

"I just moved from Canada, remember?" Nick shrugged. "All my friends are there or back home in London."

Ivy nodded, glad she had agreed. They hadn't really had time with him outside of the house, and she was curious to see how he would interact with Gavin in public.

"Besides, I need some things from the store too. Seems more logical to just go together." He nodded at her rapidly cooling food. "Eat, Ivy. I'll take care of the mess in here."

Ivy finished her breakfast, then she wriggled a squirming Gavin into some jeans, a long sleeve shirt, and a zip-up jacket. She kept him distracted on her bed with her phone as she stared at her closet. Normally, she'd just throw on some comfy clothes and tie her hair back but sleeping in had left her refreshed. Instead, she went for fitted black pants, a black and white shirt, and a red jacket. Then, after a second thought, she took a little extra time to put on some makeup besides her eyeliner and mascara. She tried to tell herself that she wasn't intentionally trying to look more appealing, but that was a lie. She wanted Nick to look at her like he had when she walked into the kitchen—like she was as gorgeous as the rose on the tray.

When she came downstairs, Nick was already there. He looked absolutely gorgeous in a pair of jeans and one of his sports coats. The sports coats seemed to dominate his wardrobe, although he did throw some jumpers, as he called them, into the mix. The one he had on was blue, with a casual maroon t shirt underneath instead of the usual button-downs, complete with red converse. He took one look at her, and Ivy knew he was *looking*.

Her ears burned slightly as she shifted her weight.

"What? Have I got something on my face?" The question bubbled out before she could think straight.

"No." Nick's eyes grazed over her face, paused at her glossy lips, and then continued down along her curves. Ivy smoothed her jacket to hide her nerves at his examination. "You look great." His voice pitched a little high on the last word, and Ivy started to think that maybe he did see her in *that* light. He glanced down at Gavin, who tugged at her hand. "Um, shall we go then?"

"Yeah, I just need to grab my wallet and phone." She didn't like carrying a purse or bag out to the park, so she dug her keys, phone, and wallet out. When she returned, Nick was kneeling down in front of Gavin, fixing his jacket. "Nick, can you hold these for me?" She held out the keys because she knew the other two items would fill her pockets.

"Yeah, sure," replied Aldwin and opened the door. He chuckled when Gavin dashed out. "Wait, Gavin!" He called before he took Ivy's keys and let her pass. Then he locked up and joined them on the sidewalk. "Where's the park?"

"This way," urged Gavin grabbing his hand and dragging him along. Aldwin grunted in surprise as he rushed to keep up with the boy. Ivy hardly seemed bothered as she fell into step beside them and reached down to let her son clasp her hand. "There's a slide and swings and monkey bars. Good morning Mr. Johnson!" Aldwin offered a wave as they passed the neighbor trimming the rose bushes.

He found he rather liked the way this felt, walking with Gavin's hand wrapped around his pinky as Ivy beamed happily. It felt like a part of him he hadn't known was empty had begun to fill. The morning was still fresh and held a slight chill. It didn't bother him in the least, but he knew the other two felt it.

Every so often, Ivy glanced over at him, and Aldwin had to try not to blurt it all out. It was a bit unfair that he knew what she was feeling, but she had no clue that he knew. He was acutely aware that she was slowly developing feelings for him, and he knew that they probably confused her. He knew she had to be conflicted and possibly overwhelmed by it. The feelings were mutual, but he couldn't tell her, not yet.

Ivy had to say it first. She had to open the door for him to step in. Aldwin knew what was holding her back, and he was perfectly fine with that. He took his time and was patient. He made sure his touch didn't linger, and that his gazes were just long enough so she knew he was watching but never long enough to be considered staring. By the time they reached the tiny park, he ached to touch her.

Gavin was off the instant the playground came into view, bee-lining for the brightly colored stairs and slide. Ivy settled on a bench nearby, and Aldwin had a choice. He'd slowly been working with Gavin, mostly when Ivy was busy, laying more of the foundation of restoring his faith. He also wanted to spend time with Ivy, to get to know more about the wonderful woman who had become his soulmate. He looked at Gavin, then at Ivy. His mind made itself up. The mission could wait a day.

"Mind if I join you?" asked Nick. Ivy looked up as he gestured to the empty space beside her. The uncertain way that he shifted made her breath catch.

"Please," she said and shivered at the cool breeze. It would warm up a little soon, but October was beginning, so the chilly weather was settling in to stay. "I doubt you could catch him anyways," she snorted, and Nick sat beside her. Gavin was all speed as he ran around the slide towards the monkey bars. Nick chuckled softly.

"He's a great kid," hummed Nick. Ivy could tell he had something on his mind, but she wasn't sure how to broach the soft tension between them. Instead, she just gripped the bench on either side of her legs and watched her son play. "And you're a really great mum." She loved hearing him talk, and his compliment brought that now too familiar warmth to her cheeks. She smiled over at him.

"Thanks." She liked how his presence beside her felt, as the warm scent of snowy pine ghosted across her face. They didn't often spend time alone, and, although they were at the park, it was the first time Gavin was truly out of earshot and distracted. "You're really good with him. I was sorta afraid he'd hate you in the beginning."

"I'm good with kids. I don't have any myself, but I've got loads of younger cousins." Nick laughed softly. "Sometimes it feels like there are thousands of them." Ivy laughed at that. She only had one cousin, Paula, who lived about forty-five minutes away. "And, you know, my Dah's business is catered to kids. So, it comes naturally." He bumped her shoulder with his, and Ivy loosened her grip on the bench some. Being around Nick was often a conundrum of relaxation and guilty tension. So far, the guilt was staying away. "I hope we didn't scare you too much this morning, letting you sleep in," he added.

"God no, I needed it," Ivy admitted. She didn't know why she blurted that out, but it felt good to tell someone. She never really told Alex or her mom that sometimes she wished for something as simple as sleeping in and breakfast already made when she woke up. "I really, really needed it." She glanced away from Gavin and looked up to find Nick was watching him too. Then his gaze shifted towards her. It was so understanding and soft that she found she couldn't help but inch a bit closer to him.

"I know. I heard you tossing and turning last night. Bad dream?" Aldwin didn't miss the way Ivy scooted almost imperceptibly towards him, and he fought to keep the excitement from showing. Instead, he chanced sliding his arm up to the back of the bench behind her. Ivy's appreciative smile faltered, and he almost pulled his arm back until she drew in a heavy breath and looked down at her hands.

"No, it's just that sometimes good dreams can be bad to wake up from," whispered Ivy. Aldwin couldn't even begin to fathom how good her dream had been for her to want to cry when she woke up. It had probably involved Aaron. "Sorry if I disturbed you at all," she huffed. His thumb brushed her shoulder, and she froze.

"Sorry," grunted Aldwin. He pulled his arm back and mentally kicked himself. He'd just been trying to ease her emotions, not make her uncomfortable. "I didn't mean to put my arm," he stuttered. "Well, I was just—" Great, he'd buggered it up. Ivy stared at Gavin and picked at her bottom lip with her teeth. He dropped his hand to his lap. "Sorry, I didn't even realize I'd done it."

"I like you," blurted Ivy. Aldwin's heart skip a beat at how direct her words had been. She didn't meet his eyes though, so he wasn't sure what to say back. How could he explain to her that he knew and that he liked her, well more than liked her, back? "I mean, I really like you, Nick."

"I *really* like you too, Ivy," admitted Aldwin. He didn't push her, because he could tell how much she struggled internally to get the words out. He chose to watch as Gavin joined in with a game of tag instead of trying to catch her gaze. "I understand, though, how you're feeling."

"Do you really?" asked Ivy. Aldwin couldn't resist the soft, rhetorical question. He looked over at her and watched as she fiddled with the rings on her finger. "Because—" he cut her off gently.

"You feel guilty for liking me,"he said, and he turned fully to her. "That's perfectly normal, and I don't want you to think it upsets me." He let the words lie as she looked back down at her hands and breathe in deeply. Aldwin waited for her to find her words and kept an eye on Gavin from his peripheral. Then he focused back on the wonderful woman beside him.

Ivy took the time to find her thoughts, which had been scattered by his tender understanding. She looked up to find Nick watching her with an open, honest, and compassionate expression that stole her breath.

"I need time," she said and reached over. She was so relieved that he knew what she was feeling without her saying. She touched his arm gently and tried to convey what a comfort it was that he hadn't pushed her.

"I've got all the time in the world," replied Nick. Then he reached up and tucked the ever-bothersome lock of hair that constantly fell in her face behind her ear. Ivy didn't hide her smile, as she accepted the familiar touch instead of moving away from it. Aaron had always done that too, usually followed with a kiss on her cheek. Nick didn't kiss her, though. Ivy was grateful, because that may have ruptured the lump of emotion in her throat that she was struggling against. "There is something, though, that I've wanted to do for the last few days. It's just a small thing really." His fingers fell away from her cheek, and Ivy swallowed when they came to rest on her wrist.

"What?" She asked and almost winced at how breathless she sounded to her own ears. She'd opened the door between them but how far would he try to push in? She braced herself until he cautiously laced their fingers together. It was the most perfect feeling in the world, and Ivy relaxed at his touch. She smiled up at him and gently squeezed their joined hands.

"Just this," chuckled Nick. His hand was warm and effortless against hers. Ivy had wondered many times if holding his hand would feel nice. It felt better than nice—like her fingers were perfectly formed to fit with his. She expected the guilt to flare up, as their joined palms rested on the small dip where their thighs met, but it didn't. "Is this all right?"

"It's perfectly all right," she answered.

Ivy squeezed his fingers again to let him know she meant it, as she glanced back out to find her son. Gavin stood at the top of the playground, and he had obviously watching them. When his intense blue eyes met hers, he grinned like a madman and ducked out of sight.

Memories Of Love

"Spill, how's the renter?" Fiona queried from across the table.

Ivy hadn't had any students show up for her class, so she had headed over to her mom's for lunch. Gavin was well settled in at Crestwood, and she didn't want to bother Nick with whatever he did while they were gone. He was probably grading papers or recording a lecture. She'd never really asked, though he'd been with them going on a month now.

"He's great," she said.

That was the biggest understatement she made in years. Nick was an absolute dream. Since their little exchange in the park a week and a half before, hand-holding had become an everyday thing. From joined fingers wedged between them on the sofa, to thumbs brushing knuckles as she took his plate to clear the table, they touched hands as much as possible. It had also been increased with long looks that made her feel radiant and texts throughout the day about random things that filled her with the familiar giggle of a new relationship.

"He's really sweet, and Gavin likes having him around."

"And he's gorgeous." Ivy snapped her gaze up from her sandwich and blinked in shock at her mom's snicker. "You're practically about to float out of your chair." Her mothers aqua eyes danced in amusement. "And Alex said he was hot, with—how did he word it—an ass meant for squeezing." Ivy groaned inwardly at her mom's words and felt her cheeks burn. Nick's butt was absolutely meant for squeezing, but she hadn't indulged in that yet. "Hang on, I know that look!" Fiona accused loudly. "Ivy Holly Moore! Are you two sleeping together?"

"What!" Ivy yelped at the accusation. "No, God, Mom. Why would you think that?" She dropped her head to her hands and tried hard to hide how red she felt herself turning. They hadn't even hugged. "We're absolutely not sleeping together."

"But you like him," said Fiona , smugly. Of course, her mom would figure that much out. She'd known Ivy was seeing Aaron before Ivy had told her about their second date. Well, she hadn't known who, just that she was seeing someone. "Have you told him yet?"

"Yeah, I have," grumbled Ivy. She picked at her sandwich, her gut twisting in nerves and that sensation of guilt that liked to flare up randomly. "And he likes me too. We haven't done much past talking though."

There had been talking all right. There had been many ten-at-night cups of tea on the sofa. He'd drawn patterns over her right hand while they talked about everything and nothing. Their conversations had mostly been about where she'd grown up, how he was only teaching because he wasn't sure he was able to take over his fathers business, and that she was afraid Gavin was going to alienate kids at Crestwood, and how he spoke over eight languages.

"We haven't even gone past hand-holding," she admitted.

"Well, I want to meet him," Fiona insisted. She crossed her arms, as Ivy opened her mouth to protest, but Ivy knew it was pointless to argue with that face. "Don't even argue, missy, I need to make sure he's not some creeper."

"Mom, Alex already ran a full check on him. He's a perfectly normal man," Ivy said as her phone dinged a text from the table. She tried to grab it, but Fiona beat her to the punch. "Mom!"

"He wants to know what kind of pizza you and Gavin like." Fiona snorted with a smirk, and then her thumb began scrolling. Ivy could not believe her mom was going through her phone. She tried to grab it, but Fiona jumped out of her chair and dashed into the living room. "Hang on. This is him?" She paused and cocked her head to look at the screen. "He's a bit skinny, but my God, is that a toupee?"

"No!" Ivy yelped. She was absolutely mortified, but she was immensely grateful that the only pictures in that particular thread of messages were ones he had snapped of him and Gavin and of her and Gavin that he texted her. "Well, I don't think it is. Haven't exactly stuck my hands in it have I? Gimme my phone!" She tried to snag it back, but

Fiona batted her hands away. "Oh, he is a bit prettier than your old type. I'm betting he's tall though. You always like them tall."

"What'd'ya mean my old type?" Ivy hissed. She definitely did not have a type. She never had. Lots of people she had gone out with when she was a teen and before she met Aaron were good-looking, but she didn't have a type. "I don't have a type."

"Yeah, you do. You like the older, tall, sort of broody, bad boys." Fiona scoffed and finally surrendered the phone. "They usually have a penchant for leather. You know, Daniel, Ashton, Marcus, and Aaron." Ivy sucked in a breath as the name stabbed into her heart. Her mom instantly froze. "Oh honey, I didn't mean that. Aaron was a good man, but you have to admit if you didn't know he was a cop or a former professor, you'd think he was a little on the rough side."

"He was only rough when he had to be," Ivy snapped. She bit her lip and shakily texted back that they liked pepperoni. She didn't like that her mother had compared her loving and devoted husband to the ones who had hurt her before him. "He was a good man, Mom, the best. I know you never liked him, but please, don't lump him in with my idiotic choices from high school."

"Ivy, sweetheart." Fiona sighed, and her mothers arms went around her. Ivy clung to her and buried her face into her shoulder. She didn't bother hiding her tears from her mother because she knew how hard it was. Becoming a widow young seemed to be an inherited part of their family. "I'm sorry, baby. I did like him. Really, I did. He was good to you, never hit you, never made you feel bad about yourself, and he never cheated. That's all I asked for, and he loved you and Gavin more than anything." Ivy squeezed her mother tighter. "But you did have a type."

"Oh, shut up," groaned Ivy. She was chagrined to admit that her mother was right, although, she hadn't known about Aaron's obsession with his leather coat until their first date. Alex had demanded an invitation to the wedding a month later when Ivy walked into the local bar with that very same coat wrapped around her rain-drenched shirt. That jacket still hung carefully preserved in her closet, waiting for Gavin to fill it. "No, I guess Nick isn't my usual type that way, but he is a bit like Aaron."

"Yeah?" Fiona asked and pulled away to tug her down onto the couch. "How so?"

"Bananas." Ivy giggled at Fiona's arched eyebrow. "He's absolutely bananas for bananas. Pancakes, smoothies, pudding, candy, you name it, he likes it in banana." She cocked her head, counting through the mental list she had subconsciously made of his similarities to Aaron. "He's really into science, chess, and reading. He and Gavin have the TV practically stuck on those docu-series. He prefers tea over coffee, with five sugars and no cream the exact same as Aaron. He even takes his pancakes the same way, and he always knows exactly when my hair's about to fall in my face." She reached up to tuck the stray lock back.

Her mothers eyes scanned over her face, and Ivy didn't understand the scrutiny behind them. Then Fiona shook her head and smiled.

"Well, I'm coming over for dinner tomorrow. I want to meet him. I won't hear a word about it. I've gotta make sure he isn't taking advantage of my babies."

Ivy knew it was pointless to argue.

"Fine, but don't slap him like you did Aaron." She snickered as she recalled the shocked look on his face the moment he'd met her mother. "That was so uncalled for!"

"You disappeared for a whole weekend. What was I supposed to think? Your job gets robbed. You go on one date, and then a week later you disappear. Cellphone's still on your dresser. Your book bag is gone with your university textbooks all over .the bed and floor." Fiona shook her head and laughed. Ivy's chuckles turned into a full-blown laugh as well. "I thought you'd been kidnapped. Where were you? In Florida, on a beach, with a man you barely knew!"

"I just meant to stay the night at his apartment. There was a lot of tequila involved." Ivy sighed in contentment at the memory.

She still couldn't remember, so many years later, what prompted that insane trip. She just remembered being half-naked in his bedroom, drunkenly hoping he had condoms, as she tried to get her bra off. Then, suddenly, they were in a taxi. She had awoken to the sound of the ocean, the light of the sun coming up, and the salt air whipping in through the curtains. She'd known then, at the precise moment he cradled her against his chest and kissed her hair softly, that he was the man she was going to marry. His sticking around after a Fiona slap had proved it.

"Can't exactly go off like that now, can I?" she asked.

"Nope, but if this Nick deserves it, he's getting smacked!" Fiona stood up and lifted her chin defiantly. "Now go finish your sandwich." Ivy rolled her eyes, returning to the table to eat.

***

Across town at the house, Aldwin was a hectic mess in the kitchen.

"Well, I just heard some unexpected news," a voice announced from the living room

He yelped in shock as his mothers voice startled him. He almost knocked the laptop over, which was paused on a tutorial for homemade pizza, as he spun. Sure enough, she was standing there with a warm smile, as the silver dust of her magic fizzled away.

"Careful, love. Don't break it!" Cateline tsked him.

"Mum!" He hissed at her, looking around the empty house.

It wasn't that Aldwin wasn't happy to see his mum, but her sudden appearance with no warning call or message was odd.

"What are you doing here?" He wiped his flour-covered hands off on the apron tied around his waist. Granted, he could have magicked the pizza into completion, but he wanted to do it by hand. "Is Dah okay?" He hurried over, hugged her tightly, and breathed in the crisp and wondrous smell of home.

"He's fine, dear." Cateline pulled back to reach up and cup his cheeks. "But what about you? Hmm? Anything you didn't mention on your call last week or the previous one." Bugger it all, she knew. Aldwin could see the amusement in her eyes, as he floundered for a reply. "Your grandmum heard from Summer, who heard from Antiope, who heard from Bartholomew, who heard from Anais that you found your soulmate." He watched as those wizened eyes glanced around the room. He knew the instant she found the mantle above the fireplace. "Oh, she is beautiful. Is this the boy?" She moved over to a photo of Ivy and Gavin on a carousel.

"Yes, that's them, and yes, I have," he admitted. There was no use in denying it. At least Lewin hadn't told her, but it seemed despite being a Supreme Cupid, Anais was just as prone to gossip as the other ones. "She's absolutely perfect, and Gavin is brilliant." Aldwin was completely enamored by the little family, and somehow he knew that if he hadn't been marked, he would have been regardless. It was impossible not to love them.

"And this is the father? Oh my, he was a handsome man," she said. His mother tilted her head and reached up to touch the bear. Aldwin had explicitly avoided contact with it, as well as the wooden train and rubber puppy in Gavin's toys. He sucked in a breath as tiny snowflakes and golden sparks burst from its eyes and glittered in the air before dissipating. "He's never played with it." His mothers voice was so heavy with sadness that he had to swallow. "But she's touched it quite a bit, even yesterday."

"Yeah," sighed Aldwin as he reached over to touch her arm. Maybe she could answer the questions Lewin hadn't. "Mum, would you like some coffee or tea? I need to get to this dough before it rises too much." He nodded back to the kitchen.

"No, but I'll come anyway. You were always a bit clueless except for breakfast." Cateline chuckled and looped her arm around his waist as he turned her back to the kitchen. "Now, Aldwin, sweetling, tell Mumma what's got your mind in such a jumble." Of course, she had seen it. His mother, the queen of compassion with a heart of pure sugar and cream, always knew when somebody was troubled. "Is it her or your task?"

"Both, I think, maybe," Aldwin said and heaved a sigh. Then he dipped his hands in the flour and began to knead the dough again. "How could we be marked? I'm Ageless and she's mortal. I thought you and Dah weren't marked?" He had wondered about the validity of the story since he had been shot. "Dah says you were human, before."

"I was, but no, we were not marked. Times were different then. The magic was stronger, and even though I was nineteen, I still believed," Cateline said with all the breathlessness of a lovesick teenager. She leaned against the pantry door, and Aldwin smiled at the absolute affection in her voice. Despite being together for nearly a thousand years, his parents' love had never dimmed. It was immortalized in the stories. "It happened quite by accident, really. I was betrothed, you see, to this baron. I didn't want to marry him, but back then there was no choice."

"Oh, so Dah-"

"Don't interrupt, Aldwin," she hissed, and he slammed his lips shut. "I had just come into my brothers home from visiting my ailing grandmother. It was late, well past midnight, but I was hungry and cold. I wasn't supposed to be there until after sunrise, so I didn't want to wake anyone up." Aldwin glanced back at her from his kneading to see that the sweet sound in her voice had caused a dusting of flurries in her hand. She gave them a thoughtful twirl. "My nieces were little, so of course, he came. I think my presence startled him as much as he scared me. Out of nowhere, he just appeared in front of the hearth, and he said 'Now, sweet Cateline, you shouldn't be here.'"

Aldwin could almost see what she described. His father was young, all of nine-hundred and five, staring at the startled face of a young woman. His mother continued to weave their story.

"Then he asked me why I hadn't written. I was a believer, but he hadn't gotten a letter that year. I told him that my betrothed had said he wouldn't tolerate such childish things, and he had demanded I grow up," his mother recited. For the first time in his life, Aldwin heard an edge to her voice, a cold shiver, like an icicle piercing the snow. "And your Dah said 'well that is no husband for you, in my opinion. What would you ask me for then? If it is in my magic, I will grant it to you.'"

Cateline grew silent for a moment, and Aldwin looked back while he grabbed the rolling pin. Her eyes were closed, and a soft smile danced on her lips. He wondered why she had never told him those details of their story before. "What did you ask for, Mum?"

"I was smitten with his compassion for me, with how he radiated pure magic and love. So I said 'Father Christmas, I should like to marry you and leave to go live high above the world and far away from all of this.'" She sighed, so softly that Aldwin abandoned his work to turn. His mother had ceased her flurries, and her eyes were closed.

"He said 'that is not in my magic, dear one. Please forgive me.' Then he kissed my brow and was gone," she said. Aldwin's mind was a whirlwind. How, then, had they married? How had she become a sprite if he'd left? He couldn't remember this part of their story. He had heard it when he was very little. "The next afternoon, as my family gathered for our meal, there was a knock at the door. My father, who was sick, but still very firm, answered the door. There stood the two most beautiful women I had ever seen. One was dressed in the richest robes of red, gold, and green. The other had skirts of silver and blue, and they both wore shining diadems. With them was your Dah, in flowing robes of red, trimmed with the purest white fur and wearing a pair of boots of shining black leather to his knees." It was rare that his greatest grandmum appeared to mortals, even rarer that Grandmum Winter would show herself, but he knew that's who they were.

"They looked at my father and said, 'we are queens of the northern lands, and our son loves your daughter. We come to ask that you to allow them to wed'," gushed Cateline with a happy hum. She opened her eyes and giggled not at all like she was as ageless as she was. "My father demanded a dowry twelve times what was being offered, and your father waved his hand and summoned it. My family was stunned when they realized they were not mortal, and my father said, 'you will marry her today.' We did, with the blessing of Gaia herself, and she and Winter turned me into a sprite, so your father and I could live together forever."

"Oh, Mum, that's amazing," Aldwin whispered. He had never asked to hear their story in full, but her retelling had eased a worry in his heart. So, he wrapped his arms around her shoulder and basked in the awe of his parents' history. "But what does this mean for me and Ivy? Will my magic, the fact of who I am, change things?" he asked. He had to admit that he was afraid, no terrified, that because Lewin hadn't seen their destinies, it would fail. "Knowing you and Dah made it work helps, but I'm so worried I'm going to mess things up with her."

"I can't say, my little snowflake, but don't rush things. Soulmates or not, love must be allowed to blossom freely. Feed it gently and let her give it the power to grow." His mother drew in a deep breath and released him. "Fear and doubt can halt its growth. Now, put aside those fretful thoughts and don't forget why you came to begin with."

Aldwin glanced at the clock and yelped when he realized it was almost six.

"Ivy and Gavin will be home soon. I have to finish this," he said and looked back at his abandoned dinner, groaning as he saw the dough was a complete waste. "Bollocks," he huffed.

"Language, Aldwin," his mother chuckled before kissing his cheek. "But I hope to meet them soon." With a flash of gold, she was gone.

The sound of Gavin's laughter from the front step had him in a panic, and Aldwin whined softly. He'd promised pizza, but there was none to be had. Desperately, he snapped his fingers and tried to work the dough flat, add the ingredients onto it, and bake it there on the counter with his magic. Distracted by the sound of the key in the door, the power came too quickly. Flour, cheese, and sauce splattered everywhere, just as Ivy's voice called out.

"Nick! We're home!"

"Pizza!" Gavin exclaimed, followed by the thud of his book bag. "Did you make cookies too? I smell cookies!"

Ivy made her way into the kitchen, and she stopped. Nick stared down at his hands, face red under a mess of raw dough, flour, cheese, and sauce.

"Oh, my, God, what happened?" she asked, barely containing her laughter. Gavin burst into giggles beside her, and the absolute despondent expression on Nick's face melted her heart. "Gavin, baby, go change out of your uniform. We're goin' out for pizza." The giggling child was gone in a flash.

Nick looked up, eyes wide in apology, as she stepped into the war zone of her kitchen.

"Ivy, I'm sorry. I don't know what happened," he said. She reached up and brushed a glob of dough from his sideburns. She, honestly, didn't care because the thought behind it was enough. She'd been assuming he was ordering dinner, not making it.

"Why don't you change too, hm?" Ivy giggled, and Aldwin thrilled at her soft stroke against his cheek. His heart soared at the amusement and adoration in her eyes. Then, to his shock, she went up on her toes and kissed his cheek. It shot electricity down his spine, and he fought hard against the urge to chase her lips with his own. "Mm, shame. That sauce tastes wonderful."

The way Nick beamed at her kiss erased Ivy's shock that she had done it. Then, with a somersault of her stomach, his lips pressed delicately against her brow.

"I'll clean it up. When we get back, of course," he said. She shook her head and felt a bit dazed as he moved past her to the stairs. The guilt only tingled for one breath, and it faded before she could feel a tear form.

Fiona's Interrogation

Aldwin fussed with his shirt cuffs and listened to the sounds of Ivy in the kitchen below.

Fiona was on her way over for dinner, and Ivy had been in a whirlwind of stress all day. He had been banished upstairs, thanks to his failed attempt at making a salad. Supposedly he had incorrectly chopped the onions, and he had gotten out of her way. How exactly could one incorrectly chop onions? They were onions. You chopped them up. Either way, he could only hazard a guess as to why such a fuss was being made over this particular dinner. Ivy must have told her mother there was more to him being there than friendship and tenancy.

Aldwin found he was unusually anxious. He'd 'dated' here and there over the last eight hundred or so years, but introductions to parents had never been necessary. He was Santa's son, after all, and no Ageless had ill will towards their family. Meeting Fiona Moore was different. It was the first time his family's reputation wouldn't precede him, and he didn't want there to be an issue.

"Mommy's going nuts." Gavin's voice made him turn, and he found the boy standing in his doorway holding a toy plane. "Can I hide up here with you 'til Gran gets here?"

"Sure buddy," chuckled Aldwin. He moved to the small love seat and patted the cushion. "I take it she's not usually like this when your Gran visits." The boy shook his head and climbed up beside him. "You know, sometimes mums just get stressed, but they calm down."

"I know," Gavin said and shrugged. "Mommy's always stressed but never like this for just Gran." Gavin zoomed his toy through the air. "Gran must be mad or something, 'cause Mommy is making her favorite cake. Do you think they had a fight?" The boy maneuvered the toy plane into a loop-de-loop.

"No, no, I just think that maybe she wants to make sure Gran thinks this dinner is extra special," Aldwin said in an attempt to reassure him. Had they had a fight? Ivy hadn't said anything, but would she say if they had? Did Fiona already disapprove of them? Had she even told her mother? It didn't matter. He needed to focus on Gavin. Aldwin realized that this was the first time he'd been alone with Gavin when Ivy was truly out of earshot. It was time to get back to work.

"Gavin, can I ask you a very serious and grown-up question?" He asked the young boy who stared at the plane in his hands as if it held the answers to all his problems.

"Yeah! I love grown-up questions," Gavin said. The plane dropped to his lap, and the boy turned to sit cross-legged and stare up at him. "I like that you always treat me like a big boy and not a baby like my old teachers.

"Well, you are a big boy, but it's a very serious question, and I don't want you to get upset, okay?" Aldwin said. Gavin nodded, and he seemed more intrigued if that was possible. "What made you stop believing in Santa?" He had to play ignorant, even though he knew. Understanding exactly where the loss of faith began was crucial. "Did you look it up or did another kid tell you?"

"Oh," grunted Gavin, and his normally excited eyes grew sad and dark. It didn't fit the face of such a loving and sweet child. Aldwin bit back his automatic need to comfort him. "Well, Mommy and Gran and Uncle Alex always said Santa would bring me whatever I wanted if I was good. They said he was magic, and that he could do anything." The boy looked down and fiddled with his sleeve. "I wrote him a letter, and I asked him to bring me a daddy. I wanted Mommy to be happy again too. I was so good all the time. I was never mean or rude to anyone, even when they were being stupid heads. I did everything adults asked me to do, even when I didn't wanna. Then when I woke up and there was no daddy. I knew he couldn't be real. That magic wasn't real."

Even though Aldwin had read the letter, the disappointment in Gavin's voice ached his heart. He knew it was the lack of getting a father that had hurt him, but he had never realized that Gavin had recognized the loss and loneliness Ivy was experiencing. He shoved the pain the boy's story brought to his heart away and tried to get his words together. He'd thought about how to present this new idea to Gavin for a while, but he hadn't expected to be so impacted by the way the boy felt.

"Hey, well, did you ever think magic has rules, just like science?" he asked. Aldwin curled his arm around Gavin's drooped shoulders and tugged him into his lap. "Or even like chess?" Gavin looked up at him, his young eyes tight below his furrowed brow.

"But if magic is magic, how can it have rules?" Gavin asked. He propped an elbow on Aldwin's shoulder and leaned his face into his hand. Honestly, the boy's mind was amazing, but Aldwin knew he had started to chip away at his doubt.

"Well, you know how in elements, each one has a specific property?" Aldwin asked. Gavin's squint tightened. It was obvious that it was slightly too advanced for him. "Okay, how about chess? While every piece does have the ability to take another or checkmate the king, they've got rules for how they move, right?" The confusion on Gavin's face lessened a bit, and Aldwin squeezed him gently. "Well, Santa isn't like the Queen. He can't go in any direction. See, he can only gift toys or other physical objects. He can't make two people love each other, and your Mum would have to love someone very much to let them be your daddy."

"That's cupid's job, right?" Gavin asked. The thoughtful question made Aldwin snort in surprise. "You mentioned him in the story, so I looked up what a cupid was." Aldwin dreaded to think what could have been found if Ivy didn't have age restrictions on Gavin's tablet.

"Exactly, buddy, cupids are responsible for love magic," Aldwin said. He had the boy logically considering magic now, even if it wasn't quite the way he planned. It was a start, and that's all he needed. "But I don't know all about their magic. My expertise is in Santa magic." He could see the questions that brewed in Gavin's eyes. He needed to think fast. The boy opened his mouth to speak, but Aldwin had an idea already. "My friend Lewin, though, he's a cupid expert."

"Can you invite him over some time? I want to know 'bout cupid magic," demanded Gavin, and the excitement was back in his eyes.

Aldwin blew out a breath in relief at how quickly the boy took the diversion. He had no idea where Gavin was going with it, but he knew it was on the right path.

"I can ask, but we have to run it by your Mum," Aldwin said. He reached up to ruffle Gavin's hair as the low sound of a knock echoed below them. It wasn't even a heartbeat before a voice carried up to them.

"Where's my favorite boy?!"

"Gran!" Gavin shouted. He was off Aldwin's lap in a flash and sprinting towards the stairs. Aldwin swallowed hard and stood up. Steeling himself, he headed down the stairs to join in with the loud exchanges occurring in the living room.

"Well, where's he at then?" A woman asked. The voice undoubtedly belonged to Fiona Moore, and the tone confirmed that she knew what was growing between him and her daughter.

"Nick should be right—" Aldwin cut Ivy off as she pointed toward him

"Here," he eased into the hallway and offered a broad smile as he took in the older Moore. Fiona had some similarities to Ivy in her full face, button nose, and just barely poutier lower lip. Her eyes were aqua though, as opposed to Ivy's caramel amber. Those must have come from her dad. "I'm Nick Claus. You must be Fiona. Heard a lot about you." He extended his hand and tried hard to pull off charming. Fiona's eyes narrowed, raking him over with the wisdom of years spent protecting her daughter.

"I'm sure you have," Fiona said. She clasped his hand, and one eyebrow arched as if she was saying she could see through him. Aldwin knew enough about an experienced mum's gaze to wonder if she did see through him. Her hand fell away, and she turned to her daughter. "When's dinner?"

"I'm about to set the table now," Ivy said. She had been silently on edge through the brief exchange, but she let out a breath and smiled as Fiona scooped Gavin up onto her hip. "I made lasagna, and there's lemon cake with raspberry frosting for dessert." It was her mum's favorite, and she hoped it would keep dinner amiable enough to make it to dessert.

"I can set the table," Nick offered from beside her. He looked cornered, and she bit back a chuckle. He had every reason to be concerned. Her mother didn't just play at being intimidating.

"Actually, can you take Gavin to wash his hands? He was playing with that glitter slime earlier," Ivy said. She was afraid her mom wouldn't surrender him, but Gavin quickly wriggled in her arms and reached for Nick. Luckily, he had experience with catching people before they fell, as she well knew.

"C'mon Gavin, my boy, let's go get cleaned up," Nick said as he pulled Gavin towards him. Like she always did anytime Gavin latched onto Nick with a grin, Ivy felt her affection for the man swell in her chest. "Get ready to fly!" With a laugh, Gavin was above his head like a superhero as they raced down the hall.

"Well?" Ivy asked as she grabbed her mom's hand and dragged her into the kitchen. "What's the verdict?" Her mom could form an opinion without even a word, and nine times out of ten she was right. That one-off time she'd been off was with Aaron, but her opinion had quickly changed.

"He's a bit odd, but I can't quite put my finger on why," Fiona said and looked back over her shoulder. "Not a bad odd, just, different. He smells a bit strange too, like-" Ivy knew what she was going to say and cut her off.

"Snow-covered pine trees. Yeah. I think it's his cologne or soap," Ivy said and shrugged. She'd always meant to ask, but she'd never gotten around to it. "I like it though; it makes me think of Christmas when you'd buy a real tree." She started to pull plates down. "But other than that, what did you think?"

"He's pretty, but he's a bit too thin for my taste. That hair though," Fiona said and flashed her an approving smile. Of course, she'd zero in on that. Fiona was a hairdresser. "That would be genetics, though. I bet you none of the men in his family are bald." She opened the fridge, and Ivy watched with a careful eye as she procured the wine. "Gavin's already attached. He doesn't even go to Alex when I'm holding him." Then her mom paused in the middle of removing the cork. "I'll tell you what is really weird, it's that I've felt like I've met him before. Like it feels like I've seen him around or something."

"I felt the same when we met," Ivy said. She had gotten so used to him, that she'd forgotten the flicker of recognition she felt when he caught her. She didn't have time to think about it, because Gavin raced by with Nick hot on his heels. The mad smiles on their faces were infectious, and Ivy smiled right back.

"You've got it bad," Fiona snorted, and Ivy's cheeks and face burned. "Like Aaron level bad." She didn't even have time to grimace at the name because the pop of the wine bottle startled her. "You know what that means," her mom said. There was a wicked glint in the woman's eye, and Ivy groaned internally. Unfortunately, she did know what it meant. "And don't even think about interrupting."

Aldwin had expected some form of maternal interrogation, but Fiona Moore was relentless. Question after question was fired at him. Most were seemingly harmless but undeniably important. He knew without a doubt that every answer was being filed away in her mind. He was barely able to chew his food under her onslaught.

"Mostly Canada, but I've traveled all over with my Dah's company," he replied to her most recent question about where he had lived.

"You don't sound very Canadian. I'd've pegged you for your parents being Scottish and English." Fiona sipped her wine, as he failed to take another bite of his gradually cooling lasagna. He didn't miss Ivy's eye roll or sigh of exasperation, and he chuckled. "What, I read romance novels and watch movies. I know some of the vernacular for the regions."

"My mum's English. My Dah was born in Scotland but raised in Ontario most of his life." Okay, so that was half a lie. He knew his mum's accent had never changed, and she was only a hundred twenty when she had him. It was definitely Old English. His Dah's mum had been a winter sprite who preferred the highlands of Scotland before choosing Kristoff. "Kids tend to take after the mums more with the accent," he said.

"Why'd you leave the company then? Ivy says you're a professor now," Fiona continued without missing a beat. He glanced at Ivy, who was silently trying to coerce Gavin into eating something other than the cheese and meat. "And why come to Ostcrest?"

"I needed to branch out on my own for a bit. I always loved science, particularly theoretical physics. Teaching it at the University of Kansas was an opportunity that came up, and I took it." Okay, that was an absolute lie, but he kept it concealed. "As for why Ostcrest, well, I've never been one for city living, and it's only an hour from the university. I liked the pictures I saw online, and I thought, 'why not.'"

"Didn't leave behind any broken hearts did you?" Fiona asked.

"Mom!" Ivy's hiss of exasperation was just the distraction Aldwin needed to finally shovel a bite of food into his mouth. God, she was a good cook. He'd have to get this recipe for his mum. "Rude."

"It's fine, Ivy," Aldwin said after he swallowed, and he smiled confidently. He wasn't inexperienced in the aspects of dating, but his last fling had been almost two hundred years before and it hadn't been even remotely serious. "No, no broken hearts. I've been single for about two years." He chanced a glance at Ivy, who met his eyes and flushed before hiding behind her wine glass. "But, I'm hoping that changes soon."

"I bet you are," Fiona snorted, and for a moment, it seemed as if her interrogation had ended.

Ivy let out a shaky breath of relief when her mom's rapid-fire test ceased. There'd be more questions for Nick, but they'd be done privately, probably with a random mid-afternoon drop-in. With Aaron, Fiona had shown up at his apartment at noon on his day off.

"So, mom, how's Paula?" Getting Fiona to talk about family gossip was a sure-fire way to distract her.

"Oh, goodness, I forgot!" Fiona exclaimed. Ivy stared at her mother in confusion at the sudden outburst, and Fiona slapped her forehead. "She's pregnant, bless her heart, by that butcher she's been seeing. They're getting married at the beginning of December, so she can fit in the dress before she starts showing." Ivy perked up at that news.

Paula had been dating Blake on and off for four years. The breakups had never been over anything bad but mostly because of her parents wanting her to 'upgrade'. Paula was absolutely gorgeous. She had the body and face of a runway model, but she was absolutely in love with Blake. "She wants Gavin to be the ring bearer, and you to be a bridesmaid."

"She hasn't called," Ivy said. She wasn't shocked at the lack of calls. Paula did work two jobs while trying to finish a degree in business. Fiona, however, called everyone and was the unofficial Grand Central Station of their family and friends when it came to information. "I'll call her tomorrow; tell her we'd be pleased!"

"Don't go getting any ideas yourself though," Fiona said, and Ivy choked on her wine when Fiona pointed her fork at her and Nick. "One baby shower at a time is the family tradition." Ivy started to drop a well-thought-out rebuttal for that, but Gavin interrupted

"Mummy," Gavin said, and Ivy froze at the way her son had affected Nick's accent almost perfectly. "I want Nick's friend Lewin to come over."

"Who?" Ivy and Fiona queried at the same time.

Ivy looked over at Nick, who seemed surprised that Gavin had blurted it out.

"Who's Lewin?" she asked. Ivy hadn't heard the name before, so she was curious as to who he was. Nick flashed her a conspiratorial look that made her think things were about to get weird.

"So you know how I'm an expert on Santa?" Nick asked. Ivy nodded, ignoring her mom's bewildered stare. "Well, Lewin is an expert on cupids. I was explaining to Gavin that Santa's magic isn't all-powerful. That different jobs call for different magic." Ivy had nearly forgotten the story he had woven his first night, and she relaxed at the news that this had to do with their ploy to get Gavin to believe again. "Gavin apparently remembered me mentioning cupids before, so he looked up what they are. Thankfully, my friend Lewin knows exactly how to explain that particular brand of magic." Nick flashed her a wink, and Ivy chuckled.

"Well, Alex is supposed to come by on Friday for dinner. I suppose we can make room for Lewin too," Ivy said, and Aldwin was relieved that she had agreed. He knew Lewin would agree. After all, he had been bugging him to introduce him to the pair.

"Yay!" Gavin cheered, and he clapped before pushing his plate away. "I want cake now!"

"I'll get it," Ivy said. She always cleared the table, but Aldwin wasn't having it tonight. She'd been on her feet all afternoon. So, he leaped up, carefully stacking the plates and forks.

"Anyone need a refill on wine?" He asked as he collected Fiona's plate.

"I'm good thanks," Ivy said and lifted the second glass she had been nursing. She never went past two glasses when Gavin was awake, Aldwin knew from experience. "Mom?" Fiona surrendered her glass, and Gavin produced a pair of toy dinosaurs from his pocket and began playing.

Fiona looked properly bewildered, as he walked away, but Aldwin kept his focus on their conversation from the other room.

"Nick said the S-word, and Gavin didn't flip. Okay, what is goin' on?" Fiona asked, and Aldwin chuckled under his breath at the disbelief in her voice. Ivy had been of the same response the very first time he'd talked to Gavin about it. He peeked back in just in time to see Ivy's smirk of satisfaction.

"Nick found out Gavin doesn't think Santa's real. Well, that just wouldn't do for him, so he's been explaining to Gavin how magic is just science we can't explain," Ivy said, and Aldwin ducked back into the kitchen before he could be seen. He didn't miss Fiona sinking back into her chair looking dumbstruck. "And he taught him that Santa is from another dimension that's more advanced than ours." Aldwin cut the cake as he listened, and he felt his heart swell in affection for the wonderful woman he'd been marked to. She sounded as proud and delighted as he felt by the success they'd had so far.

"You're joking me," Fiona scoffed. "And Gavin, baby, you really believe it?"

"I dunno yet. I have to see what I learn about cupids first," Gavin said, and Aldwin was pleased that he sounded distracted by his toys. "Gotta do my research. Professor

Marx says research's the most important part." He stacked the cakes onto the tray and carried them back into the fray of disbelief.

"Let him handle it how he wants," Ivy said and took a sip as Nick returned with four plates of cake. Fiona, for once, was shocked speechless. When he settled into his seat, she reached down to squeeze his hand.

Aldwin had heard every word of the conversation, and he couldn't help but grin ear to ear as Ivy squeezed his hand. Softly, he trailed his thumb over her knuckles before he laced their fingers together. If Fiona noticed, she kept her comments to herself.

A Kiss of Guilt

Everything had gone so well with dinner and her mom that Ivy didn't even dread the pile of dishes that waited for her after she put Gavin to bed. She stumbled to a stop when she entered the kitchen and found it was spotless. The dishwasher was running, and pots glistened in the drying rack. Nick, the gorgeous angel that he was, leaned against the counter sans coat, sleeves rolled up to his elbows, and holding a glass of wine.

"You cleaned up?" she asked, stunned by his actions.

"Yup," Nick said.

"I didn't even hear—"

"Didn't want to wake Gavin."

"Are you even real?"

"Flesh and blood."

"That for me?" Ivy asked and eyed the red liquid in the glass between his fingers with hope. She gladly took the drink when Nick surrendered it with a flourished bow. "It's a little domestic, isn't it, washing dishes while I put Gavin to bed?" she asked. Then she took a sip and savored the flavor while Nick poured his own.

"You were stressed all day. I just thought you could use a break," explained Nick. "Come here." She didn't object when he looped his arm around her waist and tugged her towards the living room. "I think you deserve a moment to put your feet up." Ivy liked the way his long arm fit around her. She went willingly with him, settling down on the sofa sideways to look up at him.

"Keep spoiling me like this, and I might just keep you," she said and poked at his ribs playfully. She had to admit she missed having this, someone to just talk to, to relax with, someone who was more than a friend, who saw past the mask she wore for everyone else.

Alex's version of giving her a break was to take Gavin for a weekend fishing or to the museum. Her mom's solution was to occasionally cook dinner or offer to babysit if she wanted to go get her hair done or have a night out for drinks. What Nick had done was different, somehow. Doing dishes, waiting with a glass of wine, saying he'd noticed she needed a break, and then giving it without her asking seemed small, but they were things Ivy had missed about her husband. He always knew.

"Well I guess I'll have to keep doing it then," whispered Aldwin. He adored seeing Ivy with Gavin and watching that unbreakable bond. He found her absolutely stunning when she was tidying up after the five-year-old whirlwind. Seeing her at that moment, genuinely happy, relaxed, and carefree had him as putty in her beautiful hands. "Maybe next time, I'll throw a shoulder massage in." He meant it as a tease, just something to make her giggle, but Ivy let out an absolutely filthy, lusty moan.

"God, I haven't had my shoulders rubbed in ages." Her voice was wistful, as she rolled her neck and raised her glass for another drink. "Probably why my neck hurts all the time." Ivy took a long drink, and Aldwin did the same to quench the heat her needy tone had lit in his throat. "Mom got me a spa trip for my birthday, but that was way back in April."

"That was a while back," he replied.

"Yeah, I wish I could get one once a week," she sighed and rested her head against the arm he stretched across the back of the sofa. "I could use one after today."

Was she asking? Aldwin took another drink to dampen his now dry throat. Mortal libations had minimal effect on him. A glass of moon-stilled thistle wine, on the other hand, was a whole other story. The thought of feeling her skin under his hands had his head spinning more than any drink had ever done.

"Well, not to brag, but I am pretty talented at shoulder rubs," he said. "I have been told that my hands are positively magical." Aldwin waggled his fingers at her in a tease. He hoped she couldn't hear how nervous he was at testing the waters to see if she wanted it.

Ivy heard the hesitancy under the faux pride. She watched him watch her for her permission. It was too tempting an offer to pass up, even though she hadn't been intentionally asking for one. Her heart did a little skip when her hands moved of their own accord. She took his glass and set her own down with it on the coffee table.

"Are you cutting me off?" Nick asked. His chuckle was light, but Ivy saw the hopeful eagerness in his eyes.

"You can't give a decent massage if you're half-drunk," she replied and turned her back to him. Her breaths came quickly as she waited to see how he'd respond, and she nearly melted when his hands squeezed her shoulders.

He was soft and gentle at first, and Ivy sighed at the wonderful sensation. Her head lolled forward, and she closed her eyes. Gradually he increased pressure, and Ivy couldn't suppress her soft moan of "Oh, God."

Nick's hands were like magic. They had instantly located the mirrored spots on either shoulder that always felt stiff when she'd had a long day, and he was giving them attention she wasn't sure even the masseuse had given her. "Jesus Christ, that feels amazing."

"I did tell you," Nick said with a chuckle, as he slowly worked her tight muscles through her sweater. Ivy found that although he was massaging her shoulders, the rest of her body was relaxing. She felt her jaw unclench for what seemed like the first time in years, and her fingers fell open on her lap. Her posture would have slumped over if he hadn't been supporting her with his miraculous hands.

"I know you did," Ivy whispered. "I just didn't expect you to be *this* good." She kept her eyes closed and exhaled in relief when his thumbs found a particularly tight area just beside her spine. She couldn't remember the last time she'd felt so relaxed and at peace. Had it been a year or maybe two? She wasn't sure. It didn't matter, so she let it go and tried to enjoy her moment.

"Blimey, Ivy, you weren't joking. You're as tense as can be," he said. Aldwin had expected some knots of tension, but Ivy had way more than he'd thought. It wouldn't do at all.

He silently cursed the fabric that kept him from really touching her skin and from releasing the small knots of stress that dotted her back. He slowly worked up to her neck, pressing with each thumb in turn. Aldwin took extra care to alternate the pressure from soft to firm to soft again. This earned him another of Ivy's breathy moans, and he had to roll his eyes and bite his lip to keep from letting out one of his own.

Aldwin wanted to touch her skin on skin, not only to feel the satin gentility of it but also so he could focus his attention for more of her benefit. He held himself in check, not even allowing himself to even graze his thumb up the side of her neck when she took a particularly deep breath. He didn't even trust himself to speak. His body was practically vibrating with the need to feel her skin. If he said anything, there'd be no way to disguise the longing in his voice.

Ivy, however, told him how much she enjoyed his attentions with a breathy moan. She had let her head loll forward, was as relaxed as she could possibly be while remaining upright,and the sighs she was making caused his heart to race. He heeded his mum's advice, though, and he didn't press Ivy to do more than just feel. Aldwin would only take what she was ready to give, and he would give her everything she asked of him.

Ivy was far more relaxed than she thought she'd ever be. Honestly, Nick's hands were nothing short of miraculous as he kneaded, rolled, and pressed along her back and shoulders. It was as if he knew exactly where she carried her stress, as if he could read her mind to get the pressure just right. Every so often, he'd push almost to the point of pain, and with a gush of warm tingles, a tight spot she'd long learned to ignore was relieved. She had lost the ability to speak, and she was reduced to soft gasps of delight or moans and whimpers of pleasure when he eliminated the remnants of her stress.

A yearning began to build inside of Ivy, and it made her stomach flutter as her hazy mind eased a new thought forward. If it felt this good with her sweater on, she wondered how it would feel if she was just wearing the thin tank top she had on underneath. She knew it would probably feel like heaven. His fingers would keep her warm, and he could probably work better. Her body agreed it was a good idea.

"Hang on," Ivy managed to sigh, and when Nick's hands drifted away the loss was tangible. She didn't even remember moving until her sweater was tossed onto the cushion in front of her, and the cool air brushed her skin. "Mm, now please continue."

"As you wish," Nick said, and Ivy could have sworn it sounded like he had been preening in his statement. "Your skin is so soft," he added, and she felt him return to the knot he was so intent on eradicating. For a moment, she longed to feel his lips on her neck, but the sensation didn't come. "You're so beautiful." His whisper sounded like near worship in the dim light of the living room.

"So're you," Ivy said. She didn't care how shaky it sounded. That feeling was brewing again, that yearning to feel more.

Her mind was even more dazed as she tried to make sense of the image-less, wordless sensation it was after. Her body knew what it wanted, even if it hadn't felt it in years. Her tongue slipped out to dampen her lips, and her neck tilted back instinctively. Back, back, and back she reclined until her head rested against his shoulder, and her nose brushed his jaw.

"Nick," she whispered. She couldn't get her leadened eyelids to open.

"Yes?" Aldwin asked. He couldn't breathe. He couldn't even work his hands with this new position. Ivy was practically laying against him, so he slid his arms around her. Her fingers found his hand and he discovered she was shivering slightly. Then, stars above, her lips grazed his jaw. He wasn't sure if it was a reflex or if she wanted it to happen. His heart skipped a beat when she did it again, and it was instinct to turn his head.

Their lips met in a feather brush. The magic in his veins erupted in fireworks, as the contact made the world turn upside down.

Aldwin had experienced his fair share of kissing, but the way he felt kissing Ivy was realms above any other. It was brilliant, no, perfect, the way her lips formed to his, yielding, breaking away, coming in again to catch his bottom one in a tender suck. Her tongue met his—hesitant, explorative—and the taste of her wine flavored it as sweet as it felt. His fingers, which had longed to draw her close for weeks, fit divinely along the curve of her waist. He slid his hands down, memorizing the smooth curve that led to her supple hips. Suddenly, she was in his lap, and he groaned when her fingers plunged into his hair.

Ivy was kissing Nick. Her whole body felt a bit light and dizzy as he broke away for a moment and moved back in.

She'd tried kissing, on one of those dates. She couldn't remember which. It had felt wrong, too forced, and far too feigned. Nick was different. His lips shot sweet, sweet bliss down her spine, and the contented sighs that brushed over her mouth and chin were delicious. It had been so long since she'd felt something so pure, so emphatically right. She didn't want to stop herself when she turned, went up on her knees, looped her arms around his neck, and let Nick catch her bottom lip in a caress.

His hair was so soft, and, just like she'd thought it would, it did stick up naturally. The silken chestnut and chocolate strands held no resistance, and Ivy reveled in its perfection. Her entire being, deprived so long of affection, trembled in bliss as his hands slid up her spine. Straddling his thighs had been a natural step, and she didn't give it a second thought. Pulling back, she managed to open her eyes. He opened his, and those burning pools of cocoa and caramel became visible with a gasp from Nick's wet lips. Ivy cupped the side of his neck, stroked his jaw with her thumb, and went back for more.

Aldwin sighed as Ivy's hands began to explore. They skimmed down his neck, as their tongues danced together and then broke away so he could catch her upper lip. One delicate fingertip trailed down his chest and explored the exposed skin at his top button. Another sent sparks down his arm where it rested on his bicep. He glided his right hand up her spine, under her shirt, to graze along her exposed skin. The other he danced down the jeans that covered her supple thigh, not to grope, but to gently squeeze it through the material. He whimpered in loss when she pulled away from the kiss, but then, moonlight save him, she began to kiss down his neck.

He groaned deeply but didn't return the kiss. Instead, he pulled her closer to him, tilted his neck to the side to give her easier access, and pressed his lips against her shoulder. Her skin was as delicate as he'd imagined, but he strove to keep his touches and caresses as tender as possible. He didn't want to push her, to take away from the natural, magical feeling, and tip her over the edge. He'd never felt anything so flawless as the way they moved together or the way their breaths broke over each others skin. He ignored the yearning that had ignited low in his core, and he willed his body into behaving itself.

Nick's skin was sweet and tangy under Ivy's tongue. That fresh, woodsy smell that always surrounded him was absolutely intoxicating, and she inhaled it greedily. His hands, which had always been tender, squeezed her thigh and tangled in the hair at the base of her skull. She sighed and trailed her lips up to curl her tongue along his jaw. She shivered in delight when he laved an open-mouthed kiss to the junction of her shoulder and neck in response. Supernovas exploded behind her eyelids, and she melted into his embrace. Ivy lifted her face from the path she was kissing along his jaw and tilted her neck to give him better access. Reaching up, she stroked his ear and opened her eyes to admire his stunning face.

Light sparkled off her hand, and the moment shattered. Shame flooded her, as she froze in horror. Nick immediately stopped the delicious exploration of her collarbone.

"Ivy, love, what's wrong?" he asked

Ivy didn't know what to say or how to explain the all-consuming guilt that burned through her. She failed to hold back a gasp and scrambled off of his lap and out of his arms to sit beside him. "Ivy, talk to me. Did I do—" he started to ask, and she cut him off.

"No, God, no," Ivy said. Her tears were unstoppable when he lifted her chin up to meet his gaze. "You're perfect. I—just—" sobbing, she looked down at her wedding rings. How could she explain that it felt like she was being unfaithful to a dead man?

She tried to stand, but everything was hazy and unsteady. Her body soared on the high of Nick's touch and affection and pleasure, but her heart and mind were heavy with guilt.

"Aaron," she whispered, and she tried to stand again. Across the room, she saw Aaron's picture, and the rock of guilt turned into a blazing boulder.

"Oh," Aldwin replied. He didn't need any further explanation. He hurried to his feet to catch Ivy before she could stumble, and he scooped her into his arms. "I know, Ivy. I know. I'm sorry." She shook her head, and the tears that soaked her cheeks were beautiful in their love for her first soulmate.

"Nick, I'm so sorry," she whispered.

"Let's get you upstairs to your bed," he suggested. "You can curl up and have a good cry. Maybe talk to him a bit." Her head rested on his shoulder as he carried her, but he didn't kiss her forehead like he longed to. He would give Ivy whatever she needed to recover, and he would wait an eternity if she asked. "Maybe we moved a little fast after such a stressful day."

Ivy didn't answer, and he didn't push. Aldwin took extreme care as he carried his crying love through the house. All he wanted was for her to feel safe, loved, and happy with him, and if that meant giving her all of the space, patience, and support while she mourned her deceased husband, then he would give it willingly.

"'M sorry, Nick. I didn't mean to..." she said, and Aldwin shushed her softly as he paused at the base of the stairs.

"Shhh, I understand," he said and squeezed her gently. "Don't worry."

Nick's unwavering understanding only made Ivy feel worse, but she couldn't do more than nod and wrap her arms around his neck while he carried her up the stairs. She hid her tears in his shoulder, choking on each gasp of air. His lips brushed her hair, just as he elbowed her door open. She wiped roughly at her face when he lowered her to sit on the bed, and she forced herself to look at him through the tears. She had to apologize for the mess she had dissolved into.

"Nick, I'm sorry, I didn't mean to tease," she whispered.

"Hey, no, I'm not upset," he murmured, and his thumb was so tender when it caught a tear to wipe away. "Tell me what you need."

What did she need?

Ivy didn't know. Her love for Aaron wanted nothing more than to curl up under the blanket and cry alone and hidden like it had for two years. Yet, this new feeling, one so fresh and so fragile, didn't want Nick to go away. The feeling was afraid that if he walked out the door, he'd go away forever too. He sat beside her, not touching her, abnormally quiet and still.

"Can I just," Ivy said, unsure of how to ask for what she needed. So, she gestured hesitantly at his lap and tried to clear her throat. He nodded and lifted his hands from his thighs. She slumped down, facing him, and fisted his shirt in her hands as she rested her head on his lap. As he stroked her arm, Ivy let the grief and pain take over.

Aldwin didn't know what to say to comfort his Ivy, but it didn't seem to matter. All he could do was sit quietly and gently rub her arm until his shirt and trousers were damp with tears, and her breathing became shallow and ragged. Every ounce of him wanted to shift her to the pillows and curl up with her, but he knew that was too much. Instead, very gently, he lifted her limp body from his lap and eased it to the pillows. Then, as carefully as he could, he pulled the blankets and sheets from under her, to tuck her snugly in. Finally, after he placed a gentle kiss on her hair, he slipped from the room.

An Amorous Amores

"I kissed Nick," Ivy blurted. The guilt had become too much to hold in on the drive to get Gavin from school. She cringed when she realized she'd interrupted Alex's story about the family of ducklings he had spent all morning rescuing from a drain. "Alex!" He had nearly rear-ended the car in front of him.

"Come again?" yelped Alex, and Ivy bit her lip. She pulled her scarf up in front of her mouth and nose to look over at him. Luckily, the light was red because he had turned to stare at her as if she'd just announced she was pregnant with alien triplets. "You did what with whom?"

"I kissed Nick—Tuesday night—after my mom left and Gavin was asleep," she whispered. Slowly, Ivy lowered the scarf, and Alex let out a noise something akin to a rubber duck being punctured. "Like 'kissed' kiss, with tongues and touching. I was on his lap, and I also kissed his neck and—" Alex cut her off with a finger to her lips.

"Hey, slow down," he said. He dropped his finger and squeezed her hand. He released it again when traffic began to move. "Now breathe," Alex coached her with a smile. Ivy pulled her scarf up again and sucked in a breath. "Okay, this is news. Let's start from the beginning." He reached over and tugged the scarf down. Ivy blew her breath out and leaned her head back against the seat. "I'm going to assume you two have been flirting, even though you didn't tell me."

"Yeah, we have. Until Tuesday night, we were just holding hands, and we spent about two hours every night just talking after Gavin went to sleep," Ivy said. Her face burned as she recalled the last two nights. There hadn't been any more kissing, but there had definitely been a change. The before-bed talk had progressed to his arm around her while she snuggled into his side and spent the chat memorizing his freckles or counting how many of the hairs in his left side-burn were ginger. "But Tuesday, after Mom practically interrogated him, he, um, well, gave me a shoulder rub."

"Oh, okay, sweater on or off?" Alex asked.

He seemed to have taken it in stride, which pleased Ivy. The fact that he was her best friend, had spent years as Aaron's partner, and was Gavin's godfather had made his opinion on the situation the one she'd dreaded second-most. The first was Gavin's, but she hadn't told him yet.

"On, at first," Ivy said, and she looked down to fiddle with her thumb. "But since I had another shirt on, I took it off after a bit." She could almost feel the sensation of Aldwin's fingers on her cheek. Alex nodded, silently, so she continued on. "Then, I dunno, him being there, it felt—Alex, it honestly felt amazing. I mean, I started the kiss, not him. I leaned back, kissed his jaw twice, and the next thing I know, I'm straddling his lap, and we're touching each other." She shivered softly and remembered how perfect it had been, how he didn't push her for more. She sighed and closed her eyes so she could remember the fullness of the moment. "And I started feeling, well, good. Better than good. I felt like it was right." She opened them again and looked over at him.

"Did you, well?" Alex asked and waved a hand. She didn't miss how he shot her a quick side glance. "Take it upstairs?"

"No," Ivy said, shifting in her seat as the guilty feeling started to rear its head again. It was a different one, an embarrassed, almost shameful, guilt, for what she had unintentionally subjected Nick to. "I was really into it, but then I saw my rings, and I sorta had a breakdown."

"Oh," Alex said, and the sympathy in his voice was evident. "I see." He blew out a breath, and Ivy tried to avoid his eyes. "How'd he handle that?"

"Like he was a freaking fairy tale prince," Ivy sighed. She fiddled with her sleeve again and thought back with a warm flicker of affection at his reaction. "He carried me upstairs, let me lay my head in his lap, and just sort of rubbed my arm until I passed out." She stared out the window at a couple walking a dog and pushing a stroller, and for the first time since Aaron's death, she didn't need to look away. "Then, I guess he tucked me in because I woke up under the blankets." She finally looked back over at Alex, who nodded thoughtfully. "When I came downstairs, he already had Gavin dressed and fed. Then he told me to go back to bed, he'd take him to school, and that he'd wake me for work."

"And did he wake you up?"

"Yeah, with a hot bath waiting. Then he made me scrambled eggs, bacon, and a cup of coffee." Ivy didn't care that she was gushing over how wonderful he had been. "When he woke me up, he just eased me awake with gentle rubs on my back and softly whispering my name. It was beyond amazing."

"Does he happen to have a gay brother who's single?" Alex chuckled, and Ivy giggled in relief. For some reason, she'd been afraid Alex would judge her or be upset that the make-out session and breakdown had happened. She should have known it had been a pointless worry, after all, he'd babysat willingly for the two dates she'd had in August. "Because I could use some pampering like that in my life."

"Only child, sorry," Ivy said. Then she reached up to rub the charm of her necklace out of habit. "But, you don't think it's too soon to, you know, be feeling like this?" She was afraid to admit that it was more than a crush out loud. What if Nick wasn't feeling it as intensely as she was? Yet Ivy was keenly aware of what these emotions were, as well as the way they had weaseled themselves deep into her heart and chest. She was falling for Nick, hard. "My mom never remarried."

"Your mom was a widow in a different era. She didn't have the safety net Aaron left you and Gavin," Alex said, silencing the flicker of doubtful guilt that had pressed up into her throat. "You aren't Fiona. You're Ivy, and if you're starting to feel more than a crush, if you really, really like him, then it's not too soon." He eased into a spot outside of Crestwood's after-school building and turned to take her hands. "I know you, and I know you're probably feeling about three hundred levels of confusion and guilt, but you don't need to. Aaron wouldn't want that. He'd want you to thrive, to love, to dance and smile, and to live the best life you can."

"How'd ya know?" Ivy asked, uncertain about the risks she knew she ran by giving in to her emotions. "He was always a little territorial." Jealousy had never been in Aaron's vocabulary because he knew Ivy would never cheat, but he had always gotten very protective anytime guys started getting a little too friendly with her.

"Because he loved you, and your and Gavin's happiness was all he wanted," Alex insisted. With a brotherly squeeze of her hands, he kissed her forehead. "But he'd also want me to make sure that this Nick is good enough, so I hope you know that's what I'll be doing at dinner."

"Judging him?"

"Like he's on trial," Alex said and started to chuckle. Ivy rolled her eyes.

"Can't be too obvious about it though, because his friend is coming, Lewin or something like that," Ivy said. She opened the car door, so she could go fetch Gavin. She cast a look back over her shoulder at her friend. "We're sorta in the middle of this elaborate plan to make Gavin believe in Santa. If Gavin asks, Lewin is a cupid expert." She snickered at the confused look on his face, before closing the door.

***

Across town, Aldwin shuffled his way around Lewin in an attempt to get some semblance of a dinner together, sans exploding dough. He'd already given his friend the details of what the dinner was about, and he was waiting for the cupid's response.

"So let me get this straight?" Lewin asked with a scoff, as Aldwin pointed at the empty stove to materialize a pile of cheesy potatoes in a pot. His mom wouldn't notice the missing ingredients from her pantry. "You want me to stay for dinner and pretend to be a cupid expert?"

"Yup," Aldwin replied and flicked his finger at a bowl to materialize corn he'd apprehended from his mothers canned goods.

"To help a five-year-old believe in cupid magic."

"Uh-huh."

"Which will, in turn, restore his faith in Santa."

"Pretty much."

"So you can bang his mom."

"Exactly, wait, NO!" Aldwin yelped and nearly dropped the pan of rolls he'd just magicked down from his mum's pantry. He rolled his eyes before glowering at his friend. "No, stars above, Lewin, restoring Gavin's belief has nothing to do with me having sex with Ivy. Kissing is just fine for now." He snapped his fingers at the chicken, nodding as it broiled to perfection in the plan.

"You kissed her!?" Lewin squealed, and Aldwin sighed. He knew he should have kept that to himself. "So, how was it?"

"Ever had someone go into a full emotional breakdown mid-snog?" asked Aldwin. Lewin made a snorting noise, so he threw a hand towel at the cupid's stupid face. "Well, it's not fun, for anybody involved. That's the truth."

"Right, yeah, I'm sorry man, that's rough," said Lewin. He leaned against the counter, and a glass of bourbon materialized in his hand. "Haven't kissed since, huh?" Aldwin knew it was more of a statement than a question. He shook his head. It had to be Ivy's decision to do that again, and he was fine with that.

"No, but the evening chats and cuddling are amazing. Which, you'd know if you'd ever had more than two or three days of a lover." Aldwin pointed a finger at the man. Cupids could be faithful, but it took a special person or polycule of people to truly satisfy their needs. "You know, though, this friend of hers, Alex, he's right up your alley."

"Oh, really?" Lewin asked. He perked up at that and looked down at his jeans and shirt. "Well, better change then." In a puff, they were replaced with the finest khaki dress trousers and a button-down dress shirt Aldwin had ever seen him in. "Do, you really think this 'magic is just science' gig is gonna work? I still don't understand how explaining my job is going to help."

"Gavin is unique like I said. You'll understand when they get here. Just, keep it G-rated, and let Ivy answer any questions that involve the 'talk'," he said and glanced nervously at the clock.

Honestly, he had no idea what was going through Gavin's mind. He knew that what he had planned seemed to be working, but there would always be a margin for error. After a quick peek at Gavin's tablet history, Aldwin saw there had been quite a bit of research into not only cupids, but dimensions, Gaia, sprites, and Yule lore. He hoped Lewin was prepared for the boy's attempt at stabbing holes in logic.

"So when do you plan on telling Ivy the truth?" Lewin asked.

"Uh, haven't thought about it yet," Aldwin said. He grabbed the plates to set the table, as the clock drew nearer to six. "I guess, I could just take her and Gavin to my parents, once he believes."

"No warning? Just pop them up there for tea?" Lewin snorted the question as he took a sip of his drink. Aldwin shrugged. "You're nuts, my friend, absolutely bonkers."

While telling Ivy he believed in Santa was one thing, coming right out and saying 'oh, by the way, Santa is my dad and I'm next in line', sounded like a good way to have something hurled at his head. He knew them enough to know that the evidence had to be there to make them believe.

"Sometimes seeing the truth has better effects than just hearing it," Aldwin said. He finished setting the five plates out before he hurried to toss some pots and dishes in the sink to make it seem as if he'd cooked himself instead of sneaking it down from his mum's kitchen. "They should be here soon."

"You should ask her out," said Lewin, stepping out of the way so Aldwin could work.

Aldwin paused where he'd been in the middle of rolling his sleeves down and slightly disheveling his hair, so he'd look like he'd be working hard. "What? Ask who out?"

"Ivy Moore, you know. She's blonde, about yea high, and your soulmate," Lewin groaned, and the cupid's sigh of exasperation had him confused. Take her out where? They were about to have dinner here. "Gaia, give me the patience." His friend huffed, crossing his arms. "Mortals go on dates, you know. They don't just go 'cool, we've been marked. Yay!' Trust me, ask her to go out. It doesn't even have to be fancy. She and Aaron got burgers on their first date, which was only like fifteen hours after they met."

"Right, dating," Aldwin grumbled. He hadn't given much thought to that either. His mum had always taught him women paid attention to actions, and that they liked affectionate gestures, like shoulder rubs or breakfast in bed or doing dishes. "Um, I could take her out for dinner. I think Fiona's babysitting tomorrow night." Why hadn't he thought of that before? Fiona took Gavin one weekend a month for 'Gran Time'. "I'll ask her tonight after Gavin goes to bed." The sound of laughter preceded the door opening, and he had to rush to make sure there was no evidence of anything magic in the kitchen

"Nick! Where are you?" Gavin shouted. He barreled into the hall, and Aldwin rushed out to catch the boy mid-jump. "Is your friend here? Did he come?"

"Gavin, calm down," Ivy said, and her giggle made Aldwin look over.

Her presence, as always, made him feel complete. A grin took over his face. She beamed in response, and Aldwin barely caught the analytical way Alex observed them. Good, the best friend knew, and that was just as good a sign as her mum knowing. He squeezed Gavin firmly in a hug.

"Good to see you, Alex," Aldwin said, and he felt Lewin come in behind him. "Ivy, this is my frie—" of course, Lewin cut him off, stepped around with an outstretched hand, and offered one of his oldest backup stories.

"Hello, I'm Lewin Miller," purred Lewin.

Ivy looked up into a smile that hit her like a steam engine, as Lewin took her hand lightly in his. His pale, blue eyes sparkled down at her from a perfectly chiseled face, and she swore the man radiated pure seduction when he raised her knuckles to his lips.

"Been dying to meet you."

"H-hello," Ivy stuttered. She wasn't really attracted to him, but his sheer presence and the implications that shone from his eyes were almost overwhelming. "Pleasure to meet you." Clearing her throat, she slid her hand free of his and saw Nick's eye roll from behind his friend. "This is my best friend, Alex Jones," she said. What happened next confused her.

"Well, hello Alex. I'm—"

Ivy watched, as if in slow motion when Alex stepped forward, hand outstretched. Then they both froze, hands nearly clasped in a shake for a moment.

Aldwin watched as Lewin turned his trademark smile on Alex, and he felt him really crank up his magic above the teasing whammy he'd laid on Ivy. Then he huffed in shock.

Out of nowhere, Anais materialized, invisible to the three mortals, raised his bow, and fired. The arrow pierced Alex's back, erupted from the left side of his chest, and slammed into Lewin. Then, with a wink of emerald eyes, the eldest and most powerful of all cupids, vanished. Unable to contain himself at the irony of what had just occurred, Aldwin laughed, and Lewin gasped.

"Sure we'll—whoa!" Lewin shouted. He stumbled over his feet, and shook his head, as their fingers met in what Aldwin knew was supposed to be a cordial shake but was now a pair of trembling hands. "Uh, hi, er, wow." Aldwin laughed harder and put Gavin down to wipe the tears of amusement pouring down his own cheeks. He'd never seen anything more brilliant.

"What's so funny?" Ivy asked. The two men had both shivered and missed their first attempt at a shake. Then they'd finally gripped each others hand. She was completely confused when Alex blushed, and his shy, flirty smile flashed onto his face. Lewin was gaping at him like he'd never seen a human before in his life, and he turned just as red. Nick laughed so hard at them that tears poured down his cheek. "Nick?"

"Nothing, just, I've never met someone who could make Lewin stutter like that," Nick cackled.

"Hello Lewin, thanks for coming to dinner," Alex said. She had seen Alex flirt before, but she knew that wasn't it. It was something different. His posture changed in a way she couldn't explain, as he stared slightly up into Lewin's eyes with a warm smile. "Excuse me, have we met?"

"No, I'd definitely remember meeting someone as gorgeous as you," gushed Lewin.

Finally, Ivy understood. The idea was brilliant! Nick hadn't said Lewin was gay, but there was no denying the sparks that flew between their best friends. She giggled in excitement, and she caught Nick's gaze as he winked.

"Move, Uncle Alex!" Gavin huffed. He wriggled in between the men, looking up in wonder. "Hi! I'm Gavin! Are you the cupid expert, Lewin?"

"Uh, yeah," Lewin said. Aldwin tore his eyes away from Ivy, to watch Lewin bend down and shake Gavin's hand. "I understand you have some questions, little buddy."

"Loads 'n loads," the little boy said. Aldwin knew he wasn't under-selling himself.

"Well, let's have dinner, and I'll answer them," Lewin replied.

"Alex, can you show Lewin to the dining room, while Nick and I set the table?" Ivy asked, and Aldwin followed her as she made her way into the kitchen.

"You didn't tell me he was gay," she hissed. Aldwin chuckled.

"Technically, I believe he prefers the term omnisexual. You'll have to clarify it with him," he replied and pulled her to him. He knew she didn't understand the reason he was beaming. "Either way, it looks like Alex knocked him off his feet. I think dinner will be a win in at least one way."

Lessons From Lewin

"**S**o what exactly brings a Canadian to Kansas?" Ivy asked as she cut up Gavin's chicken into suitable bites. She watched as Alex settled into the seat next to the man, and she giggled inwardly. It was a rare thing to see her level-headed friend flustered. Luckily, Lewin seemed to rather like the seating arrangements. "I'm sure you didn't hop a flight just to see us."

Nick had already told her that Lewin's parents had been born and raised in the States, but that they had moved to Canada when Lewin was little. He and Nick had apparently met in their last year of high school and gone to undergraduate school together. That was about all she had learned.

"I'm a pilot," Lewin answered. "I decided to take my week off after a flight into Kansas City. I had just booked my room when Nick called me actually." She watched as he glanced sideways at Alex. "Most of my flights are between Canada and the States. So I'm in the country quite often." There were heavy implications in his tone, and Ivy swallowed a giggle when Alex turned a brilliant shade of magenta.

"That was lucky for us then," Ivy said. She counted her lucky stars that Nick's friend happened to be in town merely days after Gavin's request. She was afraid to inconvenience the man, though Nick had assured her he was more than willing to help. "Because knowing Gavin, he probably has about a million questions." She didn't know if Nick had warned his friend, but they weren't kidding. Gavin had been compiling a list all week.

"And I told Lewin what questions were best suited for you to answer," Nick said, and his reassurance that some boundaries had been set was wonderful.

Ivy didn't know Lewin, but she knew from his flirtatious attitude and casual demeanor that he probably lacked a filter. While Gavin was smart, she hadn't had the 'talk' with him yet. Under the table, Nick squeezed her hand. She squeezed back, before moving her own up to her plate.

Aldwin knew the boy well enough to know he wouldn't make it past two bites. Sure enough, Gavin wore his inquisitive face. Before he could warn his friend, the interrogation began.

"What exactly is a cupid's job, Lewin?" Gavin asked.

Aldwin picked up his own fork and watched as Lewin began thinking through an explanation.

"Well, it depends. There are three types of cupids," Lewin began. Aldwin knew he, Ivy, and Alex would just be listening for a bit, so he took advantage of the moment to gauge Ivy's reactions. She believed in Santa, and he was curious to see if she would also believe in the others. It would make the truth easier if she did. "The lowest levels, well, they basically do as they please. Their magic arrows rarely last more than a month or so."

"What about the other two types?" Gavin asked.

Aldwin was relieved he didn't ask why love would only need to last a month or so.

"Well, the second level, they handle basic lifetime love. Ordinary people, with ordinary purposes meeting and falling for other ordinary people," Lewin explained. "Not that love of any kind isn't magical." Aldwin smiled as Gavin bit into a mouthful of potatoes. The boy's blue eyes were rapt with attention. "But not all of it is the kind that can cause massive changes to the course of history."

"Is that what the third level does?" Gavin asked.

Ivy had to admit that the story being woven was intriguing. She'd always pictured cupids as little cherubs in diapers, but Lewin's explanation held that same enchanting air as Nick's story had.

"Yes, the third-level members are called the Supreme Cupids," Lewin said, and Ivy took a bite of her chicken as she listened. She had to give it to Lewin that he had wound a good backstory. Nick must have slipped him some of Gavin's questions to prepare for the five-year-old's interrogation. "There are only three in all of existence, and their job is to unite the most important of soulmates."

"What's a soulmate?" Gavin asked.

Ivy hadn't expected that question, and she readied herself to interject. How could someone possibly know how to explain the love of a soulmate in terms a child could understand? Nick obviously sensed her hesitance, because he touched her arm with a soft shush and gave her a tender smile.

"It's somebody who carries a part of you with them. They will balance you out, perfectly, in every way," Lewin said. Ivy relaxed a tad, mostly from Nick's touch, but also from the way Lewin looked over at Alex, who was rapt with attention himself. Lewin looked at her friend the way Nick looked at her—the way Aaron had looked at her. She felt butterflies of excitement for Alex flutter in her stomach. "If you're wild at heart, they are calm. If you are grumpy all the time, they bring you light."

"Well, how can you be sure someone's your soulmate? Leticia's Mommy and Daddy were in love, but they got a, um, divorce. That's what Lettie called it." Gavin said.

Ivy cringed, and she wondered when Lettie had let that information slip to Gavin. She'd been adamant about not talking about marriage drama around her son.

"Oh, you'll know," Lewin said, and his eyes seemed to glow with golden dust as he leaned forwards toward Gavin. "When you meet them, time seems to stand still. Your head gets a little dizzy, your eyes go all starry, and the moment they touch you, you feel it here." He touched his own chest. "In your heart. That's the arrow, and when you look in their eyes for the first time after the arrow, you feel like you're drowning but also like you've met them before."

The description made Ivy gasp, not just at the beauty of the supposed meeting, but because she intimately knew that feeling. She'd felt it, years ago, in the empty retail store when a protective hand and the bluest of eyes stole her heart. Swallowing hard, her mind recalled a damp front stoop, a slip, strong hands gripping her close, and how Nick's caramel eyes had looked so familiar. She didn't even have time to shift her gaze before Nick reached up and brushed her hair back from her eyes. Her heart went a little crazy at the sweet touch.

"Lewin," Ivy asked before her mind could catch up. "Is it possible for someone to have two soulmates?"

"On the rarest of occasions, absolutely," Lewin replied. His blue gaze flicked between her and Nick, and there seemed to be a smug knowing in them.

"So, cupids don't pick whom they want?" Gavin asked. His voice seemed a bit sad, and it drew Aldwin's attention from Ivy. While Ivy's question had utterly distracted him because he knew she was wondering how she had experienced that thrill of soulmates twice. The boy looked down at his plate, and his previous smile had dropped. He knew that look. It was the one Gavin had when he'd lost his chess matches last week.

"The first and second levels do, but not the Supremes," Lewin said. He gave a slight shrug, as Gavin lifted his eyes. Aldwin could normally guess what the five-year-old was thinking, given his tendency to simply speak his mind. He wasn't sure, though, what was whirring behind the boy's summer sky eyes. Lewin, however, had lit up as if he'd figured out the true question the boy poised. "You could always write and ask them more about it if you don't believe me."

"How? Nobody knows where cupids live," Gavin said. He pushed up onto his knees and leaned forward, unquestionably intrigued.

"I do!" Lewin crooned. Aldwin wanted to slap him for what he suspected was coming.

Ivy was confused by the new turn of events. Why in the world would Lewin think a five-year-old would want to write to cupid?

"You do? How?" Gavin asked. Ivy abandoned her food in order to watch the exchange. She picked up her glass and took a sip.

"Well, I know all three Supreme Cupids," Lewin said. There was a sly look in his eyes that convinced Ivy that he most definitely knew them. Santa was real, so maybe cupids were too. She would and could believe anything.

"You do?" Gavin asked. He was practically on his plate, and Alex yanked it out of the way of the five-year-old's elbows. Ivy mouthed thanks to him.

"You betcha, here," Lewin said. She blinked when he dug in his pocket and produced a business card. "See, being a pilot, I've traveled all over. You meet all kinds of people, magical and human. I happen to know that one of the Supreme Cupids has a summer home in Florida." Gavin took the card and squinted down at it with a look somewhere between uncertainty and that mad, genius expression he got when he was about to raid her kitchen for experiment supplies he'd seen online. "One even told me that sometimes, they do take requests." At that, Lewin flashed her an obvious wink and then sent one to Nick. Nick must have kicked him under the table because Lewin grunted.

"Mummy," Gavin said, and again Ivy adored the way he'd begun to mimic some of Nick's vocabulary. It showed her that he loved the man too. "Can I be excused?"

"Yeah, baby," she said. In a flash, Gavin was down and sprinting upstairs.

There was a thick silence at the table because Alex and Nick seemed as confused as she was. Lewin, on the other hand, was smirking as if he'd just declared a triple Olympic victory for himself. He leaned back in his chair and draped an arm behind Alex.

"What address was on that card, Lewin?" she asked, trying to keep her voice low so Gavin wouldn't hear them.

"Mine," he replied with a soft chuckle.

Aldwin sucked in a breath as he made the connection. Lewin had given Gavin the address to the cupids' council building, but why? Cupids didn't take requests, ever.

"You think he's going to write and ask for information?" Alex finally spoke up, and there was all the concern of an uncle dripping from his voice. Aldwin was grateful such a loving and caring man had been in his loves' lives. "What're you going to do then?"

"Send him the information he needs, of course," Lewin said and grinned broadly. "And now that he's upstairs and my work here is done, I have a question." Aldwin chuckled as Lewin turned to fully look at Alex. "Would you like to get a drink after dinner?"

"Well, I—" Alex began, but Ivy threw a pea at him and hit him in the nose, cutting him off.

"Shut up and go get your coat, Alex," Ivy said. She snickered at the way her friend seemed more than a little overwhelmed by Lewin's seductive smile. Lewin wasn't Alex's usual type, but the connection between them was undeniable. Maybe it was time for Alex to toss his usual type in the trash, where their personalities and bad opinions belonged.

"I guess we're getting drinks," Alex said. He pushed his plate away and stood, and Lewin followed suit. After some brief hugs and handshakes, she found herself alone with Nick, who was clearing the table.

"I'll wash up," she said, earning herself a soft brow kiss from him. Ivy moved to the kitchen. She tried to make sense of the conversation and why she had asked about having two soulmates. She turned on the water, adding a bit of soap.

She knew Santa was real. She knew it in her gut. So maybe Nick and Lewin were right. Maybe it was all possible. She did wonder how Nick and Lewin knew so much, so confidently, about things never mentioned in folklore? Did they learn it in some tradition not taught in the U.S.? Maybe they studied rare folklore history in college.

She didn't know, and honestly, she didn't care. All she cared about was that her son was happy.

"Penny for 'em," chuckled Nick, His hands came around her to slide the glasses and utensils into the foamy water. It should have startled her, but somehow her body had known he was there. That happened, sometimes. He'd try to sneak up, but she could feel him enter the room in her chest. Just being near him sometimes stole her breath away. "You've got your thinking face on."

"Just woolgathering," Ivy replied. She recalled Alex's words in the car and wondered if he was right. Would Aaron really want her to start over? If so, would he approve of Nick? She felt him move away, probably to go upstairs and shower. On instinct, she reached back and grabbed his hand. Then she pulled it around her waist. "Stay with me a while, like this."

"Oh, gladly," Nick whispered. His other arm wrapped around her, and Ivy felt that old sensation of being secure and cared for return. His cheek rested against her hair, and Nick gave her a slight hug. "Your mum is still taking Gavin tomorrow, yeah?" He whispered, as she turned off the water and began washing.

"Mm-hmm," Ivy replied. She still had that thoughtful tone to her, and Aldwin wondered what was going through her mind. "Why?"

"Well, I was wondering, if, maybe, I could take you out," he said.

He hoped he was doing this right. Lewin had asked Alex in a similar fashion, but he didn't know if Ivy needed to be asked in a different way. He wouldn't be able to stand it if he made her uncomfortable.

"Like a date?" she asked, and Aldwin swallowed. She sounded like she didn't understand what he was asking.

"Exactly like that," he said. Her face turned, and Aldwin pulled his own back, stomach fluttering in anticipation. What if she said no? What if she wasn't ready? Just because she was okay with snuggling and even this wonderful moment of just standing together, it didn't mean she could handle going out with him, just him. Maybe dating was too much. They hadn't even had a proper kiss since her breakdown.

"I thought you'd never ask," Ivy practically purred. Aldwin wanted to croon his excitement out, but he settled for kissing the top of her head and hugging her tightly.

Ivy felt a rush of elation. A date! Nick wanted to take her out on a proper date. It would be just them, out, in public, without wondering if Gavin was about to wake up or come barging in. Abandoning the dishes, she turned and looked up at the man grinning ear to ear.

"Can I dress up?"

"Absolutely, you can," he said.

His fingers brushed along her spine, and those adoring eyes bounced between hers. His joy and excitement at her simple agreement stole her breath.

"Come here, you," Ivy groaned. She grabbed his collar and tugged him down. Their lips met in a closed press, and she sighed in relief at the perfect way it felt. Just like before, it was so familiar and flawless. Her entire body began to warm, tingling as he raised a hand to cup her hair at the same time his tongue grazed her lower lip.

She parted her lips for him, sighing at the flavor of wine on his tongue when it curled along hers. She cupped his cheek and didn't protest when he turned them slightly. She nipped at his bottom lip gently, before pressing up on her toes so she could pull him down closer.

"Mummy!" Gavin shouted from upstairs and made her jerk back. "Can I have a stamp?"

"Yeah, baby! Be right there," she called, breathlessly. She felt dizzy when she offered Nick an apologetic smile. "Sorry." She giggled at the smear of pink lipstick she'd left on his bottom lip. Gently, she wiped it with her thumb.

"Hey, Gavin comes first," he said. "Hurry back." He squeezed her waist, quickly pressing his lips to hers again.

"Two minutes," Ivy said. "Then we can pick up where we left off." She licked her lips as she ducked out of his arms. She made it halfway up the stairs before she realized she hadn't felt a flicker of guilt

Aldwin was soaring higher than he'd felt in some time. Once Ivy had given Gavin his requested stamp, bathed him, and put him to bed, she'd returned and the kissing had resumed.

When he was two hundred years young, a bit wild, and under the influence of both the Spring Equinox and more Sundew Wine than should be legal, he'd had a pretty wild fling with a base-level cupid Lewin introduced him to. It lasted about two weeks—two very intense and unforgettable weeks. The kiss that he got when Ivy came back into the kitchen effectively erased those two weeks from existence.

It had started at the sink, but somehow he'd ended up with her pinned against the refrigerator. Then Ivy was up on the counter, her fingers in his hair, and somehow they'd ended up on the sofa with her jumper on the armchair and his tie hanging from a lamp.

They hadn't crossed any lines. Hands hadn't wandered into dangerous areas, nor had he let his body take over and respond to her weight on his lap. Yet, there was a fading mark on his collarbone, and he was almost certain he'd left one just above her left breast. When she had finally broken away, lips swollen, hair mussed, eyes shining, to point out it was after eleven and she needed to get to bed, Aldwin had been loath to release her. Still, he didn't want to press her or even ask her to stay the night in his bed, which he sorely dreamed for. Instead, he'd muttered something about straightening up Gavin's toys he'd drug out Thursday night and watched her disappear slowly up the stairs.

A Family Favor

All day, while Ivy was out getting Gavin a haircut and running some errands, Aldwin had been trying to figure out where to take ivy. She wanted to dress up, so somewhere nice was a no-brainer, but the issue came with where. The solution to his problem came in the form of a phone call.

"Heya, snowflake. I'm a little upset with you," Regina Cauldrop, his cousin, said. She didn't seem upset at all, and Aldwin knew she was just teasing.

"Regina, hi," he said and flopped down on his bed to stare in vain at his closet. The feisty redhead was his favorite cousin, closest to him in age, and it was always an adventure when they got together. She was also as well-known as he was in the Ageless community, but not for the same reasons. "What'd I do now?"

"You, you skinny brat, have been living near Kansas City for a month and a week now, and you haven't called me once," Regina said playfully. "You know we have clubs out there. Also, Auntie Cateline tells me you've got a soulmate. I want to meet her! Have you told her about the family yet? Probably not knowing you."

"Regina, the babbling, that's my thing, not yours," Aldwin teased. He twirled his finger, summoning a suit to examine it. "What's that noise?" In the background of the call, it sounded like a band warming up the chatter of voices.

"I'm setting up for a Halloween Masquerade," Regina replied, but the noise soon faded. "Here at one of our clubs in Kansas City."

"You're still running The Noble? I thought you closed that down to run off with that summer sprite. What was his name again?" Honestly, Aldwin hadn't cared for him, so he'd basically forgotten the man's name immediately after the party they'd been at was over.

"Who? Miran? Ew, no. He was just a fling. You know how I get at the Spring Equinox," Regina chuckled.

Aldwin knew very well, too well, actually. Some mental images couldn't be scrubbed from a brain, even after six hundred years.

"Like parents, like daughter," Aldwin snickered.

The reason Regina was as well-known as his parents were simply because of her parents. She was, and remained, the only living half-Summer, half-Winter sprite. Seriously, Spring Equinox celebrations packed one hell of a wallop for all of the Ageless. There was a reason he'd stopped going. Dancing on a hill in Ireland and waking up half-naked in a Nebraskan cornfield was something he never wanted to do again, well, unless Ivy wanted to give it a go. He'd do it then.

With Ivy back in his thoughts, Aldwin had a wild idea. "Would you like to meet Ivy tonight?"

"Uh, duh," snorted Regina. Aldwin knew very well that if they were in person, she would have smacked him in the back of his head. "What name are you using? I'll put you on the list."

Aldwin breathed out a sigh of relief.

"Just my middle name, Nicholas Claus, and, do you mind getting the word out to other guests to not ruin my cover?" The Noble was one of the favorite gathering places in Kansas City, Kansas and Missouri for Ageless. It catered to mortals, of course, but on a highly regulated, reservation-only basis. "And you said Masquerade right?"

"Yup, and I'll make sure nobody approaches you," she said.

"You're a lifesaver, Regina. See you tonight," he said.

Aldwin had a plan. He just had to make sure Ivy was fully prepared. So, when the call ended, he quickly twirled his magic and grinned as a dress appeared, complete with a matching mask. Then he hurried down the stairs to hang it on her doorknob, with a note. It was just in time, too, because the door downstairs was opening.

"Nick, we're back!" Ivy called up, and Aldwin hurried down. When he reached them, he stumbled to a stop, shocked by the sight before him.

Ivy had apparently gotten her hair done too. It looked like her highlights had been touched up, and it was swept back in a stunning twist, with her bangs pinned back in elegant swoops that accentuated her eyes. She was stunning. Gavin's new style caught his attention too. Instead of the shaggy ear-length strands he'd been sporting, it was cut short on the sides, and the top was gelled and ruffled up in a mirror of Aldwin's usual style.

"Wow, just wow. You both look great!"

Ivy felt herself flush when Gavin proudly announced. "My hair looks like yours!" He'd begged and pleaded for the style, and she had finally given in and shown Miranda a picture before her mom dragged her into a chair to fix her hair up for the date. "Mummy said I look handsome!" She had given up on trying to correct her son back to saying Mommy because the mimicked accent was just too adorable to stop.

Nick's eyes went impossibly soft as he bent down, and the flattered tone in his voice sent Ivy's heart in a flutter. "Very handsome, buddy. You make it look way better than I do."

"Gavin, baby, why don't you go pack your costume and jimjams? Gran'll be here to pick you up in a bit," she said and watched as he raced down the hall to the stairs. Nick straightened up, and she shifted under his eyes as he gazed over her. "What? You don't like it? Is it too much for tonight? I wasn't sure what to do with it."

"Ivy, you look absolutely amazing, and it's perfect for tonight," Nick said. He pulled at his ear, in that nervous way of his that she found so endearing. "It'll go perfect with the dress actually."

"I haven't even decided what I'm wearing yet," she said, confused at his statement. She shrugged it off though. Glancing past him to make sure Gavin wasn't watching, she snagged Nick's shirt and pulled him close. "I missed you while we were out," she whispered. Then she slid her arms up around his neck and grinned while his hands slipped to her waist. Offering her lips to him, she sighed happily as he brushed a tender, light caressing kiss on them.

"I missed you too," Nick whispered into her lips and gifted her with another tender press. Ivy eagerly accepted it, loving how warm and soft his lips were. "And, as for the dress, I may have left you a little gift for tonight on your door. You don't have to wear it, but it was just in case you didn't have something to dress up in." Ivy pulled back and felt a thrill of excitement

"You got me a dress?" she asked.

She bit at her lip, unsure of whether to dash up and see it or just kiss him senseless. She had wanted to wear something special tonight, but not knowing what plans he'd made, she'd been undecided. Ivy had hoped to coax details out of him before she got ready. Thanks to him, she didn't have to choose, because Nick playfully pushed her towards the hall.

"Go see. I'll make sure Gavin's getting his bag ready," Nick whispered, and she pressed another hurried kiss to his cheek before moving out of his reach.

With a smile she couldn't keep back, Ivy hurried up the stairs. Sure enough, a dress bag hung on her knob, and she gaped at the stunning black filigree masquerade mask adorned with red crystals that hung with it. She had no idea what he had planned, but she was very excited to find out. Her heart racing, Ivy slipped inside and close the door behind her. She unzipped the bag and gasped in amazement as she pulled the dress out.

It had a black corseted bodice that was covered in maroon lace. The sleeves were designed to hang off her shoulders and rest against her upper arms. The skirt was long, with the same black material and maroon lace down the right side and around her calves. There was also a lovely, short, black cape, no doubt designed to keep the late autumn chill from her skin. Ivy drew a breath and searched for a price tag. She knew for the style it had probably cost him a fortune. She wondered how he could afford something so exquisite and where in the world he'd found it in their small town. Then she remembered he was heir to a successful company, even if he didn't work there now, and immediately she wanted to give it back. He'd also probably ordered it to be delivered from the city. Then she saw the note. Gently, she picked it up, unfolding it.

Ivy,

Don't even think about giving this dress back. It was made for you and only you.

Nick

"Well then," Ivy sighed to the empty air.

She couldn't very well give it back before dinner if he'd had it custom-made to wear to wherever they were going. She'd talk to him about giving it back after. Kissing the note, she set it down and hurried into the small en-suite to wash off and do her makeup. She wanted to look perfect, and despite having already kissed him and skirting the edges of a relationship, first date jitters had her shaking in anticipation and eagerness.

She heard her mom knock when she was halfway through her makeup but not the conversation. Ivy hoped she wasn't blasting about that it was a date in front of Gavin. She wasn't quite ready for him to know because he hadn't taken too keenly to the two previous dates. Yes, he practically worshiped Nick, but she didn't know if those feelings would turn to spite if he found out too soon and from anyone other than her. She needed to explain it to him gently.

Shortly after she heard her mother leave, she heard Nick head up the stairs, past her door, and his shower turned on over her head. She knew he never took long, so Ivy dug her pair of once-worn black heels that would match the dress from her closet and slipped into her clothes. She'd just tied on the cape and smoothed her skirts when he knocked softly on her door. Ivy picked up her mask, quickly spritzed on some perfume, and opened it. The sight that greeted her made her gape in awe and her mouth run dry.

Nick wore a suit she'd never seen. It was all black, but with a red shirt underneath. That shirt matched the red pinstripes running through the suit as well as the buttons. The black tie he wore had small red vines of ivy embroidered on it, and upon looking down, she swallowed a giggle at the brand-new red high-tops poking out. His magnificent hair was back combed, and it made his sharp features look so devastatingly delicious it made her dizzy.

"You are absolutely gorgeous," Aldwin gushed. He was proud he formed the words because the sight of her in the dress made his brain go blank. The colors suited her complexion and almost made her glow like silken cream. Cautiously, he reached out to trail his thumb just along her chin, not wanting to ruin that painted pout with a kiss. "Ready to go?" He asked.

"Mm-hm," Ivy hummed. Her cheeks flushed when he dropped his hand, and her chest swelled in affection as she dragged her eyes over him. "God, you look amazing too. I'm gonna be fighting everyone off with a bat."

Aldwin snorted at that, but he still stepped aside to place his hand against her lower back and guide her down the stairs. Their car had just arrived before he came down.

"I won't have eyes for anyone but you. I'm the one who's gonna be fighting off the competition," he quipped, as she descended the stairs first.

"There is no competition," Ivy said.

The certainty in her words took him by surprise, and he flipped off the lights as they went. When she opened the front door, he knew she expected to see a taxi or ride-share, but he hid his smile at the classic, black, two-passenger, antique chauffeured car waiting at the bottom of the driveway. Not hesitating for her to ask or say anything. Aldwin took her arm and escorted her down to the vehicle.

"What's this?" she asked

"You wanted to dress up. Well, I figured why not give you the full treatment," he said and nodded at the driver who opened the door. "After you, Lady Ivy," he chuckled and gestured for her to slide in. Then he took his own seat.

Ivy's mind was racing, and she tried to guess where they were going. She shifted in excitement when Nick pulled a mask from his inner pocket and tied it on. It was black on one side and red on the other, with swooping swirls. Giddily, she tied her own on, and the lights dimmed when the car started.

"Where to, Mr. Claus?" The driver asked.

"The Noble," Nick said.

"You got us reservations at The Noble?" Ivy gasped.

She couldn't believe it, and she had no idea how he managed to do it on such short notice. The club and restaurant were the most highly acclaimed in the city, with a three-year wait-list. She knew because Alex had been trying to take her for her birthday for the last two years, but every time he called or attempted to book online, there were never any openings. Ivy finally understood the outfits and masks. Their Halloween Masquerade was one of their biggest events of the year.

"How? It's nearly impossible to get in, much less tonight."

"Well," Nick said. His smile was hesitant, and Ivy felt a flicker of fear. Maybe he didn't know it was by reservation only? "My cousin Regina and her parents are the owners of The Noble and a few other five-star restaurants and clubs around the world. She wanted to meet you, and she was in town for the weekend. Is that okay?"

Did he want to introduce her to his family? Ivy nearly giggled aloud at that knowledge.

"I can't wait," she said. Nick seemed to relax as Ivy smiled and slipped her fingers into his. The night was going to be magical.

Ivy had worried she may be a bit out of date with her dress, as the driver pulled up to the front door. It wasn't that she didn't love it. She did, though, especially how it hugged her curves and pushed her breasts up just right. Her worry was that it wouldn't blend in with the other patrons. She should have known Nick wouldn't do that to her.

As they approached the door maître de, she caught glimpses of the two lines. Most of the women in the line to the left, who were being waved through with a smile and a nod, were dressed in similar fashions. A few were even wearing Romanesque-style gowns. The other line had the more current styles.

"Name please?" The maître de asked before he looked up. He caught sight of Nick and blinked. Then his smile lit up when he looked at her. "Mr. Claus! Haven't seen you in ages. Regina said you'd be coming." She looped her arm through Nick's while the man tilted his head as if studying her and then smiled. "This must be Ivy. Regina's just inside."

"Hello." Ivy gave a small smile before Nick led her in. They seemed to have arrived just at the beginning of the dinner rush because many seats looked empty. Following his lead, she looked around for a woman who seemed like they could be related. It was impossible to tell, but in a moment they were moving past the main tables and up to two small ones that were manned by a stunning blonde woman in a floor-length burnt orange gown with a mask designed like flames. The woman nodded once at Nick, and then Ivy found herself tucked into an intimate booth in the back corner with an unobstructed view of the dance floor.

"There you are, you skinny little candy cane!" Ivy yelped as a woman with bright red hair, a purple Roman-style gown, and a matching mask seemed to appear from nowhere to hug Nick. "Hi! You must be Ivy. I'm Regina, Nick's cousin." Catching her breath from the surprise, Ivy shook her hand. Except for the wild, slightly manic grin, she couldn't see any resemblance.

Aldwin was glad Ivy was distracted by looking around when Regina decided to pop into existence and hug him. "I said to meet her, not scare the pants off her, Regina," he chuckled. "I hope you don't mind, I commandeered your table for us."

"Nah, I don't mind at all. I'm just really excited to meet Ivy," Regina said tossing her long, red hair back as she looked Ivy over. Aldwin knew she could see it, that belief in the magic that made her glow brighter than the majority of other adult mortals. "We thought this moron would never find a woman," she said, and he grunted when she elbowed him. "Want me to send out a bottle of your favorite, Nick?"

"No," Aldwin cut her off, not wanting to run the risk of getting a little too loose. Then Ivy changed his mind with an eager smile and a soft request.

"Oh please. You never pick out the wine. I want to try it," she insisted, hugging his arm gently. He couldn't deny her anything if he wanted to.

"Okay, but you better charge me for it," huffed Aldwin. He kissed Regina's cheek before he slid into his seat and draped his arm around Ivy. "And, can you send out the off-menu Chef's choice platter?" he asked. If Ivy was about to partake of some moon-stilled berry wine, she would need something a little more filling than simply mortal food.

"It'll be right out," Regina said, and she headed down the small steps grinning ear to ear.

Aldwin relaxed as Ivy snuggled into his side.

"She liked you." If Regina hadn't, she wouldn't have been in such a friendly mood. "What're you in the mood for dinner?" he asked. He knew she'd probably gotten something quick for lunch, and, by now, she'd be starving. He picked up the menu to hand it to her. "Pick anything you want. Tonight is all about you having fun." He glanced around to make sure that none of the other Ageless who were slowly trickling in interrupted them. He wanted the night to be absolutely perfect.

Dinner, Dancing, and Decisions

Aldwin hoped Ivy didn't see him glancing around and giving pointed looks at the individuals coming up into the VIP area. It wasn't that he really had any particular status in the Ageless Hierarchy, at least, not until he took up his father's mantle. It was that with their people, everybody knew everybody or at least one of their relatives.

Given their longevity, it was absolutely imperative that everyone stayed friendly. Blood feuds were a bad idea when they could stretch millennia. That meant when they gathered in places like The Noble, for parties, or just coincidentally, there were no true social boundaries. He just wanted to make sure Ivy didn't know until she was ready. A few caught his eyes, nodding as they settled into their own booths in the VIP section, but so far Regina must have warned them off.

"Um, I dunno what I want to eat," Ivy said.

Everything on the menu looked amazing, and she couldn't choose. Somehow, despite the music being at an acceptable level, and the low hum of chatter not being too high, there was something about the atmosphere that distracted her. She couldn't quite put her finger on it, but she'd felt it before. "What're you having?" she asked. Probably half the menu if he got his way. Despite being lean and lithe, Nick ate like a fifteen-year-old boy. If it was in front of him, he'd have three helpings. "Pick me something to go with the wine."

"I know just what you'll like," Nick said. She smiled when he took the menu and set it aside. A waitress appeared from seemingly nowhere. She poured their wine and set down a platter covered in fruits and cheeses. Once it was done, he stroked Ivy's shoulder, sending warm tingles along her spine. "I'll have the braised steak, rare, with the herb and lemon potatoes. My lady would like the center cut steak, medium rare, with the flame-grilled shrimp and a side of the butter sautéed vegetables," he rattled off without even looking at the menu.

"Of course, Mr. Claus," the waitress said. Then she was gone.

Ivy was starving, so she reached forward to pick up one of the red berries she didn't recognize and dip it in a creamy cheese with lavender swirls. Popping it on her tongue, she groaned at the explosion of flavor.

"Oh my god," she moaned. It tasted like raspberry, only crisper with a bit of tart undertones. The cheese, however, was sweet with a wild accent that immediately counteracted the berry's tartness. "This is amazing."

Nick chuckled beside her, as he popped a bit of green fruit he'd smothered in some orange-looking cheese in his mouth.

"Try the round, white slices with a chunk of that pink cheese," he encouraged her with an eager tone, and Ivy did. Honestly, the combination was so exquisite, that she couldn't do more than just let it melt on her tongue while he raised his glass for a sip.

"I think the food faeries are having a party in my mouth," Ivy whimpered, before swallowing.

She reached for the wine. It was odd-looking. There was the normal reddish color of a robust flavor, but it glistened with what looked like the world's finest glitter. It must have been the club lights that made the bottle seem to glow from within. She took a sip, and warmth shot out across her body. There was absolutely no way to describe the deliciousness slipping across her lips to her throat.

"I think I'm in love with this wine," she breathed, turning to look up at Nick who beamed at her.

"It's pretty strong, so don't overindulge," Aldwin warned her. He made a mental note to keep an eye on Ivy's intake when he felt the atmosphere in the club begin to change. "You'll regret it in the morning if you do."

With the influx of Ageless patrons, the magic began to ramp up and fill the building. None of them except Regina and the wait staff would have permission to directly use it, due to the risk of exposure to the mortals, but the energy had definitely grown palpable. The magical sensation was one of the reasons The Noble was so sought out as a 'place to be' by the mortals.

"Do you really think she liked me?" Ivy asked, and Aldwin nodded. He leaned in close so none of the Ageless could overhear them.

"Oh, absolutely, Regina isn't the kind of person to lie about it," said Aldwin. He could keenly remember the time Lewin had brought a partner to one of her parties, and the sprite had been promptly kicked out. "She would have told me to get you out of her club." Ivy relaxed some, but he could tell she was still anxious.

"It's just, with Aaron, he didn't have any family to meet," Ivy said between sips. Aldwin paused and waited for the usual frown and regression into grief that came at the mention of Aaron. It didn't come, even when she continued to talk. "His parents died in a car accident, which is what brought him home to Ostcrest from teaching physics. He didn't have any siblings, and he didn't have any cousins he was close to. So, I had no family to meet."

"Well, I will definitely be introducing you to my parents soon," murmured Aldwin. He loved how, even behind her mask, she blushed slightly and smiled. "And they said they already adore you because you make me happier than anyone ever has." He leaned over and pressed a kiss to one of her flushed cheeks.

"How is Regina related to you, mom's side, or dad's? You don't look anything alike."

Ivy was trying to change the subject of meeting his parents, but she was also curious. She and her cousin Paula looked different, but their familial traits were still easy to pick out. People always knew they were cousins. Paula was a bit taller and just a tad thinner, but they had the same nose and smile from her mom's family. She knew she looked like her cousins on her dad's side too, but rarely saw them as her aunt didn't get along with her mom at all.

"My Dah's side," replied Nick. There was an odd expression on his face when he said it, but she didn't press. "Her father is my Dah's youngest half-brother, but she gets the red hair from her mum's side. Honestly, I look more like my mum than Dah too."

"That makes sense," Ivy replied. "I look nothing like my dad's side, except for the eyes. Which is great since they don't talk to us. I look just like my mom's mom though. It makes sense that Regina doesn't look too much like you."

Aldwin nodded. Discussing Ageless relationships was difficult if people didn't understand. His grandfather hadn't been married to his grandmother, but his great-uncle had fallen head over heels for Thelania, a stubborn summer sprite. While it wasn't uncommon for the different families to intermix for flings, marriage and children were rare. Usually, the bloodlines' magics weren't compatible. He needed to change the subject.

"Enjoying yourself?" he asked. Then he grinned as Ivy popped another Starberry with a bit of crumbled Hituran, a cow-like creature from the other realm, cheese into her mouth. He was glad she had gravitated towards that combination. The sugars and proteins would help absorb the wine better than the mortal dinner food would.

"Mm-hmm," Ivy hummed. He kissed the side of her head again before she continued to speak. "Feels good having a night out, just us." Her lips pressed into his cheek, and Aldwin enjoyed the tingle they left.

Their food came out in record time, and Ivy enjoyed it the way she would any steak. As they ate, though, the music began to pick up, and it made her entire body vibrate and hum.

Since the majority of the patrons were here for the dancing, the dance floors filled up quickly. The more she watched, while Nick alternated between eating and touching her tenderly, the more her body began to heat up. She couldn't explain the feelings washing through her, but she wasn't drunk. Instead of feeling impaired, everything was more intense, clearer, and more enticing. It made their conversation and other topics feel like a deep, mental seduction. All she knew, by the time her plate was mostly empty, was that she wanted his hands on her body.

"Dance with me," she teased. Then she slid from her seat and grabbed Nick's hands.

"Ivy, we haven't even had dessert," Nick protested, but Ivy wasn't hearing it.

"Don't care about dessert right now," she informed him. "I want to dance with you." She tugged at him, encouraged by the oddly warm and sultry feeling coursing through her veins.

Nick finally stood up, and he took the lead to guide her through the crowd. The music was loud, and it wasn't like anything she'd ever heard. It mingled modern hits with a wild, almost mystical rhythm. Ivy liked it, and she tried to make a mental note to ask him who the DJ was. The moment Nick's hands landed on her waist and pulled her back into him, she forgot to ask. All she could focus on was the beat of the music, the warmth in her veins, and the way Nick's very touch shot electricity under her skin.

Aldwin found it harder than ever to keep himself in check, as the wine, the food, and the magic pulsed in and around him. Ivy's face, so open, full of excitement and joy had him feeling rather intoxicated. He knew the effects of the wine were sending her senses into overdrive rather than subduing them. It was why he had wanted to avoid the wine, but as she moved against him, one hand on his chest and the other around his neck,

Aldwin was not complaining. It took a blink for him, and another pair of hands were almost covering his on Ivy's hips.

"Share with me!" A woman said. Ivy's head shifted to reveal a rather lovely Spring sprite he vaguely knew as Coralei, with golden hair and lavender eyes, smiling wickedly at him over Ivy's shoulder. "Ald-" he cut her off, by wheeling Ivy around.

"I don't share," growled Aldwin. He rolled his eyes when Ivy giggled. "Sorry, told you I'd be fighting people off." A few others were eyeing them, so he did the only thing he could think of to make sure nobody else tried to solicit attention from his lover. He bent Ivy slightly back, leaned down, and kissed her for all he was worth. Thankfully, Ivy responded enthusiastically, so he took extra time to fully enjoy the taste of the wine on her tongue and lips before pulling away.

"Let's go have that dessert," croaked Aldwin and tried to coax her into returning. He needed to get Ivy alone because the longer he spent with her delicious curves and supple body pressed against him, the more difficult he found it to behave. Luckily, she didn't protest and followed him almost giddily off the dance floor. "Having fun?" he asked, using the break to try to gauge how well she was handling the way the magic pulsed through the atmosphere.

"Oh my God, yes!" Ivy crooned. She eagerly slid back into their booth with him and pressed as close as she could manage.

She felt unspeakably alive, and something about having Nick so close made her feel things she hadn't in over two years. The cool metal of a fork pressing against her open lips caught her by surprise, and she took the proffered bite with burning cheeks. She wondered if her love could tell what was unfurling in her veins. She slid her hand to his thigh under the table, and stroked her thumb slowly and softly.

She chewed the dessert languorously, groaning at the rich chocolate cake that had a hint of rum to the icing. It spurred her on, and she shifted her hand slightly higher when Nick didn't respond to her touch. A bead of sweat trailed down his cheek, and she yearned to trace its path with her tongue. Ivy knew exactly what she wanted from him, and she felt the thrill of it in her veins. It had been years since she'd felt the way she did. She just wasn't sure how to ask him for it.

Aldwin was mid-bite when Ivy's touch shifted higher and poured warmth down his legs.

"Mm, what are you doing?" he asked in a whisper, swallowing the treat as her eyes blazed past her mask at him. He'd never seen that look on her. Her thumb slid higher, and it hit him when she smirked, why she was ignoring the dessert. She was aroused. "You're being very naughty, you know." He covered her hand, not to stop her, but to make sure she didn't slip too high. He loved the way it felt, but he didn't want to get too hard to walk.

"Am I?" Ivy asked.

"You know you are," he said. Aldwin stroked her knuckles with a thumb as she shifted her hand up another inch on his thigh. He picked up his wine to cool his blazing throat and resisted the urge to lean down and kiss her.

"What's wrong with a woman touching her boyfriend's thigh?" she asked. Aldwin tightened his fingers slightly around hers. He was already half-hard, and if she made it a few more inches up she would feel. "Nobody can see." Aldwin had to bite his tongue, literally, at the husky, heated tone of Ivy's voice. Shoving his plate aside, he leaned down to whisper in her ear.

"No, but I don't fancy anyone but you seeing what's in my pants," he said. "And if you keep it up, everyone will see the imprint when I stand up." Ivy gave a short gasp that sounded deliciously needy. Then her words hit him, and his heart stuttered.

She'd said boyfriend. She'd called him her boyfriend. He had to know if she meant it, or if it was just part of the moment.

"Boyfriend?" he asked and chanced a kiss to the spot below her ear, thrilling at how she tilted her head to give him access. "I like the way that sounds."

"Me too," Ivy said and squeezed his thigh gently. His lips felt magical, fueling the warmth that had long been pooling between her thighs, making it hard to think. Her throat and mouth were dry, and she wriggled away from him only long enough to top their glasses off. "What'dya say we have one more drink then get out of here?" she purred. The only thought on her mind was how that suit coat would look and sound like hitting the bedroom floor.

"I'd say you better drink fast," Nick growled. They quickly emptied their glasses, as he picked up the bill folder the waitress had just dropped off and stuffed a handful of cash in it. Ivy was too focused on the burn of the wine and his touch to notice how much it was.

The chilly night bit at Ivy's skin as they stepped out of the club, but she didn't have time to be uncomfortable. Nick had her against him, his arms around her tightly, and he peppered eager kisses across her lips and face. She vaguely registered the car pulling up and them getting in before she was half in Nick's lap with his mouth on hers.

There was an intensity behind it, and it had Ivy shooting higher and higher. Somehow their masks were gone, probably tucked in one of his pockets.

Nick kissed and nipped along her neck and shoulder. Time seemed to be moving a little funny, and that crisp, snowy pine essence that clung to his skin only enhanced the effect that last glass of wine had caused. She was out of the car before she could focus, loosening the tie on his neck with eager fingers.

"Get me inside first, greedy!" Nick yelped, then he laughed.

Aldwin couldn't blame her, because he wanted that dress off just as much as she seemed to want his suit gone. He couldn't believe what was happening. His heart pounded in his chest, and it took what was left of his willpower to not just transport them up to his bed. Thankfully, he managed to get the door unlocked without breaking away from her lips.

He knew Ivy wasn't drunk. The appetizers would have dampened the alcohol. What they were both riding. The humming, buzzing, electrified sparks were just their bond. The magic used to make the wine was enhancing the physical aspect and allowed it to bloom uninhibited by doubts or fears.

"Oh my stars," Aldwin groaned when Ivy reached between them to press her hand against the bulge in his pants. He kicked the door shut, and he couldn't wait any longer. "Hang on!"

Ivy squealed as she was scooped up into strong arms. She clung to his neck, giggling, and oh so ready for what was coming.

The house was dark, with only the moonlight coming in the window. So she closed her eyes against the spinning in her mind. The sensations and the moment were so familiar. Heavy footsteps echoed on the stairs, and she received a broken, breathless, passionate kiss halfway up. A heart raced against her side, pounding hard, and teeth tugged gently at her ear.

"Ivy, my Ivy, all mine," he panted into her ear. Their bedroom was right there, door open and bed waiting in the light of the moon beyond the window. "There? You sure?" he asked.

"Of course," Ivy sighed.

Why would he ask if she was sure about going into the bedroom? Men could be so silly when drunk, and she giggled at his question. In a moment, he had her back on her feet by the bed, and he was unlacing her dress. She groaned when his tongue laved a path along the back of her neck to her shoulder before his kiss lit up her skin.

"Yes, more," she pleaded.

"I could stare at you for hours," he groaned.

Ivy hadn't had this dream in ages. She could just feel it, feel him, the love, the tenderness. Everything was so sharp, so intense, better than a dream. Her white dress was pooled around her feet. Gavin was at her mom's, and they were alone for their wedding night. She forced her eyes open, sighing in contentment at the rings sparkling on her left hand.

"Say something. You're so quiet," Nick sighed into her hair, as his fingers ghosted along the swell of her breast. His thumbs brushed across her nipples, making her shiver, and Ivy was aware of herself.

It was Nick, not Aaron. It wasn't their wedding night. It was their first date. She wanted this, wanted him. Her whole body craved everything about him. She turned to look at him, to kiss him, to undo every button of that ridiculous sexy shirt of his.

Blue eyes met hers behind him, framed on her dresser, and a broad smile filled her vision. The guilt knocked her so hard that her knees buckled.

"I can't!" she cried, and thankfully Nick caught her.

What had she been doing? Those blue eyes stared out at her in accusation. They had seen her, had witnessed everything she'd just done.

Aldwin's heart sank when Ivy went limp and began to tremble in his arms. He wasn't disappointed, not in the least. That exact scenario is why he'd wanted to go up to his room, but it may still have happened. Either way, it didn't matter. His Ivy needed him in a different way.

"I know. I know. Shhh, sit here," he murmured to her lovingly. He eased her to the bed and went to her drawer to get one of her long night gowns. At least she wasn't crying, because if Ivy had started crying, Aldwin knew he might just do it too. If anything, she looked every bit like a woman who had been caught cheating. Then he saw the picture, and he knew that had caused it.

"I know is stupid to feel guilty, like I'm being unfaithful to him," Ivy whispered, her voice strained, while Aldwin helped her slide on the gown. He refused to let himself admire the frontal view because he wanted to save that for their true first time. All that mattered was getting her calm and comfortable again. "But I can't think straight. I do want you. Please, Nick, understand that. I didn't mean to be a tease. Please forgive me." Aldwin almost shook his head at the pleading tone of her voice.

"There's nothing to forgive," Nick said. He cupped her face and knelt in front of her. Ivy swallowed hard, trying to gather her scattered thoughts. "You weren't quite ready, I know. I'm not upset. So don't apologize. I'm only ever going to want to go as far and as fast as you want." He kissed her brow, and at his words, Ivy buried her face in his chest instead of pulling away from his touch. "I told you, my precious girl, I have all the time in the world for you."

Ivy was surprised she wasn't sobbing this time, but the ache of guilt nagged at her. It wasn't just the guilt from thinking of Aaron, but also because she had felt how much Nick wanted it to happen. She had a choice between a living, breathing, wonderful man who adored her and was so kind to her son and the man who had loved her unconditionally, who had cried the first time Gavin's heart was audible on the ultrasound, and who was gone.

"Can we go sit and have some tea?" she asked. Tea at night was a habit she had more than happily picked up from him.

"Of course," Aldwin said. He helped Ivy stand, and the conflicting emotions on her face were evident. He didn't press her as he took her down to the sofa. He knew it was best to allow her to think in her own space while he heated water for tea. Then he joined her.

The silence wasn't heavy, but it felt fragile. Ivy was quiet in the way she got when she was walking in her memories. He let her take her journey, as they drank their tea. When his cup was empty, he took off his tie, dress shirt, coat, and shoes. He didn't stop her when she stood, expecting her to go upstairs. She didn't. Instead, she walked over to the mantle, picked up the police bear, and kissed it. Then, to his surprise, she placed it back down, grabbed the blanket they sometimes snuggled under to hide their clasped hands from Gavin during movies, and reached up to turn off the light.

"Ivy?" he asked in the dark.

"Lay down," she whispered. He did as he was told, propping a throw pillow between his head and the arm of the couch. Suddenly, Ivy was slotted between his legs, with her head on his chest and the blanket was draped over them. "Just hold me tonight."

Nick's arms came around her, and Ivy breathed in the soothing, comforting, security of his embrace. She wanted to spend the night with him, but she didn't think she could brave his bed, and hers was not a choice. The couch wasn't comfortable, but it was somewhere she was familiar with being intimate with him. It was somewhere she could let herself be in his arms and not worry about the guilt consuming her.

"Precious girl, of course, I will," Nick whispered into her hair and curled his arms around her waist. For that moment, it was as much as her heart would allow.

Dresses and Blessings

"**Y**ou're late!" Fiona called from the back of the dress shop. Ivy groaned and rolled her eyes as checked her phone. Alex had just gotten to her house to pick up Nick and Gavin. Her friend had invited the boys out for lunch and some 'guy time'. "What took you so long?" Her mother asked.

"Um, doctor's appointment," Ivy said. She forced a smile on her face and winced at the sting in her left butt cheek where the contraceptive shot had been administered not an hour before.

After waking up from the embarrassing almost drunk sex the week before, Ivy had nearly kicked herself for being so reckless. When Ivy's cell phone had dinged, Nick had picked it up to read it for her, and it was a reminder to pick up tampons for her impending period. That had led to her and Nick having an even more awkward discussion about how he didn't have condoms in the house, and she wasn't on the pill. So she'd been extra cautious and scheduled an appointment just in case she got up the nerve to finally have sex with him.

"Hey P," Ivy said as she found her mom and cousin in a back corner with one of the salespeople.

"Ives! How are you?" Her cousin asked and came around Fiona, who was standing in front of a rack with three dresses. The girls hugged, and Ivy found herself smiling at how her cousin positively glowed. "Hope you don't mind I stole your mom. Mine's being a complete bitch about this whole thing!"

"Not at all," Ivy laughed as she stepped back to see if she could see Paula's baby bump yet. Her cousin's stomach was still as flat as always. "Trust me, I let her help plan mine, and I'm telling you, she'll make sure it all runs smoothly." She looked around, trying to spot the other bridesmaids. "Where's everyone else?"

"Moira and Sedona came in earlier so they could get to work on time," Paula said. She smiled, her hand falling to her stomach. "Honestly, I'm glad your mom volunteered to help. The doctor said all this stress wasn't good for the baby."

"You should be sitting down and relaxing," Fiona called over her shoulder. "You had finals yesterday, and you've got to work a double shift tomorrow you said." The elder Moore woman was all business as she held up a pale blue dress. "I think this is the one for Ivy. What do you think? It's the same color as the others but see how the bodice is a bit different."

"Oh, that's lovely! Go try it on," Paula said and gave Ivy a playful push. Ivy accepted the dress when her mom handed it to her. Setting her purse down she ducked into the changing room. "So, your mom says you've got a new man! She said he's super-hot but a little weird."

"Yeah," Ivy said. She giggled at the accurate description her mom had given, as she stripped out of her clothes and shimmied into the dress. The color, paired with the tiny crystals along the bodice, reminded her of the world after an ice storm. "'And he's not weird, just, different than most men."

"He's good with Gavin then?" asked Paula. Ivy didn't have a chance to respond.

"Can't separate them to save your life, I swear to you," Fiona laughed, and Ivy grinned at the memory of the night before.

Gavin had passed out on the sofa, while she was folding laundry, and Nick had somehow managed to carry him upstairs, change him into pajamas, and tuck him in without waking him. Watching Gavin's sleeping face on his shoulder had brought a terrifying thought to Ivy's mind. She was falling in love with Nick, and she didn't know if she was or wasn't ready to take that plunge.

"All you hear from Gavin these days is 'Nick this, Nick that,'" Fiona said.

"Oh, Ivy, that's fantastic! I'm so happy for you," Paula gushed, as Ivy came back out. Her cousin's face lit up, and Ivy smiled at her. "Wow! That dress is perfect! Aunt Fiona, you were right again!" The bride-to-be set the book of dresses aside. "Hang on, is that a hickey?!" Paula yelped, and her amber eyes blew wide. Fiona spun around and made an odd noise. Ivy's cheeks turned to fire, and she slapped her hand over the mark on her collarbone. She hadn't even noticed it. Although, after the intensive make-out session in the laundry room before she left for her appointment, she should have checked.

"Ivy!" Her mother chastised her. "I thought you said you two weren't having sex yet!" Ivy didn't cower under the scowl that her mom gave her.

"We're not," she snapped, then tossed her head back and turned to look in the mirror. Both women made snorting noises of disbelief. "What, I wasn't on anything until today. Like you said Mom, only one baby shower at a time." Still, Ivy thought Nick was already proving he'd make a great dad. She froze, shocked by the thought in her mind, and she shook it off before they could notice.

"Oh, stop lying Ives, you're practically glowing. You're wearing makeup, and those were the 'ass jeans' you were wearing when you came in," Paula snorted. Ivy gasped and spun around. How dare Paula bring up those jeans in front of her mom! That was a secret, granted, not a very good one since everyone except her mom knew the story.

"What do you mean, ass jeans?" demanded Fiona. "They looked nice." She bent over a rack of shoes, and Ivy continued to admire her own reflection in the mirror. The dress made her boobs look amazing, and the mermaid design showed off her waist and hips in all the best ways.

"You know, after Ivy lost the baby weight, she was upset because her favorite jeans didn't fit her butt anymore. So Blake and I took Ivy out shopping to cheer her up." Ivy bit back a smile, as she let herself be tugged into the memory. "Blake didn't know who Aaron was," Paula continued. She was giggling uncontrollably, and Ivy giggled right along with her, wondering if her cousin would be able to make it through the story without peeing herself in laughter. "So, there she is, standing in front of the dressing room, asking Blake if the jeans were a nice fit while I tried on a swimsuit. Then Aaron walks up and says 'no, they aren't a nice fit', slaps her ass, and continues to say 'They're a fucking fantastic fit. It's a shame you're engaged because that is one gorgeous—', but Blake cut him off before he could finish and shoved him away."

"I thought they were going to fight it out in the middle of the store!" Ivy blurted out, her laughter uncontrollable as she remembered the way Blake had been so angry, and Aaron had been so amused. Her mom rolled her eyes and started towards her with a shoe box. "I had to break it up," Ivy said. "But that's when Aaron said 'all right, brother. I guess you're good enough to date my Ivy's cousin.'" She sighed happily at the memory.

"I always wondered why Aaron called Blake, brother," Fiona said. Then she handed Ivy the box. "Try these on while I see if the fitting lady is back from lunch." Her mom disappeared around a corner. That was one thing about Fiona Moore—when she went into wedding/baby shower/party planning mode, she was not easily distracted.

Ivy sat down and opened the box to find a pair of silver shoes. She wasn't surprised that they matched the dress exactly.

"So, can I ask you a personal question Ivy?" Paula asked in a half-whisper.

"Paula, we lost our virginities on the same night in conjoining rooms. When have we ever not asked personal questions?" Ivy snorted and leaned over to try the heels on.

"It's just, well, if you're seeing someone, why are you still wearing your rings?" Paula asked, and her words froze Ivy in place. It took her a long moment before Ivy could sit up and stare at her in shock. Paula continued on "How are you intimate with him while still wearing them? Doesn't that make it feel weird?"

"I dunno," Ivy said. She looked down at the objects in question and turned her hand so they caught the light. She touched the diamond on the engagement ring with her thumb. "I just, well, I just can't yet. I can't take them off until I'm sure."

"Sure of what?" Her cousin asked in a low voice.

"If it's real, Paula. If what I'm feeling is love or if it's just loneliness," Ivy admitted. It felt like a secret had been lifted from her heart, and it made it easier to breathe. She hadn't admitted that to anyone, not even herself. Despite her brave face and her insistence that she was fine, Ivy had been aching with that uncertainty.

"Look at me," Paula said. Ivy met her eyes, so identical to her own passed down from their gran. They bounced between hers, and her cousin smiled. "It's love, trust me. I've seen you in love, and that's what I'm seeing right now. You have to bring him to the wedding." She squeezed her hand gently. "I want to meet him! I want to meet this strange man who made you fall in love with him and got on Gavin's good side."

"Of course, I'm bringing him," Ivy said and squeezed her hands back.

Despite Paula being the second person trying to convince her that this was real, she was still anxious about it all. It felt like she remembered how love felt, but there was so much more at stake this time. What if she was wrong? What if Paula and Alex were wrong? What if Nick didn't feel as strongly as she did. He could walk away, and she would be left to pick up the pieces of not one but two shattered hearts. Still, she forced a smile, determined not to cry while helping her cousin plan a wedding.

"Now," Ivy said, changing the subject. "We're having your bachelorette party at Mom's. We figured since you can't drink, nobody should. Mom and I have some stuff planned though."

"Really?" Paula asked, tears filling her eyes. "You guys don't have to give up the partying part for me." Before Ivy could prevent her cousin from having a grateful emotional overload, they were interrupted

"Paula, come on back to get your dress pinned for alterations!" Her mom's voice carried up to them. Paula stood up, and her face broke into a grin. Ivy waved her off then returned to strapping on the shoes. She had a lot to think about, and she needed to take it seriously.

***

Across town, Aldwin gave Gavin another push, sending him swinging up a little. They'd been at the park for about five minutes, and Alex had to step away to sit down on the bench and take a work call.

"I'm gonna go play on the slide!" Gavin called, jumping off the swing as soon Aldwin pulled it to a stop. He watched as the boy took off at a sprint, and then he went to settle on the bench beside Alex.

"We need to talk," grunted Alex as he stuffed his phone into his pocket. Then he crossed his arms. He wasn't looking at Aldwin, but his gaze was locked on Gavin. Aldwin had been expecting this, eventually. He was a little surprised it hadn't come earlier. So he let the man continue uninterrupted. "About Ivy and Gavin, I mean."

"I love them," Aldwin said bluntly. He knew it was best to get it out there right away. Alex needed to know he had nothing to hide and held no reservations about the small family he'd found himself drawn into. "I know that's what everyone's worried about, but I do. I love them."

"Yeah, but how much?" asked Alex and cast a look over at him, his face serious. "You see, by being Gavin's godfather, I've got certain responsibilities." Aldwin nodded, showing he understood what the man was implying. He knew human customs enough to know that being a godfather meant if something happened to Ivy, then Gavin would become his adopted son. "The thing is, they don't apply to just him. They apply to Ivy too. I have to make sure that you aren't going to walk away."

"I would never," said Aldwin, and he meant it. Not only was the idea abhorrent, but it was impossible for him. He was soul-mated to Ivy, bound by the most ancient of all magic. Their souls were united. He could never walk away from her. Only death could break them apart. "I'm here for the long haul, and nothing is going to make me change my mind."

"You say that now, but what about when the newness wears off," asked Alex.

At first, Aldwin was confused. It wasn't new anymore. They'd been officially a couple for over a week. The man continued, and it began to make sense, even though his facial expressions didn't.

"What about when the thrill is gone, and the sex isn't so fresh and new and exciting like now?" asked Alex and he was downright sneering at Aldwin. Aldwin didn't flinch back from the protective anger that edged Alex's voice. "What about when being a dad becomes a drain? Hmm? What then?"

"We haven't had sex," admitted Aldwin. He arched an eyebrow, confused by the statement. He wondered how Alex had come to that conclusion. The man looked entirely unconvinced. "Look, I don't know what Ivy told you, but we haven't made it past kissing and heavy petting." Gavin shrieked, and Aldwin zeroed in on him, immediately abandoning his defensive statement. It only took him a moment to find the boy. He was playing tag with a couple of kids. Secure in the knowledge that Gavin was fine, he turned back to Alex. "And as for being a dad, well, I haven't earned that slot yet. I'm sure doing my best to be worthy of that title, though."

"Then why the hell did I drop her off at an appointment for birth control this morning, after she said 'there was a close call'?" demanded Alex. Well, that explained Alex's unusually cool demeanor. A close call could be interpreted many ways, and Aldwin couldn't help but chuckle. "You think my family is a joke?"

"No, stars above, Alex, the close call wasn't a pregnancy scare. It was a 'we almost had sex while drunk' scare," he said and reined in his chuckles. "The conversation the next morning was about how we were lucky we didn't because I didn't have protection, and she isn't on anything." Aldwin's heart fluttered in excitement, as Alex's words finally connected in his mind. Ivy had gone to get birth control, which meant she was seriously considering taking the big step in their intimacy. Alex stared at him, disbelief evident on his face "What?" Aldwin asked.

"You two haven't had sex? Seriously? You've been living together, and you've been physically involved through kissing and groping for almost a month now. Ivy already told me that much." He snorted and shook his head. "You mean to tell me you haven't had sex, not even once?" The man shook his head as if bewildered by the idea. Aldwin understood why he would be. "Why not?"

"She isn't ready, so I don't bring it up," Aldwin said and shrugged. He turned away to watch Gavin as he followed some kids up to the top of the spiral slide. He didn't see the need to look back at Alex to continue the conversation. Gavin's safety was more important, and he could watch him and speak at the same time. "I know you think I'm going to up and bolt, but I'm not. I love her, really I do. She's it for me, the one, and you can ask Lewin if you need confirmation. That's what I told him, and that's what I've been telling my whole family."

"And Gavin?" Alex asked, and Aldwin resisted the urge to point out that he knew they were a package deal. "You're really okay with raising a kid who isn't yours? That's her biggest worry, you know. She can handle her heart being broken, but she can't handle watching his break again."

Aldwin hadn't thought about it from that perspective, but it didn't matter. Gavin felt like he was his. He'd come with the intention of getting the boy's faith back, and that had made him feel a special bond with the boy. Being soulmates to Ivy meant that he was destined to be Gavin's father too. His mission may have taken a back burner to develop his relationship with them, but it still felt right. He had no anxiety or worry over Gavin not believing still, because he knew they were close. It all felt connected, and he knew it would all turn out beyond amazing.

"I know," Aldwin said, and he turned back to Alex. "I love him too, just as if he was my own. I'd never hurt either of them. I swear that to you." Aldwin gave his oath and held Alex's gaze.

He didn't doubt for a second that these questions weren't just coming from the man beside him. The look on Alex's face said this conversation, this line of questioning, had been planned out years before, either over drinks or in a patrol car. He knew what the man needed to hear, and Aldwin had no reservations about saying it and meaning it with everything in his core.

"I'm not trying to replace Aaron," Aldwin swore and placed his hand over his heart. "I don't want to because nobody can. What I can do is help preserve the legacy he left behind." He nodded to Gavin, who was hanging by his knees from a ladder bar, then he looked back in time to see Alex's expression soften. "One day, I want nothing more than for that little boy to be mine, for him to see his mum loved and happy, and to hear him call me Dah. What I won't do is try to erase his past or his name. He'll always carry Aaron's name. I'll never take that from him."

Alex didn't break their locked gazes, though. Aldwin didn't flinch, and he didn't cower. He held the man's stare for what felt like ages. He wasn't sure what was going through his mind, but after a moment, Alex nodded and extended a hand. Aldwin took it, expecting a shake, but instead, he got a firm squeeze.

"Then you have my approval," Alex said, and his face broke into a smile.

Aaron's Final Request

"Okay, so he's in the tub. Just make sure he brushes his teeth."

"Ivy,"

"And it's supposed to be chilly tonight, so make sure he wears his—'

"Ivy,"

"And don't give him juice after seven or he'll never go to sleep."

"I know."

"And if there's an emergency. His doctor's number is on the fridge."

Aldwin grabbed Ivy's cheeks and pressed a kiss to her lips to end the torrid of rhetorical information she was babbling. She gave a soft sigh and smiled.

"I've got this, sweetheart. We'll be fine," he said and stroked her cheeks with his thumb. He made sure not to smudge the carefully applied blush she'd dusted on. "You go have fun at the party."

"Are you sure? It's not like I'm rushing out to the store for a few hours. I'll probably stay the—"

Aldwin cut her off and kissed her again. He loved the way she practically melted into his arms. It was Paula's hen night, though the wedding wasn't for another two weeks. It was the only night everyone in the bridal party was free.

"Call me, if he needs me," she whispered softly.

"I will," he promised. Ivy pulled away, but he could see she was still nervous "I promise, now go. Sedona's waiting outside!"

"Thank you, for this. Just don't let Gavin stay up too late, or he'll be grumpy," she said and picked up her bag with a last glimpse upstairs. Aldwin pointed at the door and tapped his foot. "Okay," she giggled. "I'm going. See you in the morning."

The door closed behind her, and he flicked his finger to lock it before peeking out of the curtains. Once the lights of Sedona's car were gone, he hurried into the kitchen and summoned a box of pizza and ingredients for banana splits. Then he queued a movie about time travel on the TV.

"Gavin! Pizza's here!" He called up, an,d as he expected, the sound of tiny feet came barreling down the stairs. Gavin skidded into the room, wrapped in a towel, and clutching his pajamas.

"But Mummy said you were gonna make chicken and veggies," hissed Gavin. He wasn't complaining, Aldwin knew, just testing to see what was going on. "Are you sure we can have pizza?"

"Your mum left me in charge, and I say we can," Aldwin insisted. Gavin cheered and tried to dash past him, but Aldwin snatched him up by the waist, towel, and all. "Whoa slow down. Jimjams first, pizza and ice cream second." He carried him over to the sofa and flopped down before easing Gavin back to his feet to dry the boy off. "Are you excited to be the ring bearer at Paula's wedding?"

"Yeah," Gavin cheered. He beamed from under the towel while Aldwin dried his hair. "I was the ring bearer at Mummy and Daddy's wedding. I told Mummy I won't throw the pillow this time." Aldwin had had to laugh out loud at the serious expression on the boy's face. He was impressed that Gavin remembered it, given he was only three at the time.

"You remember that?" he asked.

"No, but I found a DVD in my closet at Gran's, and she let me watch it. It was their wedding. Mummy looked like an angel, and Daddy looked so happy." Gavin wriggled away from the towel to grab his top. "Nick, can I ask you a question?"

"You mean besides that one?" Aldwin asked.

He ruffled Gavin's hair, before folding up the towel and draping it over the edge of the couch. One thing that Aldwin loved about the boy was that he always had questions. Sometimes they were oh so simple, but other times, they bespoke the clever, unfiltered intuition of youth.

"Are you my Mummy's boyfriend?" Gavin asked, and Aldwin cringed internally. Ivy had absolutely forbidden him from discussing this with her son. She said she would tell him when the time was right. He had to think fast to avoid being drawn further into this pickle. "Sally from chess league says you are. She said only boyfriends put their arms around girls' backs like you did with Mummy at my match on Wednesday," Gavin said, and he was as serious as any five-year-old Aldwin had ever seen. Sleighbells save him, he wasn't sure how to answer.

"Well, I'm a boy, and I'm your mum's friend," Aldwin said. He hoped it would work. "Sometimes friends do that. Uncle Alex puts his arm around your mum all the time." Ivy owed him her deluxe banana split refrigerator cake for having to deal with this on his own. The boy headed towards the kitchen, still rambling.

"Yeah, but Uncle Alex only likes boys, like Lewin! Did you know that Lewin is Uncle Alex's boyfriend now?" Gavin opened the pizza box to grab a slice. "Aunty Penny told Mummy that Uncle Alex is head into heels for him."

"Head into heels?" Aldwin snorted at the flub but added before Gavin could look too put out over his statement, "It's head over heels." He filled their plates and led Gavin back to the couch, where the boy snuggled into his side and took a bite.

"How can they have babies though?" asked Gavin, and Aldwin almost choked on the bite he had just taken. "I found a book in the library on where babies come from, and it said you have to have an um ute...uterus."

"Well, uh, you see," Aldwin stuttered. The conversation was not how he pictured the night going at all. He didn't want to lie to the boy and changing subjects did not work when Gavin got that wide-eyed, eager expression. "They could adopt."

"Wha's that?" Gavin asked through a full bite and stared up at him with that look he got when he was really fascinated. Usually, it forewarned that the kitchen was about to be turned into a kindergarten laboratory.

"Well, some kids don't have Mummy's and Daddy's, so people will adopt them and raise them like their own child," Aldwin said. He patted himself on the back for that. He was really going to have to text Ivy later and warn her about this turn of events.

"Oh," Gavin said. His eyebrows narrowed as he chewed, and he propped his elbow on his knee. Those blue eyes were heavy with thought, and Aldwin was just about to suggest they start the movie when he spoke again. "I like that idea. Uncle Alex would be good at being a dad. He can cook and play football, and he knows all the best places to fish." Gavin nodded firmly, and Aldwin relaxed. At least the subject had changed away from him and Ivy. "And, he gives good snuggles when you're sick."

"He's had lots of practice with you," Aldwin said. He grabbed the remote and passed it to the boy. "Ready to start the movie?"

"Yeah!"

With Gavin distracted, Aldwin pulled out his mobile and texted Ivy.

You owe me a deluxe banana split refrigerator cake. I'll explain later.

***

At her mom's apartment, Ivy giggled when Paula lifted the slinky, black, lace teddy she had bought her from the white tissue. Since they couldn't go out and have a proper bachelorette party, she and Fiona had decided to turn it into a 'honeymoon preparation' party. "There's a matching thong," she said, and Paula turned red as she lifted the item in question from the box.

"Oh, it's gorgeous! But, it's a bit big in the boobs, yeah?" Paula asked, and she bit her lip as she held it against her chest.

"That's because you'll be needing it bigger in a few months," giggled Ivy. She elbowed her mom, who was snickering as she took the bow and taped it to a paper plate. They were the only women present who had kids. "Trust me. You'll fit, and you'll thank me."

She could remember how she felt when she started really showing. As much as she loved being pregnant and how Aaron spent every spare moment touching her, she'd felt fat and sometimes uncomfortable in her own skin when she tried to initiate sex. When she'd confessed it to her mom, Fiona had bought one almost exactly like the one being shown off. The look on Aaron's face when she'd come into their home office wearing it had made her feel sexier than anything ever had.

"Oh, I wish I'd thought of that," Sedona sighed, from her spot on the sofa. "Go on! Open mine. It's the gold bag!"

Ivy took the moment of distraction to sneak her phone out, despite the rules. The first person caught on their phone had to clean up. It had vibrated three hours ago, but everyone had been watching each other like hawks. It was a text from Nick, saying she owed him a cake. She could only imagine what Gavin had done. She tried to type a reply, but Moira yelped.

"Cellphone! Ivy loses."

"Oh, that's so not fair. I had to make sure Gavin was okay!" Ivy cried in dismay.

"And Nick has my home number," Fiona said and snagged her phone. "Rules are rules! You get to clean up! We're gonna go get started on the pedicures."

"Pedicures?" Paula asked and looked up eagerly from tucking away a very transparent piece of pink material that had come from Sedona's gift bag. "Everything's closed already. I thought we weren't going out."

"We turned Gavin's room into a mini spa," Moira said. She stood up, grinning like a mad woman. "We've got stuff for masks, foot baths for pedicures, and all the goodies for manicures." The bride-to-be made a happy noise, and Ivy chuckled, despite being busted. There wasn't too much to clean up at all, as they'd used disposable plates and utensils. The three other women started down the hall, giggling excitedly.

"Since I already lost, can I at least ask him why I owe him a cake?" Ivy asked her mother, as she began gathering up the remains of the food. "Gavin's probably been a menace to him. Twenty bucks says Nick gave him juice when I told him not to."

"So, you two are pretty serious?" Fiona asked as she waved Ivy's cellphone. Luckily, she kept her voice low. "You changed your lock screen to a picture of him and Gavin at the park.

She felt her cheeks flush. The picture had been so gorgeous she'd had to change it to her lock screen. The picture of Aaron and Gavin passed out on the couch was still her main wallpaper though. "And you left him overnight with Gavin. Alex didn't even get overnights until after, well…" Ivy knew there was no sense in hiding it. Her mom knew her too well.

"Yes, we're, um, well, we've been officially 'together'," she said and air quoted the word before stacking more cups together. "Since we went out on Halloween while you took Gav trick or treating. We haven't told Gavin yet, so don't bring it up." Ivy shrugged a shoulder as she turned to head into the kitchen. Fiona followed after her, carrying the wrappings from the gifts to shove in the recycle can.

"Is he any good in bed?" her mom asked, and Ivy nearly dropped the cups she was juggling. "Wait, you still haven't had sex?" Fiona squeaked.

"No," Ivy hissed, turning to close up the boxes of takeout. "I mean, I want to. God, do I want to. I just can't. I dunno why." She didn't bother hiding her disappointment from her mom. "I've tried to go up to his room three times this week, but I just can't do it."

"It took me five years," Fiona said with a sad sigh. Ivy paused to look at her, stunned by the tone in her voice that was so often found in her own. "After your dad, I mean. You probably wouldn't remember the guy, Larry. He didn't stick around long."

"Hang on, was he the one with the toupee?" Ivy asked. She could vaguely remember a man sitting across the sofa, while she played with dolls. Fiona nodded. "Why'd he leave?"

"You peed on him at the store, and he decided being a dad was not something he was ready for," her mom said. "I mean, I knew he was unsure about it, to begin with, but I needed the help." Fiona had wandered back into the sitting room, and then she returned carrying the gifts. She began condensing them into piles. "Nick's still good with Gavin though, isn't he? He isn't getting distant with him?"

"He adores him, Mom," Ivy gushed, her heart swelling with affection at the man. "He always volunteers to help with him with homework or chores. Sometimes it's like he knows Gavin better than me." Ivy found herself smiling, as she thought about how natural it felt. She hadn't had to ask Nick to watch Gavin tonight, he'd just assumed it when she mentioned the party. "Like for tonight, before I could ask him to babysit he just went, 'Oh, Gavin and I'll have a boys' night in! It'll be great!'"

"You're in love with him," Fiona murmured, and Ivy jerked around at the soft words. "Don't try to deny it. I know you. I'm your mom, and I can see it now just as plain as I could see it when you stormed out after Aaron when I slapped him. It's just as plain as when you told me you and Aaron were trying for a baby after barely dating for a year."

"Mom," Ivy said, and she drew in a breath. It had only been about two months, but she couldn't deny the truth anymore.

She couldn't deny the feelings that had only been growing stronger every second of every day. She knew them too well; she had lived them for years. She hadn't thought it possible, but when she thought back, she realized she'd started feeling those things the moment they met. She just didn't understand how something so powerful could happen twice in one lifetime, so she had been fighting it back. There was no fighting it anymore.

"I do. I really do love him," she whispered.

"Then why are you still wearing your rings?" Fiona asked. Her voice wasn't accusatory in the least. It was the most understanding, gentle, and maternal tone her mom had used on her since the funeral.

"Because," Ivy said and opened the fridge to avoid the sympathetic look on her mom's face. She didn't know. She'd thought about it, even slipped just the wedding band off in the shower the other day, but it had left her feeling guilty, naked, and afraid. "I don't know."

"I do," her mother said. She looked over her shoulder at her mom, who was fiddling with the tiny diamond solitaire that never left Fiona's right hand. "Because, it feels like if you do, you're erasing your love for Aaron." It was a simple sentence, but the truth of it resonated deep in Ivy's soul. "You're not though. They're just symbols. You've got something better to remind you of how much you loved each other. You have his eyes, his hair, and even those ears of his running around your house. Aaron would want you to take them off." Fiona turned, leaving the words hanging in the air as she left to go back to the living room.

Ivy blinked back the tears and followed after her. To her surprise, Fiona wasn't cleaning. She was pulling a small, worn-out shoe box from behind some photos on the top shelf of her DVD case. That made two people convinced she should take them off. The question was, how could they be so sure? Yes, if the situation were reversed, she'd want Aaron to move on.

"How can you be sure? I mean, no offense Mom, but you never did move on past Daddy, not really."

"*I* never fell in love with anyone, not for lack of trying," Fiona said and blew some dust off the box. Ivy swore she saw tears in her eyes. "But I know he would, because Aaron came over one night with Gavin, just after you got married. He, well." She handed Ivy the box. "He made you this and asked me to keep it, just in case."

"What the hell?" Ivy yelped. She ripped the lid off and nearly dropped the box when she saw the small digital video recorder inside. "Mom! Why didn't you show me this before?"

"He gave me strict orders not to," Fiona said with a laugh. Ivy swallowed hard as she stared down at the unassuming camera in the box. "He said if I gave it to you before you needed it, he'd come back from the grave and make my life hell." Fiona sniffed, and Ivy managed to chuckle past the lump forming in her throat. "I loved him like a son, but I did not need him blowing up any more toasters."

"It was one toaster, and it wasn't his fault," Ivy huffed. She pulled the camera out, as well as the power adapter. Across the buttons, other than power and play, was a strip of tape with words written in permanent marker. "Fiona's assurance at not being haunted. God, he was insane sometimes." She laughed.

"You married him, not me," her mom said and kissed her hair as she gave her a brief hug. "You can watch it now if you want. I'm sure Paula would understand."

"Um, I dunno," Ivy said. She couldn't breathe right.

Aaron was right there in her hands. It was something new, something she'd never seen. It wasn't like their wedding video, the voicemail Gavin had accidentally deleted the year before, or even the videos saved on her computer. Those were memories. This was not, and judging by her mom's face, it was as close to a message from beyond the grave as Ivy would ever get. "I'll be in in a minute."

"Take your time," Fiona said. She hugged her once, before leaving Ivy to kneel down and plug in the cord.

Steeling herself, Ivy settled onto the sofa, opened the view screen of the camcorder, and pressed play on the only item saved. The screen was blank at first, but then her breath was stolen.

"This is a message for the woman who stole my heart," said Aaron. His blue eyes were intense as they stared out of the screen. He had the heavy, serious look he'd always gotten when he'd had a hard shift or was deep in thoughts. Then, his lips twisted up in a soft smile, and Ivy found her own lifting in response. Aaron chuckled. "Made you giggle, didn't I?"

"Yeah," she started to say, but he cut her off.

"Ivy, sweetheart, listen. This is important." That serious look was back, and she swallowed hard. "I'm going to cut to the chase. First, if you're seeing this, I'm dead." The nonchalance in his words felt like a punch to the gut and a warm embrace all at once. "I hope it was a good and honorable death. Also, if I'm not dead and you're watching this, tell Fiona I'm coming for her microwave." She heard her mother shout something unintelligible from somewhere off-screen, and a sippy cup flew past his head. "Rude, Fiona, rude. Anyways, if I am dead, I want you to know how much I miss you and my Gavin. I miss you both so very much."

"I miss you too," Ivy sniffled. She touched the screen, trying to blink back the tears as she heard Gavin whine somewhere in the background. Aaron leaned out of view and then righted himself, holding the sippy cup. He handed it off-screen.

"Secondly, if Fiona *has* given you this, it means you've met someone," Aaron said. He shifted, just subtlety, and if Ivy didn't know his every move, gesture, and expression better than her own, she'd have missed it. "And I bet you're feeling guilty, and you're probably still wearing your rings. Aren't you, Ives?" he asked. The exasperation in his voice was feigned, and she knew it. She could hear, just there, even through the distorted speakers, the love and adoration behind it.

"Yeah, I am," she tried to say, but he cut her off again.

"Let me finish, love," Aaron said with a point at the camera, and Ivy covered her mouth. The tears fell, and she knew she couldn't stop them. "I love you and Gavin more than anything in the world, and I would never want to keep either of you from your happiness." His finger lowered, but his gaze never wavered. Ivy blinked past the tears and sniffled hard. "I need you to do me a favor to help me give you that happiness. Can you do me one final favor?"

"Anything, baby. You know that. I'd do anything for you," Ivy sobbed. She wiped her cheek, as he leaned forward and propped his forearms on his knees. His broad hands dangled in the gap between them.

"Move on, Ivy. Take my rings off and move on," Aaron said. Ivy watched as he fiddled with his own band. "I don't know how old you are now, but I plan on remaking this in a few years, just in case. So, if you're seeing this, you're still young enough to not hide away, do you understand?"

"I know, I know," Ivy whispered. She touched the screen again, dying to reach in and feel that leather coat draped over his shoulders.

"Let him love you, Ivy. Let him love Gavin. He must already because I'm making Fiona promise not to show you this unless she is sure he does. Most importantly, my darling wife." He looked down at his hands and clasped them together as he drew in a breath. "Let yourself love him too."

Ivy bit her lip, preparing to replay the video, assuming it was the end, given the sudden silence, but he spoke again, his voice softer. It held that tender tone he used every time they snuggled in bed. His eyes lifted to the screen again, and Ivy found herself drowning in the love that shone through the tears in them.

"I love you, Ivy Moore Somerfield, and if you love me, then let me go." He leaned forward, and the screen turned to static.

Ivy lost it.

She closed the screen and shoved the camera back into the box as she fell back to the cushions. She bit her lips closed so she could keep her tears to herself and hugged one of the throw pillows tightly. He'd known, somehow, some way, Aaron knew how she'd be feeling. They'd taken all the cold, unfeeling, necessary precautions like wills and medical authority after she'd gotten pregnant, but never, in a million years, had she guessed Aaron would have thought this far ahead.

Let me go.

The whisper echoed in her mind, like ghostly fingers soothing the broken ache she'd carried all alone since he'd left. Even in death, he loved her enough to know what she needed to hear. He'd given his permission, and the guilt that always plagued the edges of her soul was washed away.

"I will, Aaron. I will," she whispered, hurrying down the hall. She opened the door, drawing four pairs of eyes to her. "I um, I need to go take care of something. Paula, I'm sorry. It can't wait."

"Go on," Paula said, understanding evident on her face. "Love ya!"

"Love ya!" Ivy sobbed, closed the door, and hurried to grab her phone and overnight bag. Then she ordered a ride, as she rushed down the stairs.

Midnight Fireworks

I vy tried her best to compose herself, so she wouldn't worry the driver. She tried calling, to let Nick know she was on her way, but he didn't answer. It was almost midnight, and that was usually when he was in the shower. When she got home, the door was locked. She didn't want to wake Gavin up by knocking, so she dug her keys out and slipped inside.

The house was dark, and through her tear-stuffed nose, Ivy could smell pizza. Sure enough, there was an empty box on the counter and bowls and spoons in the drainer. The TV was still on, playing a DVD title screen on repeat. It made her pause in her trip to the stairs, and when she looked in the living room the sight she found finished making up her mind.

Nick was sprawled out on the sofa, one arm dangling off, and the other wrapped around Gavin. Her son was curled up on his chest, clutching a stuffed dinosaur in one hand, and the other was wrapped around Nick's neck. Finally, after weeks of battling the guilt, of fighting against her feelings, Ivy acknowledged the reality. Nick was it. He was the one. Somehow, for a reason she couldn't explain, the universe had given her two soulmates. She dropped her bag beside the pizza box and tiptoed into the living room.

"Nick," she whispered, touching his face. "Nick, love, wake up."

Aldwin blinked, confused by the feather-light strokes to his cheek. His vision cleared when Ivy's tear-streaked red cheeks and smiling face came into view.

"Ivy," he whispered back, remembering that the weight pinning him down was a sleeping Gavin. "You okay? Why're you home? Why're you crying?"

"We need to talk, and it couldn't wait," Ivy said. For a moment, Aldwin was afraid it was bad news, but Ivy caressed his face again and leaned down to kiss his nose. "Gimme Gavin, and I'll meet you in your room."

"I've already got him," Aldwin said and waved a hand to shoo her back. "I'll carry him up." Carefully, he raised himself up, shifting Gavin so his head rested on his shoulder.

"No, really. I'll take him," Ivy said. He didn't understand the myriad of emotions in her voice and on her face. He didn't know if he should be worried or not. "You just go wait for me in your room. I won't be but a minute."

Aldwin surrendered Gavin to her arms, and he turned off the TV as she left the room. He didn't have to ask what could possibly have gotten her so worked up that she came home to talk. There was only one subject, one name, that had the ability to move her so emotionally, Aaron.

Sighing in understanding, as he passed Gavin's room, he went up to his own. At least, now, it seemed she wanted to seek comfort somewhere besides the couch. That was a big deal, and he appreciated the effort it took her.

Aldwin stripped off his shirt and trousers, quickly donning a pair of pajama pants, and set about straightening up his tiny sitting area. Then, with a hopeful afterthought, he turned back his blankets. Just as he did that, he heard Ivy's shower turn on. He suspected, woefully, she'd changed her mind. However, the water didn't run long at all.

Ivy toweled off her hair and body and drew in a soothing breath as she made sure her ruined makeup was all gone. Confident in her red-faced reflection, she opened the medicine cabinet and pulled out the box she'd picked up after her doctor's appointment. Dr. Wagner had told her if she did anything within the first month to use it as a precaution. Ivy had bought it, just in case. Now, she popped the tiny pill out of the packet, placed it onto her tongue, and chased it with two handfuls of water from the tap.

Swallowing, Ivy tried to steady her rapid breaths. She went to her dresser and found the comfortable but sultry satin nightgown her mom had gotten her when she mentioned she was thinking of dating again. Ivy pulled the tag off and shimmied it on, shivering a bit in the chill of the air. Then, she opened her jewelry box.

"I'll always love you, Aaron," she whispered. Ivy grasped her rings in her shaking fingers and slid them off. With a gasp, she tucked them into an empty slot, shut the doors, and rushed from her room. She stared at the door hiding the stairs, and she opened it quietly.

Nick was standing shirtless beside his dresser, back to her, fussing with his hair, and Ivy drew in a breath. She didn't know what to say or how to begin. She was all in, so maybe knowing he felt the same was best.

"I love you, Nicholas Claus," she said.

Aldwin jerked around, convinced he'd hallucinated the three words. Yet, Ivy was standing there, eyes wide in hope, determination, and love. Her body was barely covered by a pink night dress that hardly reached her thighs, and, holy stars, her left hand was absolutely bare.

"I love you too, Ivy Moore-Somerfield," he said.

He knew it was important he add Aaron's last name, even though she'd never had the opportunity to change it, but he wasn't sure why. Ivy's face glowed, brighter than moonlight on fresh snow, and before Aldwin could take two steps, she threw herself in his arms.

"Oh, Ivy, I've been dying to tell you." Aldwin held her tightly, letting Ivy touch his face, her eyes flicking between his own.

"You have to mean it, Nick. Because, it's not just me—" he cut her off with a soft kiss.

"I couldn't love Gavin more if he were my own," he murmured. Ivy practically melted in his arms, and Aldwin pulled her even closer. "Honestly, the moment we met, I was done for. I couldn't leave you if I wanted to. I can't imagine my future without you or Gavin in it."

"I can't fight it anymore. I want this, want us, please, Nick," Ivy said.

Aldwin sighed as she pressed up on her toes and caught his lips in a frantic kiss. He didn't resist, curling an arm completely around her waist and cupped the side of her neck with his free hand. There was something different in her movements, something he didn't quite understand, which was saying something because he thought he'd had her every gesture memorized.

Aldwin didn't want to assume, didn't want to rush things if she wasn't ready, even when her fingers plunged into his hair, pulling him down more, and her thinly clad breasts arched up into his chest. Her tongue teased his, and he chased it back for a twirling dance. Then, making his heart stutter, Ivy reached one hand between them and tugged on his waistband. "I *need* you, now, tonight, please." He groaned at her words and lifted her up by the waist.

Ivy did need him. Her body had been starving for his touch, but she'd fought it so many times. She couldn't anymore. It was time, past time, and suddenly, she was in the air. Her legs instinctively wrapped around his lean hips. His lips broke free of hers, and before she could whine, they were exploring her neck, cascading rushes of heated delight down her spine. His fingers were firm on her thighs and bare butt as he walked her to the bed. When Nick lowered her to the sheets, Ivy pulled him down too. His weight on her body was marvelous, when he groaned into her shoulder, lips moving wetly along the skin there.

"Are you sure?" Nick asked, and his whisper tickled her ear. She tightened her legs around him to bring him even closer, kissing his neck gently.

"I haven't been more sure of anything since a beach in Florida," she purred. The memory didn't bring any guilt, and Ivy sighed in contentment as she pressed an open-mouthed kiss to his bare chest. "I, love, you." She enunciated each word by rocking herself up into him. On the third rut, she felt him surge to attention against her bare center through his thin pajama pants.

"Oh, Ivy," Nick moaned.

His eyes seemed to shine down at her, so wonderfully adoring, and then his lips trailed down her chest. Electricity exploded in her core when he laved his tongue over the thin material covering her right nipple, and Ivy keened her approval when he nudged the material aside with his nose and took her breast into his mouth.

Her touch-neglected body responded immediately trembling, twitching, and sending heated dampness pooling between her thighs. Ivy clung to his back and dragged her fingers along his shoulders. It had been so long, and she needed more.

"More!" she gasped, crying softly in pleasure when Nick gave a delicate pull at her nipple with his teeth before he graced her with another seductive suck. "Yes!" She cried out, tossing her head back and pressing her body up into his eager touch.

Aldwin was in bliss with his Ivy, his love, his soulmate moving under him. Her skin was so soft, so perfect in its sweet taste. He released her and glanced down to find her face awash in pleasure, eyes closed, breaths quick and desperate. He shifted to the other side, preening when she keened her delighted approval and rocked up against him. To his own pleasure, and surprise, she felt bare against his own thin pants. It made his mouth water in anticipation.

Aldwin needed to taste and feel all of her, to explore Ivy's body in all the ways she deserved. He was reluctant to move away from the perfect, pebbled, bud he was rolling with his tongue, but he released her with a wet pop and slid his hands down to her thighs.

"You're so perfect," he whispered to her, inching his fingers into all the places he'd longed to explore. The skin beneath the very edge of the pink satin was softer than he'd ever dreamed, and Ivy's lips ghosted along his ear as he savored it. He wanted to taste her more than anything he'd ever experienced.

"Take it off," Ivy panted.

She needed to feel his skin on hers. The urge had suddenly become more important than breathing. When Nick lifted away, settling back onto his heels, she pushed herself up and trembled in anticipation. His nimble fingers seized the material and slid it up her skin. He moved slowly, his eyes never leaving her face, and she could see the love she felt radiating back to her from his gaze. She fell back to the pillows, feeling her chest and neck flush at the punch-drunk look that washed over his face when he finally stared at her nude body.

"Touch me," she pleaded breathlessly, and his hands were everywhere at once.

Ivy burned in the most delightful way, as Nick's touches, squeezes, and wet tongue mapped out her bare body. She couldn't get enough of him, either, and she eagerly began to memorize the lean, toned, planes of his chest and back. That heated, hungry sensation deep in her core only flamed higher, when his fingers curved over her hips, and his kisses set off sparks along her chest. He moved lower, burning stars in his wake, and, then, he cupped her curl-covered center, and Ivy groaned. It had been months since she'd touched herself, and years since anyone else had. The sensation was far better than she remembered, sending a jolt of delight into her core.

"You're soaked," Aldwin said, hoping Ivy could hear the pleasure in his voice.

He had expected to find some arousal, but his precious girl was positively dripping. The trimmed curls under his hands were already soaked, and the quiet sounds she made, paired with the press of her hips up into his hands, were addictive. He slipped one finger between her folds dragging the slick nectar that dripped from her with him as he sought his prize. He found it, that hooded bud, swollen and yearning, and he stroked it softly. Ivy's eyes burned into his, and she bit her lip as she keened out her wordless approval.

"I want to taste you," he whispered into her ear. He didn't have to wait for a reply, because Ivy's fingers fisted in his hair and pushed it down with a desperate-sounding whimper. "Brilliant," he crooned, his erection flexing at the thought of how she would taste on his tongue.

He slid down her body, settling onto his stomach. Aldwin pulled her right leg over his shoulder and reveled in the vision before him. Desperate for her pleasure, he slipped his tongue out, parting her dark blonde curls, and caught the sweet, but tangy, nectar dripping from her center. It was better than ambrosia, than Sunberry Wine- better than anything he'd ever dreamed. He drank her in, moaning his thirst and his love into her heated skin. Then he trailed his soaked tongue higher, searching, craving, and intent until he found her clit. Smiling to himself, he pressed his tongue against it. At her soft cry of pleasure, he wrapped his lips around it and gave a gentle suck.

Ivy slapped a hand over her mouth to muffle herself. She kept the other in Nick's hair. He was amazing. He used his lips and tongue to make love to her like he knew exactly what she enjoyed. It was better than she'd imagined, and she writhed under him, unable to keep still from the ecstasy he was laving onto her. Each suck and lick sent wave after wave of bliss through her. His own moans, sighs, and growls of hunger only intensified everything. Then, to her joy, she felt one finger circle her yearning center.

"Yes, please," she begged, and it slid into her. She cried out again, the hand on her mouth falling to grip the blanket beneath her. It felt amazing.

"Hush," Nick said. His voice was raspy, even in that one sound, and Ivy covered her mouth again as he curled his finger up. At the same time, he closed his lips around her clit and gave a gentle suck. His tongue flicked in a pressing circle, and the sensation made her whole body shudder. She couldn't think, could only feel, as he began to thrust his fingers in earnest.

After so long alone, Ivy knew she would be close soon. So she arched her hips up to him, and gave herself to his touches, letting herself be carried away in the pleasure he seemed so intent on giving her.

As if sensing her surrender to his talents, Nick's ministrations became more determined. A second finger joined in. It curled inside of her slightly, thrusting, stroking, as his determined sucking and circular licks became a steady rhythm. He was just as vocal as she was, groaning and humming in response to her. His fingers dug into her hips, and it only served to build the tension in her core and thighs with an intensity she'd forgotten was possible. She couldn't open her eyes, and breathing became hard. The deliciously wet sounds accompanied by Nick's own desperate breaths tightened the coil. Her pulse roared in her ears, and her heart began to sprint.

"Don't' stop, please, Nick. Don't stop," she begged, as she catapulted to the precipice. His hand on her hip shot up to grip hers, their fingers lacing on her stomach. His fingers thrust in, curling up, finding the spot that seemed to connect to her very soul. At the same moment, his tongue gave a circular press, and he gave one long, purposeful suck, and Ivy gritted her teeth to subdue the cry as she launched into the stars.

Oceans roared in her ears, and supernovas lit up behind her eyes. Ivy tossed her head, forcing herself to remain as quiet as possible, but the restraint only made it more intense, and she sobbed in relief when his lips crashed into hers, catching her shout of release.

Nick's lips and chin were slick with her own juices, but Ivy didn't care. She whimpered into his lips, scrambling for any sort of grip on his bare back as the aftershocks sent wave after wave of perfect delight through her body. She felt one of Nick's arms slide under her, as their frantic kiss broke into the open mouth, almost desperate pants. She couldn't open her eyes.

Aldwin kicked his pants aside as he cradled Ivy with one arm under her back. She trembled under him, her skin flushed from her cheeks down to her breasts, and he muffled her whimpering cries with his tongue once more. She had been glorious, almost making him finish at the very sound and sight of her, and he wanted nothing more than to sink into her velvet heat and make her explode like that again and again. Yet, he restrained himself. He wanted to lull her gently back to herself, so he kissed her tenderly and stroked her cheeks with his thumb. Ivy's eyes finally fluttered open.

"There's my love," he whispered, as he nudged her trembling legs further apart with his knee. "You are so perfect, so beautiful."

"So are you," Ivy said in a breathless whisper. "'Nick, please, I need you." That was what he'd needed to hear, as her legs wrapped around his waist. Aldwin grunted when his hard, arousal slipped through her wet folds. He could feel the hooded bud at the apex of her folds still pulsing against the underside of his erection. "God, you feel amazing," Ivy moaned in his ear, and he slid himself back, trying to coat himself in her slick, wet, nectar. "Please make love to me. I want it. I want you."

"You have me, forever," Aldwin promised her. She'd know soon enough that that was their ultimate truth. They were bound for eternity. For now, at the moment they were in, he would show her as best he could. Reaching between them, he took himself in hand and slid down between her soaked folds, until he reached his goal.

"Please look at me, love" Aldwin said, and those amber eyes were full of stars when they fluttered open. Drowning in them, he slid into her, slowly, savoring each breath-stealing second until he was sheathed completely inside of her. "You okay?" He asked when she dug her nails into his spine and keened through pursed lips.

"Oh yes," she murmured, and at her assurance, Aldwin pulled back and slid in again.

This time, she rocked up to meet him, and Aldwin fed his addiction to her lips as he set his pace. Her body seemed to welcome him, encasing him in a perfect caress of a hot, soaked, fluttering embrace.

Ivy was stretched and full in the most amazing way. Years of nothing but senseless, quick, self-pleasure in the shower for stress relief had made her body forget how marvelous it felt to be filled. She had forgotten what it was like to experience the magic of the man she loved rocking into her, kissing her, squeezing her thigh, and groaning above her in love. She yielded to him, but she also gave back everything he was giving her. It was paradise, a euphoria she'd never imagined she'd experience again.

She rocked up to meet each of his thrusts, catching his moans and whimpers of pleasure with her own lips. Ivy tightened her thighs, sliding her hands down his shoulders and up to cup his cheek to pull him away for a moment and stare into his eyes. He gave a particularly deep thrust and groaned, and she answered him with a gasp of her own and a nip of his lower lip with her teeth.

"I love you," she said, earning herself a falter in his thrusts and a smile so bright she thought she would go blind.

"I love you too," Nick replied. Then he kissed her again, and she lost herself to his touches.

Aldwin couldn't think about anything except the woman fluttering around him and clinging to his back. Ivy panted into his lips, his neck, his shoulder, anywhere she could get her lips as she rocked her hips up with each of his thrusts. Nothing, ever, in his life held the power, the magic that this was bringing to him. It burned in his veins, yearning for release, but it also begged for her pleasure all at once.

"One more, for me, darling," he groaned. He slid his hand down her thigh, dipping between them, wetting his fingers in the slickness she'd left on his skin. "Come for me one more time." He pushed himself up enough to maneuver his hand, and he found what he was after.

"I don't think I can," Ivy panted. Then when Aldwin rolled her clit with his thumb, he caught her shout of pleasure with a kiss. "Yes, just like that!" Ivy cried into his parted lips, and Aldwin obliged. He didn't alter his intensity since she'd said to stay just like that and continue to stroke the pulsing bud in time to his thrusts. He was starving to feel her explode around him.

Three strokes of his thumb and three deep, determined thrusts, were all it took for her euphoric heat to begin to tighten around him. Aldwin didn't stop, he pulled at her neck gently with his teeth, but he immediately moved back to let their tongues explore and dance together when she cried out a little too loudly. Ivy arched under him, thighs tightening around his hips as she clenched down, and her nails bit into his shoulders. It was just as stunning as the first, and Aldwin felt his own release building in response to her.

"Come for me, darling," Ivy pleaded. "I'm yours, only yours," she keened into his neck and curled her tongue along the pulse point there. "Come inside of me. I want you, love you, need you." She tightened her legs around him again, and he could feel the aftershocks of her second orgasm making her shake and flutter under and around him.

"I love you too," Aldwin groaned. He was nearly there, after two hundred years of nothing, he was so close, dancing dangerously on the edge. Everything low in his body tightened, and he fed himself shamelessly on her lips as he scooped an arm under Ivy, holding her in place. Then he buried himself inside of his lover, over and over. "My Ivy, my love, forever."

"Forever," she murmured.

He didn't care that she didn't know the full truth of those words, but they did it. The spring low inside of him snapped, and Aldwin cried out his release into Ivy's neck as his completion surged inside of her, filling her. Ivy stroked his back, pressed tender kisses to his shoulders, crooning incoherent soothing words to him, as he shivered over her. He grunted at the aftershocks that shot through him until he felt himself grow soft.

Ivy whimpered when Nick slid from her and fell to the side. It felt foreign for him not to be over her and inside of her, like a part of her was missing. She almost protested, almost lifted her head to complain, but he stopped it all with a simple whisper

"Come here, precious girl," Nick said and pulled her up and over to sprawl across his chest with her legs tangling in his. "That was beautiful and wonderful," he murmured into her hair.

Ivy couldn't speak. Everything inside of her was too much, in the best way. The lingering aftershocks of her nearly back-to-back orgasms and the wonderful feeling of Nick's own completion slowly dripping from her were a perfection she'd only felt once in her life before. She gasped for air and tried to make the world stop spinning while she listened to Nick's powerful heart under her ear.

She'd done it. They'd made love, and it had been perfect, better than anything she'd been afraid to hope for, and the perfection of it burst out, trailing rivulets of joy down her cheeks.

Aldwin rarely felt winded or spent, but he was. Sleep, something he only needed every other day, had seemed impossible to get again once Ivy woke him up. It was lured close to him by Ivy's warm, shuddering body, curled up in his embrace. He was about to surrender to it, to doze off as they both cuddled through the content glow of their lovemaking when something hot and wet hit his chest. Then another hot, wet, drop splashed against him, and he realized that Ivy's trembling had shifted from post-coitus bliss to tears. His heart sank.

"Ivy, love, it's okay. Please don't cry," Aldwin said. He cupped her chin and lifted her face, dreading the look of shame and guilt he knew he'd find. Instead, she was smiling. Ivy wiped her eyes as she gave a shaky giggle and sniffled hard.

"I'm not sad, Nick. I'm really, really happy," Ivy reached up, as Nick's face glowed in understanding. "Because this was perfect, and I want this, want us together, every day." She licked the tears from her lips and laughed softly at the wonderful gift she'd been given. "I want to sleep up here tonight. Is that all right?"

"That's more than all right, you silly woman," Nick snorted.

Ivy giggled when he scooted her off of him and scrambled off the bed to grab one of his shirts from a chair and his pajama pants. She collapsed back into the pillows, as he ducked into his en-suite. She rubbed her sticky thighs together, contemplating asking him for a wet cloth when he reappeared holding one. God, she loved him.

"But if you sleep here, you've gotta wear this," Nick said. He handed her his shirt, and Ivy pushed herself up to pull it on. She'd just gotten it over her head when the warm, wet, soft cloth touched her skin in a tender stroke. He used it to caress her thighs, wiping gently up to her curls, where he parted the sticky, wet folds. Ivy gasped in relief and let her head loll back. "Blimey, that look on your face is gorgeous," Nick practically crooned.

"Oh stop it," Ivy said, but she willingly laid back and let him finish wiping her clean before he disappeared back into the en-suite. When he returned, he turned off the lights and crawled next to her. "Hold me," she sighed and snuggled into his pillows as his arms went around her to pull her back tightly to him. One of his legs wriggled between her thighs, and his lips pressed into her shoulder.

"I'll hold you forever," Aldwin promised. He smiled into her hair, as Ivy gave a hiccupping yawn. Then her fingers laced with his against her chest, and in a few minutes of silence, her entire body went lax. Smiling at the perfection of his life, he followed suit, determined to resume his mission with Gavin in the morning.

The Hope of Morning

Ivy was only confused for half a moment when she awoke. It was just after six according to Nick's alarm, and she sighed happily at the dead weight wrapped around her and the soft snores behind her. She wanted to stay there—so warm, safe, and loved—but her bladder was being rather intrusive. So she gently slipped from his arms to take care of that, and, for good measure, snag his toothbrush to banish her morning breath. Then she tiptoed back to the bed and hummed happily as she curled up with her face to his chest.

"Good morning," mumbled Nick. His slurred voice was thick with amusement, and to her surprise, his breath broke across her face with that same scent of pine his skin carried, only it seemed to be enhanced by peppermint. He had to have woken up before her and had the same fear of morning breath. His toothbrush hadn't been damp, had it?

"Good morning indeed," Ivy giggled and shoved the thought aside. She wanted to waste no time. She went for his lips, slotting her leg between his thighs, and plunged her fingers in his hair. "Sleep well?" she asked, between their clumsy, drowsy kisses. "I sure as hell did."

"Are you always so foul-mouthed this early?" mused Aldwin. He didn't care in the least that she was. He rolled her over, keeping the blankets over them to block the chilly air as he knocked her knees apart playfully and settled between them. "Not that I mind, but I'm curious."

"Maybe," replied Ivy. She hooked her ankles over his calves, and he could feel her bare center already growing damp against the leg of his pajama pants. "I'm definitely dirty-minded right now, that's for sure." She pushed at his shoulders in what he assumed was an attempt to roll him onto his back.

"Oh yeah?" Aldwin asked as he fell onto his side, and, under the blanket, he grabbed her knee to hitch it back up over his hip.

He was starving for her again, and obviously, she was too. He rocked against her center, letting her feel how eager he was to make her come undone. He tried to reach down and free himself but got distracted by the pebbled nipples his own shirt was covering. So he paused to roll one with his thumb through the fabric. He chuckled and kissed her playfully when she batted his hand away.

"Shut up," Ivy said and rolled her eyes, but she took his kiss. She moaned when he rocked against her, and she knew it wouldn't be long until she was wet and desperate for him again. "God, I love you, Nicholas Claus."

"I love you too," Nick sighed, and his fingers stroked her arm under the blanket. His nose grazed along with hers, and his thumb rubbed tenderly against her thigh. "I'm so glad you came home last night."

"Me too," Ivy said. The urgency to feel him subsided as his lips slowed and turned to gentle, tantalizing caresses. Maybe it was a good thing because Ivy had started to feel the aching reminder that she'd gone over two and a half years abstinent, and their first time had been double-orgasmic in its intensity. "I'm so lucky I met you," she whispered into his parted lips. He pushed the blanket down to her hips and kept her naked half covered to ward off the chilly morning. "Say it again," Ivy said before their tongues met for a tentative twirl.

"I love you, Ivy Moore-Somerfield," Nick murmured, and one thumb trailed her jaw.

"I love you, Nicholas Claus," Ivy breathed.

The way he once again acknowledged Aaron's name with hers, even though she never legally changed it, reaffirmed her decision. She hummed as his fingers tangled in her hair, and the kiss that followed was so tender she felt like he was kissing her soul. The world seemed to fade, and nothing but the sound of their kiss and breaths filled the room. The need to make love to him again calmed into a deep desire to just lay in his arms and savor this new beginning.

"Does this mean Nick is my daddy now?" Gavin's sleepy voice made Ivy yelp. She broke away from the kiss and yanked the blanket up to her chin.

Gavin stood in the archway between the bedroom and the sitting room, rubbing his eyes and yawning. Ivy couldn't speak, as embarrassment and fear flickered through her.

She was sure they were about to experience a full-on Gavin tantrum, and she wasn't prepared. Nick started talking before she could even formulate a sentence.

"Uh, well," Aldwin stuttered. He fumbled for an explanation, glad he'd had the forethought not to toss the blanket off completely. Ivy was frozen beside him, as red as Gavin's pajamas, staring at her son in dread and horror. "Gavin, erm, Ivy?" He nudged her in the arm, and she shook her head as if coming back to herself.

"Honey, we haven't decided that yet," squeaked Ivy and gave him what he thought was an apologetic look, but Aldwin just squeezed her hand on the sheets. "But, well, baby bear, well, Nick and I are in love, and—" Her explanation was cut short with a shout from Gavin.

"You are?" Gavin asked, his eyes blown wide. Aldwin had never seen a kid go from half asleep to awake so fast.

"Yes, we—" Ivy tried to say, but she was cut off by Gavin again. Aldwin was too stunned to laugh.

"It worked! It worked!" Gavin cheered, jumping around in a circle and clapping. Before either of them could speak, Gavin took off for the stairs, shouting as if he'd just solved light speed travel. "It worked! It worked! It worked!"

"Well fuck," Ivy groaned. She had no idea what Gavin was shouting about, but at least he wasn't pitching a fit. She rubbed her face, trying to abate the horror at being walked in on by her five-year-old and find some way to make sense of what had happened after. "Sorry, Nick. I should have locked the door."

"I'm not upset. Are you?" asked Nick. He bumped her shoulder with his, and Ivy shook her head. "Seems like he's okay with it." He didn't look half as bewildered as she felt when she fell back with a strained groan. Nick leaned over her, bracing himself on one hand beside her head on the pillow. Somewhere below them, Gavin continued to cheer, and he was banging around with something. "Tell you what. Why don't you go take a nice," he pressed a kiss to her nose, smiling as she opened one eye, "warm," he kissed it again, and she opened the other one, "shower," at the third peck, Ivy giggled and looped her arms around his neck. "While you're in there gather your thoughts, and I'll distract him with dinosaur pancakes. Then we'll see what other questions he's got, together."

"See, brilliant ideas like that are why I love you," Ivy said and stared up at the goofy grin Nick was giving her. She tugged him down to pull that delicious lower lip between her own. "Go on." She slid her hands down to his chest and playfully shoved him off. "We can pick this up tonight when he goes to bed." Nick's eyes flashed with heat before he rolled off of her, literally leaped out of bed, and swaggered off to the stairs. From this angle, Ivy got a clear view of the fading red scratch marks she'd left on his back, and heat flooded her veins.

She waited a good minute, before tiptoeing down to make sure the hall was clear and hurried to her room. There she grabbed her phone and texted Alex and her mom.

Told Nick I loved him. He said it back.

Biting her lip, she quickly added to Alex's text, remembering he had said he was inviting Lewin to stay the night for the first time.

He fucks like a god. Hope your night was as satisfying ;-).

Then she ducked into the shower.

Aldwin hummed under his breath, as he pushed open Gavin's door. He wasn't sure what he was going to find, but what hit him made him lose his breath. Gavin was seated on his bed, notebook in his lap, pencil flying over the page. What stunned Aldwin was the unmistakable glow that radiated from him, one he hadn't had before. It was totally and completely breathtaking. He believed! Gavin believed!

"Gavin," said Aldwin, hesitantly. Those blue eyes met his, and Ivy's wide smile beamed up from that tiny face. "Whatcha doin'?" He knew. He could see the word on the first line but hearing it seemed so important.

"Writing a letter to Santa!" Gavin exclaimed and turned the page to show him. "Are you making breakfast?"

"Yeah, want banana pancakes shaped like dinosaurs?" Aldwin asked. He could feel his magic surging in response to the powerful belief infusing the room. He was dying to know what had done it, how in less than ten hours Gavin had changed his mind so extremely.

"Yea," Gavin said and scrambled off the bed to run past him. He had never seen the boy that happy. "Come on! I'm so hungry!" He followed after him and watched as Gavin settled onto the sofa to resume his letter writing. Then, for the first time in his life, Aldwin heard it, a Christmas wish, in Gavin's tiny voice, echoing into his mind.

A train table or maybe a puppy. I think a train table.

"That isn't gonna open itself," Ivy said. Her words made him jerk in shock, as she reached past him to snag the box of the mix he had blindly pulled out of the cabinet.

Then she pressed a kiss to his cheek. At the contact, another whisper floated into his mind. It was Ivy's voice, younger, an echo of a whisper. Instantly he knew it was her last wish as a youth because he'd seen his Dah deliver it years ago.

Yellow roller skates, so I can go to the park with my friends.

"Nick, earth to Nick," Ivy said and tapped his shoulder with a free hand. He had a strange look on his face like he was listening to a distant conversation. She finally rescued the box of mix from his grip. "You okay?"

"Uh, yeah," he said and shook his head, smiling broadly. "Just, a bit shocked." He nodded towards Gavin, who was scribbling away on a notepad. "Guess what he's doing?"

"What?" Ivy asked. She popped the box open and turned to get a bowl down. She yelped in surprise, as Nick caught her waist in his arms and whispered in her ear.

"Writing a letter to Santa," he said. His sentence made her heart skip.

"You're kidding me!" Ivy half-shouted. She spun in his arms, looking over Nick's shoulder at her son. Gavin chose that moment to glance up, take one look at them, and then giggle. "Whatcha doing, blue eyes?" she asked and held her breath.

"Writing a letter to Santa!" Gavin announced, before returning to his work.

"Told ya," Aldwin said. He laughed as Ivy gave an excited squeal, set the box and bowl aside, and kissed him furiously. When his head stopped spinning, he kissed her cheek and pulled out the frying pan. "So, have you guessed what he meant by 'it worked'? Because I have no clue." He set the pan on the stove to open the fridge and retrieve the bacon and milk.

"Let's find out," Ivy said.

She took the milk from Nick. Excitement and joy bubbled in her chest. Not only did Nick love her and Gavin, but her baby boy believed again. She tried to keep her voice even.

"Gavin, baby, what did you mean by 'it worked'?" she asked. Ivy was dying to hear his explanation, to find out what he thought had happened, and how it had made him believe in Santa again.

"I wrote a letter to the cupids and asked them to make you and Nick fall in love," Gavin said. Ivy gasped, as Nick nearly knocked the pan off the stove. "Today you love each other, but last night Nick said you were just friends." Her son beamed proudly at them, wriggling on the seat in his excitement. "And that means cupids are real. If cupids are real, then so is Santa, right Nick?"

"That's right buddy!" Aldwin cheered. He was not going to tell Gavin the truth, that they had been marked months ago. He had to arrange the big reveal first, and that meant a trip home to ask his parents' permission to bring mortals to Yule Town. After the reveal, they could tell Gavin his letter had been answered before he even wrote it.

Gavin ripped the page out and hurried towards Ivy who was cutting up bananas. "Mummy, can I go to your office and get an envelope and stamp?" Aldwin ruffled the boy's hair and winked at Ivy.

"Sure baby," Ivy said. Gavin darted from the room. He moved out of the way, so she could bring the banana pieces over, and he laughed when she smacked him on the butt playfully afterward. "Look at you. The way you're smiling, you'd think you were Santa himself."

"Maybe I am, Ms. Yellow Roller-skates," Aldwin quipped, and at Ivy's stunned noise, he quickly added, "I saw a photo of them in one of the albums upstairs." The shocked look faded into a giggle. "Scared you for a second, though, didn't I?" He asked with a laugh, reaching around her to squeeze her tightly to him. He couldn't wait to show her everything, and, most of all, to hear her say his real name.

"Just a bit," Ivy admitted.

She stirred the batter, trying to get the banana bits evenly mixed in. For a moment, she'd thought Nick had read her mind since she'd thought about the skates while wondering if Gavin would want a pair. It was a silly notion, of course. Santa didn't teach online classes.

"So, I've got some things to do today, picking up my dress and Gavin's tux, and I have to get the wedding gift. Do you mind coming along and keeping us company?" She asked, even though she knew what he would say.

"Is that a rhetorical question?" Nick snorted. He reached and tugged a lock of her hair gently. "How about we do what you have to do, and I treat you both to lunch? That sound like a plan?"

She batted his hand away, so she could find the dinosaur-shaped bits of metal he had somehow procured to make Gavin pancakes.

"I'd like that, and I know Gavin would too," Ivy said.

She was so relieved that her son was as ecstatic about this change as she was. The fact that he'd actually wanted it, had been hoping for it, made the feelings inside of her all the more perfect.

"About what he asked this morning when he walked in," she said and looked up at Nick. "We should probably talk about that."

Aldwin felt his breath catch as he scooped the bacon onto a napkin to drain.

"The D-word?" He asked softly, moving so she could get to the stove. Ivy nodded and chewed at the side of her thumbnail. He knew when Ivy wasn't ready for something or wasn't certain if that step was right. "I mean, that's a title I plan on working really hard to earn." Her relieved expression spoke volumes, and he was happy she took his words well.

They knew it was something Gavin wanted, but Aldwin also knew that it wasn't a position to be taken lightly, and it was totally in Ivy's court when the decision was to be made. Light footsteps announced Gavin's return, and he looked over to see the five-year-old clutching his letter.

"We'll mail this today, okay?" Ivy smiled as she took it from him and waved him to the table. Aldwin smiled at the pair. "Breakfast is almost done, then we're all gonna go out."

Breakfast was the best one Aldwin had had so far since arriving. Now that Gavin knew, Ivy was open in her affections and just as open with receiving them. Well, it was good at first, but Gavin's demeanor changed a little. While he was talkative and eating, he wasn't up to his usual energy.

"I want Nick to help me get dressed." He said, but his voice lacked its usual exuberance.

"Okay, baby. You two do that, and I'll clean up," Ivy said and ruffled his hair as she picked up his plate. His skin felt warm, but he had just been laughing. And she had the heat on. "You have a headache, baby bear?" she asked, pressing the back of her palm to his forehead again.

"No ma'am," Gavin said and shook his head. He always got one with fevers, so she let the brief worry go. "Come on Nick!" He exclaimed, climbing from his chair.

Aldwin followed Gavin up the stairs.

"Okay, buddy. Let's find you something warm." While the cold didn't phase Aldwin, Gavin would need to have at least two layers for the late autumn chill. He picked out a black long sleeve shirt, a short sleeve one with an astronaut, and some dark jeans. Aldwin was just tying the boy's shoes when Gavin gave a pitiful whine.

"Hey, what's wrong?" asked Aldwin, looking up to see Gavin's face pale and drawn.

"My tummy hurts. It hurts really b—" Gavin's sentence was cut off, and Aldwin was drenched in orange juice and banana pancakes.

Acting on instinct, he scooped the boy into his arms and dashed across the hall, through Ivy's room, and into her bathroom. He made it to the toilet just in time for the second wave of vomiting. He sat cross-legged and cradled Gavin in his lap as the boy sobbed and retched. As he brushed Gavin's hair from his face, he felt the beginning of a fever forming.

"Ivy! Need you!" He shouted towards the door. He heard a pot drop downstairs, and Ivy's footsteps were on the stairs in a flash.

Ivy raced up the stairs and found her door open. The unmistakable sound of vomiting came from her bathroom. She darted in, finding Gavin in Nick's lap, and Nick was rubbing his back soothingly. Both were covered in Gavin's breakfast.

"Oh no!" She cried. Ivy half expected Nick to be disgusted, cringing away, but it didn't seem to phase him. "My poor boy. I've got him. Go get washed off." She tried to kneel down, but Nick waved her away.

"He already got me. I don't need you getting it," Nick said. Ivy didn't know what to do. She wanted to take the problem onto her own shoulders, but she could also see the comfort that Gavin was taking from Nick's embrace. "I just need some clothes from my room. I'll get him and his floor cleaned up."

"Are you sure?" Ivy bit her lip as Gavin finally sank back into Nick's lap, looking pale and clammy. "Baby, are you okay with Nick taking care of you." Gavin gave a little nod before resting his head on Nick's shoulder and curling a tiny hand on his neck. "Okay, Nick's gonna wash you off. I'll be right back." She hurried up to get Nick some clothes, and when she returned, he had stripped Gavin down to his underwear and placed him in the tub which was filling up slowly. "Guess we're staying in, huh?" She asked. Ivy didn't have to check the water to know Nick didn't have it too hot or cold. He'd have it just right to ease her baby boy's fevered skin.

Aldwin knew Ivy would throw the whole day away if he let her, but he could tend to Gavin just fine. He also didn't want her to get sick. Being Ageless, mortal illness had no impact on him, so it was much safer for him to tend to the small boy shivering with fever in the warm water.

"Why don't you go run the errands, love, and I'll stay in with him. That way you can get stuff done," Aldwin said.

"You have to mail my letter," Gavin whined, from where Nick was propping him up with one hand and gently wiping his face clean with the cloth he held in the other. Her baby boy flinched and grabbed his stomach with a sob. Ivy tried to grab him, but Nick didn't miss a beat. He had the tiny blue trash can by the toilet emptied on the floor in a flash, and it was under Gavin's face in the nick of time.

"Ivy, I've got him," Nick said over the sound of Gavin being sick. Ivy bit her lip, torn by wanting to comfort her son, but also seeing that Nick had the situation under amazing control. "Really, Ives. I know what to do. I'll get him washed up, put him in something comfy, and we'll camp out on the couch with ginger ale and saltines."

"And the sick bowl," Gavin said. He lifted his face away from the trash can, whimpering and wiping his snotty nose. Ivy expected him to hold his arms up for her, but he leaned into Nick's chest again. "Please mail my letter, Mummy."

"Okay," conceded Ivy. "But I won't be gone long. Want me to bring you home some of that chicken soup Uncle Alex brought over when you had a cold?" She asked. Gavin nodded, his eyelids drooping.

Aldwin waved Ivy out, so he could have room to pick Gavin up and wrap him in a towel, and set him on the closed toilet. "Sit here for a minute, okay buddy? My turn to wash off," he said. Then he turned on the shower, draping the striped pajama pants Ivy had brought him and a towel over the curtain, then he ducked in. He only stayed in long enough to wash clean, rinse the bottom of the tub out, dry off, and slide on his pants. Then he carried Gavin out to Ivy's bed, where she had left him some pajamas.

"Can we watch Land Before Time?" Gavin asked through a sniffle, as Aldwin dried him off and eased him into his clothes. "Daddy used to cuddle me and watch it when I was sick." Aldwin looked up, both shocked and extremely moved by his quiet request.

"You remember him doing that?" He asked. Aldwin wondered if the boy really did, or if it had just been something Ivy or Fiona had told him.

"It's one of the only things I remember 'bout him," Gavin said. Those blue eyes were filled with tears, again, and Aldwin wiped them as they fell down his cheeks. "I had chicken pops, and he let me sit in his lap and rubbed pink stuff on me 'cause I was itchy." Aldwin had to swallow at the way Gavin looked down at his hands. In his fever, the usual proper grammar and enunciation faltered into something far more like children his age. It was adorable. "So can we?"

"Yeah, Gavin boy, we can do that," Aldwin said. He pressed a kiss to his brow before turning away to throw the towel over the mess on the floor. Then he scooped Gavin up in his blanket to carry him gently downstairs. Ivy was starting the dishwasher, and she had set out the ginger ale, a pack of saltines, and a huge bowl covered in blue dragons with top hats. "Thanks, love." He smiled, dropping a kiss on her cheek as he passed.

Ivy followed her boys, setting the bowl, Gavin's favorite cup, and crackers down on the coffee table. To her surprise, Nick eased Gavin to a cushion and then headed to the shelf with the DVDs. Her heart swelled and ached as he ran his finger along them before pulling out The Land Before Time. She knew it was one of the two clear memories Gavin had, but how did Nick guess? "Did you know that—" he cut her off with a nod.

"Gavin told me, upstairs.," Nick said. He shifted and looked down at the movie case as if nervous. "I mean, he asked. Is that okay? If it was their thing, I don't want you thinking I'm trying to take it."

"I don't," insisted Ivy. "I don't think that at all." She squeezed his arm before turning to kneel in front of Gavin. "Mommy will be back soon. I love you, sweetheart." She kissed his nose as he snuggled deep down into his blanket. Then she stood up, and Nick grabbed the remote. "There's some Tylenol in the cupboard. If he throws it up, don't give him another dose."

"Got it," Nick said. He brushed her hair back from her face and leaned in to kiss her softly. She accepted his soft brush of lips and smiled when Gavin giggled weakly from his blanket cocoon. "Go on. We'll be right here when you get back."

"I love you," she sighed as she pulled back. "You didn't have to offer but thank you."

"I know I didn't, but I wanted to," Aldwin said. "I told you. I love him too. There's no need to thank me. This is what I signed up for, remember?" He spun her around and gave her a gentle push. "Now go, and don't forget his letter." He watched as she looked back one more time, nodded, and left them alone in the house.

A Visit and A Remedy

Aldwin shifted Gavin off of his lap onto the cushion. His fever had gone down some, but after the last round of puking, the boy had drifted off and had been sweating on Aldwin's chest for a good ten minutes. He hated seeing him like that, and he had been thinking of a way to ease his little tummy. There was a remedy as well as a preventative to keep Ivy from getting sick, but he didn't have any of the ingredients present. He could try summoning them, but he wasn't sure about an accurate dosage for a child.

Ivy wouldn't be back for another two hours, and Gavin was sleeping peacefully. Since his stomach was empty, Aldwin knew he wouldn't wake up to puke again for a bit. If he hurried, it would only take about five minutes. Also, since his powers seemed to have fully blossomed, given the whispers he'd gotten glimpses of whenever a kid must have walked by the house, he could just listen to hear when the boy woke up.

He pressed a finger to his nose. In a blink, the warm aroma of his mum's cooking, fresh pine, and the teasing magic of their realm encompassed him.

"Aldwin!" Cateline Claus exclaimed. "I knew you'd be coming back, but not so soon." His mum was carefully moving her hand over one of the sprites who worked in the toy shop. "Why are you in human pajamas?" The cut on the sprite's hand sealed itself, and with a wave, it was gone. "Would you like some cookies? I just made a fresh batch."

"Can't stay long," replied Aldwin. He grinned when she raised an eyebrow. "Ivy is out running errands, and I left Gavin alone for a minute. He's got a horrible stomach virus. Even ginger ale and crackers won't stay down." He hugged his mum tightly for a moment before turning to the cabinets where she kept her medicinal stores. Magic could heal physical injuries, but when it came to illness, the herbs and oils from their realm worked best. "I need a tonic for a five-year-old boy, and one to make sure Ivy doesn't catch it."

"Well let's see," Cateline said and shuffled him out of the way. "Get the pot and two vials. Then grab some cinnamon to flavor it for them while you're at it." He did as instructed and kept his mind opened for Gavin's thoughts. "Your Dah says Gavin regained his faith this morning. He told me Ostcrest lit up on the sleigh's navigational charts like a supernova. How'd you do it?" Aldwin flicked some fire into the small alcove on her preparation table with magic and set the pot over it.

"Well, believe it or not, I had to make him believe in cupids first," Aldwin admitted. His mother burst into laughter. "Well, actually I started by explaining how magic is really just science. That got him thinking. Then, I told him that Dah couldn't give him a new daddy because that was a cupid's job."

"Oh, that's right. Lewin mentioned it when he popped round to bring me the news that he found his soulmate," said Cateline with a happy sigh. She measured out herbs into the pestle bowl as she continued. "Alex is Gavin's godfather, right?"

"Yup." Aldwin uncorked the two vials and sprinkled a pinch of cinnamon into each. "Well, as I was saying, Gavin wrote a letter to cupid, asking them to make Ivy and I fall in love. We, well, we hadn't told him that we were together yet." He felt his face flush in embarrassment. Even if he was almost nine hundred, some things he knew his mother didn't want full details on. "Ivy came home last night, and she told me she loved me. We, well, made love," he said in a hurry but couldn't stop the smile that took over his face. "This morning, he caught us kissing in bed, and he heard us saying that we loved each other. He assumed a cupid must have done it at his request, and therefore they were real. If they were real, then Dah is real, according to his logic."

"Oh, he's a clever boy isn't he?" His mum asked and dumped ingredients into the pot. "I can't wait to meet both of them. Have you thought about when to tell them?"

"Christmas Eve. I wanted to bring them up before Dah and I left," Aldwin said. He swallowed hard because his next words were ones he had contemplated all day. "And I'm going to propose to her just as Christmas dawns."

"You better ask her mum first," Cateline said firmly. "Just because she's mortal, for now, it doesn't mean you can't adhere to her traditions. Ask her mum to bless the proposal."

"Oh, I planned on it," said Aldwin. He had to admit that he dreaded that talk. Fiona wasn't going to give her blessing easily, since it had been such a short time, but he knew he could convince her. "We'll have to tell her, too." Well, he'd have to show more than tell, but not before he got her blessing. If she knew the truth, what would have to happen to Ivy for her to be with him forever, she'd probably try to kill him. He took the first vial his mum passed it to him and watched her mix up the second batch. "This one Gavin's?"

"Yes. He'll have to drink the whole thing, and he can't have anything to eat for ten minutes," she said. Aldwin nodded, and he heard Gavin begin to stir.

"He's waking up," Aldwin said.

"Nearly done," Cateline replied. She poured out the second vial, and he took it. "Mix hers with some tea, and it'll get right to work." He leaned down and kissed his mothers cheek in thanks. "Now go!"

"Love you!" Aldwin called as he touched his nose. He pictured the upstairs hall so Gavin wouldn't see him appear, and he breathed a sigh of relief when he found himself staring at Ivy's door.

"How did you do that!?" Gavin's surprised shout made Aldwin turn. The boy stood at the door to Aldwin's room, eyes wide in shock. "You just appeared out of nowhere!"

"I well, uh, you see," Aldwin stuttered.

It was the second time in less than six hours that the five-year-old had left him speechless. He swallowed hard, floundering for an explanation, and scrambled to explain without completely revealing everything.

"Oh my gosh, you're magic!" The boy shouted. He hurried over and stared up at him. His face was still flushed, and Aldwin could see the thin sheen of fever sweat on his brow.

"Don't tell your mum!" Aldwin blurted out and knelt. "You can't tell anyone, okay. Not until I tell you its okay." Aldwin squeezed his eyes shut, but then he remembered the vials in his hand. He uncorked the one meant for Gavin. "I went to get you some medicine. It'll fix your tummy and fever right up. I wanted to be back before you realized I was gone." He held it to Gavin's lip. "Drink up, buddy." Gavin swallowed, making a face for a minute, but then he licked his lips.

"That's yummy," Gavin said. Aldwin pocketed the vial and picked the little boy up. "Nick, how do you have magic?"

"I was born with it," he said as he carried him downstairs and headed for the sofa so they could talk. "But, it's a secret, okay." So far the conversation wasn't as bad as he feared, but he needed to emphasize the point about not telling anyone. "If you tell anyone, even your mum, Santa will put you on the naughty list."

"He really has a naughty and nice list?" Gavin asked with a gasp, and Aldwin was pleased to see his color returning to normal. His skin was cooling down. "How do you know? Have you seen it? Have you met him? What's he like? Is Ruby real?"

"Whoa, whoa, slow down," Aldwin said. He laughed as Gavin covered his mouth and gave a little burp. Good, the medicine was working. "Yes, Ruby is very real. As for how I know about the list, well." He drew a breath and looked around to make sure Ivy was not coming in early. "Santa is my Dah." Gavin yelped and nearly fell out of his lap, but Aldwin caught him. "Careful!"

"Santa's your dad?" Gavin whispered and covered his mouth as he giggled. "Really? Can I meet him?"

"Well," Aldwin hesitated, but then he remembered what his mum had just said about meeting them. "I suppose as long as we're back before your mum." He snapped his fingers, and Gavin was bundled up in heavy winter clothes. The boy gave a little yelp, as he patted the thick, down coat. "And you have to pinky swear not to tell her or anyone. I'm going to, soon." Aldwin held up his finger, and Gavin linked his with it for a shake. "Okay, put your arms around my neck." Those tiny hands clutched at the back of his shirt in a flash. Aldwin stood up, shifted him to his hip, and then he touched his finger to his nose.

Gavin yelped, and Aldwin appeared in the kitchen he'd so recently vacated. Now, it was empty, barring some biscuits cooling on a rack.

"Here, they're banana," he said and plucked one up for Gavin, handing it to him. "You won't throw it up now." He lowered Gavin to the floor and took his hand. He couldn't sense his Dah's magic, but his mum's was coming from the library. "Come along."

"This place is so cool!" Gavin squealed, as he stared around the house with that wide-eyed expression. It had all the inner trimmings and trappings of a comfy cottage, but with so much more to offer. "How is that doing that?" He pointed at a floating plant on display in the hall.

"Hovering Cloud vine," Aldwin answered. He slid his hand under it to show the empty air beneath the dirt-covered roots. "It levitates during the day but settles back into the pot at night." He chuckled as Gavin kept half turning to drink it all in. "This is the library. I have a feeling it's gonna be your favorite room. It's one of mine." Aldwin pushed open the door and smiled when Gavin darted ahead and skidded to a stop.

"Bloody hell!" The boy exclaimed, and Aldwin winced. Ivy was going to slap him good when she learned Gavin had picked up that particular phrase from him.

"That's not proper language for a little boy," Cateline Claus said. He turned to find his mum in her favorite chair with a thick volume in her lap. "You must be Gavin." She set the book aside, smiling, and Aldwin beamed at her. Gavin glued himself to Aldwin's left leg. "Do you know who I am?"

"Who do you think she is, Gavin?" Aldwin asked. He gently pried him off and nudged him forward.

"Are you Mrs. Claus?" Gavin asked in a whisper. "I didn't mean to be rude. Please don't let Santa put me on the naughty list!"

"It'll take a bit more than that to end up on the list," she said. Then she held out her hands, and Aldwin knew exactly what was coming. His mother adored children, which is what made her such a perfect match for his Dah. "Come give me a hug, little snowflake." In a flash, Gavin ran towards her and was hauled in her lap. "Did my Aldwin give you one of the cookies?"

"Who's Aldwin?" Gavin asked.

"That's my first name," Aldwin said and shrugged. "Nick's my second name. Like how Michael is your second name." He watched as his mum placed her hand on his forehead and then smile in a satisfied way. "My mum's the one who made your medicine."

"Oh, thank you, Mrs. Claus," Gavin said and hugged her tightly. Cateline chuckled lovingly as she squeezed him back. "It made my tummy feel much better."

"Is Dah in the workshop or the stables?" Aldwin asked and looked out the window at the latter one in the distance. "Because Gavin wants to meet him too."

"We can' tell Mummy though, 'cause it's a secret," Gavin whispered. He put a finger over his lips. Then his eyebrows narrowed as if he'd had a thought. "If Nick marries my mummy, will that make you my gran too?"

"Yes, yes it would," Cateline said and kissed Gavin's cheek again. "You can call me Nana or Nan or Grandma Cateline. I know you call your other grandmum Gran." Aldwin had to admit he loved the way it looked to see his mum with Gavin. He'd known, of course, that he'd have to have kids to carry on the line, but he hadn't ever really thought about all it entailed. Knowing that soon, be it weeks or months, the boy was going to be his officially, erased any reservations he had been harboring at ever being a father. "And, Win, your Dah is on his way to his office. He just went to fetch the mail." Almost instantly, he felt the shimmer of his Dah appearing in the house.

"Come on, buddy, we've only got a bit before we have to go back," Aldwin said. He held his hand out to Gavin. "See you later Mum." He smiled, as Gavin hurried over to take it. With a press of his nose, they were in the workshop.

"Aldwin Nicholas, is that a mortal child?" his father asked. Aldwin looked over to see Santa was seated at his desk with a stack of envelopes piled halfway to the ceiling. The stern look was just an act, he knew because his mustache twitched in a smile.

"Yup, we've just been to see Mum," he said and nudged Gavin forward. "Uh, I'll explain why he's here but Ivy isn't later."

"Gavin Michael Moore-Somerfield," Kristofer Claus said, and Aldwin watched as his Dah set his letter aside and pushed back his chair. "You've gotten bigger since last Christmas. Come here, my boy."

"Go on," Aldwin encouraged. Then his eyes traveled to the massive scroll on a nearby desk. "I need to see something."

He walked over, and Gavin scrambled onto Santa's lap. He extended his hand. Finally, he felt the humming tingle of the parchment, and with a wave of three fingers, it unraveled. The list was blank, and Aldwin drew a breath. Holding it in, he touched it and watched as the enchanted ink began to materialize in a shimmer of gold and silver.

"Yes!" He crooned in victory.

His fathers booming laugh made him turn. He was standing, with Gavin's hand clutched in his, pointing at the massive globe suspended between two spiraling racks of old letterboxes. "This is how I keep track of everyone. It's enchanted and linked to my list, so it automatically calculates who is naughty and who is nice."

Aldwin closed the list to watch Gavin spin around in wonder. He looked on proudly as the boy took it all in stride, but he could see he was bubbling with questions and aching to touch everything and see how it worked. He half-expected him to go for the model sleigh and reindeer that levitated on a nearby shelf, but instead, he moved towards a wall of hooks with keys. "What're these?"

"These," Aldwin said and rushed forward, as Gavin pulled one down. "Are old keys. See, back in the old days, a lot of people were afraid of magic. We couldn't just pop back and forth, or we might be hunted down." The pulled free one of the Keys of Winter Aldwin used to carry, back before the mortal world grew in technology and therefore less prone to believe in magic or question someone suddenly disappearing from a crowd. "You can put this in any closed door's lock, turn it to the right, and it will open right up to the main house."

"That is so cool," Gavin said in awe.

Aldwin's pocket buzzed, and he pulled out his cellphone. It was a text from Ivy.

Hey, forgot my house keys, and I'm almost there. Can you come and let me in?

"We gotta go," Aldwin said. He handed Gavin the key to hang back up. "Put this away. Your mum's almost home."

"Now, Gavin, you know the secret. Think you can keep it quiet?" His father asked and crouched down to look Gavin in the eye.

Gavin yanked his hands out of his pocket and nodded.

"Cross my heart," the boy said firmly. "Santa, can I come back and visit?"

"Of course! After all, you'll be my grandson very, very soon!" The two hugged, and Aldwin held his hand out for Gavin. The little fingers slipped into his.

"Later Dah!" He called. In a blink, they were in Gavin's room. "Get out of those clothes and into some jimjams. Remember, not a word." He ruffled Gavin's hair, and the boy giggled uncontrollably. "Next time, you can see the reindeer." He snapped his fingers so Gavin was back in his clothes from before which only made the boy giggle even harder.

Ivy expected the door to open, but not as swiftly as it did. Nick stood there, shirtless, despite the cold.

"Here, let me take this," he said and grabbed the bag of take-out that included Gavin's soup, and the primly wrapped box of dishes she'd bought at the mall for Paula's wedding gift. With her burden relieved, she moved her dress bag off of her shoulder and the hanger containing Gavin's tux stopped digging into her palm.

"Thanks, babe," she said. "How's my boy?" She'd been worried all morning but hadn't wanted to continuously call or text. Nick didn't need her doubting she trusted him enough to handle it.

"He's much, much better," Nick said. He leaned in and kissed her. The patter of bare feet announced Gavin coming down the stairs. "Spoke to my mum, and she gave me a remedy to get rid of it, as well as one to keep anyone else in the house from catching it."

"My tummy feels loads better, Mummy!" Gavin exclaimed as he skidded into the room. "Is that lunch! I'm super hungry!" She laughed, relieved that he did look much better. She draped the clothes over a chair and nodded for Nick to set the bag down on a table. Then she scooped Gavin up.

"Mm, you smell good," Ivy said. His skin was saturated in Nick's piney cologne, but there was also a pleasant aroma she couldn't describe, like cookies, old books, pipe tobacco, and peppermint. It was probably from whatever remedy Nick's mom had given him. Nick smelled the same when he hugged her. "And so do you."

"Why thank you," Nick said. He kissed her gently before he held out a vial. "Mix this in some tea, and you won't get that stomach virus."

"Thanks," she said, as she carried the food to the dining room. She opened the bag of take-out, while Gavin slid into his seat, and pulled out the container of soup and a plastic spoon. "One chicken soup for Gavin." While he dug in, she turned to Nick. "So, how did playing nursemaid go before the remedy?"

"Well," he said and drug the word out. His smile never faded. "We cuddled, I caught about three bowls of puke, then he took a nap. Once he woke up and took the medicine, he was right as rain." Those chocolate pools twinkled down at her. Something was different about him, in a wonderful way. She couldn't explain it, but as he reached up to cup her cheek, she loved it instantly. "He did talk to my mum and dad a bit. That all right?"

Ivy didn't see any harm in a friendly phone call, so she shrugged.

"That's great," she said. "How'd they take you dating and living with a single mom anyway?" She had yet to talk to the distant Mr. and Mrs. Claus. The thought of their names made her giggle.

"Oh, they can't wait to meet you," Nick said, and his smile grew broader. "They're beyond happy that we're together. I was thinking, actually, about all of us getting together on Christmas Eve."

"Oh! That'd be wonderful." Ivy pressed a kiss to his cheek as she stepped around him to go get some tea for the tiny vial in her hand. She did not like the idea of spending her second night in Nick's arms running a fever and throwing up. "Let me go take this, and I'll come eat."

"Hurry back," Nick said. Ivy looked back, as Gavin and Nick shared a look and conspiratorial smiles. She didn't know what her boys were up to, but she had a feeling, she'd find out soon enough.

A Night Alone

I vy groaned in relief as Nick's hands rubbed her feet. After spending all afternoon in heels at Paula's wedding, the massage was wonderful.

"Your hands are like magic," she hummed and nuzzled deeper into the pillow.

It was barely after nine at night, but Gavin was at her Mum's for their monthly sleepover, the house was clean, and she and Nick were both freshly showered. It hadn't been a joint shower, because she needed to scrub off the makeup and wash the hairspray and gel from her hair. Still, she didn't see the point in bothering with clothes, so she'd come up to his room in nothing but a towel.

"Well, maybe they are." Aldwin chuckled and pressed just below her ankle with his thumb. She looked absolutely edible, sprawled out on his blankets, bare except for the red cotton towel that barely covered her lower back and bum. "Or maybe," he continued. "I just know what makes you feel good." He leaned down to press a kiss to the back of her calf, grinning when she made a breathy noise. "Anything else sore? Maybe here?" Releasing her feet, he slipped his hands up her calves and squeezed them firmly.

"God yes," Ivy said with a positively sinful moan, and Aldwin preened.

They'd made love twice since the first time, but it was always late at night, quiet, and quick. Tonight, though, they were alone, and he planned on putting that fact to good use. He hadn't at first, expecting her to proclaim she was tired and just wanted a cuddle, but Ivy had wandered in wearing just a towel, and that had pleased him to no end.

"Mm-hmm, my thighs are sore too, you know," she said.

"Oh, better fix that then," Nick said, and Ivy bit her lip.

His hands danced up to firmly grip her thighs. She'd been fantasizing about this all day. How could she not, with him looking so sexy in his tux that it should have been illegal? While that outfit had been mouthwatering, seeing him damp from his shower with nothing but a pair of boxers had been just what she'd hoped for. His fingers shifted higher, one set stroking her inner thigh while the other teased along the edge of the towel.

"How's this?" he whispered.

"Much, much better," she said, lifting her face just enough to look back at him. "This getting in the way?" She asked and reached back to pat the towel. His eyebrow arched, and that talented tongue darted out to dampen his lips. He nodded. "Well, guess it should go." She lifted up, giggling as he practically ripped it out from around her.

"There we go, now I can do this," Aldwin said.

He moved up onto his knees, straddling her thighs, and he fed his need to touch her skin eagerly. He pressed his fingers into her back, kneading firmly, but gently, eager to hear more of those gorgeous noises. He was careful to avoid actually touching anywhere that would get this moving too far too fast. He wanted to savor it.

"Mm, that's lovely, but," Ivy drew out the word. Aldwin pulled his hands back as Ivy started to roll over. He didn't bother trying to conceal how hard simply touching her, being with her, had made him. "I think you've earned a good back rub more than I have," She propped herself up on her elbows and grinned wickedly at him. "Lay down."

"If you insist," said Nick. Ivy giggled when Nick promptly fell beside her, face down, and buried his face into the pillow. "Not gonna hear me turn down a back rub from you, ever."

"Well, these have gotta go," giggled Ivy and knelt beside him, tugging at the waist-band of his pants.

Honestly, they didn't have to, but she really wanted to get her hands on that gorgeous, biteable, tempting ass of his. In a flash, he had wriggled out of them and hurled them across the room. "Much better, thanks."

Without preamble, she swung her left leg over his thighs, splayed her hands on his lower back, and slid them down to squeeze. "How's that."

"Bloody brilliant," sighed Nick. Ivy took her time groping, squeezing, and kneading his rear. She wanted to fuel the desire for her deeper in his veins. She moved her hands up, massaging along his spine. "I'm pretty sure you're the one with the magic hands," he said with a throaty groan.

"Oh yeah?" Ivy asked. Her chuckle was accompanied by her moving, and her thighs framed his hips as she settled half onto his back and half onto his bum. It pleased him to no end to find how hot and wet Ivy already was. He had intended to make tonight a bit romantic when he found out they would be alone, but Ivy had been pretty aggressive in the second-floor hall before departing to her shower. "Well, let's see what spell I can cast on you." He groaned as she pressed down and slid forward, her tongue trailing along his spine.

"Sounds promising," Aldwin said. She pressed her hands up, rubbing down his arms, pressing her chest against his back so she could place a kiss on the side of his neck. To her delight, he gave a shiver of his own, and she pulled playfully at his skin with her teeth. The yearning growl he gave in response made her core tighten in reflex. "You're soaked already. I can feel it."

"Can't help it." She purred in his ear, before nipping the lobe with her teeth. "I love you. Love touching you and tasting you. It feels so perfect." She squealed as he rolled suddenly under her with an agility Ivy hadn't known he possessed. She didn't fall, though, because he had his hands on her hips in a flash. "We don't have to be quiet tonight," she said and managed to chuckle after regaining her balance. Hoping to emphasize her point, she dragged the tip of her nail down his chest. She bit her lip when he rocked under her and pressed his hard length against her rear.

"Oh, I know." Aldwin reached up and tangled his hand in her damp hair. He pulled Ivy down for a fierce kiss. With his other hand, he cupped her breast and rolled the perfect, pink, pebbled nipple with his thumb. When she pulled away to pant for air, he tested a playful tug of her hair and a pinch of that same nipple between his fingers. He preened when she arched over him and let out a hiss of pleasure. "I plan on you being very, very loud."

"How do you intend to make sure of—"

Aldwin cut her off by lifting up from the blankets to take her right breast in his mouth, sucking, and flicking his tongue across the nipple before he tugged it with his teeth. This time, Ivy ground down on his hips, crying out. He had no complaints about their other three times. Each one had been perfect in its own way, always sweet, always quiet, and always a race to get off in case of interruption.

"More," she gasped when he released her with a wet pop, and he didn't give her time to whine before he had the other one on his lips.

Ivy had been wanting something a bit more passionate or more intense, and it seemed she was going to get it. She temporarily lost her ability to think from the way he was handling her with just the right level of roughness to make her pant and yelp and cry out. The one remembered what she'd wanted to do. She wanted to taste him. There hadn't been an opportunity until now.

"Lie back," demanded Ivy and pushed him down. Nick growled and pulled just a bit harder at her already tingling nipple. Pleasure blazed to life in her core. "Now, fuck." Normally she didn't swear, but it was hard to keep her language clean when she felt like this.

"Rude, I wasn't finished," Nick huffed before he fell back.

Ivy smirked, leaning down to kiss him quickly, before shifting her lips to his chest. Just the thought, as she licked, nipped, and kissed her way down his body, of watching him watch her had her already dripping center and nearly gushing.

"Mm, stars above you're perfect at that," Nick praised her. Ivy shifted her hips lower, sliding her folds along his thick, hard, erection. She gave a twist of her hips and ground down. "Ivy, please, I want you." She giggled when he bucked up against her. She slipped further down, ignoring his plea, to kiss her way along his stomach.

"No," Ivy said. Aldwin blinked as Ivy slid further down, looking up from his navel where she'd been teasing the fine hairs with her tongue. "Be patient, my love."

He bent his knees when Ivy pushed them apart with her own, and those mesmerizing eyes met him as she paused just above his pulsing erection. He could see the precum shining as it dripped from the tip. He groaned in surprise when she took him in hand and slowly curled her tongue across the head, pulling back to reveal the glistening strand stretching from her tongue to his erection. He swore under his breath when she smiled, broke the strand with a finger, then tucked it between her lips. Ivy hummed in delight.

"God you taste amazing," she moaned and took him on her lips.

Aldwin bucked in pleasure, fisting her hair in his hand as she gave a determined suck.

"Fuck!" The expletive came out without thinking when she pressed her tongue along the underside of his shaft and took him halfway in her mouth. "Yes, gods, you're so—" he tried to say, but he lost his voice when Ivy looked up from under her lashes, stroked her fingers down, and then took him almost to the hilt in one swift motion. He couldn't help himself from thrusting up, feeling her swallow when he hit the back of her throat.

"Ivy!" he cried out.

Ivy preened internally, as she worked him. She was a bit out of practice, but Nick didn't notice or care. She squeezed her fingers, pulling her lips in over her teeth, and then she bit down with the slightest pressure before she dragged them up to his tip. The noises she ilked out from him had her entire body burning in need. She loved his taste and the texture of his silky skin over the iron hardness.

She didn't stop. She unleashed every skill and trick she knew. Ivy wanted to drive him to the edge, to see if she could push him into losing control. She had no intention of making him come like this, but she wanted to get him to the edge. She groaned when he tugged at her hair, and bucked into her mouth, shouting, hissing, and gasping out incoherent words. At least, she thought they were words. When she pulled up to the very tip, only to slide back down and nearly gag on every inch of him in her mouth, he shouted something that sounded like it may have been German. When she twisted her fingers and stroked down as she sucked up, his groaned voice sounded Gaelic. She giggled when she remembered he was fluent in several languages. With a flash of pride, she realized she was making him lose control. Her body hummed with pleasure at the way he cried out her name and a string of syllables she didn't recognize the accent for.

Aldwin was nearing the edge. Ivy's talented mouth had totally scrambled his brains. He couldn't think, couldn't even be bothered to translate his Ageless thoughts into English, letting them come as whatever language popped out. He honestly didn't think it could get any better, feel any more intense, and then his little minx cupped his balls and squeezed them ever so gently.

"If... you... don't—Holy fuck!" he shouted, interrupting his warning that if she didn't stop, he was going to come. She had done the teeth thing again and made his brain short circuit. "I've, I'm gonna... if you don't stop." He felt that tension growing, felt himself tighten in her hands. No, he had no intentions of finishing in her mouth. Ivy sucked again, bobbing her head, humming around him as her hips shifted, gifting him with a prime view of her supple rear. "No!" He tugged at her hair, not too hard, but enough to pry her away just before the coil snapped. "Not in your-" his words were cut off as she released him with a wet pop. Then she practically pounced on top of him, groaning into his lips, her tongue grazing his. Ivy's short curls were hot, sticky, and soaked as they slid against his bare skin. He wanted them on his lips, now.

Aldwin rolled her over, pushing her thighs apart, and pinned them to the bed as he dove between them, laving a lick from her dripping center to her pulsing clit. Ivy cried out, her legs trying to close, but he pressed them back down, sucking furiously on the hooded bud with a growl. Then he slid his hands down, grabbing her calves, pushing her legs until her heels hit her rear. With a growl, he lowered his weight onto her feet, pinning her in that position, and thrust his tongue into her.

Ivy mewled at the sensation. She tried to move, to look, to arch into his lips, but she couldn't. The only thing she could move was her hands, and it was mind-blowing.

"Yes, more!" She pleaded, grabbing the blankets when his tongue swirled, curling up, dragging out only to thrust in again.

His nose grazed against her clit, sending a jolt of pleasure from the hooded bud straight to her spine. The position was new to her, and it made the sensations more intense. His lips were around her clit again, sucking, flicking with his tongue. She still needed more. She needed it all.

"Nick!" She cried out. He had thrust two fingers into her, curling them up as he circled his tongue before she could ask.

Ivy couldn't think, and she didn't want to. All she wanted was to feel everything Nick was giving her. She had hoped to tease this side out of him, and she'd gotten it. Her lover was voracious, and he never ceased the attention he was giving to her. Usually, he would pause every so often to compliment her or smirk when she'd given a particularly active wiggle, but she was getting none of that. He seemed determined to drive her mad with pleasure.

"Again," she cried, and his teeth grazed ever so gently against her clit before his tongue drew a circle around it. She shouted his name, fisting the sheets in her hand, seeking some outlet for the intensity of the pleasure that rolled through her body like a thunderstorm. This earned her a vibrating hum, and he did it again.

Aldwin knew Ivy was close. He had already memorized her tells. She was trembling, tossing her head on the pillow, fluttering around his fingers, and her gasps had become a string of run-on pleading. He redoubled his efforts, desperate to be inside of her, but also needed to hear and see her come undone first. It was crucial to his plans.

It didn't take long, and her trembling grew more intense. He could feel her tightening around him, that hooded bud started to pulse harder under his tongue. He thrust his fingers in deeper, deeper until her drenched entrance stopped his knuckles, and then he curled them up again, pressing. He flattened his tongue against her and sucked desperately.

Ivy exploded under him, screaming out as her lower body lifted from the sheets and her slight flutters turned to intense clenches around his fingers. Aldwin pulled them out, pushing himself up. There he grabbed her hips, and he rolled Ivy onto her stomach. Finally, he lined himself up. He dropped a hand to her upper back, pushing her torso down, and before her shaking legs could slip, he thrust into her and dug his fingers into her hip. It made him cry at the perfection he found, the way her orgasm still tightened around him as he sank into her completely.

Ivy gasped a strangled cry when Nick thrust into her from behind. She clung to the sheets, trying to rock back into him with her legs that were slowly regaining feeling.

"Yes, love, yes. More, harder," she said. Nick's hand was in her hair, pulling just right, forcing her head back and up, and the sensation made her groan in delight.

"More? You want more?" He asked and gave a noticeably harder thrust that made her keen from the intensity. "I'll show you more."

The wicked promise in his tone when he pulled slightly harder at her hair made Ivy whimper. Suddenly his other hand was pushing her down further, forcing her knees wider apart, and his hand left her hair to grab her arms. She surrendered them to him willingly, and soon he had both in his grasp, against her lower back, and his rhythm changed. He wasn't so much as thrusting into her now, as he was pounding.

"Put your ankles over my calves, now Precious Girl!" The usually sweet pet name held a commanding tone that made her head swim. She did as she was told, and the slight change in angle was impossibly more pleasurable.

Aldwin knew he wasn't hurting her, and he grunted as she fell into a stream of incoherent cries. He buried himself inside of her, over and over, as hard and fast as he could. Ivy was literally gushing around him, filling the air with seductive, thrilling, wet noises as her sweet arousal dripped down his groin to his thighs. Keeping her hands pinned with his left hand, he dipped his right around, cursing an Ageless swear at how it coated her own thighs. He wanted more, and he knew she could give it. He slid his fingers up from her thighs, finding her still pulsing clit, and he rolled it quickly in time to his thrusts.

"Oh my god!" Ivy howled, tossing her head side to side, and panting under him. "Don't stop, please. Please. Nick, God, need, want, fuck!"

Aldwin chuckled, reveling in how marvelous she felt around him. He worked her fervently, forcing her higher, groaning as she began to clench around him again. The closer she got, the better she felt around him. He nearly had her there, and on a whim, he caught her swollen bud in the softest pinch.

Ivy snapped, her whole body feeling like she was careening over a ledge. She slammed her eyes shut, shouting out for him to hear her release. His fingers left her, but her climax wasn't waning. It was filling her, making her jerk, overwhelmed by the utter ecstasy he had driven her to. She could barely breathe, gasping, stars dancing in her mind as her whole body filled with fire. He didn't stop thrusting into her, didn't slow his speed at all. She loved it all.

With Ivy awash in her climax, Aldwin lost himself in her body. He released her hands, gripping her hips to pull her back into him. He was nearly there himself and could feel his own release building. He chased after it, seeking it in the nirvana of his beautiful soulmate. She had him riding high on his need for her.

"So close, love! Just a bit more. Can you take it?" He asked and squeezed her hips as he buried himself into her, again, and again.

"Yes, come for me, please. Just like this," Ivy begged. She didn't want him to slow down, to lessen the power behind his desperate pace. She lifted her head, casting a glance back at him. Nick was panting behind her, jaw clenched, eyes closed as he tossed his head back. It was glorious. "I need it." His eyes snapped open, as he yanked her back so hard she was forced to drop her head to the pillow.

"Good!" Aldwin howled out.

That's what he needed to hear, and with Ivy's encouragement, he gave it to her without reservation. He was nearly there, dancing dangerously on the edge, and Ivy squeezed around him, intentionally he knew from experience, and that did it. Shouting out in completion, Aldwin buried himself as deep as he could, pushing Ivy flat, covering her back with his body, and groaning into her neck as he felt his release spill out inside of her.

"Love you. I love you so much, my Ivy," he mumbled into her skin, twitching as his heart pounded and his head spun.

"Love you too," Ivy whimpered, unable to stop the trembling in her body at the relief that followed the furious coupling. "Feels so good."

She could feel him pulsing inside of her, sending tiny jerks of delight against her sensitive body. Then he moved, sliding from her, and the sensation made her clench in his absence, aching to be stretched and filled again. She didn't understand how her body could want more after that. Ivy didn't care, she just scrambled to grab Nick as he rolled off of her.

"Come here," Nick said and hauled Ivy onto him, catching her cheek in one hand and kissing her. "Hello," he said with a chuckle, as those glittering eyes met his.

"Mm, hello," Ivy giggled, and she felt him still hard under her. Maybe she could get more, but first, she needed to catch her breath. "That was fucking amazing," she, kissing his chest and humming in delight as he wrapped his arms around her.

Despite how deep his orgasm had been, Aldwin wasn't going soft. His body was screaming for more. He didn't understand how that was possible. Their lips broke apart, and he groaned as Ivy shifted flush over him instead of sprawled half onto his chest

"Yeah, it was amazing," Aldwin said. He stroked her back and bit a gasp as she gave a soft rut against him. It made his eyes roll back for a moment, feeling how drenched she was from not only her arousal but his release. "Sorry, I'm still—guh." He grunted when Ivy repeated the motion, and it felt so wonderful he had to close his eyes to keep from sliding into her again.

"Me too," Ivy said. She reached up to stroke his cheek, as she remembered the decision she'd made waking up in her own bed this morning. Despite being together, being like this, she hadn't spent every night in his arms. She wanted to change that. "Nick," she kept her raspy voice low, and those intoxicating eyes met hers. She hoped he would say yes. "I want to move up here, with you."

"You do?" Aldwin gasped. His heart skipped, as the after-glow flush on her skin darkened just a bit. His beautiful Ivy bit her lip and nodded. He knew what a big decision this was for her. "I want that very much too," he assured her. Then cupped the back of her head and pulled her to him for another slow, lingering kiss. With a sigh into his parted lips, his Ivy shifted again, sliding back, and with a whimper, she had taken him into her again. "Sweetheart, let yourself recover." He grabbed her hips to hold her steady, biting back a grunt at the pleasure of her around him.

"Shhh." Ivy put a finger over his lips to silence him. She held herself still, just feeling the perfection of the way they fit together. She smiled at him and then rested her cheek against his shoulder as she stroked his chest. "Just feel with me. I need this, after that." She hoped he understood what she was asking him for. "Nick, I love you. You know that right?" She rolled her hips slightly and sighed her pleasure into his jaw.

"Yes, love. I know," Aldwin said. He stroked her back and held her to him as she gave small, slow, tender rocks of her body. He kept his touches against her light and soothing, helping her find her center within herself again. "And I love you. Gods, I love you. I want you, with me, forever." He kissed her brow and trailed his palms along her rear.

"Good, because if you ever left," Ivy said, and gentle, slow rocks faltered

"Never," Nick said.

Ivy didn't even have time to reply before Nick rolled her onto her back and began to drop tender kisses along her skin. He pulled back only to slide slowly, languorously into her. It was so perfect, that Ivy had to swallow back a sob.

"One day," he whispered into her ear. "When you're ready." He pulled back and gave another languid thrust into her. "I plan on proposing to you." Ivy squeezed her eyes shut as she lifted her head to bury it in his neck. She knew she could say what she needed to say, and he would accept it without scoffing.

"Nick, I think you're my soulmate," she whispered, letting her head fall back to the pillow so she could watch as those adoring eyes softened above her.

"Oh, Ivy, I know you're mine." Aldwin stroked her side and pressed a kiss to her brow as she hooked her legs behind his knees and rolled her hips up against him. He thrilled at hearing her admit it, even if it was just faith on her part.

"Make love to me," Ivy whispered and kissed the underside of his chin. She wrapped her arms around his back. Aldwin sighed, nuzzling her hair back from her face, and he began to move.

Nick was so gentle and tender as they moved together, luring another double climax from her, which left Ivy whimpering in his arms. He cradled her up to him when he filled her again. At that moment, as Nick smiled and pressed kiss after kiss into her cheek, Ivy knew that when he asked her to marry him, she would say yes.

Secrets Revealed

I vy zipped up Gavin's coat, and he bounced eagerly in place.

"Hold still, little monkey," she said and giggled. She didn't remember ever seeing the coat he had handed her. Then Gavin said Nick gave it to him. Things like that were what solidified her decision to plan Nick's Christmas present.

"But Mummy, Nick's ready to go!" Gavin fussed. He looked over to where Nick leaned against the stove, a long coat the only extra layer against the slushy snow coming down outside. She rolled her eyes and chuckled under her breath.

"There, now go get your hat. Hurry," said ivy and shooed him to the stairs. She wandered over to Nick, who looped his arms around her waist. She smoothed his jacket lapels, grinning up at him. "Well, you've got one dad aspect down," she teased. He arched an eyebrow, mouth opening. "Last minute Christmas shopping for Mum," she explained and mimicked his accent. "Well, almost at least, real dads wait until three in the afternoon on Christmas Eve. You picked the day before Christmas Eve."

Aldwin laughed out loud and leaned down to kiss her gently. It had been twenty days since she'd moved most of her clothes and things up to his room. Yet, in that time, she hadn't given him the impression he'd earned the title she was dangling in front of him with a grin.

"So, how many more aspects before I'm promoted?" he asked, tightening his arms around her lightly.

"Have to check the handbook, but." Ivy paused, obviously pretending to think. "I think only a few more." She danced back out of his arms towards the almost completed Christmas tree against the wall. She looked back at him, as she picked up an ornament. "When he comes back down, we can check off one more."

Aldwin perked up, curious as to why she was suddenly discussing it after avoiding it so long. He kept his mouth shut while she hung a blue bulb on a branch. Then she turned to a box.

"What do I have to do to check it off?" he asked.

"Help him with this," said Ivy.

Aldwin blinked in surprise when she lifted a large, golden star from a box. The sound of Gavin's snow boots coming down the stairs had his heart racing.

"Ready!" Gavin proclaimed as skipped into view. Aldwin watched his already smiling face glow even brighter as he saw the star. "Oh! That's my job! Let me! Pick me up, Nick. Pick me up!"

"Well, you heard him, Nick. Pick him up," giggled Ivy.

he was so glad that Gavin had understood the plan, even if Nick didn't. She watched in delight, her heart-melting when Nick's face split into a grin. He scooped Gavin up by the waist, and she handed her son the star. She blinked back the tears of happiness that had been bursting out at random all morning when Nick expertly lifted Gavin up over his head for him to set the star in place.

"It's perfect!" Gavin exclaimed, and Aldwin lowered him back down. "Now can we go! I know just what I wanna get Mummy!" He looked over at Ivy again, who was closing the storage boxes.

"You sure you don't wanna come?" he asked. Ivy had been working all week to get the house ready for Christmas morning. It would do her some good to get out, even if he and Gavin were going to sneak away.

"No, I've gotta wrap gifts, and there are a few more loads of laundry," said Ivy.

She brushed her hair back and smiled to hide her nerves. She wanted everything to look perfect when she met his parents. Also, she had to get his present boxed up and wrapped. It was hidden in her old closet behind a box of photo albums.

"Okay, we'll text you when we're headed back," said Nick. He kissed her cheek before taking Gavin's hand and leading him to the door. "Okay, Gavin. Do you remember what I told you? We're doing today?" She heard him ask, as the door shut behind them

"Get my present for Mummy super quick, then go to your house and set up your present for her, and then stop by Gran's to ask for her blessing," Gavin said, and he counted the tasks off with his fingers. Aldwin squeezed his tiny hand proudly.

Once they were out of sight of the house and obscured from the street by bushes, he lifted Gavin into his arms. There was no need for a cab when it was just them.

"To the shops," he chuckled and pressed his finger to his nose. In a blink, they were in a crowded store.

As Ivy carried the ornament boxes up to her office, she smiled. She stuck them in the closet and brushed her hair back. She let herself feel the excitement building inside of her. She skipped to her room to dig out the things she and Nick had bought for Gavin and stashed in various places. Then she settled on the floor to wrap them up. Nick was in charge of assembling the bike hidden under the bed, but that would be done tomorrow.

As she worked, carefully cutting the papers, folding them primly, and neatly taping them in place on each gift, she replayed the last week or so over and over in her head.

She'd gone and had a long talk with Alex, where they discussed just how perfectly their lives were going. He'd told her to go for what she wanted to do for Nick's Christmas. Finally, she'd talked to her mom, who was naturally hesitant at first, but after seeing how much Nick loved Gavin and how much Gavin loved him, she, too, agreed it was the best decision. Waiting for Christmas morning to tell her boys was hard, but she applauded herself for not letting the surprise slip. It was also why she was anxious to meet his parents.

She had yet to talk to them, but Nick had relayed their happiness at the relationship and their assurance that they would accept her and Gavin with open arms. Once all Gavin's gifts were wrapped, Ivy reached up into her closet to pull out the box containing the parts for Nick's gift.

The first gift was a frame, with the very first picture she'd taken of him and Gavin. He was seated on the living room floor, Gavin in his lap, looking at a book on astronomy. She set it aside and pulled out the papers beneath, waiting on signatures to be turned in. It was the Emergency Contact Card for Crestwood, Gavin's medical release forms for his pediatrician, and the authorized pick-up form for his daycare. Carefully printed on each form, above Alex and her mom's name, was Nick's name. At the bottom of the box were a notebook and an envelope. She'd meant to already put the letter in, but Nick had snuck up on her in the office before she could. The letter wasn't long at all, but it carried the weight of her entire world on it.

Dear Nick,

All Gavin wanted for Christmas last year was a new daddy. This year, all I want is the same thing. Will you make both of us happy by saying yes to our wish?

Love,

Ivy and Gavin

Carefully, Ivy tore the page out to fold it up. Then she neatly tucked it into the envelope, sealed it, and wrote the number two on it. Picking up the documents, she stacked them neatly and wrapped them in tissue paper. On the paper, she wrote the number three.

She settled them back in the box, followed by the envelope, and using a bit of scrap wrapping, Ivy wrote one and taped it to the frame. Then she neatly wrapped the box, signing the label from her and Gavin. Satisfied with her work, Ivy carried the gifts downstairs to tuck them around the tree.

With that done, she turned her attention to the buzzing dryer. She pulled out Gavin's clothes and put them in a basket to fold in a bit. Then she transferred over his sheets that had been washing and headed up to get hers and Nick's clothes. For the most part, they were in the hamper, but some of their various shirts, pants, and hoodies were tossed about. She smiled because she knew they were scattered due to their eagerness to get in the shower together.

Ivy picked up the items and put them into the hamper. She spotted one of Nick's numerous sports coats half-under the bed. He'd assured her, in the beginning, that they were machine washable in the delicate cycle. She pulled them out and dipped her hands into the pockets to make sure they were empty.

After seven years of doing first Aaron's and then Gavin's laundry, she had learned this was imperative to her sanity and the integrity of her washer and dryer. In the left inner pocket, her fingers brushed paper.

"Men," she snorted, pulling them out, and tossed the coat in with the others. She was amused to see she had found two envelopes, faded, crinkled, and ripped at the top. Shrugging, Ivy went to toss them on his side of the dresser, until she saw what was written on them.

Santa Claus

1 North Pole Ln.

North Pole, Arctic Circle

She recognized the sloppy writing on the first, then the neat cursive on the other. The writing was hers and Gavin's.

"Impossible, no," gasped Ivy. She glanced at the return labels, and they were the ones she had used up last year. The letters were postmarked last year, though they held no stamp. "What the hell!" She shouted. She remembered for a fact that she hadn't put stamps on them before Gavin had mailed them, but they were clearly stamped and postmarked.

Ivy yanked the letters out, and her heart raced as nausea twisted her gut. They were their letters, unmistakable in their requests and signatures. The papers felt like they burned her skin, and Ivy dropped them. Her hands flew to her necklace as she flopped onto the bed, and she flailed for a logical explanation.

It struck her, hard, the memory of their first encounter. Nick had looked familiar, but she couldn't place it. Her mom said he looked familiar too like she'd seen him around. Had she seen him before, maybe in passing? She squeezed her eyes shut, chest tightening. He had been so familiar and known her and Gavin so well almost immediately. Two thoughts warred in her mind.

Thought one was that Nick was actually Santa. The thought seemed absurd, though. Santa was real, but he didn't look like Nick. He was old and bearded and married. How else could he have known about her necklace? Ivy shook her head as her world spun. That beach in Florida had been packed, but she'd been glancing over the faces, watching for suspicious people like Aaron had taught her, while she kept an eye on Gavin. Had his face been in the crowd? Ivy couldn't remember.

The second thought was more plausible, more realistic, and he made her sick. Nick was a stalker. Ivy's stomach churned, as her mind began stringing everything together. Nick had their letters.

Someone had bought Gavin a police bear, but nobody remembered doing it. Somehow her necklace, lost on a beach, had been primly wrapped under the tree. Someone had bit into the cookie. He had responded to her ad a mere two hours after it had been posted, and only he had. Nick had suddenly shown up, just as she was walking in the house, close enough to startle and catch her. He'd known exactly how Gavin liked his pancakes. Not only that, but he also knew exactly what Gavin's interests were, and, he'd had so much cash on hand that day. His record was clean.

Too clean, Alex had said.

She'd never talked to his parents, but they were supposedly okay with everything. That woman, Regina, had said something about the family thinking he'd never find a woman. He had been single for two years, and she'd lost that necklace two years ago. Ivy shot to her feet and raced to the photo albums on the shelf. There was only one with pictures of her as a kid. She flipped through it, heart pounding. There was no photo of her with her yellow roller skates, but back in August, she had told Morgan, on one of the two dates, that her most memorable gift as a child was a pair of yellow roller skates that she got for Christmas when she was twelve.

"Oh my god," Ivy whispered.

She felt a stab of pain in her stomach, and she raced for the toilet. Her lunch came up violently, choked by fear and horror. What had she done? How had she been so stupid, so naive? Stumbling to her feet, she felt panic and disgust well up. Nick was a stalker. It was more plausible than anything. Why else would he be so keen on encouraging her and Gavin's belief in Santa? If they did, she wouldn't question other things. Ivy had fallen in love with a stalker and had let him in her home, around her son. She hated herself to her core for being so incredibly stupid.

Ivy tried to calm herself, as she planned her escape. She needed to get Gavin and get somewhere safe. She couldn't let Nick know she knew, not until she had her son protected. Ivy raced down the stairs to her cellphone and was about to dial Alex when a horrible thought coursed through her.

What if Nick had put one of those bugging apps on her phone? He had her password. He could have done it any time. Swallowing she set the phone down, her vision spinning as she fought back the panic. Getting Gavin to safety was her most important priority. Steadying herself, Ivy picked up her phone again and pressed Nick's number. It rang twice.

"Hey beautiful," he said. Ivy wanted to vomit again.

"Hi, where are you guys?" she asked trying to stay as calm as she could. She stared at the clock. It'd been two hours since they left.

"Um, we were just going to swing by your mum's and say hi. Gavin's idea," explained Nick. The sound of traffic was audible around them. "Ivy, love. You're crying. What's wrong?"

"I, uh, I just got some bad news. I need you to come home. It's an emergency," she said. It wasn't a lie, and that made it so much easier for her to act the way she needed to.

"Be there in fifteen," Nick replied soothingly. "Just, sit down, have some tea. We're coming. Love you." The call ended.

Ivy immediately called a local cab service instead of using her ride-share app. She didn't want Nick to see her order a car. Someone answered. "Yes, I need a cab ASAP. Please, in the next ten minutes. I'll pay your driver triple," she said, hoping the man on the other end of the line could hear the panic in her voice.

"We'll be there," he said.

Pocketing her phone. Ivy raced up the stairs to grab her and Gavin a bag. She shoved three sets of clothes in each and made sure she put important documents like their passports in hers. She wanted to call Alex, her mom, or anybody, but she was terrified he would know. If he knew, he may take Gavin. He may even hurt him. Her stomach churned, and Ivy barely made it to the toilet as she heaved again. How did this happen? Why did this happen?

Wiping her mouth, she answered her ringing mobile. It was the cab, outside. Ivy yanked her boots on, grabbed the bags, and sprinted out the door. She reached the cab and opened it.

"Please, you have to help me,"

"Hey, sweetie, you okay?" The woman behind the wheel asked as she turned around. "You look like you've seen a ghost."

"No, no I'm not. I need you to do something for me, okay?" Ivy pleaded. The woman nodded. "My son and boyfriend are going to be here in five minutes. I'm going to send my son out to you alone. If I'm not out of that door within three minutes of him getting in, you get him out of here and to the Creekwood Apartments on Candle Drive, apartment thirty-two B, That's my mom, Fiona Moore."

"Honey, are you in danger? Do I need to call—" the woman tried to say, but Ivy cut her off.

"No!" Ivy screeched, and she winced back to calm herself down. "No, no, he has my son. If he sees the police, he may take him and run. Please. Just, please, help me."

"Okay, honey. I will, What's you and your boy's name?" She asked.

"I'm Ivy Moore, and he's Gavin Moore-Somerfield," Ivy told her. She sent up thanks to the universe as she slid the driver the money and a substantial tip. Then she raced back inside, wiping her face, pacing the hall. Time seemed to crawl; each frantic heartbeat felt like ages. Finally, the key turned in the lock.

"Mummy! We're back!" called Gavin. The accent he was still using made her want to cry.

"Ivy! What's happened?" Nick asked, coming around the corner.

Ivy turned around, trying her best to mask her anger and her fear. "We have to go. It's why there's a cab waiting. I don't want to speak in front of Gavin," she said. Choosing not to lie made it so much easier to play her role.

"Gavin, go wait in the cab," Nick said and patted his head.

Gavin rushed out the door obediently. Ivy looked at the clock. She had three minutes.

"Ivy, love, what's wrong." Nick's hand came forward. Ivy snapped.

"Don't fucking touch me!" Ivy shrieked. Aldwin barely had time to register Ivy was angry at him before her fist collided with his jaw and sent him stumbling into the wall. "You fucking pervert! You sick, fucking, freak!"

He staggered upright, only for her foot to collide with his shin, and the pain sent him ducking out of her reach. He didn't understand what was happening.

"Ivy, what the hell?" yelped Aldwin. He spat his own blood on his sleeve, trying to figure out what was going on. "What happened?! I don't understand!" What had scared her so badly was attacking him? It wasn't right. Aldwin felt fear bubble up inside of him.

"I found the letters. Yeah, I did. The ones Gavin and I wrote last year. They were in your coat pocket." Ivy sneered. She backed slowly to the door, her eyes full of hatred and rage. Aldwin felt his blood run cold, and he didn't understand what she was accusing him of. "When did you pick me out? It was Florida right when I lost my necklace?"

"What? I—Ivy, what are you saying?" stammered Aldwin. he wanted to reach for her again, but he knew if he did, she would just go berserk again. He froze as her words clicked. She found the letters, oh holy night, he understood her fear. "Ivy, no, it's not what you think. I'm not a stalker."

"And I'm a virgin," Ivy snapped. She was opening the door, slowly, trying to make it inconspicuous, but he noticed. Aldwin needed to explain and fast. "Fuck off Nick, if that's even your name!"

"Listen, I'm not a stalker!" he cried. He had to do it. He had to show her, but he was aching from her attack. The panic and fear made it hard to concentrate. Then he saw it, and it stunned him. Ivy didn't believe anymore. She was cold and lightless. The reality poured glaciers into his stomach. "You don't believe anymore?"

"Your lies, no, fuck you!" Ivy screamed. The door was opening more, she'd nearly be able to fit if he didn't stop her.

"You're right. My name isn't Nick. It's Aldwin Nicholas Claus! I'm Santa's son," pleaded Aldwin.

He grabbed for her, intending to teleport her to his parents, but Ivy delivered a solid kick right to his groin. Shouting, he went down. Tears stung his eyes, as he gasped for air.

"You're completely insane!" She screamed. The door shut behind her with a terrifying finality.

"Ivy! No! Please!" Aldwin sobbed. He stumbled to his knees. "Please! Come back!" Tears poured down his cheeks, as he stood and gripped the knob.

This couldn't be happening. It couldn't. Aldwin ripped the door open, and he watched in anguish as the cab sped away, carrying his future inside.

A Mother's Worst Fear

"Ivy, what is going on?" Fiona gasped as Ivy shoved her way into the apartment, slammed the door with her foot, set Gavin down, and locked it. "Why are you both crying? Did Nick leave?"

"No! Mummy left Nick," sobbed Gavin, his voice raw from screaming, pleading with her to go back.

"Gavin, baby, go sit down and watch TV," demanded Ivy. Gavin stomped his foot, screaming wordlessly at her as he dropped his bag. "Now, God damn it!"

Ivy couldn't ever remember a time she'd truly raised her voice at him, but it snapped past her lips. Her mom made a noise, and Gavin's screaming went silent. In a blink, he had disappeared and the TV came on, but his sobs weren't muted.

"Kitchen, now." She croaked and grabbed her mom's arm.

"Ivy, what happened? You look worse than when Aaron died." Fiona pulled her into a hug and rubbed her back. "What happened? Did Nick hit you? Did he do something? Tell me."

"He was stalking me, Mom, since the Florida trip. I found..." Ivy paused, the pain in her core was so real she thought she was being kicked. "I found proof." Ivy sobbed into her mom's shoulder. "I'm scared, Mommy." She could call the police, but by now he'd probably already run from the house. "He had the letters to Santa from last year, mom. I asked for this necklace, remember how I lost it in Florida? It was under the tree, and nobody can remember who gave Gavin the bear."

"Oh my god, Ivy," gasped Fiona. She sank down across from her and grabbed her hand. "You don't think he snuck in and..." Her mom didn't need to finish that sentence.

"I do. It had to have been. Unless he's Santa Claus," Ivy snorted, as she wiped her tears hard.

"No, Nick's not Santa,." Gavin's trembling voice drew their gazes. He was crying, huge crocodile tears in the doorway to the kitchen. "He's Santa's son! He took me to meet Santa and Mrs. Claus. We were there today too! He said not to tell you, 'cause it's a secret."

Ivy ran a hand through her hair. Nick had taken Gavin somewhere and told him not to tell? That just proved it. She hated doing this, hated the words she was forming, but Gavin needed to know. It would be safer that way.

"Gavin, Santa isn't real. I lied, okay! I lied because I hated seeing you so sad!"

"He is real! I met him! I met him!"

"Gavin, Nick isn't—" her mom started to say, but Gavin interjected

"He is! He is!" her son shouted. He stamped his feet, screaming again. The behavior was unlike him, and it terrified Ivy. "I want Nick!"

"No!"

"I hate you!" Gavin shouted. Ivy gasped as Gavin threw the remote at her feet. "You ruined everything! I want Nick!"

"Go to your room!" Ivy screamed, and she surged to her feet. Gavin glowered up at her, hiccuping, sobbing, as he clenched his fists. "Now Gavin, or I'll—I'll—I'll ground you!" Her heart broke when his entire posture dropped. She hated Nick. She hated what he had done to her son's poor heart. She hated herself for falling for it.

"I hate you both!" Gavin shouted again before he disappeared down the hall to her old room that was now his for sleepovers. The bedroom door slammed.

"Jesus Christ, Ivy Holly Moore!" Her mother gasped. "Tell me everything."

Ivy looked into her mom's eyes, and finally, after an hour of panic and confusion, she broke down. She fell to her knees, sobbing at her stupidity and her naivety. Pain shot through her, turning her stomach, and making the world spin around her. Her mother was on the floor beside her in an instant, wrapping her tightly in her arms.

"Mommy's here. Shhh, you're safe. You're safe," Fiona murmured in her ear. Ivy didn't know if she really was or if she ever would be again.

***

Far away beyond the protective magic of the Arctic Circle, Aldwin materialized in his mothers kitchen.

"Aldwin, sweetling, what happened to your face?" his mum asked.

Aldwin stumbled into the counter, his panic and desperation had made him unsteady in his landing. He groaned at his sore shin, which protested again being smacked into a drawer. Soft hands caught his arms, steadying him, and his mothers face swam into view.

"Aldwin, your lip is bleeding! What happened?"

"Ivy happened," he said. Then he touched his lip, pulling his finger away to look at the vermilion liquid stuck to it. He winced and wiped it on his pants.

"What? What do you mean?" she asked again. Aldwin sighed in relief as his mum gently touched his lip, and her magic mended the split with a tingle.

"She found the letters," groaned Aldwin. "I tried, Mum, I tried to explain, but she thought I was stalking her. She attacked me, and then she ran off with Gavin." He worked his sore jaw, swallowing. One thing was for sure, Ivy packed one hell of a wallop. "I need to talk to Dah." He started limping towards the door when it flew open.

"I'm going to Ostcrest, now. Gavin is almost on the naughty list, and Ivy isn't showing on the tracker," his Dah's booming voice preceded him into the kitchen. "Aldwin!" His Dah paused eyes wild in panic. "Aldwin, what in the blazes happened to your face?"

"Ivy did, Dah," grunted Aldwin. His father grimaced and pointed to a chair. Aldwin fell into it, just as his mum knelt down to roll up his pants leg. "Ivy found the letters. She wouldn't listen. She ran. I need to find them!"

"She thinks he was stalking them," Cateline added, and her palm pressed against the bruised shin. In a shiver, the aching pain was gone. Then she cupped his swollen jaw.

"Well, Gavin's at his gran's. I'm assuming Ivy is there too," his Dah said and reached over to pat his arm. "Take a second, Aldwin. Think about this."

"I won't lose her. I can't." Aldwin shook his head.

He could feel their absence like a wrenching pull to his gut. There was no thinking about it, at all. This was his future at stake. She was his soulmate. He needed her as much as he needed to breathe and eat. The thought of being without her felt like a thousand icicles were ripping apart his very being. The throb in his jaw dissipated.

"I'll be back, with them both. Okay, I'll be back."

"Aldwin, think it through boy!" Santa bellowed. His fathers voice, normally so calm, boomed with the authority of one of the Ageless council. Aldwin fell back to the chair, his mind reeling. "She thinks you were stalking her, and she ran off. More than likely she's got police there."

"I don't care,." Aldwin shook his head, staring down at the hands that had so recently held Gavin up to help him put a star on the tree. "I'll just pop in, grab their arms, and bring them here. Once she sees—" he was cut off again.

"No! Don't be stupid," his mother snapped and shoved him back down into the chair. "Do you want to start another hunt?"

"I won't start—"

"If you show up there, just appear in an apartment full of cops, you'll reveal us all," his father said. Dah slammed his hand down on the table. "You were a child, Aldwin, during the last global hunt! You don't remember what it was like! It wasn't just Ageless who suffered. Thousands of innocent humans were burned, hanged, beheaded, and drowned!" Aldwin tried to open his mouth, to protest that the cops wouldn't even have time to realize what was happening, but he didn't have a chance. "I forbid it!" The power of Santa's magic sizzled in the air, and Aldwin swallowed, shuddering at the magnitude.

"But Dah, she's my soulmate!" Aldwin shouted back. He met his fathers eyes, pleading with him, begging him silently to undo his edict. The frozen knives twisted tighter in his gut. He wanted to curl up and sob. "Imagine if you were separated from Mum but a million times worse! You know this is hurting us—me and Ivy."

"Kristofer, he's right. Look at him. He can barely control his magic," said Cateline. Aldwin looked down, watching in shock as ice frosted across the table from his palm. "Aldwin, calm down, love. Just breathe and focus" His mothers touch on his cheek was gentle, soothing.

"It's nearly Christmas Eve, Aldwin," his Dah said. His voice softened slightly, and he reached out to cover his hand. "Here's what we'll do. We'll go on the journey, like always. This will give Ivy time to calm down and for the police to leave. Then, when we get to Gavin, I'll speak with her." Aldwin shook his head. It wouldn't work. It couldn't work. Ivy would just attack him too, and Fiona would join in. That was if Alex wasn't there. If he was, then things would be bad.

"Aldwin, listen to your father. You have to calm down. You have to accompany him on this trip, and you know it. Trust him." She stroked his hair, and then she kissed his brow. "Come on, my little snowball. Come have some tea."

"You have to promise, Dah. Do you promise to take me to her?" Aldwin asked as he stood. His whole being ached at the thought of Ivy's hatred for him. His father nodded. He let his mum take his hand. Silently he followed her to his room and settled onto the massive bed. He stared numbly at the floor.

What if this was the end, though? Lewin had said he didn't know how the magic would react with her being mortal and Aldwin being Ageless. What if the bond had broken because of her rage and doubt? What if that was why it hurt so deeply and why it was driving his magic out of control as tiny flurries spun in the air?

"Mum, I feel like I'm dying," he whispered, looking up at her when she summoned a tea tray.

"I know, Aldwin darling, I know. Your Dah will get you to her. He's very persuasive," she said. He took the cup she offered but couldn't taste it at all. He felt as if his entire world was falling to pieces, just like how the hot liquid was turning to ice in his grasp. "Aldwin, stop. You have to focus. Come now, breathe."

"Mum, I'm terrified. I can't lose her. I can't lose Gavin. They're my everything," he sobbed. He tried to push his tears away. Then he drew a shaky breath, attempted to center himself, and with a herculean effort, his magic settled to a barely restrained level.

"It'll all work out," Cateline said. His mother stroked his hair, reminding him of when he was a child. There was always a soothing quality to her presence. "Now, there we go. Why don't I show you what I made, hmm? It's your very first Santa suit."

"Sure," said Aldwin.

He set the cup aside and dragged his hands down his face. His mum was right. Dah would help him fix this. Aldwin just had to pull himself together until they got there.

"Look, love. I know you don't normally like the vests, but," his mother said.

Aldwin looked up, and what his mum was holding made him blink. He'd expected a variant of his fathers suit, but it wasn't like that at all. She was holding up a red three-piece suit and running down the material were thin white pinstripes. Underneath was a white shirt, a matching pinstripe vest, and a red and white tie with swirling ivy vines. In her other hand was a pair of black high-top sneakers.

"Do you like it?"

"Mum! I love it!" He half cried in surprise.

He was moved by the thought and consideration she must have put into it, how she had taken careful consideration that he had never really been one to want to wear the heavy, ceremonial furs like his Dah except at council meetings. He shot to his feet.

"It's perfect. It's so perfect." He reached out and took the hanger, holding it up.

"It's you, Aldwin. I knew you would want something unique," she said. "I knew you would want to look like yourself." She rubbed his back, and Aldwin swallowed. He had to get his head on straight. Millions of children were counting on him and on his Dah. "Go put it on. You'll be steadier when you do."

"Yeah, yeah. Right." He took the shoes and stumbled to his en-suite.

There he pulled the suit on by hand, not trusting his magic quite yet. The last thing he wanted was to destroy it with tiny icicles. He and Dah would get to Ostcrest, and Ivy would know the truth. How could she not believe it then? If they were at Fiona's, then he'd be able to tell her too, get her blessing. Breathing deeply, he tied his tie, smoothed his coat, and combed his hair. Then he walked back out to his mum.

"Oh, Aldwin. You look perfect," she gushed. He hugged her tightly and leaned down to bury his face in her shoulder. Even at nine hundred years old, her scent radiated comfort that made the world seem a bit less insane. "Now, love, go down and help your father harness the reindeer." She held up the long, fur-trimmed red coat he always wore. The cold of the mortal realm didn't bother him but jumping between realms could get chilly.

"Yes ma'am," Aldwin said. He kissed her cheek, then he forced his feet to move to the hall. He just had to hold on. In a few hours, he'd have Ivy again. He'd have Gavin. His world would be perfect once more. As he approached the waiting sleigh, he took Ruby's halter from one of the stable sprites. "Come on, Ruby. It's time to fly."

***

Back at Fiona's apartment, Ivy paced the kitchen, wringing her hands.

She stared at her and her mom's phones on the table. She needed to call the police; she knew that. Yet, she was uncertain. The world felt wrong. The rage and fury had faded, and in its place, she felt like her soul was being shredded. She couldn't think right. Everything was hazy and unfocused.

"Are you gonna puke again?" her mum asked and sat down with a can of ginger ale.

"No, maybe." Ivy whimpered and pulled at her hair. Gavin's never-ending sobs from down the hall twisted her heart. She shouldn't have shouted at him and threatened to ground him. "Mom, I feel like I'm dying." She leaned against the sink and whined when her stomach rolled again, making her clutch it.

"Ivy, you're not pregnant, are you?" her mom yelped.

"Fuck no!" Ivy sobbed.

The idea was impossible, and the image it conjured in her mind horrified her. Thank heavens she'd gone on the shot because Ivy didn't think she could handle this if they had slipped up like that. What was he going to do to her? Nick, or whatever his name really was, had access to everything—her house, her laptop, and her work schedule. Hell, he could be outside right now, waiting.

"You have to call the police. Who gives a shit that you left the proof at the house," urged Fiona. She shoved a phone at her. "You need protection! Gavin needs protection!" Ivy took it, but her stomach ripped again, and she heaved frothy foam into the sink. "Oh my god, did he give you anything to eat before you left?"

"No, he was out. God, I hurt. I hurt all over," groaned Ivy. She rinsed her mouth, gagging at the cold water. "Need to think. Please, Mom, I need to think."

She spun from the sink. Gavin's muffled sobs made it so hard to concentrate. She didn't know what to do first. Ivy knew she never should have screamed at Gavin. It wasn't his fault, and he didn't understand. She'd go calm him down, apologize to him, and then she'd call Alex. The apartment was suddenly silent, and Gavin's sobs stopped. Her poor boy had probably cried himself to sleep.

"I'm gonna go get Gavin tucked in and make sure he's asleep. Then I'll call Alex."

"Okay. I'll make you some chamomile tea and some broth for your stomach," Fiona said with a soft rub of Ivy's back.

Ivy nodded, wiping her sore face roughly. She staggered into the hall and tried to compose herself. Quietly, she turned the knob and stepped into the dark room.

"Gavin, baby, are you asleep?" The smell of baking cookies washed over her, and with it came the aroma of pine and pipe tobacco. Ivy knew that scent. Three times Gavin had gone out with Nick and came back smelling like that.

"Gavin!" She slammed the light switch up and her gaze landed on the empty bed. "No! No! Gavin!"

Ivy ripped open the tiny closet, but it too was bare, holding only the clothes her mom kept.

"Gavin? Gavin? Come out right now!" Spinning around, she dropped down to check under the bed. All that was there were a few books. "Mom! Gavin's gone!"

"What!" Fiona shouted. The sound of glass shattering from the kitchen filled Ivy with panic. "Check the bathroom!"

Ivy scrambled to the bathroom door, ripping it open, yanking the shower curtain back so hard it ripped from the rings. It was empty.

"Gavin!" she screeched. Ivy spun, yanking open the cabinets under the sink. "Mommy! I can't find him!"

"He's not in my room either!" Fiona shouted. There was a brief silence. "Ivy! The window! The fire escape!"

"Shit!" Ivy cried out.

She tripped over her feet as she raced back to Gavin's room. She yanked the curtains open, freezing when she found the latch was still locked from the inside. She flipped it and leaned out to look at the metal steps. There were no prints in the slushy snow gathered on them.

"Mom! It was locked! There are no prints!" Ivy shouted. She turned in the empty room and howled out the pain and anguish and fear in her soul. "Gavin!"

Ivy couldn't breathe.

She raced back into the hall. Shoving her mom aside, she grabbed her phone. She pressed her thumb to the contact that would mean help, which had always meant help. It rang four times before a cheerful voice answered.

"Ivy, hey. Sorry, it took so long to answer. I was, err, busy." Alex sounded happy and breathless.

"Alex, Nick kidnapped Gavin," gasped Ivy. Then she slid to the floor and began to sob. "From my mom's. Please, please. I need you, Alex, he has my baby."

"Don't move! Don't go anywhere. I'm coming," said Alex, all happiness gone from his voice. The call ended, and Ivy looked up at her mom. Fiona dropped to her knees beside her.

"It's all my fault. It's all my fault." Ivy clung to her mother. "It's all my fault!" Ivy felt like her world had just been blown to pieces. "I should've called first. I should have, Mom, I should have protected him." Fiona held her tightly, as they both sobbed and waited.

***

Gavin had been tired of Mummy crying and puking. He liked calling her Mummy, like how Nick said it. He missed Nick. It wasn't fair. Nick wasn't a liar, and he wasn't a bad man. She wouldn't listen to him, though. He hated crying, but Mummy had shouted at him. She was scared, and Mummy never got scared. He had to fix this. He had to bring Nick back so he could explain. How, though?

He gasped for air and sat on the bed. He shoved his hands in his pockets. Mummy always left tissues in his pockets. He needed a tissue for his snot. He froze when his fingers wrapped around a piece of metal. Why was there metal in his pocket? Gavin pulled it out, blinking at the old, faded key. Why was there a key in his pocket? Oh yeah! It was one of Santa's keys! Nick said it would take him to the North Pole!

"I'll get Santa. He'll 'splain to Mummy. She has to believe him," Gavin said to himself. Wiping his nose on his sleeve, he scrambled off the bed. "I'll make Mummy love Nick again. Then we'll be a family." Sniffling, he raised the key up and slid it into the lock.

It fit! Of course, it did. Nick said it would.

Eagerly, Gavin turned it, and the door changed. It was a huge wooden one now, with a big golden, metal handle. He pulled it open, shouting in triumph as he saw the long hallway and the plant slowly drifting down to its pot.

"Nick!" he shouted, shutting the door behind him. "Nick! Where are you?" Gavin hurried down the hallway, listening for Nick's voice.

"Gavin, my little bluebird, is that you?" Nana Claus asked, and she came into the hall.

"Nana!" he cried. Then he sprinted to her and threw his arms around her skirts. "Nana! Nana! I need help! Mummy and Nick had a fight! Mummy said he's bad, but he's not!" He blinked back tears as she pulled him up for a hug. "Where's Santa? He can fix this! He can prove to Mummy that Nick's his son!"

"Gavin, love, Aldwin, and Santa already left," said Nana. She carried him to the kitchen and put him on the counter. "There we go, calm down." He sucked in a shaky breath when she wiped his cheek with a tissue. He looked up into her blue eyes. She looked sad too, sad like Mummy and Gran. "How did you get here? Did Lewin bring you?"

"No, I had a key. See," he said and pulled it out of his pocket. "I didn't mean to take it, but I'm glad I did." He let her pull it from his hand before she softly stroked his cheek. "Can you come with me then, to show Mummy?"

"Honey, I can't leave until they get back," said Nana. She turned, pointing to a wall that had a huge map with a blinking red dot. "I have to track them in case something happens. All the workers have gone home until summer. It's just me right now."

"Oh." Gavin didn't know what to do then. He had been counting on them going back with him. "Mummy's gonna be worried. Nana, can you call her?"

"Do you know her number?" asked Nana. Gavin shook his head. He knew the house number, in case he had to call nine-one-one, but not Mummy's cell phone. "Okay, well. Let Nana see what she can do. Why don't we go get you washed off and some food?"

"I'm starving," announced Gavin.

He hadn't had lunch, and then Mummy had sent him to his room before dinner. Mummy was so mad. He was gonna be in trouble when Nick or Santa took him home. He'd never been grounded before, but Mummy had said she would do it. He hoped it didn't mean he couldn't go to the chess league.

"Sit here, little bird," said Nana and carried him over to a big chair. With a flip of her hand, a plate of grilled cheese and a glass of milk appeared. "I'm going to go run you a bath, and then I'll get you some clean clothes. Can you watch that map for me and shout if it starts flashing red all over?"

"You betcha!" Gavin exclaimed. Then took a bite of his grilled cheese, and Nana did that poofing teleportation thing. She wasn't gone long, and he'd just finished his milk when she reappeared.

"You remember where Aldwin's room is, yeah?" She asked. Gavin nodded and wiped his mouth off. He felt better with a full tummy, but he'd feel much better if he knew Mummy and Nick were happy again. "Well, I ran you a bath in there, and I left some nice, warm pajamas for you. Go on then, and then come right back."

"Yes ma'am," Gavin said.

He slid off the chair, hurrying down the hall, up the stairs, to the second door on the left. He pushed it open, and he smiled because it smelled like Nick. Sure enough, Nana had run him a bath, with shiny, blue bubbles that smelled like Christmas trees. He stripped down, struggling with his boots, then jumped in to wash off.

"Mummy and Nick have to make up," he said to the rubber ducks floating in the bubbles. "They're soulmates. That's what he said. Soulmates have to love each other."

It was nice to be clean and to have his snot and tears all gone. Gavin climbed out, drying off as best he could. Mummy or Nick usually helped, but he could get most of the water. There were some jimjams folded on the counter, and he pulled them on. Then he hurried back down to Nana.

"All clean," he announced to her. Then he yawned. Gosh, he was tired. Crying took a lot of energy, and what he really wanted was to snuggle up with Nick and Mummy in bed like he had the other day.

"Oh, look at you. Come here. Nana will rock you, while we watch the map," said Nana. She made a big, comfy-looking chair appear and sat down. Gavin liked that idea. "Don't you worry your precious little head about Mummy and Aldwin. Santa and Aldwin have a plan for your mum." He climbed on her lap, yawning again as she snuggled him close to her. Nana always smelled so nice, like cookies and Christmas trees.

"Where are they now?" he asked. He didn't know much about the maps, but they were over some big water.

"Almost to Japan," whispered Nana. Then she began to hum, and she rocked in the chair. It was nice, so comfy, and she had a pretty voice. He really tried to stay awake, but his eyes were so heavy. He'd just rest them for a minute, and then he'd check the map again.

The Truth At Last

"**D**rink Ivy."

"No. I can't," said Ivy.

She threw her phoned aside and knew Alex was going to be pissed. She'd broken the cardinal rule of kidnapping. She'd called Nick, but it had gone straight to voicemail.

"I can't, not until my son is home!" She stared out the window and watched as the wind whipped the nasty, wet, slushy snow past. Gavin had wanted snow for Christmas, even if it was like this. It was mere hours away from Christmas Eve, and her baby was somewhere with a lunatic.

The room was suddenly awash in the aroma of cologne, melted chocolate, and something inexplicably seductive that made her heart flutter. She spun, trying to locate the aroma, and then Alex appeared right in front of her, with a puff of pink and gold glitter. He wasn't alone, either. Lewin had him wrapped in his arms.

"What the hell!" Ivy shouted at the same time as her mom.

Alex stumbled out of Lewin's arms, looking a bit stunned. Her mind tried to point out that two men had just appeared out of thin air, but her maternal instinct locked in on Lewin. Lewin was Nick's friend, and Nick had Gavin. She charged at him.

"Where's my son?" She howled, grabbing him by the shirt and slamming him into the wall. "Where did that bastard take him?" Suddenly Ivy wasn't holding anything except a fistful of glitter. "What the f—" she stuttered and turned around

"Nick didn't kidnap Gavin." Lewin huffed, rubbing his chest. He was hovering cross-legged over their heads. "He would never hurt Gavin or you."

"Okay, what the hell is going on!" Fiona screeched, and Alex gaped in shock at Lewin.

"How? How?" Alex pointed behind him then back at the room. "Okay, what the hell just happened!"

Ivy didn't care what happened. She cared about finding her son.

"Everybody needs to calm down," Lewin said. "Now, can I come down or will you try to kill me again?"

Ivy sank to the sofa, her mind flailing to think of an explanation, a logical one. She was hallucinating, delirious from throwing up.

"Please, Lewin. Gavin's gone. He didn't come past us, and he couldn't get the window open on his own. Nick has him! I know he does. I smelled him."

"Ivy, um, you are aware that my boyfriend just teleported me from my living room to your mom's, aren't you?" Alex asked as he hurried over to touch her shoulder. "Maybe we should let him speak…" his voice trailed off. Then she jumped when he shouted. "No, fuck that. What the hell Lewin? How!"

"Uh, magic, duh," snorted Lewin. He sank down to the floor, and he twisted his hand in the air. A bottle of scotch and two cups appeared in it. "I think Ivy needs one of these." He tapped the bottle to the glass, and Ivy yelped when it filled without even opening the bottle. "And Fiona." He handed off the glasses to them, but Ivy didn't drink. "Now, everybody just take a breath."

"What are you?" Ivy gasped the question out in stereo with Alex, who had sunk to the arm of the sofa and was rubbing her shoulder.

"Cupid," Lewin said. He shrugged, and massive gold wings spread behind him, gusting them as he flexed the feathers. "Well, technically a cupid, one of the three Supremes." He shrugged again and the wings were gone.

This couldn't be happening. Ivy was losing her mind. She passed out and hit her head. That was the only explanation. She'd wake up in a minute.

"Where was Gavin last?"

"Ivy's old room," whispered Fiona, gaping in shock.

"Show me," Lewin said.

Ivy nodded, stumbling to her feet.

"I sent him in here. Uh, I found out Nick was stalking me," she said. Then she tucked her hair behind her ear and curled into Alex's side as they opened the door. "Since Florida. I found these letters."

"Nick wasn't stalking you, Ives," said Lewin as he stepped into the room. She watched him pause, tilt his head back, breathing in. Then he smiled, a broad thing that made him giggle. "And his name isn't Nicholas. It's Aldwin Nicholas Claus, the only child of Kristofer Claus, currently known as Santa."

"Hang on, you're Cupid, and Nick is Santa's son?" Alex barked out a laugh. "Oh, great. This is one hell of a prank. Good one Ivy."

She blinked up at him, letting her tears fall again. How could he even dream she would pull a prank like this with her son?

"They're all crazy, Alex," Ivy said. "He has to be in on this!" She tugged his sleeve, her mind refusing to accept it. Ivy's stomach jerked painfully, and she went down on her knees, gagging up froth onto the carpet.

"Stop trying to sever your bond! Do you want to rip your soul in half?" Lewin shouted before he hauled her up, and Ivy shoved him away. "You're hurting Aldwin too! A soulmate bond can only be safely broken by death! Stop fighting it."

"Fuck off!" Ivy howled. Then she swung at him, and that tearing, stabbing sensation shot through her. Alex caught her when she fell. "Where did he take my son? I want my son!"

"Gaia's crown," snapped Lewin and threw his hands up with a groan. "He didn't take Gavin. Aldwin and Santa are—" he paused, glanced down at his watch, and Ivy finally regained her legs again. "Probably starting on China."

"My grandson's in China?" Fiona shrieked and pounced. Ivy shouted as Lewin disappeared, making her mom crash into Gavin's bed. "Jesus Christ! How?"

"Magic, Fiona, magic, what don't you all get about that?" Lewin asked with a huff from behind her and Alex. Ivy spun, and the room tilted dangerously. "And, no, Gavin isn't in China." He drew in a deep breath again. "Naughty boy that he is, he ran away, and I know where, too."

"Why would he run away?!" Alex cried. he looked down at Ivy, but before she could explain, Lewin's words sank in. He knew where Gavin was.

"Where? Where did he run away to?!" She pleaded. Ivy snatched his hand and stared up at him from her spot on the floor. "Lewin, where's Gavin? Please, I need my son!"

"He ran away to the North Pole," said Lewin as if it was the most obvious answer in the world. Why did he keep sniffing like that? "Yep, those are definitely Mama Claus' cookies and Kris's pipe tobacco. How though?" Ivy didn't believe a word of this, at all.

Then Lewin touched the door and closed his eyes. "Gavin, you sneaky little monkey," Lewin chuckled. "He stole a Key of Winter."

"What?" demanded Fiona. She looked murderous, but Lewin was laughing loudly. "This isn't funny."

"The North Pole isn't real! Stop laughing!" Ivy screamed. She tried to hit Lewin, but her abdomen twisted again, harder, more intense than before. She swore she heard Nick shout in pain just behind her. When she looked back, she found nothing but the wall. Then, her knees buckled.

"I believe you, Lewin," said Alex. He sounded so confident, but Ivy couldn't think anymore. "Ivy, stop fighting this. You saw us appear, and you saw his wings."

She shook her head, gagging. This wasn't possible.

"I believe you too. Now take us to my grandson!" ordered Fiona.

"Give me Ivy," murmured Lewin. Then she was in his arms. Ivy tried to scream, to fight, but the pain was unbearable. "Fiona, Alex, take my elbows and hold on tight." The world exploded.

Ivy's chest felt tight and stretched all at once. Lights burst around her, and her heart tumbled as she spun. A kitchen formed around them, full of that rich aroma she'd always smelled on Gavin when Nick took him out and in the bedroom.

"Lewin Amoriel, what have you—oh my stars, Ivy!" A woman shouted. A pair of wizened, kind eyes met hers, wide with concern. "Can you stand, my girl? Lewin put her down."

"Who are you?" Fiona snapped.

Ivy was glad her mom asked because it was taking all her energy not to fall over. The woman smiled, and she took Ivy by the waist. She smelled so lovely, like cookies and pine trees and peaceful nights.

"My name is Cateline, Cateline Claus," the woman said, rubbing Ivy's back. "And I believe you're here for Gavin. Come with me."

"Alex!" cried Ivy. She flailed for her friend, clinging to his arm as she followed the woman up the stairs. All around her, the house was marvelous, filled with impossible things like floating plants and mini constellations above pedestals. Her mum and Alex gasped in awe as they followed.

"Gavin, showed up about two hours ago, a right mess. I couldn't bring him home, sorry," explained Cateline. She opened a door, and Ivy gasped. Gavin was curled up on a massive bed, under a warm-looking blanket. He looked so peaceful, freshly bathed, and sleeping soundly. "I fixed him some dinner and put him to bed. I was going to have Kristofer or Aldwin bring him back when they returned."

"Gavin!" Ivy sobbed. She stumbled forward to the bed. He was here! He was here and safe and sleeping. "Gavin, baby, Mommy's here." She leaned down and dropped kisses all over his face and hair, but she froze as she smelled his skin and the blankets he was under. It was the same scent Nick carried. She hauled her son into her arms and gazed around the room. Her stomach hurt too much for this to be a dream.

"Ivy, you know who I am, don't you?" asked Cateline as she eased her way forward to stroke Ivy's sweat-soaked hair.

"You're Mrs. Claus," she whispered.

There was no denying what was around her or how she had gotten there. It was true. It was all true. She was actually at the North Pole with Mrs. Claus.

"But Nick! He...the letters...the necklace!" Ivy didn't know how to explain the confusion in her soul.

"Aldwin is next in line to be Santa," said Mrs. Claus, sitting down beside her. "Kristofer gave him the letters, and Lewin tracked your love for Aaron to find the necklace."

Ivy kissed Gavin's hair and cradled him in her arms. Nick wasn't Nick. Nick was Aldwin. He wasn't a stalker. He was Santa's son.

"What've I done?" Ivy whispered in horror. The pain in her soul vanished, but it was replaced by guilt and regret so deep it choked her. "I hit him. I screamed at him."

"Mummy," Gavin whispered. His eyes fluttered open. "Mummy! You're here!"

"Hey, so am I!" Fiona snorted.

"Gran! Uncle Alex! Lewin!" Gavin exclaimed. He wriggled in excitement, hugging Ivy so fiercely she thought his enthusiasm would choke her. "Nana! Nana! Look! It's my family!"

"Nana?" whispered Ivy and looked over at Cateline, who smiled sheepishly. She would talk about that later. At that moment she had more important things to say. "Gavin, baby, I'm sorry I shouted and cursed at you. I'm so sorry. I wasn't myself. Please forgive me."

"It's okay Mummy. I know, and I'm sorry I ran away. I just wanted to get Nick and Santa. I wanted you to believe," her son said. He snuggled into her neck, sniffling softly.

"Oh baby, I believe. I believe," Ivy said. She stroked his messy hair, squeezing him tightly. "Listen, why don't you lay back down, 'kay. Mommy just needs to talk to Mrs. Claus for a minute." She shifted him back to the sheets and tucked him in.

"I'll lay with him, Ivy," her mom said. She was toeing off her shoes, and Ivy smiled her thanks at the offer. This was one conversation she'd rather have in private.

"And I think Lewin and I will go have a nice chat about things like secrets," added Alex. He smiled, but Ivy could see Lewin was about to get an unpleasant tongue lashing. They disappeared into the hall.

"How are you feeling?" asked Cateline. Ivy took Cateline's hand, and the woman led her into the hall. "Your color's back, and you aren't falling over."

"Bit better, but I'm just overwhelmed." Ivy glanced over at her, drawing a breath. She ran a hand through her hair, trying to wrap her mind around all of this. "Mrs. Claus, I'm so sorry. I thought he was dangerous."

"Shhh, pet, I know," said Cateline. Ivy sighed as the woman patted her cheek. "Aldwin told me all about it. Don't worry about his face and leg. I healed them right up. You reacted how any frightened mum would."

They were back in the kitchen, and Ivy blinked in awe at the magic coming to life around her. With simple waves, the woman summoned a kettle from the fire and a tray of cups from a shelf. A bowl appeared, filled with steaming soup.

"I've never actually witnessed someone trying to sever a soulmate bond, but I imagine you're properly famished. Have a seat."

"Mrs.—"

"Call me Cateline or Mama Claus. Missus is too formal for the woman my son loves," Mama Claus said while she poured the tea. Suddenly a beep went off, and Ivy watched her hurry to a huge map on the far wall. She was staring at a blinking red dot. "I told them not to fly too close to that airport. Bet my left arm Aldwin's driving tonight," she sighed, shaking her head. "He's had more near-crashes in seven hundred years than his father's had in a thousand." Ivy choked on her soup, as she gasped for air.

"Seven hundred? Nick is seven hundred?" Ivy asked. The shock nearly made her dizzy.

"Eight hundred and ninety-nine actually," Cateline said. She had settled back across from Ivy. "His birthday is Christmas Day, fifteen minutes after sunrise." She smiled, but Ivy's mind was racing too much to return it.

He was nine hundred! Nick, or well Aldwin, was nine hundred years old. No wonder he was so good with Gavin. He probably had dozens of kids that were grown.

"I know that look, Ivy. Any mum would. What's troubling you?"

"He's nine hundred, and I'm only twenty-five. He has kids older than me," whispered Ivy. She stared down at her soup and tried to hide her fear.

"Aldwin doesn't have children, Ivy. You're the first woman he's ever truly loved." Those soft, patient hands covered hers. "He does love you, and Gavin, with all his heart. When you left, he was barely in control of his magic."

"We're really soulmates?" Ivy's head spun as she processed that. "Oh, God. I hurt him! Mama Claus, I said so many horrible things."

How could he ever forgive her? She'd ruined everything. How could he ever want her again, after she dismissed him so easily? Her stupid, horrible doubts that had always threatened to overwhelm her had violated their love. "Oh my God, what if I severed the bond? What if the pain is gone because I ruined it?"

"You'd both be in comas if that were the case," murmured Cateline. "Eat, Ivy dear. Then we'll get you and your mum some fresh clothes and warm baths, hm? Trust me, Aldwin will be over the moon to find you waiting here."

Ivy nodded and picked up her spoon. She did have one thought, something she was afraid to ask. If Nick was nine hundred and barely looked a day over thirty-five, what would happen when she aged? Shoving that aside, she yielded to her angry stomach, filling it with the stew.

***

Far below in Ostcrest, Aldwin materialized in the house he'd begun to call home.

"Where are they?" he asked and groaned in dismay as he stared around the empty house. Fiona's apartment had been empty too, as had Alex's. Since the pain that had been torturing him all night had subsided, he could catch his breath and control his magic.

"Hospital maybe? There were multiple vomit-soaked towels at her mum's," his Dah said, setting Gavin's gift under the tree. It was a train set, just like he'd wanted. "You're magic, so the pain from the bond won't be as bad as it is for a mortal. Could be the pain stopped on your end because she's sedated."

"Or maybe she severed it." Aldwin rubbed his aching throat. Hours before, while crossing the Sea of Japan, he'd been racked with pain so badly he'd nearly fallen out of the sleigh, and he swore he'd heard Ivy sobbing in agony. Shortly after that, the pain ceased altogether. The thought was killing him.

"Pretty sure you'd be unconscious, Aldwin," his father said and clapped him on the back. "Come on, son. You can pop around the hospitals as we go. I have a few gifts to deliver to each one."

Aldwin nodded, shooting up to the sleigh. He didn't trust himself to drive, after accidentally veering them into the no-fly zone between North and South Korea. Dodging anti-aircraft weapons was not fun. The distraction of their journey was helping him some, but he found himself reliving the horror on Ivy's face.

It was all his fault. If he had just taken her as soon as Gavin knew, then this would never have happened. She'd be with his mum, having cocoa, watching the map while Gavin slept. Ivy would be waiting, bundled in furs, outside the stable come Christmas morning, holding the Hearth Light for the reindeer to find. They'd kiss, hug, and he would drop down on one knee to ask her to be his wife and to let him be Gavin's father. That wasn't happening anymore, and it was killing him inside.

Ivy and Gavin were all he wanted, but they were gone. He couldn't find them anywhere, not in any of the hospitals, not even at any of Gavin's classmate's houses. As they jumped over the realm gap, Aldwin felt his hope waning. He hadn't felt Ivy or Gavin anywhere in all of Ostcrest.

Gavin's bright belief hadn't glowed like the millions of other children. Ivy had somehow severed the bond, and she had somehow crushed Gavin's faith. It was the only explanation. In the frigid air, he wiped his tears and did his best to ignore the pointless box he'd tucked in his pocket just in case.

It was over.

Hearth and Home

"Here we are then," said Cateline Her voice startled Ivy out of dozing off. Ivy shook her hair from her face, tearing her eyes away from the map. "I tried to catch them, but they were off to Fort Leavenworth before I could." Ivy blinked as she saw the woman was carrying a massive, red, sack. "But I managed to get these. Where are they?"

"Uh, Texas," whispered Ivy. She rubbed her eyes, standing up as Mama Claus set the sack down and waved her hands.

Ivy squeaked in shock when it opened, and her Christmas tree slowly rose into the air to come to rest in the furthest corner by the door. The stockings came next, hangers and all, to neatly settle on the mantle of the fireplace beside the map and chair. The lights swirled up to drape from the rafters above them. "Oh, Mama Claus, you didn't." Tears stung her eyes as the presents, all of them, including Gavin's bike which was now assembled, came spiraling out.

"Oh, well, of course, I did," chuckled Mama Claus. She snapped her fingers, and the sack disappeared. "Can't have our first Christmas without all of this!"

"First Christmas?" asked Ivy. She was confused. They were literally Mother and Father Christmas. They were the perfect embodiment of the holiday. "Surely you've had Christmas."

"Well, no, not since I was mortal. Our Christmas usually consists of the pair of them eating breakfast the size of Alaska and then passing out." Cateline kissed her brow, before sitting down in her rocking chair.

At first, Ivy had been a bit unnerved by Nick's mom. She was just so loving, so likable, and she talked as if Ivy was already her daughter and Gavin was her grandson. After a few hours, it had felt as natural as breathing. Her words took Ivy by surprise though.

"You were mortal, like me?" She asked

"Yes, about a thousand years ago," said Cateline. She waved her hand, and another chair appeared.

This one was thicker, bigger, with pockets on the side filled with books. Ivy didn't even have to smell the rich leather to know it was Nick's. She curled up in it, giggling as a blanket popped into existence and draped over her. She would never get over how marvelous the magic was.

"It's a long story, but in short, I accidentally caught Kristofer delivering my niece's gifts. We weren't marked by a cupid, like you and Aldwin, but it was still 'love-at-first -sight'. He came back the next morning, with his mother, Winter, and his grandmother, Gaia. Well, you know her as-"

"Mother Nature. Aldwin told us about her," yawned Ivy. In her mind, he was still Nick, but Ivy loved how his name felt on her tongue. It was beautifully odd like him, ancient but brand new. "How have you lived so long?"

"Kristofer and I married Christmas morning. As a wedding gift, Gaia and Winter used their magic to make me into a winter sprite, so I could spend eternity with him," Cateline sighed wistfully. "They'll offer you the same when you're ready to remarry. I imagine it's probably hard to think about, after losing your other soulmate."

Ivy jerked upright again, head spinning. She'd known it, felt it in her entire being that Aaron had been her soulmate, but hearing it was altogether different.

"So, Aaron and I, we were shot by a cupid too?"

"Mm-hm, Lewin actually. You're his one and only repeat mark," said Cateline. "Oh, snowflake, he apparently had a proper fit when he marked you and Aldwin. Mostly, I think, out of fear that Aldwin was going to pluck his wings."

"He knew?" asked Ivy. That was news to her. "Nick, he knew from the beginning that we were soulmates?" Cateline nodded, and Ivy's heart fluttered in adoration. "He was so patient with me. It must've been driving him nuts knowing but watching me fighting it."

"No, Ivy, no, Aldwin was happy with just being near you," said Cateline. "He would have waited forever if you needed him to." The woman chuckled. "Now, get some rest. It's almost midnight, and you've been up since seven yesterday! I'll wake you up when they start coming back."

She was right. Gavin and her mum had both slept from the night of the twenty-third until six in the morning on the twenty-fourth. Ivy had been unable to sleep much herself, what with Gavin dragging her here and there, inside and outside, to the snow gardens, the greenhouse, the stables, the main workshop, Santa's office, and so much more.

She'd caught the odd nap here and there when her mom distracted him with food and making cookies with Mama Claus—or Nana—as he called her. Mama Claus had been more than happy to feed them and clothe them in rich, luxurious furs that made her own mom drool.

"Mama Claus," said Ivy as she snuggled deeper into the chair, pulling the blanket around her. "I'm glad Gavin came to find you." That earned her a gentle chuckle.

She was too tired to think about things like whether or not it was possible to turn someone immortal. Her first concern was getting some rest before it was time to go out and greet Nick and his father. Fiona and Gavin were slumbering peacefully in a guest room since her mom said it was weird to sleep in Nick's bed. Ivy had only stayed up to watch the map in case something happened while Cateline went to try and catch them in Kansas.

"Me too, Ivy, me too," Cateline said. She reached over and tucked the blanket more snugly around her. "Sweet dreams, love."

Ivy sighed in contentment, floating in that crisp pine scent that reminded her of Nick. Just as her eyes were almost closed. She swore she saw Mama Claus pull a smartphone from her plethora of pockets. That was impossible though. There wasn't any reception here. She'd checked.

The demanding mistress, Sleep, refused denial any longer, and Ivy knew nothing.

***

In Washington, Aldwin watched Dah pull his mobile out of his pocket.

"That Mum?" He asked as he jumped back to the sleigh. His Dah had already finished the houses on his side of the street, and he was smiling at the screen.

"Yes," his father said. "She said she's starting breakfast and your cake." His Dah chucked his sack into the sleigh and took up the reins. Aldwin settled in next to him, setting the navigation controls for Fort Stewart. "She's doing triple banana pudding icing." His father chuckled, elbowing him.

"Don't think I can eat," grumbled Aldwin. He leaned his head back, watching the dimensions spark and twist as they slipped through them. "I can't get her out of my head." All he wanted to do was finish their route and get home so he could go find Ivy and Gavin.

"It's love. Of course you can't," chuckled Santa. The reindeer banked a hard westerly turn, as they came out over the base. "Get that radar scrambler up, or we'll set off every alarm."

Aldwin flipped the switch, sighing as they flew in low, under the clouds, towards post housing. Then he went to work. They'd learned long ago, to not lollygag on military installations in any country, particularly in the United States. It was a sure-fire way to end up sending them into a panic. He had to be extra sneaky, as he came down into one house.

Three boys were curled up with Star Wars blankets in front of the tree, with a pair of Dobermans sprawled between them. Luckily, animals recognized magic, particularly peaceful magic, and though the dogs sniffed and eyed him warily, they didn't bark. Waving his fingers, he dropped two bones under the tree and was back on the roof.

Aldwin had always enjoyed the journey, delivering gifts with his Dah, and learning when to reveal enough to one child and when to stay silent. Aldwin couldn't find the thrill in it anymore. Every little boy reminded him of Gavin. Every star topped tree drug him back to that morning. It was halfway through Oregon that he realized something that shook him to his very core.

The aching guilt, the torturous longing that ate him alive and swallowed him whole, was what Ivy had lived with for years. He truly understood why she had been so resistant to his advances, why she had taken so long to open up to even hand-holding.

The idea of even flirting with another person made him recoil in guilt. It would be expected of him, to move on, if she had somehow severed the bond. The line must endure. Christmas had to continue. He tugged at the harness he was adjusting.

"Aldwin, the harnesses are fine. Come on," his father said. Aldwin patted Prancer's neck and scratched Dasher's ear as he headed back to the sleigh. "Nearly done. We just have to finish the rest of Canada, then the eastern pacific islands, and up through Alaska."

"Sorry, Dah. I'm trying," Aldwin said.

He settled into the seat and typed in the next coordinates. The ring box in his pocket felt immensely heavy, but he couldn't throw it away. He couldn't drop it into the icy oceans below. Aldwin just continued on, going through the motions, forcing a smile and a wink when he accidentally woke a little girl with black braids. Snapping three bikes into assembly for a pair of triplets, he glanced down at his watch. They were cutting it close. The mortal dawn was fast approaching.

"One last stop, then home," Santa said. Aldwin waved the reins away when his Dah offered them. "Aldwin, I promise. As soon as we get home, I'll find them, and you'll work it out."

"Uh-huh," Aldwin said. He looked down at his hands, but he couldn't hope. He'd traversed the globe in the last twenty-four hours, but not once had he even caught a whisper of Gavin's thoughts. It was over. He knew when they got home, that Gavin would once again be a non-believer.

***

Back at the North Pole, Ivy was shaken softly.

"Ivy-Ivy wake up," said Cateline. Her voice combined with the alluring aroma of breakfast, coffee, tea, and cocoa drew her back to consciousness. "Look right there," Mama Claus pointed at the map. Ivy rubbed her eyes and stared at it. The blinking red dot was soaring out of Canada towards the big, four-point star that marked where they were.

"Oh my gosh. How long will they take?" asked Ivy and kicked her blankets aside. She stared down at her wrinkled pajamas. "I need to change."

"Hold still, love," Mama Claus said with a laugh, and Ivy froze.

In a flurry of snowflakes that smelled of cookies and cinnamon, she gasped as she felt her clothes change. The warm, flannel pajamas were replaced with thick, soft, black, fleece-lined leggings that disappeared into knee-high red boots trimmed with black and white fur. Over that was a rich, velvet dress of matching red with the same fur along her collar and cuffs. A quick look in the window showed her hair had been tousled to perfection, framing her lightly made-up face, where her lined eyes and red lips drew focus.

"Now, come and have some tea. We need to get you warmed up because you have a very important job to do."

"I do?" Ivy asked. She picked up a cup of tea, sipping it, as the excitement filled her veins. Nick, Aldwin, her soulmate was almost home. It was almost his birthday and Christmas, and she could tell him she was sorry, that she loved him.

"Yes." Mama Claus grinned. "Did you see that post between the main house and stables?" Ivy nodded. "Well, early dawn makes it hard for the team to see where to land. Now, normally I go out and hold the Hearth Light, but I have to finish up in here."

"I'll do it," Ivy said and squirmed anxiously. The map on the wall flashed blue and white. Bells chimed out from it as well, as if heralding their arrival. She chugged her tea, ignoring how it slightly scalded her tongue.

"Here, it's snowing. Put this on."

Ivy put her cup down, and Mama Claus draped a thick, black cloak on her shoulders and pulled the hood up.

"It's enchanted. The wind won't blow it back, and you won't feel the cold either." Then an ancient lantern appeared in her hand. It didn't burn with a flame, so much as it glowed like a star was harnessed inside. "This is The Hearth Light. No matter where you are in the world, as long as the one who loves you holds it, you'll see the light, and you can find your way through anything."

"It's beautiful," crooned Ivy. She took it gently in her hands. "It's tradition, isn't it?" She knew that Nick had installed all sorts of fancy tech into the sleigh.

Gavin had told her all about it, how he had got to turn them on. Ivy didn't even care that those three separate day trips to the museum, park, and shopping had actually been here. She didn't care about anything, except seeing Nick.

"Yes, it is. Now hurry out there and keep your hood up."

Ivy pulled the hood over her hair.

She dashed into the snow. The wind whipped around her, not too roughly, but where her cloak didn't cover it stung from the freezing cold. Holding the Hearth Light ahead of her, she sought out the post in the early morning glow. The clouds blocked the sun, turning the white world shades of gray and orange. Off, in the distance, Ivy saw something. At first, she thought she'd imagined it, but then it appeared again. There was a tiny, glowing red dot headed towards her.

"Find me," she said.

Holding the lantern aloft, she held her head high and the lantern burned in an intense, dazzling glow. She squinted against it, her heart pounding as she heard bells, followed by a faint shout. He was almost there, and Ivy poured all of her love into the lamp.

"Think she missed us?" Aldwin asked his father. He managed to chuckle because the Hearth Light blazed the brightest he'd ever seen.

Rays of gold and silver shot into the air. Dawn had just broken, and it chased them as they approached the North Pole. The reindeer tossed their heads and bellowed out their eagerness to get home. No doubt his mum had filled their stalls to the brim with fresh hay and warm oats, the spoiled brats.

"Oh, I know she did," his father said. Santa barked out a laugh, as he aimed the team into a descent pattern. "Look at her glow. She's a keeper."

"Well, I should hope so. You've been married to her for a thousand years," Aldwin said. He elbowed his Dah, who flashed him a wild look. "What? Oh, I'm sorry, one thousand and one years."

"Happy birthday, Aldwin," his father said. Aldwin looked over in surprise when his Dah handed him the reins mid-turn. "Take us home."

"Dah, are you okay?" He gripped the reins and braced his feet to keep himself center. There was something off about the look on his fathers face. "Dah."

"She's beautiful. That's all. I didn't expect her to be that powerful," whispered Santa.

"Blimey, did you sneak some eggnog at that last stop?" Aldwin rolled his eyes, then returned his focus to the Hearth Light.

Ruby bayed and huffed, stirring up the team into a frenzy. His mum's dark, enchanted cloak came into view. She hadn't needed it since her third year as a sprite, but she always wore it because it was their tradition. He angled the team to the wide path, clucking his tongue.

"Easy now," he called to the team. "The wind's picking up. Donner, Blitzen, keep Ruby center! Dasher, Dancer, prepare to brake!"

Shoving his heavy thoughts aside, so the reindeer would have his undivided attention, Aldwin kept himself centered with the light. Ruby made first contact, kicking up the thick snow. Then the whole team landed, galloping forward, straight towards the Light.

Something was nagging him about the house, but he couldn't look. He had to bring the team to a stop. Aldwin threw the brakes down, as he pulled back hard on the reins. Sighing in relief, he relaxed as a gloved hand reached out and stroked Ruby's cheek when the reindeer came to a halt.

"Thanks, Mum, but I don't think I can eat," said Aldwin before she could ask.

Ivy watched as Nick landed the sleigh like he was one with the reindeer themselves. The one at the lead came to a halt just beside her, and Ivy giggled in disbelief. Ruby really had a red nose, and it glowed a brilliant vermilion. Before she could speak, Nick jumped from the sleigh and walked away, and Ivy was staring up, up, up, into the smiling beard of Father Christmas himself.

"Happy Christmas, Ivy Moore," he murmured before kissing her brow. His beard tickled her nose.

"Merry Christmas, Santa," she said. Then she stepped around him.

"Aldwin, wait," called Santa.

Nick turned, and Ivy's mouth ran dry at the utter devastation on his face. It did not belong there, not with that absolutely gorgeous suit, not with her standing right in front of him.

"Go to him," Santa whispered and took the lantern from her.

Ivy surrendered it, as Nick looked at his father and kicked dismally at the snow. Her heart pounding, Ivy threw back her hood and ignored the biting wind and snow.

The transformation on his face was breathtaking. She saw it turn from grief to disbelief and finally to a broad smile. She couldn't help herself, and she took off at a run to him.

Aldwin's First Christmas

Aldwin's feet were moving before he could register it. It was Ivy, his Ivy. He didn't give one flying snowball how she was there.

All that mattered was that she was. Tears streaked her face, despite her smile, and Aldwin felt his own burst free and course down his face. She jumped, and he caught her, sobbing in relief when her legs wrapped around his waist.

"Oh, Nick, I'm so sorry. I'm so, so sorry," sobbed Ivy. Aldwin didn't give her a moment to say more because he pressed his lips to hers. The relief that filled him was unexplainable, and he sighed when her tongue brushed his.

Ivy whimpered in relief when Nick's lips silenced her.

She lost herself in the sensation, gripping his hair, parting her lips for his tongue to dance with hers. She caught his sob of joy, and the parts of her that had so recently been in agony rejoiced at his touch. She was in his arms, and all the empty pain in her soul was soothed.

"Aldwin," she whispered into his lips.

"Say it again," sighed Nick, and he set Ivy down gently, pulling her tightly against him.

"Aldwin, my Aldwin," Ivy laughed. She couldn't stop touching him.

They'd been apart less than two days, but it had felt like decades. He peppered her face with kisses, his hands moving constantly as if trying to see if she was real.

"I'm sorry. I was so scared, but I'm so, so sorry I hit you." His lips crashed into hers again, and their tears mingled into the kiss. "And kicked you." He gave a wry chuckle, squeezing his fingers into her hips to pull her impossibly closer. "And for whatever pain I put you in when I almost severed the bond. Please, please forgive me."

Ivy has said his name, his real name, and it was as brilliant as he imagined. Stars, she looked amazing, and his mothers magic mingled with the smell of his own scent. At her touch, the agony, guilt, and fear dissipated in a blink. He caressed her face, basking in the love glowing out at him.

"There's nothing to forgive." Aldwin cupped her face, sniffling hard as he wiped her tears away. "I should have told you sooner, but I wanted to wait until Christmas. I wanted to surprise you."

Ivy shook her head, as she looped her arms around his neck, and Aldwin hugged her tightly into his chest. The wind was picking up, and he could see it forming little crystals of ice in her hair.

"Come inside, before you freeze!" He laughed, and, without waiting, he scooped her into his arms. "How did you get here? I looked for you everywhere!"

"Lewin brought us," explained Ivy. She looked down, shame flooding her face. She knew it had been a logical reaction, but she was so embarrassed that she had let her doubt nearly destroy their love so easily. "Gavin had some key, and he came here. When I found him missing, I thought you had kidnapped him. I called Alex, and Lewin sort of popped into the middle of Mom's living room."

"Bloody show off," snorted Aldwin. He made a mental note to quite possibly snog Lewin for revealing it all to her.

"He figured it out, and he brought us here." She buried her face in his neck, as he ambled through the snow. There was an elegance to it like the cold and snow were a part of him instead of a hindrance to his path. He didn't seem to struggle through it at all. "Your mom's been making us feel right at home."

"I told you my parents would love you," murmured Aldwin. He giggled, too happy to care about the pain and anguish he'd been in. They were together on Christmas, on his birthday. "This is the best birthday of my life!" He cheered. Aldwin kissed Ivy deeply when he reached the door, then he waved his hand to open it. He carried her inside the kitchen, breaking free of her lips to take in the scene waiting for him. "Oh, my stars!"

The kitchen had been decorated in the same colors Ivy had done her house—all blues, silvers, and whites. Her tree sat primly in the corner, and the stockings adorned the small hearth where his mum liked to make fire-baked bread and cakes. Under it was a pile of presents, all of the ones from Ivy's house, and the shiny blue and white bike he'd picked out for Gavin. The lights that had been strewn around Ivy's living room adorned the kitchen rafters. Fiona stood with his mum, pouring coffee, and she smiled broadly at them. Gavin was nowhere to be seen.

"Aldwin put her down and get her some cocoa! She's freezing," his mum chided with a loving smile. Aldwin laughed out loud and spun Ivy around.

"I don't want to get down," Ivy protested. She clung tighter to him, afraid if he did then he would disappear. To her delight, Nick simply squeezed her tighter. Yes, her face and neck were cold, but she didn't care. He gave her another mind-blowing kiss, and she tightened her arms around his neck.

"I can't have my lady cold," chuckled Nick. He eased her down, but he never let go of her waist. The door opened behind them, and Ivy didn't have to turn to know that Santa had come in. Her mom gave a little shriek of shock, and his mum beamed. "Ivy, love, this is my Dah, Kristofer."

"We met outside," Ivy said. She looked up at him again, though. She knew the whole story now. Mama Claus had explained it all, the necklace, the bear, and how Nick had been sent to restore Gavin's faith. She pressed closer to Nick and rested her cheek against his chest. "Thank you, for everything, Santa."

"Call me Dah, or Papa Claus, my dear," said Santa. Ivy felt her cheeks flush as he patted one. "Now, the reunion is short one very important person."

"Gavin!" Aldwin exclaimed and kissed Ivy's hair. "Can I go wake him up?"

"Let's go together," giggled Ivy.

Aldwin didn't waste time. He grabbed her hand, unable to stop smiling, as he followed Gavin's slumbering glow up to the guest room he'd claimed as his own during the last visit. "I missed you and him," he said. He paused outside of the door, needing to hold her again, to touch and taste her. Ivy responded with open enthusiasm. "This, who I am, you're really okay with it?"

"Nick," Ivy whispered as he brushed their lips together and filled her with warmth and joy. "Aldwin, you're my soulmate, but I know, even if we weren't, I'd still love you. This is just more of you to love." She reached for the door, easing it open. Gavin was still peacefully asleep.

Aldwin followed Ivy into the room, and his heart felt so full he thought it would burst. She crouched down, and he followed her. With a nod from Ivy, he reached out and shook the boy gently.

"Gavin, wake up."

"More minutes," the boy mumbled and rubbed his cheek on the pillow.

"Gavin, baby, wake up. Somebody's here for you," murmured Ivy.

"It's Christmas, Gavin. Wake up." Aldwin leaned forward and kissed the boy on the brow. Those drowsy blue eyes fluttered open, blinked, and then Gavin went berserk.

"Nick! Nick! You're back! You're back!" Gavin shouted. Ivy laughed, falling to her butt, as Gavin half jumped off the bed onto Nick, dragging the blankets with him.

"Gods, I missed you." Aldwin hugged the boy close, squeezing his eyes shut as Gavin practically choked him. "Easy buddy, I can't breathe!"

"Nana and Gran made breakfast. Are you hungry?" asked Ivy. She carefully untangled her boys from the blankets, as Aldwin lifted Gavin up onto his hip.

"Mummy, you've been crying again," whimpered Gavin. He looked suddenly worried, as he clung to Nick. "Nick's back, aren't you happy? Or are you still fighting?"

"Your mummy was crying because she's really, very happy," chuckled Aldwin. He reached out to stroke the bits of smeared mascara on her cheek. With a gentle brush of his magic, he fixed the small mess. "We aren't fighting anymore."

"Exactly." Ivy breathed in relief as her fingers laced with his. "Mommy and Nick are never gonna fight again." She was so giddy with her love for them both that she couldn't stand still. "Now, Nana brought us all a surprise. It's in the kitchen. Want to see?"

"Yes!" exclaimed Gavin.

Ivy pulled on Nick's hand. She was still having difficulty thinking of his real name. Nick was who she fell in love with, just as she had never taken to calling Aaron, Ron, like most of his friends. She knew he wouldn't mind if she saved Aldwin for special moments.

The boys were so busy chatting about their Christmas Eve adventures, that Ivy didn't want to interrupt. So she led them back to the kitchen. She understood, finally, why he had commented that the kitchen was the center of the home.

Despite living in a massive, never-ending house. It seemed that this room held the most love. Ivy knew that the kitchen was where the tiny, powerful family spent most of their time together. It was obvious as Nick, Cateline, and Kristofer fell into a comfortable rhythm, dancing around each other to grab plates and cups and settle in at the cozy table.

She loved how well her mom fit in, how she had quickly become friends with Cateline, amiably arguing over who would serve who and how the other should sit down and relax.

Aldwin couldn't remember a time when he'd been so at peace. The two families felt as if they had been a part of each other for decades, not days, as his Dah laughed and tossed a bit of fruit into Gavin's mouth, before snagging bacon off of Ivy's plate.

Fiona kept rubbing Aldwin's back, constantly refilling his orange juice and laughing with his mum over their mutual stories of raising stubborn kids. For centuries, he'd known Christmas was about love, peace, and coming together. Living this, experiencing it for the first time with three mortals he adored, truly showed him how important it was.

"Presents," crowed Gavin. "'Let's do presents!" The boy wiped his mouth clean of syrup and scrambled off his chair. "Can we?"

"Sure, baby." Ivy tossed her napkin down, and Aldwin and Papa Claus both stretched and yawned. "Before Santa and Santa Junior pass out on their plates."

"Actually," said Nick as he touched her arm. "As of dawn, well, I'm officially Santa. Dah's retiring." Ivy gasped in surprise. Nobody had told her that. It didn't upset her; she just hadn't thought about it. Papa Claus looked so full of energy that he didn't seem to be a day over fifty under his thick beard and sparkling eyes.

"Actually, Aldwin, I was thinking," interjected Papa Claus, and Ivy looked over at him. "I could put it off, for another few years or so. Maybe thirteen or fourteen." Those kind eyes flickered over to Gavin. "You're going to have your hands full, and it's a hard job." Ivy knew what he was implying, and she almost cried at the gift her love was being given.

"Oh," gasped Aldwin. He was confused at first. "Oh!" Aldwin shoved aside his sleepiness as Dah's words sank in. He was giving him the freedom to return to the mortal realm and to make his new family the priority until Gavin was out of school. "That means a lot to me. Thank you!"

"Come on, Aldwin." Ivy yanked on his hand, as she watched Gavin begin digging in the presents under Fiona's watchful eye. "You've got some under the tree, too."

"I do?" Nick yelped. It occurred to Ivy, as he lit up just as brightly as Gavin, that this was quite possibly the first time in his life that he'd gotten Christmas presents. Cateline had explained that while they exchanged birthday and anniversary gifts today, it wasn't the same as a human Christmas.

"Here," giggled Ivy.

Aldwin sat down cross-legged as Ivy handed him a box. She looked ready to rip it open herself, as she knelt beside him. Heart racing, he carefully pulled apart the snowflake-designed paper and pried the flaps open. Inside was a framed picture of him and Gavin. He didn't remember her ever taking it.

"Oh, love, it's perfect. I love it." Then he spotted the bit of paper labeled one. "One?" he asked

"There's two more in there," explained Ivy. He set the picture aside, as he saw the envelope marked two. Carefully, he opened it and tugged the letter out. "Gavin, come here and listen," his soulmate said and pulled her son close. Then she nodded to him, and Aldwin smiled. "Read it out loud."

"Dear Nick," Nick recited, and Ivy could barely contain her joy as Nick began reading the letter to the now quiet room. "Last Christmas, all Gavin wanted was a daddy. This year, all I want is the same. Will you make—" his voice caught, and tears pricked her eyes at the way his fingers trembled, and he swallowed hard. "Will you make both of us happy, by saying yes to our wish? Love, Ivy and Gavin."

There was a thick tension in the room, as Nick covered his eyes and drew a shaky breath. The letter fell to his lap, and she felt Gavin begin to wriggle as he realized what the letter was asking.

"Well, Aldwin? Will you?" She asked and past the emotions in her throat.

"What do you think?" gasped Aldwin. He wiped his cheeks and pulled both of them into a hug. He kissed Ivy with an ecstatic laugh, as Gavin wriggled where he was trapped between them. His heart had never felt so full.

"Daddy, I can't breathe," complained Gavin, his words muffled by the group embrace. The three words made Aldwin's heart explode, as Ivy pulled away, her happy tears streaming down her face. "Are we happy crying again?" The room burst into laughter, and Aldwin realized his son's eyes were the only dry ones in the room. "Give Mummy her gift now, Daddy!" His tiny hands began searching Aldwin's pockets. "Where'd you hide it! That's not it." A wooden flute went flying, and Ivy let out a hiccuping giggle. "Why d'ya have three-D glasses?" Gavin snorted, as he pressed them onto his little face.

"You're in the wrong pocket buddy," sniffled Nick. Ivy wiped her face as her brushed Gavin away. She was about to point out he'd forgotten the third item in his box when her mom and Cateline pulled her to her feet. "There we are." His hands were closed when they emerged from inside his coat. He shifted, and Ivy expected him to stand, but to her shock, he simply went up on one knee and opened the red, engraved box. "Ivy Moore, you just asked me to be your son's father, and I will." The earnestness burning in his eyes stole her breath, as the firelight reflected off the ring nestled in the pile of silk inside. "All I could ever need now is for you to be my wife. Will you marry me?"

"Yes! God, yes," Ivy cried. She sobbed as Nick took her hand and slid the ring onto her finger. Then he stood and pulled her into his arms. Her heart soared as their lips met. When they parted, she nuzzled her cheek into his neck and clung tightly to him. Beyond his shoulder, by the window, she swore she saw someone move.

Looking up, she gasped, as sparkling blue eyes met hers, and those soft lips pulled up in a smile.

Aaron stuck his hands in his jacket pockets, his eyes shifting to Gavin, and then, he looked back at her. She couldn't move or breathe when nodded at her.

"Goodbye, my precious girl," he whispered. "I love you." Then he faded from view. At the sound of his voice, Ivy's knees buckled, and the smell of his cologne and leather jacked washed over her.

"Ivy? Ivy!" Aldwin yelped. He was glad he was hugging her because she went down without warning. "Ivy! Look at me." Her eyes had rolled back, so he lowered her to the floor, but then she gasped. An unfamiliar scent drifted past him—cologne and aged leather. Those beautiful eyes fluttered open, and Ivy turned into him, sobbing. "What happened? Are you feeling ill?"

"I saw Aaron. He was standing by the window. He was right there," Ivy sobbed. Aldwin cradled her against his chest, as she pointed. He looked back, but the room was empty. The unfamiliar scent was fading, but Aldwin knew she had seen him. "He came to say goodbye."

Christmas magic had given his love one more gift, the one he never could.

"Are you gonna be okay?" asked Nick. His whisper, as the other adults in the room began to babble in shock, was so soft Ivy barely heard it. "Can you stand?"

"I can but will you just hold me for a moment?" she asked, and she wriggled until she was sitting in his lap instead of laying in it. Ivy rested her head on his shoulder and basked in his love, as well as Aaron's, which burned inside of her stronger than ever before. She marveled at how they didn't impede on the other, equally filling but different in their taste on her lips. Finally, wiping her cheeks, she looked down at her new ring.

It was just as beautiful as her other one, but it was also entirely different. The single stone, which she had a suspicion wasn't a diamond or any other human-cut gem was nestled into a stunning, silver metal that dazzled like white gold but seemed to glow from within. The band was etched with leaves, which looked as if they would burst into life any second. It was so perfect, and the love behind it made her melt.

"I love you, Aldwin Nicholas Claus," she murmured, lifting her hand to cup his face.

"And I love you, Ivy Holly Moore-Somerfield," said Aldwin.

He knew he didn't have to acknowledge the name she'd never gotten to legally take, but he did anyway. He needed to get used to it because that was something he'd never take away from Gavin. He'd never met Aaron, but if his spirit had come across from the Realm of Bliss to give his blessing, then Aldwin would honor him.

The name would pass to Gavin's future children.

Immortalized Love

"So, nine hundred," hummed Ivy as she drew her fingers along Aldwin's bare chest in the dim firelight. He tingled all over, as their skin slid together, slick with sweat from their passionate lovemaking. The massive house was silent around them, except for the blizzard that blew outside the windows. "That's a pretty large age gap." She giggled, as he snickered.

"Does it bother you?" asked Aldwin.

He pulled his flushed-skinned fiancée onto him, sighing when her legs slipped between his, and her palms rested against his chest. She was practically glowing, and her hair was a halo of messy waves and ruffled curls. He'd been entirely too pleased to wake up from his four-hour nap to find Ivy wearing only his new suit coat and leaning against his locked door.

"Nah, it's kinda hot actually." She giggled, as she placed a kiss against the spattering of his dark hair below her fingers. Nick sighed, and she hummed in delight at the way his eyes fluttered shut, and a smile played along his lips. "I've ways had a thing for older guys who dress weird, according to my mom." This earned her an abrupt laugh and a pleasant squeeze of her butt. "But it does have me wondering. What does it mean for us? I mean, I can't just abandon my family and friends. Gavin's only five. If I became like you and did what your mom did, would I have to live here?"

"Of course not," said Aldwin. He sighed in relief, glad he didn't have to explain the gifts he knew his grandmothers would offer. He'd have to thank his mum for already telling her. "Come here." He inched up to recline against the pillows, pulling Ivy up to wrap her legs around his hips as he tucked the blanket over her like a cloak. "We could live in Ostcrest and raise Gavin until he's old enough to decide if he wants to become a sprite too. I'm sure they'd offer it to your mum if you asked." He stroked her hair, fiddling with an errant curl. "I want to add to your life, Ivy, not take away from it."

"You'd be happy, pretending to be normal," Ivy asked, and Aldwin didn't have to think for a moment to find his answer.

"It wouldn't be pretending. It's *our* normal," he said. "Plenty of other Ageless do it. Regina, for example." Aldwin leaned forward to kiss Ivy's nose, chuckling as she crinkled it and giggled. "My happiness is your happiness. If that means things like carpets and windows and coaching little league, I'll take it."

"Can you even play baseball?" snorted Ivy. She trailed her fingers along his shoulders, tracing the fading marks from her teeth. "Don't answer that." She chuckled as his left eyebrow arched, and he made that face like he was about to quip something witty at her. "So it's all true then, about the realms and crossing rifts?"

Ivy had thought it was just a story he'd made up, but there had been books in the library, written in a strange, elegant script that had seemed like it glowed and twisted on the page.

"Yes, I'd love to take you fully to our realm, but you couldn't make it as a mortal," Nick said. She had already learned that he didn't often spend time there. "Our house, along with a few other places like the Cupid Palace, well, they're gateways. You'd love the Ageless Realm and our planet." His words summoned up images of herself in flowing, fantastic robes that reminded her of fairy tales. Nick was still rambling on, and she listened to him again. "Guess I can't really call it mine. I only went to school there. I've spent more time on Earth than there."

"You went to school?" Ivy laughed aloud at that and shook her hair back. He snorted under her, but she cut him off. "Sorry, it's just. That's so adorable! Did you have uniforms, too? That where you got your obsession with suits?" He rolled his eyes, and with a wave of his hand, a picture appeared. It was Nick, most definitely, but younger and looking more like a gangly teenager in flowing red and gold robes with a high collar. "Oh, you were so cute as a teenager. Bet you were one of the brainy kids, too. Did they have a chess league?" She teased.

"Ivy, I'm a hundred and twelve in this picture, not sixteen," scoffed Aldwin. Then he laughed, as he returned the frame to its shelf in the library. "Chess club was in my primary school. I was more of a troublemaker once I got older." He squeezed her bare thighs and lifted his head to press a kiss on her soft shoulder.

"Oh, you were?" Ivy teased. "I don't think forgetting to turn in homework or returning library books late counts." Aldwin nipped playfully at her collarbone, earning him a soft tap of her fingers to his chest. "Hey!"

"You know good and well I can be bad if I want," Aldwin whispered. He knew she was teasing, and he was pleased that she was being so accepting of it all. "If you must know, I got suspended for a whole year for making the headmaster's clothes invisible during a speech." Ivy's eyebrows shot up to her hairline. "He was a right git, and it was so worth it!"

"Think you're in the mood to be a little bad right now?" asked ivy. She bit her lip and tugged his hair playfully. She loved this feeling, that insatiable hunger that always existed at the beginning of a relationship. "Unless you're tired, old man." She giggled as he growled, rolling her onto her back. "At least now I know why you've always had an above-average recovery time."

"Oh, you've got no idea, Ivy, no idea," hummed Nick as she hooked a leg around his waist. "Just wait until our wedding night, when you're like me, and you can really keep up." He lowered his lips to her ear, and Ivy crooned out her approval at the delicate tug of his teeth. "That record we set last week of four orgasms will be nothing." He chuckled as she squirmed under him and gave a little gasp. "Try more like forty." The thought made her head spin and her body burn with the need for this touch.

"Speaking of weddings," said Nick. Ivy tried to pay attention to something besides the way he rocked against her. Each gentle motion was rubbing her in all the right ways. "I was thinking New Year's Eve. Is that too soon?"

"Sounds perfect to me," she said, reaching between them to stroke his hard length with her a finger. "Are you up for round two of being a little extra naughty?" Nick made an absolutely sinful noise and with a snap of his fingers, she found her wrists tied loosely to the headboard.

"You want me to be naughty?" chuckled Aldwin. He smirked when Ivy's eyes turned deliciously dark, and she tugged at the soft ropes around her arms. "Now, you have to be quiet, and do you remember what the safe word is?"

"Jingle bells," Ivy groaned. Her other leg hooked around his waist, and he could feel her wet and ready beneath him.

"Good girl," Aldwin praised her. Then kissed her deeply, before he made it very difficult for Ivy to keep silent.

***

The six days until New Year's Eve blew by in a flash, while Ivy, her mom, and Cateline planned the small ceremony. Alex had eagerly agreed to walk her down the aisle, and Lewin was officiating.

It was only fair since Nick would be doing their wedding in a few months. Alex was taking the fact that his soulmate was an immortal superbeing better than Ivy had at first. The best part was, that he had already been changed. Which Ivy found out when he popped up in the library with white wings instead of answering her phone call. Cupid's life suited him more than being a cop ever did.

"Mom, don't cry. It's not like I'm leaving." Ivy pulled a tissue from the box on the table and handed it to her. "We're still gonna live in Ostcrest." She smoothed her skirts, feeling comfortably warm in the luxurious gown and long coat that Cateline had made for her.

"I know, it's just that I always cry when you get married!" Fiona sobbed. Then she gave a watery laugh, and she wiped her cheeks.

"Well, this will be the last time," laughed Ivy. "So don't worry." She drew in a shaky breath. She was nervous, which was pointless. Then again, she'd been nervous when she'd married Aaron, even though they'd been engaged for a year and had a child.

"They're ready!" Alex exclaimed as he popped into the foyer in a burst of silver and purple smoke. "Wow, Ives, you look gorgeous!" She blushed and reached to brush her hair back before remembering her mom had twisted it up. "Gaia and Winter just arrived, with some of the other sprites."

"Paula and Blake too?" she asked.

Lewin and Alex were supposed to fetch them. They were in on the secret, and both had vehemently sworn they wouldn't tell a soul. Alex nodded and extended his arm. He would be giving her away, which was apparently a promise he'd made to Aaron the same day Aaron had made the video message.

"Okay, Mom. Are you ready?"

"Yeah, baby," sniffled Fiona and more tears threatened to ruin her makeup. "Go ahead, I'll fix your skirt."

Ivy drew a steadying breath, as Alex waved his hand and the doors creaked open. She blinked at the bright light. The sun wasn't the cause, because it only spent a few hours a day this time of the year on the horizon. When she stepped out onto the top step, she gasped. Floating balls of light hung in their air, like miniature suns, illuminating the small crowd waiting at the edge of the ice garden. More appeared, settling on either side of the red velvet that had been laid on the snow like an aisle. The creators of these were the two most beautiful women Ivy had ever seen.

One was tall—voluptuous in her curves—and clad in stunning robes of green and gold and blue and browns. She had chestnut hair that hung in curls to her waist, full of flowers and tiny birds and colorful butterflies. On her head was a diadem of branches and blossoms, and it radiated light. The flowers bloomed and withered and bloomed again, while honeybees fluttered between them.

The other woman was thin and lithe, with hair so black it stood out against her blue and silver robes. Her crown seemed to have been carved from ice, reflecting the lights as they appeared in her hand. Her skin glistened and glittered like it was made of frost and mist. Ivy immediately knew who they were.

Nick waited at the front of the aisle, in the amazing red and white pinstriped suit again. Instead of his fur coat, however, he had on a massive cloak that stretched behind him. It was whiter than the snow, trimmed in red and black fur, and it came up in a high collar. Those warm and love-filled eyes met hers, and everyone else disappeared. She didn't even feel Alex leading her onward.

Aldwin couldn't breathe as Ivy came up the aisle towards him. His mum had outdone herself, and he was eternally grateful. Ivy was wearing a form-fitting white gown that dragged the ground. The bodice was covered in blue and silver crystals sewn onto lace that was the softest pink color he'd ever seen. Over it, Ivy had a long, stunning white coat with a soaring, white fur collar and sweeping sleeves, and the fur had been decorated with holly and mistletoe springs. Her waist was accentuated with carefully applied white nebula diamonds. They sparkled as she glided towards him on Alex's arm.

"She looks like a goddess," said Lewin, and he whistled softly. "You're welcome, by the way."

"Shut up," retorted Aldwin, trying not to laugh. Alex brought Ivy to a stop and kissed her cheek. Then he lifted her gloved hand, and Aldwin took it from him. "Ivy, you look breathtaking."

"So do you," Ivy said. Her smile was full of warmth and love, and Aldwin knew she could see his own in her smile. Beside them, Lewin raised his hands. The crowd behind them fell silent.

"Friends and family, we are brought together today to officially join Aldwin Nicholas Claus and Ivy Holly Moore in marriage," began Lewin. Aldwin squeezed her hands, and Ivy gazed up at him with shining eyes. He could have drowned in the melted topaz of her irises if she didn't keep him anchored to reality. "They've already been bonded as soulmates, but they wanted you all here to share in their outward promise to keep that bond."

Ivy couldn't think as Nick's eyes never left hers. They were glowing in love and wonder, as he pulled her closer, so their joined hands pressed between their bodies. She thought she might sink into his smile and never come back.

"Do you, Aldwin Nicholas Claus, promise and swear to love Ivy, to honor her, cherish her, and be faithful to her from this moment, until the moment when time is no more?"

"I do," swore Aldwin. He knew, without reservation, that he would never break the vow he was making. He would never do anything to wrong Ivy.

"Do you, Ivy Holly Moore, promise and swear to love Aldwin, to honor him, cherish him, and be faithful to him from this moment, until the moment when time is no more?" Lewin asked, and Ivy found her answer in less than a breath.

"I do," Ivy said. She was as sure of those two words as she had been with Aaron. Aldwin, Nick, was hers forever, and nothing could take that away from her.

"Then, by my right as a Supreme Cupid." Lewin's voice and hands raised up. His fingers brushed their hair once before pulling back. "I now pronounce you husband and wife. You may kiss—" Aldwin didn't wait for Lewin to finish.

He hauled Ivy against him and claimed her lips as the crowd of witnesses clapped and cheered. She sighed into him, and he held her tightly as her lips parted beneath his. Her fingers curled along his chest, and he smiled against her lips. Then, reluctantly, he released her. When they parted Gavin was dancing around, in his red suit and boots identical to Aldwin's, while Fiona hugged his mum and cried.

His grandmothers stepped forward, smiling broadly, he drew in a breath.

"My Ladies," said Aldwin. He bowed low, though he'd never done it for them before. Relatives or not, the moment was special.

"Now, Aldwin, formalities are not needed," said Gaia and kissed his brow.

Ivy gasped as she took in the women up close. Gaia, Mother Nature, radiated warmth, and she was equal parts awe-inspiring and terrifying. Being near her reminded Ivy of the purest summers and the most terrifying of tornadoes. Winter looked cold in her features only, and the smile she wore was like sunrise on fresh snow. She was the world after a blizzard, and her presence made Ivy shiver.

"I've heard so much about you both," she said, her voice a whisper.

"So have we," said Winter. She reached out and stroked a chilly finger along Ivy's cheek. "Tell me, child, are you afraid?"

"No, ma'am," Ivy said, and she meant it. She didn't care if it would hurt. She was willing to do it if it meant having Nick's forever.

"Destiny chose well for you, Aldwin," said Winter, and Aldwin squeezed Ivy as Gaia touched her hair. "You must release her now." He kissed Ivy's cheek, and he unwrapped his arms from her waist. Then he stepped back.

"Gaia," said Winter. He watched as she raised her hand, and Gaia clasped it firmly. Ivy closed her eyes, and Aldwin ordered everyone back.

Ivy swallowed, not out of fear, but because she was so eager her throat had run dry. Then, she felt it.

A warm, motherly hand touched her head, and a cold, tender one slid past her coat to rest on her chest. She was burning and freezing all at once, but it didn't hurt. It filled her, coursing through her veins as her mind spun. Suddenly, she couldn't feel the frigid air anymore. It was cool, but not biting, and her skin tingled and popped as she moved her hands. The touches disappeared, and Ivy blinked her eyes open.

Everything looked different, more defined and vibrant. The ache in her left shoulder she'd come accustomed to feeling since a gymnastics accident when she was seventeen was gone. There were other missing twinges and such that had vanished, as well. She felt energized like she'd slept for twelve hours and then chugged a pot of coffee.

Nick's face came into view, and she sucked in a breath at how there seemed to be a light emanating from his very soul and radiating out of his eyes.

"Am I like you?"

"Yes," said Aldwin. He was speechless at the way her magic danced pink and cream in her smile. "How do you feel?"

"Amazing! Better than, actually!" she cried. Then she threw her arms around his neck, turning to the women. "Thank you, thank you so much."

"It was our pleasure." In a blink, they were gone.

"Mummy!" Gavin came sprinting over, and Ivy swung him up into her arms. "Are you magic now too? You were glowing all sorts of pretty colors when the ladies touching you!"

"Yes, Gavin, she is," said Aldwin. He took his son from his wife and swung him up onto his shoulders. "And maybe, when you're all grown up, you can be too!" He looked over at Ivy, who was positively radiating her love, and laughed as tiny flurries of fluffy flakes began swirling around her head. "You know, though, I think she's gonna need some practice keeping her magic in control."

"Oh, I'll show you control," growled Ivy.

She squeezed her eyes shut and felt that new, unfamiliar essence surging into her hand and fingers. She struggled to contain it, trying to understand the way it whispered in her veins and fingers until she felt snow crunching against her gloves. Then she promptly threw it at his chest.

Epilogue

"Call me, if you need me to pick you up," said Ivy, as she straightened Gavin's collar under his sweater. She looked up into his exasperated face. "And no drinking. I don't care if anyone else is, you're only fourteen."

"I won't, Mum," her son said and rolled those summer sky eyes. He looked so much like both his dads that Ivy had to laugh. "There won't be any alcohol. Mary's mom's gonna be there the whole time." He brushed her hand away. "Mum, it's just a party." Even years later, he reserved Nick's accent for calling her and only her, mum.

"It's a date," said Ivy. She stepped back to look over the outfit he'd chosen.

The dark trousers and maroon sweater over a white, button-down shirt really made his features stand out. He was Aaron's mirror image, except he still had some of his baby fat in his cheeks. Gavin's sudden four-inch growth spurt over the summer had made him taller than her, and it turned his legs and arms gangly and awkward. Ivy thought he looked very handsome, but she knew she was biased.

"Mary asked you in person, not with a written invitation, to Valentine's Day party. It's a date."

"Your mum's right," said Aldwin as he popped into the room and leaned against the wall. He chewed on the banana he'd nicked from the kitchen. "I dunno if I like her though." He flashed his wife a playful look, before he added with a smirk, "Mary, I mean, not your mum. Love your mum. That's why I married her."

"Why don't you like her?" demanded Gavin. His sharp query, combined with the way he puffed up his chest made Aldwin wink at Ivy. "She's smart and funny, and sweet, and she has the prettiest hair."

"See, it's a date," giggled Ivy. She swatted her son's chest playfully as she went to get the black bag she'd laid on his bed. Carefully, she opened it up, and then she lifted the leather into her fingers. "Here, you'll need this. It's always chilly this time of the year." His eyes went wide, and she saw Nick smile sweetly at her. "Happy Early Birthday, baby bear."

"Mum is that—" gasped Gavin, but he cut himself off as he took it from her. Ivy surrendered it to him and stepped back into Nick's arms as their son shrugged it on. It was still a little too big, but it suited him, just like it suited the man who'd owned it. "Is this Dad's jacket?"

"Yes, you're old enough for it now," Ivy said. She had to wipe her cheeks and loop her arm around Nick's waist. Seeing her son in his father's jacket felt like a circle had been completed. Nick kissed her hair, and Ivy yelped as she was seized by her arms and lifted into a hulking bear hug by her son. "I love you too, baby."

"Mum, you're the best," whispered Gavin. Aldwin laughed when their son set Ivy down. It was kind of sad that they were the same height now. He missed being able to pick him up and let him ride on his shoulders. "You too, Dah. I love you both."

"Here," said Aldwin as he vanished the banana peel and dug into his pocket. "This is from me. Your mum was against it, but I sweet-talked her." He pulled out the sleek, red phone. Gavin had a basic prepaid one, in case of emergencies, but he was old enough and responsible enough to have a real one. "Now, this is on the Ageless network, like ours, so don't lose it." When Gavin reached for it, he yanked it back. "And, it goes on charge downstairs on school nights."

"Yes sir," said Gavin.

Ivy rolled her eyes as Nick finally surrendered the phone. She thought he was still a bit young to have such an expensive model, but she had been assured it was virtually unbreakable, waterproof, and drop-proof. All were necessary, given her son's inherent ability to get in trouble. He had most definitely gotten that from Aaron and not her. Okay, well maybe a little from her.

"Got your cab money?" she asked. Then she picked up his wallet and passed it to him. He took it and looked relieved. "Now, Gran's expecting you at her apartment by eleven, not a minute later!"

"Mum, you know Dah and Papa can track me anywhere in the world. D'ya think I'd risk breaking curfew?" chuckled Gavin.

Aldwin and Ivy shared a long look, shaking their heads.

"Yes!" They both laughed

"Now, go on. Have fun, and if you think Uncle Lewin would do it, don't!" Aldwin called after Gavin, who had hurried down the stairs. When the door downstairs closed, he dropped his chin on Ivy's head and sighed.

"Aw, honey, are you sad?" teased Ivy. She turned around and rubbed his back, biting back a chuckle at the pout she found him wearing. She had been feeling the same earlier, as she watched their son paw through half a dozen outfits and colognes before choosing 'the one'.

"No."

"Liar."

"Maybe," Aldwin admitted. He pulled back to look down at Ivy, and he followed her when she headed into the hall. "It's just, he's going on a date, Ivy. Where'd my little Gavin go?" He stared at the now-closed door. The dinosaurs and stars had been replaced by a 'Keep Out' sign and band stickers. "I swear I was just teaching him how to do calculus, and now he's going to parties and hanging out with friends." Ivy's soft chuckle brought him back to her from his memories. "Oh, right, I promised you dinner in Paris."

"Paris can wait." Ivy grinned. "Come with me." She laced her fingers with his, leading Nick up the stairs to their room. "I know how to cheer you up." She reached up to loosen the intricate knot she'd magicked her hair into for dinner, letting it fall around her shoulders in a gust of snowflakes against her maroon, skin-tight dress when they were halfway up the stairs.

"Oh, really?" growled Aldwin. He shoved his blue feelings away as she looked back at him with a wicked smile. His blood pooled south as he kicked his shoes off and grabbed her by the hips as soon as they reached their room. "How's that, hmm?" He raised one hand to grip the zip of her dress, inching it teasingly down

"Well." She shrugged the dress off, stepping out of it and back into his arms. "Aldwin, we've been married seven years now." She sighed as he hummed confirmation into her shoulders and danced his fingers along her lace-covered stomach. "Well, Gavin's almost grown, and, uh—" His teeth nipped at her shoulder cutting her off for a moment. "I kinda miss hearing little feet coming up the stairs, and buying cute outfits, and hearing that sleepy sounding 'good night, Daddy.'" She smiled as his lips and fingers froze. "And Dah is retiring in four years, so, maybe it's time we well..." She let her voice trail off.

"Ivy," Aldwin gasped. His breath caught as the words registered in his brain. He slid his hands lower down her stomach, seeking to see if there was even the slightest change in her body. "Are you...love are you pregnant?" he asked.

He hadn't even known she'd stopped taking the pills she'd gotten from the Ageless midwife, Helenia, that handled all of the needs of the Ageless women in this realm.

"Not yet." Ivy spun in his arms. She grabbed his tie and loosened it, and then she went up on her toes to curl her tongue along his pounding pulse point. "But I could be if you wanted. I stopped taking my pills while you were away at the New Year Council." She squealed as he picked her up and threw her onto the bed, watching as he waved his clothes away in one go and pounced on her. "Is that a yes?"

"That's definitely a yes." Aldwin laughed when she wrapped her arms and legs around him. Ivy was right. She definitely found a way to cheer him up. That's why he loved her, and why he would always love her. She always knew just how to make his perfect life just a little more complete.

About the author

Tabitha is a queer, neurodivergent author from Florida. She is the mother of one human child and one fur-baby. She achieved her MFA in English and Writing with a concentration in fiction from Southern New Hampshire University in May of 2022. She has been teaching English Composition, American Literature, and Creative Writing since February of 2023.

www.ingramcontent.com/pod-product-compliance
Lightning Source LLC
Chambersburg PA
CBHW010742310726
48971CB00010B/2917